"That goddess of vengeance, Lucky, strides again."
—*New York Daily News*

Married Lovers

"The fabulous *Married Lovers* has plenty of Hollywood women kicking ass with a trio of new heroes."
—*New York Post*

"Sexier, steamier, and more scandalous than ever. Love and lust, where the good get what they deserve and the bad get their comeuppance." —*London Daily Express*

"Nothing says summer like lathering on the sunblock, lieing on a lounge chair, and pulling a very steamy novel from the queen of romance from your beach bag—Jackie Collins's latest romance, *Married Lovers*."
—NBC's "The Today Show"

"A mood elevator comparable to anything her characters indulge in." —*Heat* magazine

Lucky Santangelo Novels
BY JACKIE COLLINS

Goddess of Vengeance
Drop Dead Beautiful
Dangerous Kiss
Vendetta: Lucky's Revenge
Lady Boss
Lucky
Chances

Also by Jackie Collins

Poor Little Bitch Girl
Married Lovers
Lovers & Players
Hollywood Divorces
Deadly Embrace
Hollywood Wives—The New Generation
Lethal Seduction
L.A. Connections—Power, Obsession, Murder, Revenge
Thrill!
Hollywood Kids
American Star
Rock Star
Hollywood Husbands
Lovers and Gamblers
Hollywood Wives
The World Is Full of Divorced Women
The Love Killers
Sinners
The Bitch
The Stud
The World Is Full of Married Men

THE
POWER TRIP

Jackie Collins

St. Martin's Paperbacks

This is a work of fiction. All of the characters, organizations, and events portrayed in this novel are either products of the author's imagination or are used fictitiously.

THE POWER TRIP

Copyright © 2013 by Chances, Inc.
Excerpt from *Confessions of a Wild Child* copyright © 2013 by Chances, Inc.

For information address St. Martin's Press, 175 Fifth Avenue, New York, NY 10010.

ISBN: 978-0-312-56983-9

Printed in the United States of America

St. Martin's Press hardcover edition / February 2013
St. Martin's Paperbacks edition / October 2013

St. Martin's Paperbacks are published by St. Martin's Press, 175 Fifth Avenue, New York, NY 10010.

10 9 8 7 6 5 4 3 2 1

To all my readers across the world.
Love . . .
Passion . . .
Friendship . . .
and
Power! Live it!

Prologue

The couple on the bed had sex as if it were their final act.

And for one of them it was.

Neither of them heard the door slowly open.

Neither of them observed the shadowy figure enter the room. They were too caught up in the throes of passionate lovemaking.

Until . . . one single gunshot.

The blood flowed.

And for one of them, death and orgasm happened at the exact same moment.

Life has a strange way of taking you on an unexpected trip.

This was one of those times.

Book One

THE INVITATION

1

Dateline: Moscow

The Russian billionaire Aleksandr Kasianenko admired his supermodel girlfriend as she stepped, unabashedly naked, out of the indoor swimming pool in his luxurious Moscow mansion. Her name was Bianca, and she was known across the world.

God, she is a beautiful creature, Aleksandr thought. *Beautiful and sleekly feline—she moves like a panther. And in bed she is a wild tigress. I am a very fortunate man.*

Bianca was of mixed race: her mother was Cuban, her father black. There was no doubt that Bianca had inherited the best of both her parents' looks.

She'd been raised in New York, was discovered at seventeen, and now, at age twenty-nine, she was the most sought-after supermodel on the planet. Tall, lean, and agile, with coffee-colored skin, fine features, full natural lips, piercing green eyes, and waist-length glossy black hair, Bianca captivated both men and women. Men found her irresistibly sexy, while women admired her sense of style and raunchy humor, which she exhibited every time she appeared on the late-night talk shows.

Bianca knew how to handle herself in front of the cameras, and she certainly knew how to plug her brand. Over the years, she'd created a mini empire that included a fine-jewelry line, exotic sunglasses, a stunning makeup collection for women of color, and several bestselling scents.

Bianca had mastered the art of the sell, making a fortune doing so. But recently, she'd decided that rather than be a one-woman band who worked hard for her money, she was looking for more. She was looking for a powerful man who would take care of her and parlay the money she'd earned into super-rich status.

Aleksandr Kasianenko was just such a man, because Aleksandr was not only a powerful, super-rich businessman, he was also tough and rugged, with a steely reserve.

Bianca was sick of the long list of pretty boys she'd dated over the years. Movie stars, a clutch of rock stars, a half dozen sports heroes, and a politician or two. None of them had really satisfied her—in bed or out. She'd always been the dominant force in whatever relationship she'd been trapped in. The movie stars were all insecure and fixated on their public image. Rock stars were mostly into drugs and getting fucked up, not to mention totally vain. The sports stars were publicity crazy and never faithful. And as for the politicians—sexually incorrect. All horn and no blow.

Then, at exactly the right time, she'd met Aleksandr. And she'd fallen for his silent strength.

Only one problem.

He was married.

They'd met on Aleksandr's home turf. She was in Moscow doing a cover shoot for Italian *Vogue,* and since it happened to be her twenty-ninth birthday, the flamboyant photographer, Antonio—an Italian gay man who knew absolutely everyone who was anyone in Moscow—had decided to throw her a massive party.

The party was a blast. Until she was introduced to Aleksandr.

The moment she saw him, he took her breath away with

his brooding dark looks and aura of control and power. He was big and strong, and there was something magnetic about him, something incredibly masculine. One look and she was hooked.

He didn't tell her he was married.

She didn't ask.

An hour after their first encounter, they were making fast, ferocious love on the floor in her hotel suite. Their lovemaking was animalistic in its intensity, so overpowering that they'd never made it as far as the bedroom. It was all clothes off and straight at it.

After their night of unbridled passion, they were both swept up and addicted to each other. And so began their steamy affair, an affair that had them meeting all over the world.

Now, after one year, and in spite of Aleksandr's marital status, they were still very much together.

Aleksandr had assured Bianca that he was in the throes of divorcing his wife, but due to several massive business deals that could affect his wife's settlement, it still had not happened. He also had children to consider. Three daughters. "The timing has to be right," he'd informed her. "However, it *will* happen, and it will happen soon. You have my word."

Bianca believed him. He was separated from his wife, so that was a promising beginning. Still, she couldn't help wanting more. She wanted to be Mrs. Aleksandr Kasianenko, and the less time wasted, the better.

In the meantime, Aleksandr wished to celebrate his love's upcoming thirtieth birthday in a big way. He'd recently taken delivery of a new, luxurious four-hundred-foot super-yacht, and to christen their maiden voyage, he planned on throwing Bianca a once-in-a-lifetime special event she would never forget. The celebrations would include inviting several of their friends on a weeklong cruise to enjoy the best of everything. What could be better?

When he informed Bianca of his plan, she was excited,

and immediately started thinking about whom they would invite on this very exclusive trip.

"How many can your new yacht accommodate?" she inquired.

"Many," Aleksandr replied with a dry laugh. "But I feel we should invite only five couples."

"Why only five?" Bianca asked, slightly disappointed.

"It's enough," Aleksandr replied. "You make your list, I make mine. Then we will compare and decide who gets invited."

Bianca grinned. "This is gonna be fun," she said, already planning her list.

"Indeed it will," Aleksandr agreed.

2

Dateline: London

Ashley Sherwin stared at her image in the ornate mirror above the vanity for a full ten minutes before her husband, Taye, entered their streamlined bathroom with the marble counters and fancy rock-crystal chandeliers—designed by Jeromy Milton-Gold, one of London's most sought-after interior designers.

"Whatcha lookin' at, toots?" Taye asked cheerfully, taking the opportunity to lean over her shoulder and check out his own image, which was, as usual, totally fine.

"New makeup," Ashley muttered sulkily, annoyed that he'd caught her, wishing she'd locked the door.

Taye had no concept of the word *privacy*. Well, he wouldn't, would he? He was a superstar footballer used to stripping off and basking in all the glory (not to mention the women) that came his way. Cheap nasty little tarts, ready and willing to chase any famous man. She hated them all.

"Well," Taye said, stretching his arms above his head. "You look hot an' horny."

Ashley had no desire to look hot and horny; her aim was to look like an elegant fashion icon, a fashionista with style to spare. Taye simply didn't get it. He thought he was tossing her a compliment, but as far as she was concerned, it was exactly the opposite.

She sighed. After six years of marriage, Taye still had

no clue who the person was that she aspired to be. Didn't he realize that she was no longer the pretty, blond, twenty-two-year-old TV presenter he'd married? She was now the mother to their six-year-old twins, Aimee and Wolf. She was older, more mature. She knew what she wanted, and it was certainly not enough to be known as Taye Sherwin's trophy wife.

They'd gotten married because she was pregnant—never the best of ideas, but better than being knocked up without a husband. And Taye was a major catch. Black and beautiful. A sports hero. A moneymaking machine, what with all his various endorsement deals and superstar status.

They'd met on a TV show she'd been cohosting with Harmony Gee, a former member of the girl group Sweet. Harmony was all over Taye, but it soon became obvious to everyone that he only had eyes for Ashley.

Before long, they were a staple in the U.K. newspapers, billed as *the* new hot couple. They were even given a nickname by the press: Tashley. It had a ring to it.

Ashley was thrilled; she basked in the attention. For six months she'd been pushed into the background while Harmony scored most of the big interviews, but with all her newfound PR, her bosses at the TV station were suddenly regarding her with new respect, while Harmony was staring at her with daggers in her eyes.

Then Taye had managed to impregnate her, and that was that.

Good-bye, career.

Hello, marriage.

Taye was a superstar in all respects. The moment he found out she was pregnant, he'd insisted they get married. Never mind about his playboy past; Taye was all about doing the right thing. Besides, he loved Ashley. She was perfect for him—a true English peach with her widely spaced blue eyes, flawless skin, long blond hair, and curvy figure.

Taye's mother, Anais, a heavyset Jamaican woman, was not so pleased. "You should be marryin' one of ya own kind," Anais had complained, her accent heavy with disapproval. "This Ashley gal's nothin' but a fancy show pony. She not gonna make ya a satisfyin' wife."

"Your mama's right, son," Taye's dad had agreed. "Ya wanna grab yourself an island woman—more meat on them bones. Juicy dark meat. Delicious!"

The last time Taye's parents had visited Jamaica was forty years ago, so Taye chose to ignore their sage advice. Instead, he forged ahead with elaborate wedding plans.

Ashley's mom, Elise—a faded blonde who worked behind the makeup counter in a department store—was torn. The good news was that Taye was rich and famous. The bad news was that he was black.

Elise tried not to think in a racist way, but, unfortunately, she'd been raised to regard the black race as inferior beings.

Fortunately, Ashley had never harbored any hang-ups about Taye being black. He loved her more than any man ever had; in fact, he kind of worshipped her, which she didn't mind at all. Being worshipped by a very famous man whom every other woman lusted after was quite a kick.

Their lavish marriage made headline news. So did the birth of their twins three months later. Taye bought them all a magnificent house near Hampstead Heath, and everything was well in the world. Except shortly after moving into their new home, Ashley suffered from a bad bout of postpartum depression and refused to go near the twins for the first six months of their lives. This forced Taye to move his parents and Ashley's mother into their house, which turned out to be a most unhappy situation, because the two women soon discovered that they loathed each other—especially when Anais accused the thrice-divorced Elise of making a play for her husband, an accusation Elise hotly denied.

The Sherwin household was not a happy one, with Ashley locked up in the master bedroom refusing to come out, the twins demanding attention day and night, and the mothers-in-law at war.

Taye attempted to keep the peace, but it wasn't easy. And since Ashley shied away from any sexual contact, he was becoming increasingly frustrated, not to mention horny.

So it came to pass that Taye cheated. And as luck would have it, the girl he cheated with (a Page 3 model with outrageous boobs) couldn't wait to run to the tabloids and sell her story for a ridiculous amount of money.

The headlines were relentless:

MY ENDLESS NIGHT OF LUST WITH TAYE SHERWIN

HE'S A STAR IN BED TOO!

IS TASHLEY OVER?

Oh, the humiliation! The fury! The shock that Ashley experienced.

She'd hauled herself out of hiding and confronted her husband in a simmering rage.

His excuses were weak: No sex for months. A depressed wife. Crying babies. Warring mothers-in-law. And a buxom babe throwing herself at him during an aftershave commercial he was shooting.

Taye wasn't made of stone. He'd fallen into those giant tits like a man starved for sustenance. He'd wallowed in them. Then, after wallowing, he'd screwed the random girl, immediately regretted it, and run for his life.

The newspaper story shocked Ashley into action. She'd hurriedly hired two maternity nurses, banished both mothers-in-law to their own homes, and set about getting herself back in shape.

Meanwhile, Taye presented her with a ten-carat diamond ring, assured her his indiscretion would never happen again, paid for the boob job she demanded, and normal life resumed.

Only it wasn't that normal. Ashley forgave; the problem was that she had no intention of ever forgetting.

As the twins grew, Ashley began to think about her future, and what she could do to become more than just another footballer's wife. She'd started by informing Taye that any ads or endorsements he did in the future should include her. He'd agreed. Having rocked the boat once, he was damn sure that he wasn't allowing it to happen again. Ashley meant everything to him, and he wasn't about to risk losing her.

So, ad-wise, they gradually became a team. The Taye and Ashley show. He with the shaved head, muscled body, and killer smile. She with the baby-blue eyes, lush body, amazing boobs, and tumbling blond curls. They got together with the best photographers, and soon created a partnership brand.

Ashley worked hard on her body, toning and tanning, losing any excess fat and gaining muscle, until she looked almost as fit as Taye, only in a womanly way.

She adored her new breasts; they gave her so much more confidence, and Taye loved them too.

Would he ever cheat again?

He'd better not, because if there *was* a next time, she'd leave him, take the twins, and make his life pure hell.

Eighteen months previously, Ashley had decided that appearing in ads with Taye was not enough for her—it was time she had her own career. The twins were getting older, and she'd been thinking about doing something that was all hers. Since she'd always fancied herself an interior designer, she'd approached Jeromy Milton-Gold, the designer who'd worked on their house. Jeromy was the older boyfriend of Latin singing star Luca Perez. She'd asked Jeromy if she could be part of his team. Jeromy, who was always looking for ways to up his profile, told her it was a fabulous idea, and that if Taye was prepared to invest in his business, they could definitely work something out.

Ashley went to Taye and asked him to put up some money.

To keep Ashley happy, he'd obliged, in spite of his business manager telling him he was nuts.

Ashley was delighted that Jeromy wanted her to work alongside him.

Before long, there was a *new* hot show in town. The Ashley and Jeromy show. Interior designers to the stars. Both with famous partners. Both with endless ambition.

It started out as a winning combination. Lately, things had not been so good.

"Got somethin' to show you," Taye said, waving a large cream envelope in the air.

"What?" Ashley asked, moving away from the mirror and drifting into the bedroom.

"Wouldn't *you* like t' know," Taye teased, following her.

Taye enjoyed teasing his wife; it gave him a feeling of power. And he was holding power in his hand, for in the envelope with the embossed gold border and exquisite calligraphy was an invitation that, if he knew his wife, she would positively cream over.

"Don't mess about," Ashley said, still slightly irritated.

"Give us a kiss, then," Taye said, putting his arms around her from behind.

"Not now," she said, wriggling out of his grasp.

"What's wrong with you?" Taye complained. "The kids are at me mum's. Nobody's around. It's the perfect time."

"No it's not," Ashley argued. "We're about to go out to dinner, and I don't want to ruin my makeup or my hair."

"I'll make it a quickie," Taye promised.

"Don't be disgusting," Ashley responded. "If we're going to do it, then we should do it in our bed like normal people."

Taye shook his head. Sometimes Ashley acted like a total prude. "Normal" people! What was *that* all about? Made her sound like her racist mother, whom he barely tolerated.

"I suppose a blow job's out of the question, then?" he ventured, edging closer.

Ashley's look of disapproval informed him that indeed it was.

Whatever happened to the girl he'd married? Free and easy, up for all kinds of sexual adventures. They'd had sex here, there, and everywhere. Now he had to practically plead to get any sex at all. It wasn't right. He still loved her, though; she was his wife, and nothing would ever change that.

"Later?" he asked hopefully.

"We'll see," she responded. "Go get changed, and hurry up. We're meeting Jeromy. He's off to Miami tomorrow, and we can't be late. You know how prompt *he* always is."

"Jeromy's such a borin' wanker. Do we *have* to go?"

"Yes, Taye. In case you've forgotten, I work with him, so stop bitching and go get ready."

"Okay, okay."

Since she appeared to have forgotten about the envelope, Taye decided not to show it to her until they came home. He knew it would put her in an excellent mood. That and a couple of glasses of wine, and he'd have no trouble getting a piece of what was rightfully his.

Yes, Taye knew how to handle his wife.

Carefully.

That was the secret.

3
Dateline: Paris

There was never enough time in the day for Flynn Hudson to achieve all the things he wished to accomplish. As a respected, somewhat maverick freelance journalist and writer, he was always on the move, traveling wherever the latest disaster took him. Over the last year alone, he'd been in Ethiopia, Haiti, Indonesia, Japan, and Afghanistan. He'd covered tsunamis, earthquakes, floods, wars.

Flynn was always front and center of the action, reporting on events, government corruption, human rights. He was an activist who answered to no one except himself, with a Web site that had almost a million followers, because when Flynn wrote one of his essays, his faithful readers knew they were getting the real deal, not the fake bullshit that most news stations fed the gullible public.

Yet Flynn preferred to keep a low profile. He turned down TV interview requests, avoided being photographed. Home was a small apartment in Paris, where he lived alone.

He did have girlfriends. Several. Although none of them had ever gotten close.

Flynn Hudson was a loner. That's the way he liked it.

Born in England thirty-six years ago to an American mother and British father, he'd been educated across the world, as his father was a diplomat. They'd traveled extensively, until at the age of twelve he'd witnessed his parents killed by a terrorist car bomb in Beirut. Miraculously, he'd survived the tragedy, and he had the scars to prove it.

After the death of his parents, he'd led a double life—spending half his time with his American grandparents in California, and the other half with his British kin, who resided in the English countryside. He didn't mind flying back and forth; it was an adventure.

After attending a U.K. university for a year, he'd switched to UCLA in California, before dropping out when he was twenty-one and setting out to roam the world.

And roam the world he did. He backpacked across Asia, mountain climbed in Nepal, learned martial arts in China, joined a fishing boat in Marseilles, worked as a bodyguard for a Colombian billionaire who turned out to be a drug lord, until finally, at the age of twenty-five, he'd sat himself down and written a successful book about his travels.

Flynn could have been a media star; he was certainly handsome enough. Six feet two, strong and athletic, with longish dark hair, intense ice-blue eyes, and ever-present stubble on his sharp jawline.

Women loved Flynn. And he loved them back, as long as they expected nothing permanent.

Once upon a time, he'd made a lifetime commitment. It hadn't turned out the way he'd expected. No more commitments for Flynn. He was done.

As an alpha male, he respected women, enjoyed their company on a short-term basis, and never tried to control them. He wanted what was best for them, especially women in Third World countries who had to fight every day for their very survival. He helped out when he could, writing about the places he went, exposing corruption, using whatever resources he could get his hands on to assist the not so fortunate.

Money had one meaning to Flynn, and that was helping others.

* * *

The girl crawled on top of Flynn like a particularly ener-
getic spider monkey, all long gangly legs and arms, small
breasts, cropped hair, and enormous kohl-outlined eyes.
He thought her name was Marta; he wasn't sure. Sometimes he felt he wasn't sure of anything anymore, not after
some of the atrocities he'd witnessed. He'd recently returned from Afghanistan, where he'd watched a photographer colleague of his caught in the crossfire between border
guards and a car carrying two suicide bombers. The guy
had gotten his head blown off—literally by getting too
close to the bombers simply to catch the best shot.

The image of the car blowing up, and that of the head-
less body of his friend lying in the mud, was embedded in
Flynn's mind. It was a photograph he couldn't erase.

After returning to Paris, he, who didn't drink much,
had gotten hopelessly drunk two nights in a row.
Marta—or whatever her name was—happened on night
two, and he wished he'd never picked her up and brought
her home.

After reaching an unsatisfactory orgasm, he managed
to slide her off him.

"*Et moi?*" she said indignantly.

"Not tonight," he mumbled, feeling the onslaught of a
major hangover. "Go home."

So she did. Reluctantly.

In the morning, nursing a massive hangover, he discovered she'd taken his wallet with her.

No more drinking.

No more slutting around.

It was his own fault. He should've known better.

Lately, things were getting on top of him: his recent
visit to China, where in some places it was deemed acceptable to drown baby girls at birth. Another trip to Bosnia,
attempting to give aid to women who'd been raped. And
then to Pakistan to write a story for *The New York Times*

about an American citizen who'd been drugged by a prostitute and had his kidney cut out and stolen.

Flynn needed a break.

Sorting through his mail, mostly bills, he came across a fancy envelope addressed to "Mr. Flynn Hudson & Guest."

Extracting the invitation, he scanned it quickly.

It wasn't his kind of thing, but then the thought occurred to him—why the hell not?

Maybe this was exactly the break he'd been looking for.

4

Dateline: Los Angeles

Being the girlfriend of a huge movie star did not sit well with Lori Walsh's ego. Oh yes, in one respect it was all strawberries and cream: her name was out there, and people were exceptionally nice to her—important people. All the magazines featured photos of her frolicking on the beach in Malibu, or walking her significant others, two large black Labradors. She was always included in the endless red-carpet interviews at premieres and award shows, hovering beside the famous one, looking like the adoring, albeit slightly awkward, girlfriend.

But *why* was her name out there? *Why* were influential and powerful people nice to her?

Because . . .

Because she was the live-in girlfriend of Cliff Baxter. *The* Cliff Baxter—the man with George Clooney's charm, Jack Nicholson's acting chops, and irresistible good looks. Mister Movie Star. No mistake about *that*.

Mister "I get my ass kissed every time I fart."

Mister "Everyone wants to be my friend."

Mister "Even when I'm full of shit you're still gonna love me."

Lori—an actress herself, although much to her chagrin she was constantly referred to as "former waitress"—had been Mister Movie Star's girlfriend for the past year. "A record," his friends had informed her, as if she'd won some kind of amazing race. "You must have something special," his friends' wives had whispered in her ear with slightly puzzled expressions, because in their minds surely Cliff could do better.

Yes, she had something special, all right. Patience. And the knack for pretending not to know when her famous boyfriend ordered in a call girl for a midnight snack in his pool house office, or spent time on his computer watching porn.

Apparently his former girlfriends *had* objected, and with the objections came banishment. After they were gone, it was on to the next.

However, Lori was smarter than all of them. She was going for the prize. The ring on her finger. She was one canny girlfriend who was sticking it out.

Cliff Baxter was heading full-tilt toward fifty, and he'd never been married.

Lori was twenty-four—half his age, which was the perfect Hollywood age difference. Besides, she loved him, in a kind of screwed-up way. He reminded her of the father who'd dumped her and her mom when she was only twelve, leaving the two of them with no money, no home, and a ton of bills to pay. Lori felt safe with Cliff; she felt protected, and sometimes she even felt loved.

The truth was that she wanted to be Mrs. Cliff Baxter even more than she wanted a career, and that was saying something, as she'd been harboring an ambition to be the next Emma Stone. She and Emma even looked a little alike, with the same athletic body and slightly toothy grin, although Lori considered herself to be a sexier version of the talented actress. Cliff was very into Lori's amazing mane of red hair, but what *really* turned him on was her matching pubes. She'd offered to do a Brazilian for him, but he was having none of it. "I like a woman to be natural," he'd told her. "Enough with the shaved pussies, they're not sexy. Keep it real, babe."

So be it. Whatever Cliff wanted, Cliff got. It was quite

a relief not to have to go through the agony of having the hair ripped from her crotch by a bad-tempered Polish woman with a penchant for inflicting pain.

However, being just the girlfriend was risky. A year was a long time. What if Cliff got bored with her? What if he discovered that the porn and the call girls were enough to keep him satisfied?

She didn't care to think about it. She dreaded going back to being just another Hollywood starlet begging for a job. Oh no, that was not about to be her future.

To protect herself, she'd made it her mission to find out all of Cliff's dirty little secrets—facts that nobody knew about him. She was determined to discover the real Cliff Baxter, not the adored icon with the starry image and self-deprecating charm.

Lori was extremely adept at underground activities. She'd learned from her mom, Sherrine, at an early age that it was useful to dig out people's secrets and use them to your advantage. That's how they'd gotten by after her dad had done a midnight runner. They'd survived because Sherrine had known how to manipulate people—such as their randy landlord, who was cheating on his wife, the supermarket checkout clerk who was padding customers' bills and pocketing the cash, and the cable guy who was into making money on the side.

Free rent. Free food. Free cable. They got by. Her mom juggled a series of boyfriends who also contributed to their survival.

Lori hadn't spoken to her mom in eight years, ever since Sherrine had caught her making out with one of her transient boyfriends. At the time, Lori was sixteen. Sherrine's boyfriend was twenty-five and a total stud. And Sherrine was thirty-five and beyond pissed. She'd thrown Lori out, along with the boyfriend, who'd allowed Lori to camp out at his place for a few weeks until she'd run into Stanley Abbson, an elderly gentleman who drove a Bentley and was very partial to underage girls.

Stanley Abbson was seventy-five years old, but thanks to Viagra, he was still able to get it up. They'd met on the boardwalk in Venice when Lori had skateboarded into him and almost knocked him flat. He hadn't minded at all, and after a couple of lunches, he'd invited her to move into an apartment where he kept two other teenage girls. It was a decent apartment overlooking the ocean; Lori could hardly believe her luck.

Stanley—who, she'd found out, lived elsewhere in a large house—gave the girls a generous allowance, and all he asked in return was the occasional girl-on-girl show, which was doable, until he started bringing along a few of his pervy old business acquaintances to watch and sometimes participate. That's when Lori decided it was not the life for her, so she'd packed up and left, taking with her Stanley's solid-gold watch and the stash of cash he'd kept hidden in the apartment. The money was enough to pay six months' rent on a run-down beach shack in Venice, where she lived for the next four years, taking acting classes, working as an extra, waitressing, doing some escort jobs that did not involve sex, and generally getting by.

Boyfriends came and went. A car salesman. A burned-out comedian. Several out-of-work actors. And a low-rent showbiz manager who offered her a career in porn, which she politely declined.

At twenty-two, Lori had realized she was getting nowhere fast, so she'd decided to move to Vegas.

Because she was a pretty, fresh face, with luxuriant red hair, long legs, and a winning smile, she immediately scored a job at the Cavendish Hotel as a cocktail waitress. The pay wasn't great, but the lavish tips made up for it.

The customers loved Lori, and so did the manager, because she could persuade almost anyone to order the best champagne, the most expensive cocktails, and the high-priced caviar hors d'oeuvres.

It wasn't long before the manager promoted her to chief cocktail hostess in the VIP lounge, and that's where she met Cliff. He'd come in one night pleasantly drunk, accompanied by an entourage of six and a skinny, model-type girlfriend, who kept crawling into his lap and tongue-kissing his ear.

Lori tried not to look impressed at the sight of such a famous man, although she remembered Sherrine taking her to see one of his movies when she was eleven, and she clearly recalled Sherrine stating at the time that Cliff Baxter was the sexiest man on two legs. Lori reckoned that even though he must be in his forties now, he still looked pretty hot.

She played it cool.

He flirted.

His girlfriend gave her the stink-eye.

She ignored the skank.

When Cliff and his entourage left, he slipped her a thousand-dollar cash tip.

She shoved the money down the neckline of her skimpy outfit and didn't share with the other staff, even though she was supposed to.

He came back two weeks later, sober and alone. He sought her out and asked if she had a boyfriend. She said no, although at the time, she was living with a hunky bar-man who worked at The Keys.

He invited her to dinner.

She said no.

He invited her to visit him in L.A.

She said no.

He invited her upstairs to his suite.

She said no.

Instinctively, she'd known that Cliff Baxter could be her big break, and that to make it happen she had to play hard to get. So she'd strung him along for several months, and each time he made the Vegas trip she'd continued to play it cool. Then just when she'd sensed he was about to give up on her, she'd accepted his dinner invitation.

That night they'd ended up in his suite, where she'd given him the blow job of his dreams.

Just a blow job. Nothing else.

Two weeks later, she was living with him in his L.A. mansion.

"Mr. Baxter, they're ready for you on the set," the young second AD called out, peering into Cliff Baxter's trailer after knocking on the door twice.

When the star didn't respond, she tentatively ventured inside and saw that he was asleep on the comfortable couch, snoring loudly, wearing nothing but a robe that had fallen open to reveal solid tanned thighs and chocolate-colored underwear.

The girl squinted at the sleeping movie star and wondered what she should do. She was new on the job and intimidated by being in the presence of such a big star. Fortunately, she was saved by the arrival of Enid, Cliff Baxter's personal assistant, a fierce older woman clad in a no-nonsense Hillary Clinton–style pantsuit and Nurse Ratched running shoes.

"What's going on here?" Enid inquired, taking in the nervous young girl and her boss's half-exposed lower half.

"Mr. Baxter is needed on the set," the girl said, an agitated quiver in her voice. "I'm supposed to tell him."

"Then I suggest you wake him," Enid said briskly, placing a large messenger bag filled with papers on the table.

"Uh . . . uh . . . how should I do that?" the girl stammered.

"Like this, dear," Enid said, leaning over and giving Cliff a vigorous shake on his shoulder.

The girl took a hurried step back as Cliff sat up. "What the fuck . . ." he mumbled. "Where am I?"

"You're at the studio," Enid announced. "You're wanted on set, so shift your ass."

"For a rehearsal, Mr. Baxter," the girl said, bravely joining in.

"Must've dozed off," Cliff announced with a big yawn. "Friend's bachelor party last night. It ended late, so I had my driver bring me straight here."

"And how did Little Miss Live-In like *that*?" Enid questioned caustically.

"*C'mon,* Enid," Cliff said, standing up and laughing. "What did Lori ever do to you? She's a sweet kid. Why do you always have to put her down?"

Enid pulled a face, and began extracting papers and mail from her messenger bag and piling them on the table.

"Shall I tell Mr. Sterling you're on your way?" the young AD asked, trying to avert her eyes from Cliff's open robe.

"Yeah, yeah, tell Mac I'll be there in five. And next time, I'd appreciate a fifteen-minute warning. You can go get me coffee now. Black. Plenty of sugar. Have it waiting on the set."

"Yes, Mr. Baxter."

Cliff threw her a jaunty wink. "Run along, unless you're planning to witness me bare-assed naked."

The girl blushed, and hurriedly backed out of the trailer.

Cliff chuckled. "They get younger every day," he ruminated, shrugging off his robe. "And you know what, Enid? Here's the crap part—*I* get older."

"We all do," Enid said crisply. "Stop feeling sorry for yourself, and for God's sake, put some clothes on. I've seen better packages at the post office."

"You can be such a mean old bag," Cliff said, seemingly unfazed. "Mean and ornery. Dunno why I put up with you."

"Because," Enid answered matter-of-factly, "I have worked for you for almost twenty years, and I am one of the few people who can break your balls without getting fired. And speaking of balls, yours are hanging out."

Cliff grinned. "Surely you know that hanging out's my thing?"

"If you're not careful, your *thing* will be out too."

Cliff grabbed his pants from the back of the couch and pulled them on. "Don't you wish," he said, still grinning.

"No, Cliff," Enid said sternly. "I am one of the few women in this world who has no desire to see your cock, your balls, or anything else you might have to offer."

"Dyke!"

"Yes, dear. And I'm proud to say that I enjoy pussy almost as much as you do."

"Except for Lori's."

"She's not pussy, she's a predator," Enid said sharply. "Not good enough for you."

Cliff shook his head. "For crissakes . . ."

"Just don't marry her, that's all."

"Marry her!" Cliff exclaimed with a throaty chuckle. "When did the *m* word raise its ugly head?"

"You should get going," Enid said, folding her arms across her chest. "It's unprofessional to keep people waiting."

"No shit?"

"And when you have time, there are a few things I need your answers on," Enid added, waving an expensive-looking envelope in his face. "This is an invitation you might like."

"Not another black-tie event," he groaned. "I've attended enough of those to last me a lifetime. This is award-show city. No more. I'm over it."

"This invite is something different," Enid said. "I'll show you when you get back. Now it's your turn to run along."

"And she talks to me as if I'm twelve," Cliff said, shaking his head again.

"And sometimes he acts as if he is," Enid retorted.

"I might be forced to fire you when I return," he threatened, reaching for a shirt and putting it on. "You have no respect."

5

Dateline: Miami

Luca Perez stretched out on a striped lounger wearing a barely-there powder-blue Speedo, his well-toned thirty-year-old body oiled to perfection, not an inch of flesh spared. On the table next to him stood a tall glass containing a mojito. Next to his drink was a Lalique dish filled with ripe red cherries, a pile of the latest entertainment magazines, his iPhone, his platinum diamond-encrusted Chanel watch, and several crucifixes attached to thin leather cords.

Luca, his eyes covered by Dolce & Gabbana shades, was almost asleep, but not quite. He enjoyed lying there in a drowsy state, allowing his mind to run riot. Nothing to disturb him. No one to bother him. Just a lazy day of doing nothing except perfecting his tan. And what a beautiful day it was: hazy sunshine, a light breeze. He'd recently returned from a demanding world tour, so life at his Miami mansion was good.

Tomorrow, his significant other, Jeromy Milton-Gold, would arrive from London, which meant good-bye to peace and quiet. Jeromy was a social animal; he always wanted to go out and be seen at leather bars and gay clubs—something Luca preferred not to do, even though they'd met at a notorious rubber fetish club in London two years ago. Meeting Jeromy had changed Luca's life. Before Jeromy, he'd been firmly closeted, living a secret gay life lest his legions of female fans find out, because Luca was a huge Latin heartthrob, a singer women worshipped and adored.

And he was married. And he had a son.

At the time.

He still had a son, Luca Junior, who was now nine years old. But he was no longer married to the larger-than-life Latin superstar Suga—the woman who'd discovered him as a teenager, nurtured his talent, married him, had his baby, and made him the star he was today.

Suga was twenty years older than Luca, yet still a voluptuous beauty with a huge following in South America. She'd accepted the fact that her husband was gay with humor and understanding. Divorce—no problem. "Ah, but Suga had you at your best," she'd joked. "Go do what makes you happy, Luca. My heart goes with you."

Suga was an amazing woman, and to Luca's delight, they'd remained best friends, sharing custody of their handsome young son, who'd inherited the best of both his parents.

So, against the advice of everyone else—his agents, managers, record producers, and label bosses—Luca had made the leap into gaydom. If Ricky Martin could do it and survive, why couldn't he?

And survive he did. His fans were fiercely loyal; they adored him. Gay or straight, it didn't matter to them. He was Luca Perez. He was their god. Now he was their gay god.

Still, Luca didn't wish to flaunt his coming-out. No threesomes or kinky goings-on in public, although once in a while he allowed Jeromy to throw a wild party at the mansion—no cameras allowed.

Jeromy Milton-Gold was not the partner people would expect Luca to choose. Jeromy was a tall, slim, very English old Etonian, with patrician features, a longish nose, floppy brown hair, and a somewhat snobbish attitude. At forty-two, he was twelve years older than his sun-kissed, blond, buff-bodied, famous boyfriend. They made an incongruous couple; however, it seemed to work for them.

The envelope addressed to Luca Perez and Jeromy Milton-Gold looked like it contained something interesting. It was of excellent stock, with intricate embossed gold calligraphy, and it appeared tasteful and expensive.

Sitting at his David Armstrong-Jones desk in his London showroom adjacent to Sloane Square, Jeromy Milton-Gold pried open the envelope with a silver letter opener and extracted the enclosed invitation.

He read it carefully. Twice.

A satisfied smile crossed his face. This was one invitation they were *not* turning down.

He slid open the center drawer of his desk, carefully placed the invitation back in its envelope, and put it next to his passport. Tomorrow he would show it to Luca and insist that they accept.

Sometimes Luca could be stubborn, only this time Jeromy refused to take no for an answer. This time it was a done deal.

6

Dateline: New York

The politician and his lovely wife were invited everywhere; they were one of the most popular couples in the city. He, so honest-looking and upstanding with his regular features, well-cut brown hair, and "I will do everything I can for my people" attitude. She, both delicate and strong at the same time, slender, with shoulder-length honey-coppery hair, a beautiful face, and widely spaced, warm brown eyes.

Her name was Sierra Kathleen Snow. His name was Hammond Patterson Jr., although—much to his father's chagrin—shortly after getting into politics, he'd dropped the *Jr.* "It doesn't sound right," he'd muttered.

"I'll tell you what sounds right," his father had raged. "Using the family name and the family reputation. *That's* what sounds right to me."

Hammond Patterson Jr. wasn't so sure. His father had been a congressman for many years, and that was not the role Hammond was planning to play. Instead, after college he'd gone straight to law school, then pursued a career as an attorney, and in time he'd parlayed that career into becoming, at thirty-six, one of the youngest senators in Congress.

Representing New York as the junior senator, he was full of ambition. He had high hopes that eventually he would become governor of the state, then, after that, possibly make a run for the White House.

Why not? He had all the right credentials. And, most of all, he had supreme confidence.

Hammond was an extremely driven man. Nothing was about to stop him.

Sierra, on the other hand, possessed a warmth and candor that attracted men and women alike. She was smart and compassionate, with a generous soul. As far as Hammond was concerned, she was the perfect political wife, an asset to have by his side at all times, which is exactly why he'd picked her.

Recently, Hammond's climb to the top had come across an unexpected stumbling block. And that stumbling block was the disturbing realization that he'd fathered a child in his younger years. Apparently, he'd gotten some girl pregnant, and that girl had gone ahead and given birth to a daughter, named Radical.

Radical had arrived at his office one day, fifteen years old and determined to meet her father.

Hammond was furious and shocked. When the girl finally got in to see him and announced she was his daughter, he didn't believe her. This couldn't be happening to him. It was impossible.

But Radical produced a birth certificate with his name on it and informed him that her mom had died from a drug overdose, and that she had nowhere else to go.

Two paternity tests later, Hammond was forced to admit that this strange, unruly teenager with streaks of green in her dyed black hair, multiple piercings, and a snotty attitude was indeed his.

Sierra, being the kind and thoughtful person that she was, had insisted that Radical join the family.

"We have to take her in," Sierra had lectured him. "She's your daughter. You have no choice. Think of your public image if you don't."

Finally, Hammond had agreed, terrified that the sudden appearance of an illegitimate teenage daughter would wreak havoc with his carefully projected image.

The public still loved Hammond and Sierra. They were accepting of his youthful transgression. Sexual scandals involving politicians were nothing new, and with Sierra next to him, Hammond could do no wrong.

Radical turned out to be a nightmare. Rude and willful, she caused trouble wherever she went. She hated her father, and he hated her right back.

Angry that he was stuck with her, Hammond soon packed her off to boarding school in Switzerland, even forcing Sierra to agree that it was for the best.

Radical went. But not without a fight.

When Hammond's assistant, Nadia, entered his office and showed him the fancy invitation, he didn't hesitate. Without checking with Sierra, he instructed Nadia to accept immediately.

Hammond smelled big money, major campaign contributions when the time came for him to run, and Hammond was well aware that important connections were everything. Plus this was a fine chance for him to start planting the seeds of his unstoppable ambition.

Yes, Hammond knew a viable opportunity when it came his way. He was no fool.

Sierra Kathleen Snow was born into great privilege. Her father was the respected Pulitzer Prize winner Archibald Snow, an academic and a renowned writer of history tomes, while her mother, Phoebee, was a true New York society beauty whose family dated back to the founding fathers.

Sierra had an older sister, Clare, who was married to a pediatrician and had written a series of bestselling books about parenting. Clare and her husband had three young children and resided in Connecticut. Sierra also had a brother, Sean, who lived in Hawaii with a woman he'd picked up on the beach.

Clare was the darling of the family, while Sean was the dark side. Sierra was somewhere in the middle.

At thirty-two, Sierra was still not sure where she fit in.

She was Archibald and Phoebee Snow's daughter. She was Hammond Patterson's wife. She was Clare Snow's sister. But who was she really?

Every morning, upon waking, she asked herself that question.

Who am I today?
Am I the politician's wife?
The dutiful daughter?
The loving, supportive sister?
Who am I?

It was a question that haunted her, because she honestly didn't know the answer.

Her illustrious parents disapproved of Hammond. Although they'd never actually said it out loud, she knew that they did. When Radical had appeared on the scene, the expression on her mother's face had said it all. *We always suspected that Hammond was a rogue. Now we know for sure.*

A rogue who harbored aspirations to eventually become president of the United States. With her by his side.

The very thought made Sierra shudder. She'd been married to Hammond for eight years, and she didn't love him. She'd started off thinking that she did, but after a while, she'd realized that she'd married him to get over a broken heart, and he'd married her because of her impeccable pedigree and family connections. Hammond was not the man he'd pretended to be.

He was a psychopath. A very clever psychopath.

To the world, he presented a smiling, honest face, was seemingly a nice-looking man filled with empathy and caring. With his brown hair, regular features, and captivating smile, he seemed like such an open book. However,

Hammond's public persona was a far cry from how he was in private. Sierra knew for a fact that he was a bigot and a misogynist and hated gays. He had a cruel tongue and a nasty, sadistic streak. He talked about everyone in a disparaging way, including her family, and he loathed his own father. He was forever voicing his wishes that the man would drop dead of a sudden heart attack.

At first she'd tried to dig into his psyche, to discover where all this anger came from, but it was a lost cause. The charming, attentive man she'd married had turned into a secret monster who actually scared her, which was why she hadn't left him.

Two years into their marriage, she'd realized what a fraud he was, and she'd threatened to divorce him. Very calmly, he'd informed her that if she ever left him, he'd arrange to have her entire family killed, and that he would make sure she was maimed for life.

Shocked and horrified, she'd considered going to the police. Then she'd realized that nobody would believe her. She was Sierra Patterson, wife of the up-and-coming politician Hammond Patterson, a man who fought for everyone's rights—including gays and women.

It was an impossible situation, and to make it even worse, Hammond was continually unfaithful, sleeping with any woman he could get his hands on.

When she'd confronted him about his indiscretions, he'd sneered at her. "What am I supposed to do?" he'd said with cold indifference. "Fucking you is like fucking a dead fish."

Sierra knew she should leave, but Hammond's threats were all too real, and she simply couldn't summon the courage to get out. What if he went through with his foreboding words and actually harmed her family? She knew without a doubt that he was capable of anything.

So Sierra stayed and threw herself into helping people. She visited children's hospitals, formed a rape prevention group, rallied for battered women, and did everything she could to take her mind off her miserable home life.

Hammond was pleased. He'd been right about Sierra: she was the perfect politician's wife. A beautiful and gracious woman who was also a do-gooder.

What could be better for a man on his way to the top?

7

Bianca reached for a towel, wrapping it around her smooth, gleaming body as she moved closer to Aleksandr.

He seized a corner of the towel and roughly pulled it away from her. The towel fluttered to the ground.

"You are so beautiful," he said, his voice a throaty growl as he began rubbing his thick fingers against her extended nipples. "Such a fine woman, and all mine."

Bianca experienced a shiver of delight and responded accordingly. Whenever Aleksandr wanted her, she was ready.

Early on in their relationship, she'd learned from Aleksandr that his wife was a sexually cold woman who'd informed him shortly after they were married that his very touch repulsed her.

Apparently his money hadn't.

Bianca didn't care that he was so enormously rich. She genuinely cared about the man, and she loved the way he was able to turn her on with nothing more than a glance. His dark eyes were deeper than a glacier; she could never tell what he was thinking. His touch was strong and manly. As for his equipment—perfection. Long and thick and solid, the best she'd ever experienced. Plus he knew what to do with it, a true bonus after a series of famous men who considered erectile dysfunction totally normal.

Aleksandr pushed her to the ground and dropped his

pants. He never wore underwear, something they had in common.

The cold tile against her skin made her shiver even more as she spread her long legs for her lover. Glancing up, she noticed the red light on the security camera and wondered if they were being watched or filmed.

It didn't matter. Aleksandr controlled everything, and he would never allow anyone to use her or anything bad to happen.

His solid body crushed her beneath him as he entered her. He was a big man, big and powerful. She took a deep breath, inhaling his overpowering masculine scent.

"Oh . . . my . . . God . . ." she murmured. "You feel so amazing, so damn hard."

"Only for you, my little *kotik*. Only for you."

"Yes," she sighed, shifting her body to accommodate him. "You know, Aleksandr, you're the only man who has ever truly satisfied me."

He was heavy on top of her. She didn't care, the sex was that exciting. She got off on the way he thrust himself inside her as if he was determined to own her.

Nobody had ever owned Bianca. She was a free spirit. With Aleksandr, she had no desire to be free. She yearned for him to possess her in every way, and possess her he did with his strong arms, full body weight, and hard penis.

At the beginning of their relationship, she'd tried to assert herself in the bedroom, but Aleksandr would have none of it. He expected total control. Sex would take place his way or not at all.

Bianca was cool with that. She was so used to calling the shots with men, it made a refreshing change to allow someone else to be in charge.

Groaning with pleasure, she flexed her thigh muscles, causing Aleksandr to grunt his appreciation.

He made her feel like a little girl, a naughty little girl. It turned her on in a big way.

8

Sometimes Taye Sherwin's mind wandered, especially when Ashley was in one of her haughty moods—a personality trait that seemed to emerge every time they had dinner with Jeromy Milton-Gold. It pained Taye to watch his wife try so hard to act as if she'd been born in Mayfair as opposed to in the modest seaside town of Brighton. Ashley tried desperately to shrug off her roots, even though everyone knew she was not to the manner born. On the other hand, Taye was proud of where he came from, the Elephant and Castle. He was a true Cockney lad who'd done well for himself, and he was happy to tell anyone and everyone about his not-so-fancy beginnings.

Taye had no clue where Jeromy Milton-Gold had originally sprung from, but he was well aware that Jeromy was not averse to dropping names and carrying on as if he were the king of the castle. Or queen. *Yeah,* Taye thought with a wicked grin. *Shouldn't that be queen?*

"What are *you* smirking at?" Ashley asked, catching him mid-smirk.

"Just thinkin' about a joke one of the lads came up with today," Taye said, quick as a flash.

"Do share," Jeromy said, tapping the side of his wineglass with long, elegant fingers.

"You wouldn't find it funny," Taye replied, wishing they could get the hell out of the fancy restaurant and head for home, where he planned on showing his wife the coveted invitation before banging her brains out. Man, he was feeling way horny.

"I can't stand jokes," Ashley said with a slight sniff of distaste. "They're always so sexist and never funny."

"I must say I'm forced to agree with you," Jeromy drawled. "Unamusing, and yet some people feel as if they're obliged to laugh."

"I think people only tell jokes when they run out of conversation," Ashley said, shooting Taye a snarky look. "It's as if they have nothing else to say."

"That'll never happen to you, toots," Taye retorted. "You're a world-class gossiper." He nudged Jeromy. "Never off the freakin' phone, this one. Always got a girl chat goin' on."

Jeromy curled his lip, a habit he'd developed when he wasn't quite sure what to say.

Ashley glared at her husband.

"Luca and I are going on a simply marvelous trip," Jeromy said at last, filling the sudden silence.

"That's nice," Ashley said, taking out her compact and applying more lipstick. "Where to?"

"Somewhere hot and exotic, I suspect," Jeromy said with an airy wave of his hand. "We've been invited by Aleksandr Kasianenko on the maiden voyage of his new yacht."

Ashley's eyes widened. "How fabulous," she sighed. "Lucky you."

Taye was speechless. Dammit, Jeromy was messing with his surprise. What was he supposed to do now? Blurt out that they were invited too, and risk a tongue-lashing from Ashley, who'd be livid that he hadn't told her?

"I can certainly use the break," Jeromy said with a patronizing smirk. "I'm expecting that you'll keep an eye on things in the London showroom, won't you, dear?"

Ashley bobbed her head and turned to her husband. "*You* know Aleksandr whatever-his-name is, don't you?"

Taye nodded. "Yeah, we met a coupla times. He's a big football fan. There's a rumor goin' around that he's thinkin' of buyin' one of the clubs."

"Bianca is a dear friend of Luca's," Jeromy allowed, once more sipping his wine. "They met years ago at a fashion show in Milan. Luca was singing for a paltry million dinero, and Bianca was busy strutting her stuff. They have a history."

"Nice," Ashley said wistfully. "I bet it'll be a fab trip."

"Yes," Jeromy agreed. "I am sure it will be."

Taye and Ashley left the restaurant and drove home in silence—an uncomfortable silence, finally broken by Taye, who couldn't stand it when Ashley slipped into one of her moods.

"What's up, toots?" he said, one hand on the steering wheel, the other patting her on the knee. "You've gone all broody on me."

"Why do you always try to put me down in front of Jeromy?" she complained, her cheeks flaming. "I'm in business with the man, and you do your best to make me look like a fool."

"What're you talkin' about?"

"You know full well." And then, attempting to imitate him, she added in a mock-up of his voice, "This one's always on the phone gossiping."

"I'm not makin' it up," Taye said, withdrawing his hand from her knee. "You *are* always on the blower carrying on 'bout this an' that."

"I am so not," she said in an uptight voice. "I *do not* gossip. And even if I did, that's no reason for you to announce it to the world."

"C'mon, toots," he pleaded. "Let's not make this into a fight."

"No. *You* come on, Taye," she said crossly. "I hate it when you disrespect me. It's not right. I'm upset."

"Don't be, sunshine," Taye said, eager to placate her.

"'Cause I got a big surprise waitin' for you when we get home."

"I'm not interested in surprises," she said, staring out the window.

"You will be in this one," Taye assured her.

"You're so annoying," she said irritably. "Why do you always have to try and get me off track?"

"'Cause I love you, toots. You know that. An' I can't stand seein' you upset."

Ashley seized the opportunity to say something that was always lurking in the back of her mind. "I suppose you *really* loved me when you were *fucking* that big-titted tramp," she spat, her voice filled with venom.

"Ashley," he said, groaning. "That was freakin' years ago. How many times I gotta say I'm sorry? That bird meant nothin' to me. I've told you a million times."

"A million times isn't enough," Ashley muttered, still holding on to a major grudge. "How'd you like it if that'd been *me* in bed with some bloke? How would *that* grab you?"

"You wouldn't do it. Anyway, I trust you."

"Yes," she snorted. "And *I* trusted you, and look where *that* got me."

How had their conversation veered so off track? Every so often, Ashley brought up the one time he'd been unfaithful, but why was she doing it tonight?

Best to stay silent and let her vent.

Which she did.

Nonstop.

All the way home.

9

Flynn had a few things to take care of, two or three hard-hitting pieces to write, several follow-up calls, and a decision to make.

Aleksandr Kasianenko, an old friend from back in the day, had invited him on what seemed like it might be a spectacular trip. He'd been invited with a guest, and therein lay the problem. Who to bring with him? And, even more important, did he want to bring anyone at all?

Certainly not one of his casual girlfriends who were available for light relief and nothing else, which was one thing he always made clear up front *before* he slept with them. Flynn did not care to have any broken hearts on *his* conscience. He knew what a broken heart felt like only too well. He'd experienced the pain, abandonment, and downright misery that came with heartbreak, albeit a long time ago, but the feeling of loss had never really left him.

Yes. True heartbreak existed. And Flynn knew all about it, so he was always careful to warn women that if they were after anything more than a casual fling, he was not the man for them.

As he thought about who to take, one name came to mind: Xuan, an exquisite Asian who was beautiful, strong-minded, and conveniently more into women than men.

Xuan would definitely get a kick out of such a trip, and he would enjoy her company—he always did.

Xuan was a fellow journalist who'd escaped from a Communist regime when her parents were accused of being spies, then brutally taken away and murdered for their supposed crimes.

Xuan had arranged to get herself smuggled out of Communist China eleven years previously, and like Flynn, her special talent was writing about the injustices in a world gone crazy. They'd bumped into each other over the years in many different countries, and formed a close, nonsexual friendship, a friendship that suited both of them.

Flynn knew many of her stories: how she'd been gangraped on her way out of China, then rescued by a man who'd kept her locked up and beaten; how after a devastating miscarriage, she'd made another daring escape, going months with hardly any food, begging for sustenance along the way, until eventually she'd reached Hong Kong, where she'd been taken in by distant relatives.

The difficulties of trying to make a life for herself and discover her own identity had not been easy. But Xuan was strong; she'd prevailed and finally forged a career for herself as a fearless journalist.

After mulling it over, Flynn sent her a text inviting her. Together, exploring the extraordinary lifestyles of the rich and overly privileged could be an extremely memorable experience, one they might both benefit from.

Or not.

It didn't matter. At least it would be a welcome change from the horrors of the world they'd both seen up close.

Flynn waited for Xuan to respond; he hoped her answer would be a resounding yes.

In a small hotel room in Saigon, Xuan and her sometime lover, Deshi, lay on the bed fully sated, a ceiling fan whirling noisily above them. The sex had been satisfying, although not mind-blowing by any means. However, Xuan found Deshi to be an intelligent man with interesting tidbits of information about government activity that he let slip her way. Conveniently, Deshi happened to work for the government.

Sexually, Xuan preferred women, although when the occasion called for it, she was not averse to bedding down with a man. Information was information, and Xuan gathered it any way she could.

Her cell phone bleeped, indicating a text.

She leaned across Deshi to reach it, her small breasts grazing his chest.

Deshi took this as an indication that maybe there was more sex in his future. To his disappointment, it was not to be.

Xuan read Flynn's message. She was pleased to hear from her friend. Of all the knowledgeable and attractive men she knew, Flynn was number one. A solid guy with admirable values and an adventurous spirit.

The first time they'd run into each other, she'd told him she was bisexual, leaning toward the female sex. She was determined there would be no sexual tension messing up a friendship that she'd sensed could be quite precious. She was right. Sex had never interfered with their close relationship.

Now Flynn was inviting her on a trip.

How nice.

With rich people. Insanely rich people, because she knew who Aleksandr Kasianenko was. *Everyone* knew who Aleksandr Kasianenko was—the Russian billionaire steel magnate with the famous supermodel girlfriend, Bianca.

How intriguing.

To go or not to go? She would have to think about it.

"Anything important?" Deshi inquired.

"Nothing that cannot wait until later," Xuan said.

In a few hours, she would respond. It was not something she felt obliged to make an instant decision about.

10

Cliff Baxter happened to be a much-loved movie star. He had his faults, but overall he was the consummate professional, very aware of the people who worked on his movies, always making sure they were well taken care of. He considered his stand-in, Bonar, a loyal friend—they'd worked together for a solid twenty-five years, ever since Cliff's first big break in the 1987 movie *Fast Times on the Fast Track,* a film about a marathon runner and his dysfunctional family.

Cliff had hit pay dirt on that one. At the time, he was young, virile, and hot—*very* hot. Plus he could really act. The director had liked him and pushed him to do some great work. To Cliff's delight and surprise, he'd gotten his first Oscar nomination. He hadn't won, but what else was new?

He'd been nominated three times since then, and only won once. Better than not winning at all.

He and Bonar were the same age, both creeping close to fifty. But Bonar had a wife and three kids, while all Cliff had was an amazing career.

He didn't mind. He had no desire to be trapped in an institution called marriage, a soulless place where there was no escape unless you were prepared to part with half of your hard-earned assets.

Cliff liked knowing that, basically, he was a free man

who could go wherever he wanted and do anything he cared to do, and that there was no one around to stop him. Only his agent and his manager could tell him what to do, and usually he didn't listen.

Cliff considered most of his male friends totally pussy-whipped, or if not whipped, miserable divorced fathers paying alimony and only getting to see their kids every other weekend.

He was well aware that they all envied him. They *should* envy him. In their eyes, he was the one living the life.

Over the years, he'd had a series of live-in girlfriends, and he'd learned exactly when it was time to move them out. There was always that moment in time when they started becoming overly clingy and needy. He knew the signs only too well. Suddenly they started talking marriage, and marriage was strictly not on his agenda; it never had been.

So far, Lori had lasted longer than the others. She was a fun girl, and he was quite fond of her. Plus she gave the best head ever. He often thought that she must've studied at the famed Academy of Deep Throat—if there was such a place. And if there wasn't, there should be.

The truth was, he couldn't get enough of Lori's expert oral skills.

Usually he counted on professionals to do the things his girlfriends balked at, but since Lori, the midnight call-girl visits were getting fewer and fewer, and Internet porn failed to grab him.

Lori, it seemed, was up for anything.

Lori had a thing about running, and not through the staid streets of Beverly Hills. No, she liked exploring the hills, finding a hiking trail, and hitting it hard.

There were no paparazzi where she went. No spying eyes with cameras affixed to them.

Sometimes she took the dogs, sometimes she didn't.

Today she was on her own, high up in the mountains, running like a crazy woman, earbuds and iPod in place, Drake and Pitbull keeping her well entertained.

Then it happened. She went flying over a log and hit the ground with a sharp thud.

She sat there stunned, feeling like a fool, finally realizing that, fortunately, there was no one around to witness her embarrassment.

After a few moments of pure dizziness, she attempted to stand. Her ankle immediately gave way, and she fell back down with a yelp of pain.

Now what was she supposed to do? Call her movie-star boyfriend to rush to her rescue? He wouldn't come. He was currently on the set, filming, which meant he'd send people. One of them might tip off the paps, and then she'd be trapped not looking her best. Wouldn't want that.

Her eyes filled with tears. Why was this happening to her?

She fished out her cell phone from her shorts pocket, and just as she was about to call for help, she saw it and froze. "It" was a raggedy coyote emerging slyly from the bushes, standing stock-still and staring at her with haunted red eyes.

She met the animal's malevolent stare right on and felt fear course through her body. Recently, she'd read about a pack of coyotes savaging a couple of German shepherds. If *they* couldn't defend themselves, how could she?

Then a second coyote came loping out of the bushes, and she knew for sure that she was done for.

After rehearsing his upcoming scene, Cliff returned to his trailer, where Enid had made herself quite comfortable: stretched out on his couch, shoes off, TV on, soap opera in full swing.

"Make yourself at home," Cliff said caustically. "Can I get you anything? Coffee? A drink?"

Unfazed, Enid sat up, slipped on her Nurse Ratched

shoes, and said, "It took you long enough. I almost fell asleep."

"So sorry my rehearsal kept you waiting," Cliff said, full of sarcasm.

"I've got to get back to the office," Enid said, thrusting a sheaf of papers at him. "Sign these."

"What am I signing?"

"For God's sake, if you want me to explain, I'll be here all day. Your business manager sent them over. They're for your recent real-estate acquisitions."

Cliff knew he could trust Enid; she would never try to put anything past him.

"If I sign, will you give me my couch back?"

"My pleasure," Enid snorted. "This trailer smells like feet."

"You're not supposed to speak to movie stars like that. Our feet do not stink. Besides, you're the one who had her shoes off."

"Oh, please!" Enid said, waving an invitation at Cliff. "What do you want me to do about this?"

Cliff took the elaborate invitation and scanned it quickly. "Hey," he said. "Wouldn't miss it. Go ahead and accept."

"Just for you?"

"Put your bitch back in the bag, Enid," he said. "Answer for me *and* Lori. She'll get a kick out of a trip like this."

Enid sighed. This one was lasting longer than the others; Lori must have hidden talents that only Cliff knew about.

"Whatever pleases my lord and master."

Cliff chuckled. "Get the fuck outta here before I kick your crusty old ass to the curb."

Enid packed up her papers and left.

After a few minutes, Cliff put his head outside his trailer to see who was around. Sometimes he was able to pull together a bunch of the guys to play softball.

Today there was nobody around. Except . . . who was that approaching?

Oh shit, it was his costar in the movie, Billy Melina, a hot young actor with naked ambition eating away at him. A ready-to-rock stud at the top of his game. *Exactly like I used to be,* Cliff thought wryly.

They had only a few scenes together, so they were hardly friends.

Cliff watched Billy approach. He couldn't help wondering if Billy was headed for an almost thirty-year career like his. He doubted it. Everything was different today. The paparazzi ruled. The magazines printed anything they felt like. There were no rules left. No studio heads and powerful managers to protect their clients. TMZ ran riot on any star who left the sanctuary of their home.

No. In ten years, when Billy hit forty, he'd be long forgotten, while Cliff would still be in the game, because he had no plans to retire. He was an up-and-at-'em kind of guy. Like Redford and De Niro, he had no intention of ever quitting; he was in the race until the end.

"Hey," Billy said, all bronzed hard body and dirty-blond surfer hair. "Wassup?"

"Nothing much," Cliff responded. "You?"

"Same old crap," Billy said, flexing his muscles. "Just tryin' t' stay outta the rags."

"Yeah," Cliff said, thinking that Billy Melina was one handsome son of a bitch. "I know the feeling." He hesitated for a moment. Should he invite the younger actor into his trailer to shoot the shit, or should he let it go?

Let it go, his inner voice warned him. *Do you really want to hear all about Billy's divorce from the very famous Venus? Or the Vegas murder scandal Billy was vaguely involved in?*

No. He had better things to do.

"See you on the set," he said, retreating back into his trailer.

"Yeah, man," Billy said. "Later."

Cliff hit the couch again and reached for his cell. Might as well see what Lori was up to. Maybe even invite her to visit him on set.

Yes, he'd do that, tell her about the invitation.

Little Lori was going to be so excited.

11

"Aha!" Suga exclaimed, descending on Luca like a full-blown cyclone, all mountains of blond curls, bouncy breasts and jiggling hips encased in a bright-orange-and-green low-cut jumpsuit, with sky-high gold Louboutins on her tiny feet—the only small thing about her. "How's my favorite baby daddy?"

Suga was an over-the-top voluptuous diva with a steam-roller personality. She looked exactly like her fans would expect her to look, and they adored her for it.

Luca rolled off his sun-bed and stood up, allowing his ex-wife to envelop him in her generous curves. He got a whiff of her strong signature perfume, and many fond memories came flooding back. Ah yes, the day she'd discovered him and plucked him from obscurity. The day they'd first made love. And, most important of all, the day he'd stood in her recording studio and cut his first single.

Suga hugged him so tightly he could barely breathe, showering him with wet jammy kisses, as was her way.

Luca was glad Jeromy wasn't around to witness his ex-wife's display of affection. He knew it pissed Jeromy off that Suga was still such a big part of his life. Too bad—as far as Luca was concerned, it was something that would never change. He owed everything to Suga. Without her, there was no way he would have risen to become the star he was today. The blond, blue-eyed Latin singing sensation that Suga had introduced to the world.

"You're back early," he remarked, gently extricating himself from her clutches. "Thought you weren't due home until next week. What happened?"

Suga pulled a face. "My manager—he canceled the São Paulo concert. The ticket sales were not so fantastic."

"Must be the economy," Luca said without missing a beat. "Ticket sales are down across the board."

Suga patted his cheek affectionately. "Not for you, *mi amor.*"

"For everyone," Luca assured her, although he suspected it wasn't true. On *his* last concert tour, ticket sales had hit an all-time high.

He hated the fact that Suga's star was starting to fade. What could he do about it?

"Where is my other *tesoro*?" Suga demanded, hands on ample hips. "I have to hug my little Luca Junior."

"He's out playing soccer with some of his friends."

"Too bad," she said, pursing her lips. "I must go fetch him."

"No way," Luca said, hurriedly shaking his head. "The kid's nine—he'll be embarrassed if you descend on him. You know what he's like."

"Embarrassed! Ha!" Suga snorted. "I am his mama. I could *never* embarrass my little baby."

"Let's get together for dinner tonight, just the three of us," Luca suggested, knowing that Luca Junior would be mortified if Suga turned up at his soccer game in all her glory. "We'll have fun."

"*Sí?*" she said, raising an artfully penciled eyebrow. "And where is Mister Stick Up His Ass?"

"If you're talking about Jeromy, he's in London, back tomorrow."

"Ah." Suga sighed. "*Me vuelves loco!* You have so many beautiful boys to choose from, an' yet you stay with someone so . . . dry."

"You need to get to know him better," Luca said calmly. "We should hang out, spend more time together."

"I don't think so, *mi amor*," Suga said, shaking her curls. "He doesn't like me. I don't like him."

"Why can't you two get along?"

"Because Jeromy is *not* the man for you." After a meaningful pause, she added, "You will see. You will learn."

Luca shrugged. "Nothing to learn. I know everything there is to know about him."

Suga smiled before leaning over and lightly caressing her ex-husband's package. "Do not waste what you have, *cariño*. You are far too young and far too beautiful."

Luca couldn't help grinning. "You think?"

"Ah, *mi tesoro*, Suga knows," she cooed. "An' *you* know that Suga is always right."

Jeromy Milton-Gold groaned as he reached orgasm. When he was done, he roughly shoved the boy's head away from his crotch.

The boy, a sulky eighteen—if that—wondered aloud if Jeromy would now like to blow *him*.

"No," Jeromy snapped, as if the very thought disgusted him. "You can take your money and go."

"But I thought—"

"Don't think," Jeromy said sharply. "I am not paying you to think. Pick up your filthy money and get the hell out."

"Fucker!" the boy muttered under his breath.

Unfortunately, Jeromy heard him. "What did you say?" he asked, narrowing his eyes.

The boy grabbed his money from the table and made a run for the door.

Jeromy thought about chasing him and roughing him up, then thought, *Why bother?* The kid might be a fighter, and the last thing he needed was to arrive in Miami with a nasty black eye.

If only he could curb his desire for random satisfaction.

No, that would be asking the impossible. Besides, after a night out with Ashley and her boring (although admittedly gorgeous) husband, surely he was entitled to some light relief?

And what Luca didn't know . . .

Jeromy was excellent at burying any guilt he might feel. Besides, he'd never promised Luca that he would be faithful, and allowing some random boy he'd ordered off the Internet to give him oral was hardly being a slut. It was more like he was taking care of business in a purely uninvolved way.

Yes, that was it. No emotion. No connection. Merely a swift sexual transaction for money. In the morning, he'd be on a plane to Miami, then straight back into the arms of his superstar boyfriend.

He hoped that Luca's fat ex-wife, Suga, wasn't around. The woman was a joke with her huge floppy breasts, loud voice, and ridiculous blond curls. It was surely time that Luca disassociated himself from her.

The thought of his young partner ever having been with Suga made Jeromy physically sick. He tried not to think about it; however, there were times he couldn't stop himself from imagining them together. Suga rolling on top of Luca, crushing his perfect body with her outrageous tits, opening her legs for him, sucking his delicious cock. The images were unbearable.

What he couldn't understand was why Luca encouraged the cow to still be in his life. True, they had a son together, Luca Junior, but why couldn't Luca start putting some distance between them? Suga's Miami mansion was five minutes away from Luca's mansion. In Jeromy's eyes, it was not a happy situation.

Jeromy had made up his mind that when they were on the Kasianenko yacht, he would insist that they sell the Miami mansion and move far away from Miss Suga Tits, the title he'd bestowed on Luca's ex.

Ah yes, perhaps a house in London's Belgrave Square,

a house that he could decorate and transform into an amazing palace for his young lover.

Jeromy gave a thin smile at the thought of how envious all his London acquaintances would be if he persuaded Luca to move to London. With his prince in tow, he could lord it over everyone. He could certainly lord it over the affluent gay brigade who'd dismissed him as an old man when he'd hit forty.

Old man indeed! Meeting up with Luca had been a lifesaver. He'd shown every one of his so-called friends that Jeromy Milton-Gold still had it.

Jeromy had scored the perfect prize, and they could all go fly a kite. He had a rich, famous boyfriend, a revitalized business, and he was on top of the world. So fuck 'em all.

12

Hammond waved the invitation in Sierra's face as if it were a weapon. "We're taking this trip," he said brusquely. "And you'd better be sure to look your best. Aleksandr Kasianenko is an extremely rich and influential man. In case you're too stupid to realize it, I need to have people like him on my side. Aleksandr can help us a lot."

"You mean he can help *you*," Sierra muttered, wishing she were somewhere else. She hadn't wanted to visit Hammond at his office; however, he'd insisted she come, and as usual she'd complied.

She had a dull, throbbing headache, which lately was becoming a daily occurrence.

"You're such a miserable bitch," Hammond snarled. "My God, you're starting to look your age too. For crissakes, get yourself together."

"Maybe you should get rid of me," Sierra replied with a flash of her former self. "Find yourself a newer model— I'm sure there's plenty of fresh meat around to accommodate you. How about the young intern I saw in the office when I came in? She seems a likely candidate."

"Shut the fuck up," Hammond said with an icy glare. "You're my wife. Try to act as if you deserve the position."

Sierra was about to respond when Hammond's chief aide, Eddie March, entered the office. Eddie was the complete opposite of Hammond. A genuinely nice man, excellent at his job, and full of boyish enthusiasm. Eddie was the real deal.

As soon as Eddie appeared, Hammond's attitude changed. Suddenly he became Hammond Patterson, the smooth and charming man of the people.

"You should run along now, darling," he said, turning to his wife and kissing her on the cheek. "I want you to buy anything it takes for you to be the most beautiful woman on our upcoming trip. Here," he added, fishing in his pocket and producing a black American Express card. "Buy whatever you deem suitable. I know your taste is impeccable."

Sierra nodded. She was married to Jekyll and Hyde. She was married to a man of many faces.

"That's generous of you," Eddie said with an admiring chuckle. "If I gave my girlfriend a card like that, she'd zip out of town and never come back!"

Sierra smiled politely, while thinking, *I wish I could leave town and never come back.* But she knew that escaping from Hammond's clutches was impossible. Somehow or other he'd make good on his threats; she had no doubt at all about how far he would go.

"You look beautiful, as always," Eddie said, smiling at Sierra. "Morning, noon, and night. How do you do it?"

"You'd be wise to stop flattering her," Hammond said with an affectionate glance at his wife. "Too many compliments will go straight to her head. And that'll cost me."

Sierra couldn't take any more. Hammond's Mister Nice Guy act in front of people sickened her.

"I'd better get going," she said.

"Always a pleasure," Eddie said.

Sierra plastered on an empty smile and exited. She'd taken two Xanax in the morning to dull the pain of her false existence. Now she needed another pill to get her through the day.

The outer offices were full of people who worked for Hammond. His supporters, his team, most of whom had helped get him elected.

She wondered what they'd think if they knew the real man who lurked beneath the facade. Would they ever find out?

No. Because Hammond was too adept at concealing his real self.

Nadia, Hammond's assistant, stopped her on the way out. "Mrs. Patterson," Nadia said. "Our newest intern is such a huge fan. Would you mind if I introduced you? It would absolutely make her day."

"Not at all," Sierra said graciously as Nadia ushered the girl over to her.

The girl was ripe and young, slightly overweight with large breasts and a toothy smile.

"This is Skylar," Nadia said. "She's joining the team for the summer."

Yes, Sierra thought, *exactly the way Hammond likes them: enthusiastic and naive. He'll soon ruin all her illusions.*

"Hello, Skylar," she said with a warm smile. "Welcome."

"Thank you, Mrs. Patterson," Skylar replied, totally thrilled to be meeting the senator's popular wife. "It's an honor to be working for Senator Patterson. I feel so lucky."

I'm sure, Sierra thought. *And will it still be an honor when he grabs your ass and asks you to go down on him? Will you fall in love with him like a legion of foolish girls before you?*

"Enjoy your summer," Sierra murmured. *Enjoy giving the senator head and getting nothing in return. It's inevitable. A fact of life. Poor little girl, you'll be powerless to resist his honest brown eyes and ready smile. Tread carefully, for he will use you and then abandon you like he did all the others.*

She made it outside and fell into the town car waiting

for her, Hammond's black AmEx card still clutched in her hand. What to do with that?

Go shopping, of course. Infuriate him by spending more money than he intended. He'd only handed her the card to look like the generous husband in front of Eddie; it was all for show.

"Barneys," she said to the driver. "After that we'll make a stop at Bergdorf."

"Yes, Mrs. Patterson," the driver said, starting the car.

Sierra leaned back against the leather upholstery. What was she going to do about her life? How was she ever going to get away from Hammond?

The answer always escaped her.

13

The invitations had been sent, and Bianca waited impatiently for the replies to come in. She'd left Moscow and Aleksandr for a *Vanity Fair* cover shoot in Madrid. It wasn't the perfect situation leaving her man by himself, but the *Vanity Fair* photos were to accompany a lengthy story commemorating her successful career and her thirtieth birthday. Such excellent and prestigious coverage was very special.

Bianca had been a top model for almost thirteen years, ever since being discovered at the age of seventeen by a legitimate modeling agent, who'd noticed her waitressing at her parents' deli in Queens, New York. The man had told her she had potential, then slipped her his card.

It had taken her two months to get up the courage to phone him. And when she'd set off for her initial interview, she'd asked her Latino gang-banger boyfriend to go with her. This did not please the agent, who'd insisted her boyfriend stay in the waiting room, a move that didn't sit well with her boyfriend at all. He'd scowled all the way back to Queens, and they'd broken up a few weeks later.

The day she did her first test shots, she'd taken her mom with her. Her mom was an attractive if slightly work-worn Cuban woman who'd always kept secret her own ambition to be a model.

Bianca was a natural in front of the camera. Instinctively, she had it down, posing this way and that, making love to the camera.

And so began her brilliant career. A career that hadn't been without its ups and downs.

When Bianca started modeling, she was young and striking, with a strong personality. It didn't take long before she became the favorite of several top designers. This infuriated some of the older models, who felt she was a pushy girl with way too much attitude for such a newcomer.

Her rise especially angered the small but tight group of ethnic models. One in particular, Willow, did everything she could to sabotage Bianca's photo shoots and modeling gigs. Willow was a great beauty herself, also of mixed race, and she didn't feel there was room for the two of them. However, the more Willow tried to sabotage her, the more Bianca fought back. Eventually, when Willow realized that Bianca was not going away anytime soon, they reached a truce, and after a while they became friends, even doing a cover shoot for *Vogue* together, posing side by side.

Along with Naomi Campbell, Tyra Banks, and Beverly Johnson, they were the most famous women of color in the modeling world.

Bianca embraced her new life. She soon got into drugs and men and parties, sleeping with whomever she felt like, doing whatever she pleased. They were fun times that included snorting cocaine for breakfast and clubbing the night away.

It didn't affect her work. She was a star in her own world, and she enjoyed every minute of the decadent lifestyle she'd so readily embraced.

Her various affairs with rich, powerful, famous, and sometimes titled men were the stuff the tabloids loved. She used men for her own pleasure, and when she was bored with them, she moved on.

In her late twenties she'd gotten hooked on heroin

thanks to a world-famous rock-star boyfriend who didn't give a damn about anyone or anything. Her family and friends—including Willow—conducted an intervention, and she'd ended up in rehab for a torturous six months.

It was while she was in rehab that she'd taken a long, hard look at her life and decided it was time to think about what would really make her happy. It wasn't fame—she had that in spades. It wasn't money—she was quite comfortable in that respect. It was something more. She finally desired a real relationship that didn't take place on the front pages of the tabloids.

Yes. She needed someone who cared about Bianca the person, not the fantasy image.

Then along came Aleksandr, and it was as if she'd been reborn.

Ah . . . Aleksandr. She smiled every time she thought of him.

Aleksandr had never touched drugs, and he couldn't care less about seeing his photo in a magazine; in fact, he hated it. He preferred staying out of the limelight, although he'd had to get used to the fact that being with Bianca meant constant attention.

Aleksandr was a man in every way. He cared about her for her own self, not the icon she'd created.

Now he'd invited a select group of people to join him on his new luxurious state-of-the-art yacht for a trip to celebrate her upcoming birthday, and she was excited.

Of course, they'd argued about whom to invite, until eventually she'd given way to Aleksandr's suggestions. He didn't want any of what he referred to as "trashy people." He insisted that they invite only the crème de la crème.

So be it. Whatever Aleksandr wanted, he got. Although she had insisted on inviting her best gay friend from way back, Latin singing sensation Luca Perez. And she'd also invited Ashley Sherwin, who'd helped decorate her London apartment.

Aleksandr hadn't argued about Ashley, for he was a longtime admirer of her footballer husband, the very handsome Taye Sherwin.

With a slight flash of guilt, Bianca remembered hooking up with Taye some time ago, long before he'd met and married Ashley. It was a one-nighter at an out-of-control party in London. She doubted if Taye would even remember, and she'd certainly never mentioned it to Ashley or Aleksandr. God forbid!

Aleksandr's choice of guests was more sedate. They included the movie star Cliff Baxter and his current girlfriend; renowned Senator Hammond Patterson and his wife, Sierra; and Flynn Hudson, a writer whom Bianca had never met, although Aleksandr spoke highly of him.

It promised to be a stellar group. Bianca was all set to make this a trip to remember.

14

Ashley could not stop gazing at the invitation. It was so elegant and simple, yet at the same time it reeked of money and class. She couldn't wait to tell Jeromy that they too were on the guest list. Mr. and Mrs. Taye Sherwin. Jeromy had tried to one-up them, as was his way, but now they had a legitimate invitation of their own.

She wished Taye had given her the invitation before they'd had dinner with Jeromy. For some unknown reason, he'd held back, not showing it to her until they got home. Then he'd had the nerve to expect sex.

Too bad. She wasn't in the mood.

Sometimes Taye could be too demanding when it came to sex. She'd discussed it with some of her girlfriends, and to her surprise they'd all said the same thing: "You're lucky he gets it up at all." It seemed that most men who'd been married for over five years allowed their sex life to slip. Or at least their sex life with their wife.

Ashley did not consider herself lucky at all. Taye's never-ending pawing at her in bed was an irritant, one she could well do without.

Actually, Ashley did not find sex that appealing. It was messy and dirty, a chore she forced herself to do every so often simply to satisfy her husband. As far as she was concerned, Taye was insatiable. However, he was also a famous footballer, so she knew that if *she* didn't oblige, there were plenty of slutty girls who would.

Football groupies. Slags. They were everywhere, with their shorter-than-short skirts skimming their tight little bottoms, skimpy tops, ridiculously high heels, over-the-top makeup, and a burning desire to hop into bed with one of "the boys," as they referred to their prey.

Yes, Taye was one of the boys, all right. He was top boy. The big prize.

Ashley sincerely doubted he'd cheat on her again, not after the last time. The incident with the Page 3 girl had almost cost him his marriage, and one thing she was sure of: he adored her and the twins, and he wouldn't risk it, because she'd warned him countless times that if he ever cheated again, they were over. *Finito.* Good-bye. She'd take the twins and half his money too. She meant it. Oh yes, she certainly meant it.

After turning the invitation over in her hands, she decided that it must've cost a pretty penny to print. She wondered how many people were invited, and who they were other than Luca Perez and Jeromy.

Royalty might be on the list. Kate and William. What a coup *that* would be, sailing the high seas with bloody royalty!

Perhaps she'd text Bianca and inquire who was going. Or was that bad manners?

Probably.

There was a reply card enclosed, stamped and ready to go. No cheesy Evite for *this* couple.

Bianca had landed herself a winner, and Ashley was pleased for her. They'd become vaguely friendly when she'd been involved in helping to decorate Bianca's London penthouse a couple of years ago. They'd found that they had something in common. Bianca was famous, while Ashley was married to fame.

Over a few gossipy lunches, Bianca had regaled her

with stories about some of the men she'd bedded. It was exciting stuff, and although Ashley hadn't seen Bianca since the supermodel had hooked up with the Russian billionaire, she was obviously still on her radar, hence the invitation.

Ashley picked up the phone and called her mum. She had to tell *someone* about the invite. Besides, she didn't want Taye's annoying parents moving into the house while they were away; it was better that her own mother was in residence to keep an eye on the twins, even though they had a live-in nanny.

Elise was less than thrilled to hear from her. "You only call me when you need something," she whined.

So? Ashley thought. *Isn't that what mums are for?*

"Take a look at this," one of Taye's fellow players said, thrusting a cell phone at him. "Feast your eyes an' get a load of *those* knockers."

Taye took the phone and stared longingly at the photo of a naked, extremely busty brunette, sitting in a chair facing the camera with her legs spread. She was pretty in a slutty way, but it was her tits that caught his attention. They were huge with dark extended nipples, so very different from Ashley's. Although since she'd had the boob job, Ashley's were pretty spectacular; he couldn't complain.

Taye felt the rise of Mammoth (a name he'd given his penis when he was twelve) and attempted to hide his embarrassment at getting a hard-on simply from checking out some random slag's tits.

"Who is she?" he muttered.

"A fan," his fellow player replied. "Sends me a new filthy photo every week. Nice pair of bazangers, right?"

"Better not let your wife see 'em."

"My wife wouldn't give a fast shit. *You're* the one who's pussy-whipped."

"Watch it," Taye warned.

"C'mon, mate," his teammate said with a knowing

chuckle. "Everyone an' their dog knows Ashley's got you by the bojangles."

"Do me a favor an' give it a rest," Taye mumbled, glaring at him.

"Go have a wank," his teammate sniggered. "Looks like you're gonna need it."

Mammoth was definitely on course. Taye made it into the men's toilet, locked himself in a stall, and helped Mammoth do its thing.

Balls! This wouldn't be happening if Ashley ever let him within ten feet of her precious pussy. She was depriving him of his conjugal rights, and that wasn't fair. He needed sex. He craved sex, but what was a guy supposed to do when his wife's thighs were locked together tighter than David Blaine's handcuffs?

Fuck! It was a shitty situation.

He loved his wife, that was for sure. But did she honestly think that he was going to sit back and accept her once-a-month sex rule?

Bullshit. He was Taye Sherwin. Women lusted after him. They wrote him adoring and explicit letters, flooded his fan Facebook page and Twitter account, hung around outside every match hoping to get lucky. He could get laid twenty times a day if he so desired.

Things would have to change, and what better time and place to sort everything out than on the upcoming Kasianenko trip?

Yeah, it was confrontation time, and Taye was finally ready.

15

Xuan sent Flynn a terse text. *Of course,* her text read. *Where and when?*

In ten days, he texted back. *Meet me in Paris. We'll go together.*

Flynn was pleased that Xuan had agreed to accompany him on the trip. He found her company to be stimulating, and he had a feeling that Aleksandr would too.

For once he had something to look forward to that didn't involve work, and it made for a welcome change; he needed the break.

He'd first crossed paths with Aleksandr several years previously when he was in Moscow investigating a notorious criminal gang. The mastermind of the group, Boris Zukov, resided in a luxury apartment just outside Moscow with his French stripper girlfriend, who wasn't averse to giving anonymous interviews in exchange for money to feed her secret drug habit. Flynn had a contact who put him in touch with her, and during the course of an extremely interesting and informative one-on-one, he'd discovered that apart from drugs and arms running, there was a plot afoot to abduct one of Aleksandr Kasianenko's three daughters for an enormous ransom. Six months earlier, another rich man's daughter had been kidnapped, and even though that ransom was paid, the child had ended up brutally murdered.

Flynn absorbed the information, and instead of going to the police, he'd done what he considered to be the right thing and gone straight to Kasianenko. It was the smart thing to do, and it turned out to be a wise move, because the Russian oligarch had handled things in his own way and no kidnapping had taken place.

Twenty-four hours later, Boris Zukov had accidentally fallen to his death from a fourteenth-floor window in his tony apartment building.

Nobody seemed too concerned about the "accident"; nobody except Boris's younger brother, Sergei, who'd been outraged that the police had done nothing. It appeared that they didn't care. To them the death of Boris Zukov was a bonus. One less vicious criminal to deal with.

It occurred to Flynn that although Aleksandr was a legitimate businessman, he was also a man who knew how to take care of things in a don't-fuck-with-me kind of way. Flynn admired him for that.

They'd met several times over the following years, and bonded as only two strong men can. Neither wanted anything from the other, and that suited them fine.

It had been a couple of years since they'd last gotten together, and Flynn was looking forward to seeing Aleksandr again. He still admired the man. Ruthless but honest. An interesting mix.

He'd been surprised when he'd read about Aleksandr hooking up with the famous supermodel Bianca, since he'd been under the impression that Aleksandr was a happily married man. Apparently things were different now.

The last time he'd seen Aleksandr, the Russian had taken him to a fancy club around the corner from his hotel, and offered to buy him one of the gorgeous women lounging on bar stools and sitting at tables. The place was full of stunning women and very few men.

"Is this a brothel?" Flynn had asked, faintly amused.

Aleksandr had chuckled. "If it was, it would've been shut down years ago," he'd said. "This is a private club, and if a man should want to rent a room upstairs for the night, then it's between him and the lady in question."

Flynn had laughed. "I've never paid for it, and I'm not about to start now," he'd said. "But you go ahead."

"Me?" Aleksandr had replied, stony-faced. "I am a happily married man, Flynn. I do not cheat. Too expensive. Too complicated."

And now it wasn't so complicated anymore.

Spending half her life on a plane was nothing new for Xuan. Besides, she enjoyed flying. One of her unfulfilled ambitions was to take flying lessons and obtain her pilot's license; it was something she had promised herself she would do sometime in the future.

Martha, a Dutch woman who resided in Amsterdam, had offered Xuan anything she wanted if only she would give up traveling the world and move in with her.

"Including flying lessons," Martha had promised.

"When I am seventy-five," Xuan had joked.

Martha was fifty, divorced, affluent, and attractive, with acceptable bedroom skills. Xuan was not tempted—she relished her independence too much.

Finished with Deshi, she hailed a taxi and visited a group of impoverished women and their children who lived in nothing more than a jumble of run-down shacks on the edge of town. She took food and clothes and as much money as she could spare, then spent several hours with them, playing with the children, laughing and chatting with the women, who were—in spite of their circumstances—surprisingly upbeat.

Back at her hotel, she thought seriously about Flynn and their trip. It was bound to be excessive and over-the-top. Spoiled rich people vacationing knee-deep in luxury.

Would she be able to stand it?

For Flynn's sake, she'd try. And if it all got too much, she'd simply take off.

That was the cool thing about having no roots—when it was time to go, there was no one and nothing to stop her.

16

Lori made a firm decision: she was not allowing herself to give in to fear. She was a survivor—she could deal. It wasn't like she hadn't dealt with enough crap in her life. Why be frightened of two mangy, red-eyed wild animals?

She stared the coyotes down with a purpose, then, when they didn't move, she started yelling and frantically waving her arms in the air like a crazy person.

"Fuck off, you little monsters!" she screamed. "Get the fuck outta here!"

It was as if she had an angel watching over her, for the two coyotes suddenly turned around and slunk back into the bushes. Just like that.

"Holy shit!" she marveled. "I did it!"

Then, as she was about to use her cell phone to call for help, a young jogger appeared. He was wearing board shorts, a cutoff UCLA tee, and a sweatband to keep his blondish hair from falling into his eyes.

For a brief moment she was mesmerized by his legs standing over her, tanned and strong, athlete's legs. He couldn't be more than eighteen, so she forced herself to shift her gaze.

"I heard yelling," he said, jogging in place. "You okay?"

"I am now," she said, relieved to see him. "Damn coyotes looked about ready to eat me for breakfast."

"Bummer," he said, scratching his chin. "You hurt?"

"It's only my ankle. I'll live."

"You need help?"

"I guess so," she said tentatively, attempting to stand.

"Right," he said, holding out his hand to help her up. "You shouldn't jog by yourself. I tell my mom that all the time."

His mom! Lori was twenty-four, for crap's sake. Why was he comparing her to his mom? Maybe Cliff's advanced age was rubbing off on her.

"I jog by myself all the time," she said, enjoying the intense smell of fresh sweat emanating from his armpit. "Usually I bring my dogs."

"Big dogs or little dogs?" he inquired. " 'Cause if they're little, the coyotes're gonna wolf 'em down."

"Big dogs," she said, leaning on him.

"Big is good," he said.

She wondered how many girls had uttered those words to him, for his package in board shorts left little to the imagination.

"Yes," she managed, holding on to his arm and wincing as her foot hit the ground.

"I could carry you if you can't make it," he offered.

Nice one. She wouldn't mind at all. She could sniff his armpit all the way down to the parking area.

"You're sweet," she said. "If you don't mind me hanging on to your arm, I think I can do it."

"Gotcha," he said.

"Are you *sure* you don't mind?"

"Naw," he said casually. "I was about to turn around anyway."

"What's your name?"

"Chip. You?"

"Uh . . . Lori."

"Okay, Lori," he said, placing her arm around his neck, and getting a grip on her waist. "Let's do this thing."

* * *

Lori did not answer her phone. Voice mail picked up. Cliff was not about to tell her that they'd been invited on the Kasianenko yacht until he could watch her quiver with excitement. She'd be so thrilled.

Where was she? What did she do all day when he was busy working?

Girl things, he supposed. Shopping, mani-pedis, Pilates, spinning, shit like that.

He knew she was desperate for him to get her a job as an actress, but it didn't seem right for the star to put his girlfriend in the movie. Although he could've if he'd wanted to. He didn't; he had to be careful that she wasn't using him in that way. Besides, what were actresses? Nothing but egomaniacs with tits and stylists. He'd had a few, and they always ended up causing hysterical scenes and running to the tabloids with a totally made-up story.

No more actresses for Cliff Baxter. Hell, no.

He called Enid and told her to book him a garden booth at the Polo Lounge for tonight. He'd tell Lori then, and later she could show him her appreciation in her own very special way.

Yes, Cliff Baxter didn't do anything unless it suited him.

17

Once Jeromy was in the house, the staff scuttled around on red alert. Jeromy was a fierce taskmaster; he expected perfection at all times. He was also a stickler for rules—*his* rules. Everything had to be just so, even the way the pots and pans were laid out in the kitchen. Every single thing had to be spotless, not a speck of dust anywhere.

On the other hand, Luca was totally laid-back. He couldn't care less if the outdoor cushions weren't arranged just so. It didn't bother him if a painting was crooked or the bed wasn't made to Jeromy's strict specifications.

When Jeromy was away, all was mellow. When he was in residence—look out!

The staff adored Luca.

The staff loathed Jeromy.

After arriving from London and enjoying a mojito on the terrace with his younger boyfriend, Jeromy flashed the coveted invitation, and informed Luca that they simply had to go.

Luca checked it out and inquired who else would be on the trip.

"How would I know?" Jeromy said with a casual shrug. "Although you can rest assured that they will be people of quality."

Luca wrinkled his nose. There were times Jeromy said things that didn't make any sense. What did "people of quality" mean, exactly? It must be one of Jeromy's strange English expressions.

"Sure, we can go," he said, leaning back on his lounger. "I'm not in the recording studio until September, so it works for me."

Jeromy was delighted. "We should go shopping," he announced, eyes gleaming at the thought of an entire new wardrobe. "The Valentino leisure wear this year is divine. We must both get fitted out. Perhaps matching white tuxedos?"

"Why not?" Luca said.

Jeromy nodded, fantasizing about how hot they'd look in matching tuxedos.

"Maybe I'll call Bianca an' see who else is going," Luca said. "Could be they'll have room for Suga and Luca Junior."

Jeromy sat up ramrod straight, almost spilling his drink. Had he heard correctly? Was Luca mad? Did he honestly think he could inveigle an invitation for Suga Tits and the child?

No. It simply wasn't right. Luca had to be stopped immediately.

"That's not acceptable," he said, the words almost sticking in his throat. "It would . . . ah . . . make me most uncomfortable."

"Uncomfortable?" Luca questioned, trying to ignore the fact that Jeromy couldn't stand Suga. "How's that?"

"You were *married* to the woman," Jeromy said with a supercilious sneer. "Her presence on the trip would definitely be awkward. Besides, it's not proper etiquette to start adding guests. This is obviously a very special trip, and I am sure everyone who's been invited was handpicked by our host."

Luca shrugged. "I thought it would be a welcome surprise for Suga," he said, not thrilled by Jeromy's attitude. "She needs cheering up."

Cheering up, my English arse, Jeromy thought with a

bitter twist. *The bitch could light up Times Square with her phony cheeriness.*

"Exactly why does she need cheering up?" he asked through clenched teeth.

"Her ticket sales are down," Luca explained. "Kinda a blow to her ego."

Ha! Jeromy thought. *It would take more than a blow to crash Suga's enormous ego. It would take a nuclear explosion.*

"I'm sorry about that," Jeromy said tightly. "Surely you can think of something else to lift her spirits?"

"Like what?" Luca said blankly.

Like who gives a damn.

"I don't know," Jeromy admitted. "We should think about it. Between us we'll come up with something."

Luca nodded, although he wasn't sure he trusted Jeromy to do the right thing.

Meanwhile, Jeromy had no intention of coming up with anything; the annoying diva wasn't *his* problem.

Then, deciding a change of pace was in order, he leaned over, gently tweaking Luca's nipple. "Did you miss me?" he cooed. "Were you a well-behaved boy?"

"Were you?" Luca retorted. He might be the superstar in this relationship, but he more than suspected that Jeromy was the slut. It didn't bother him, because he knew that Jeromy was into things he wasn't. He simply hoped that Jeromy was careful and never came home with any kind of disease to pass on.

"I would *never* cheat on you, my little pumpkin," Jeromy crooned, completely out of character, his long thin fingers caressing Luca's oiled abs.

"Sure you would," Luca said mildly, feeling the beginning of a hard-on.

He stood up. It wouldn't be cool to have Jeromy suck him off while there were staff lurking around. "Let's go inside," he suggested.

"I'm right behind you," Jeromy said, thinking of the

young boy in London, the young boy with the talented tongue and surly attitude.

In his relationship with Luca, Jeromy had found that it was always *him* who had to perform fellatio on Luca, it was always *him* in the subservient position.

But that's what Luca was into. And since the one with all the money held all the power, then ultimately it was Luca who called the shots.

Jeromy had yet to challenge him.

18

"Surely you realize that you have it all?" Clare, Sierra's sister, said with an envious sigh. She was a pretty woman, but nowhere near as lovely as Sierra. Clare's hair was brown, not golden copper. Her eyes were quite close together, not widely spaced like Sierra's. Clare had compensated by honing her intellectual skills, and creating a warm and wonderful family life. "And on top of everything," Clare added, "you're about to take off on an incredible trip."

Sure, Sierra thought. *Incredible.*

"I wish *I* was going," Clare said wistfully. "You have to tell me all about it. Oh yes, and be sure to keep a daily journal. I need to know *everything,* all the details." She let out a long, drawn-out sigh. "You're *so* lucky."

No, you're the lucky one, Sierra thought. *You with your comfortable house in Connecticut. Your teddy bear of a husband and your three terrific kids. Not to mention a successful writing career.*

"Um, yes," Sierra murmured. "I will."

"Do you have any idea who else is going?" Clare inquired, leaning across the restaurant table, agog for some juicy news.

"Not a clue," Sierra said, taking a sip of her martini. A bold move for lunch, but what the hell—getting drunk could be exactly what she needed.

Oh yes, Hammond would *love* that, she thought, stifling an inane giggle. A drunken wife on his arm. A wife dressed to impress and totally loaded.

"What are you laughing at?" Clare wanted to know.

The insanity of my so-called perfect life, Sierra thought.

"I don't know," she answered vaguely. "Nothing. Everything."

"For God's sake, please do not drift off into one of your weird moods," Clare begged. "And why are you drinking in the middle of the day? What's *that* about?"

"Because I am a political wife," Sierra retorted grandly. "We shop. We drink. We shake hands. We pick up babies. That's what we do."

Clare shook her head disapprovingly. "I don't know what's up with you today," she said, frowning. "You're not yourself."

"I wish," Sierra murmured sotto voce.

"Excuse me?"

"Nothing," Sierra said, taking another sip of her martini.

"Any news on the baby front?" Clare asked. It was the same question she'd been asking ever since Sierra had married Hammond.

"I guess I'm just not fertile," Sierra said, unwilling to tell her sister that she and Hammond never had sex. He didn't want her in that way, and she certainly didn't want him.

"Or maybe *he* isn't," Clare suggested. "Sometimes it's the man's fault."

"Might I remind you, he already has a child."

"That doesn't matter," Clare said, intent on getting her point across. "He should still get tested."

"I'm not sure I even want a family," Sierra murmured, gulping down the rest of her martini.

"That's ridiculous," Clare said firmly. "Of course you do."

Sierra felt herself losing it. Why couldn't Clare leave the subject alone? "You know what?" she said.

"What?"

"I wish you'd do me a big favor and stop bringing it up all the time."

Clare knew when to change the subject. "I got a text from Sean," she said, lowering her voice and glancing furtively around as if the middle-aged waiter standing nearby was even remotely interested.

"What did he want?" Sierra asked, thinking about her twenty-nine-year-old dropout brother who lived in a run-down beach shack with a forty-two-year-old Puerto Rican divorcée in Hawaii.

"What do you *think* he wanted?" Clare said pointedly. Then, answering her own question, she added, "Money, of course."

Actually, on reflection, Sierra realized that she quite envied Sean. How relaxing to do nothing but sit on a beach all day and beg for handouts from your family.

"I sent him five hundred two weeks ago," she said.

Clare's frown deepened. "I thought we agreed that we weren't sending him any more money."

"He told me that he had a dental problem and was in horrible pain. I couldn't ignore him. What was I supposed to do?"

"Oh my God, Sierra, you're *so* gullible," Clare scoffed. "How could you fall for that? You know he's a blatant liar."

"Yes, I do know, but show some heart, Clare. He's also our brother."

"I am not sending him one more red cent," Clare said, with a stubborn shake of her head. "I don't care how much he begs. He's a grown man, and it's about time he started acting like one. Furthermore, *you* should stop enabling him, because that's exactly what you're doing."

"I'm not enabling him," Sierra objected. "I'm helping him."

"No, you're not helping him at all," Clare argued.

Sierra was too tired to fight with her sister. She had a strong urge to go home, crawl into bed, and sleep.

Depression was creeping over her like a black cloud; she could feel it coming on. Once life had held such shining promise. No more.

How had she allowed herself to reach such a miserable place?

Was it because she'd married Hammond?

They were all questions she could answer if she wanted to. However, it was simply easier to forget.

"How old are you, dear?" Hammond asked, leaning back in the chair behind his desk, his eyes inspecting every inch of the latest intern to join the staff.

Skylar blinked rapidly. She couldn't believe that she was in Senator Patterson's presence, that he actually knew she existed. It was all so exciting. Earlier that day she'd been introduced to Mrs. Patterson, and now this!

"Uh . . . I'm going to be nineteen next week," she said, fidgeting nervously. "And uh . . . may I say that it's such an honor to be working here. I am a big admirer of yours, Senator, and of course of your wife too."

"That's nice," Hammond said, his honest brown eyes shifting into X-ray mode as he skillfully removed her clothes. He noted that she had large real breasts and wide hips. She wasn't perfect like Sierra. Not a beauty, but attractive enough.

And she was young. He preferred them young.

As he sat behind his desk, he imagined placing his penis between her big breasts, then slowly moving up and coming all over her startled face.

After the initial shock, she would love it. They all did.

"Well, Skylar," he said, pressing his fingers together, forming a little arc, "welcome to the team. We all believe in working together here. Sometimes late into the night." He took a long beat. "Does that bother you?"

"Excuse me?" Skylar said, still blinking.

"Does working late bother you?" Hammond asked patiently, thinking this one seemed a little slow.

"No, no, not at all," Skylar said, full of enthusiasm. "That's what I'm here for."

No, Hammond thought. *What you're here for is to satisfy me sexually. And you will. Oh yes, you will. Your turn will come. And soon.*

19

Divorce is never easy, but Aleksandr Kasianenko was prepared to give Rushana, his wife of seventeen years and the mother of his three daughters, whatever she wanted. Unfortunately, what Rushana wanted was to stay married to him, so she and her lawyer were making things as difficult as possible, unnecessarily so.

Aleksandr was beyond irritated. He had offered Rushana everything she could desire, and yet there always seemed to be another roadblock.

The divorce wasn't his fault. He hadn't planned on falling in love with Bianca, only it *had* happened, and Rushana should simply accept it.

Aleksandr was determined that on the forthcoming yacht trip, he would propose to Bianca. He was doing it whether he was free or not. He'd already purchased the ring, a two-million-dollar rare emerald surrounded by diamonds. It was a ring fit for the woman he planned to marry. Bianca would love it, just as she loved him.

He'd never met a woman like Bianca before. So beautiful and yet so independent and strong. And passionate. In the bedroom, she was a roaring tigress; she fulfilled him in every way.

Yes, Aleksandr enjoyed everything about her, although he could do without her fame. The pesky photographers who followed her everywhere. The annoying fans who had no sense of keeping their distance. The hangers-on who often surrounded her. And the Internet, where people made up ridiculous stories every single day.

After a year with his love, he'd learned to ignore the chaos around her. Bianca was his, and nothing could ever change that.

However, he would be lying if he said he didn't relish the peace when Bianca was in another country. He could walk down the street unmolested and be happy that there were no photographers trailing him.

His faithful bodyguard was always in attendance. Kyril, a solid brick of a man who watched his every move, for one could never be too careful. Aleksandr was well aware that he had enemies; it came with the territory. He was a billionaire businessman who along the way had attracted his fair share of haters. People who were jealous of his wealth. Business rivals. His wife's two needy brothers, who felt that he should've done more for them. It wasn't enough that he'd bought them both houses and given them jobs at which they'd both failed. Was he supposed to support their lazy asses forever?

No. With the divorce came freedom from Rushana's clingy family.

The only regret that Aleksandr had was that he was no longer living with his three daughters. They'd remained with their mother, and rightly so. He could see them whenever he wished to, but since they resided in his former home fifteen miles outside of Moscow, it wasn't that easy to make the time.

He had yet to introduce them to Bianca, although in the following months he hoped to do so. It didn't help that the last time he'd seen them, Mariska, his youngest, had said, "Mama told us you have an American whore girlfriend. What's a whore, Papa?"

Aleksandr was furious. Rushana had better learn to control her mouth. He would not stand for her insulting the love of his life.

* * *

After Madrid, Bianca headed for Paris and a full-out spending spree. She knew all the designers, and they were delighted to accommodate her, because whenever Bianca was photographed in one of their outfits, sales soared. Bianca was adept at negotiating outrageous discounts, plus she also managed to get many things for free.

Her excitement about the trip was building. She had a feeling that something special was going to take place. She had no clue what, but knowing Aleksandr, it would be major.

Bianca had legions of friends in Paris—mostly in the fashion business and mostly gay. She planned on flying on to Moscow the next day, but in the meantime, she called several of her friends, and they all met up for drinks at the Plaza Athenée, before moving on to a decadent dinner at her favorite dining bistro, the well-established L'Ami Louis, where everyone pigged out on the heavenly potato cakes sautéed in duck fat, and the amazingly tender grilled beef. For dessert they indulged in dishes of wild strawberries piled high and topped with crème fraîche. It was a decadent feast.

Bianca ate everything. Usually she watched her diet, but tonight she felt like letting go.

After dinner, her sometime hairstylist Pierre suggested they move on to a club. So they ended up at Amnesia, a mostly gay bar with incredible sounds.

Bianca danced the night away with no inhibitions. When she was out with Aleksandr, she felt as if she had to behave herself, keep her wild side strictly for the bedroom. Tonight it was all systems go, and since the ever-lurking paparazzi had no idea she was in Paris, she was free to be herself.

Ah . . . freedom from prying photo lenses! Oh, how Bianca embraced it.

What she didn't take into account was so-called friends with cell phones. And while she was letting it all hang loose, one of them was capturing images that would soon be for sale.

Her friend Pierre might be gay, but did the rest of the world know it?

Absolutely not. So photos of Bianca hugging and kissing him, dancing in a skirt so short anyone could see she was not wearing panties, grinding on a stripper pole, and generally cavorting . . . well, those photos were pure gold. Soon they would hit the Internet with a vengeance.

Bianca was blissfully unaware of the clandestine shots being taken. She danced the night away with a smile on her face, and had herself a fine old time.

20

If there was one thing Ashley hated, it was when her mother spewed forth a mouthful of dumb advice, as if Elise had any clue what she was talking about. Three failed marriages and a job in a department store at her age. Exactly who would listen to her?

Certainly not Ashley, because she considered herself way smarter than her mum. She'd moved up in life, far, far away from her humble beginnings. Not only was she married to a famous footballer, she was part of a successful interior design team. Partnering with Jeromy had been a clever move on her part. Jeromy had a stellar reputation, and so did she now that they were working side by side.

Well, kind of side by side, because they weren't exactly equal partners, even though Taye had put money into the business. When she'd first started working with Jeromy, he had bestowed the title of creative consultant on her. She'd been a bit miffed, but so far it had worked out. Whenever Jeromy had a celebrity client, he allowed her input. It was fun at first, but then she'd begun noticing that he always introduced her as Ashley Sherwin, Taye Sherwin's wife.

It pissed her off. Wasn't being Ashley Sherwin enough? Did Jeromy have to tack on that she was Taye's wife? What was *that* about?

When this had happened a couple of times, she'd

brought it to his attention, pointing out that it certainly wasn't necessary to give Taye billing.

Jeromy had gone all confused and gay on her. "I'm so sorry, sweet thing," he'd purred. "I would *never* do *anything* to upset you."

After that he'd stopped bringing up Taye's name in front of her, although somehow or other all the clients seemed to know she was Taye's wife.

Eventually she'd complained a second time, causing Jeromy to adopt a frostier attitude. "Is it my fault that you and Taye are photographed wherever you go?" he'd said with an imperious curl of his lip. "People recognize you, dear. Besides, it's good for business. Get used to it, or may I suggest that you stay out of the magazines."

It was true; she couldn't argue with Jeromy's logic. She and Taye *were* a staple in every magazine. *Heat* and *Closer* often featured them on the cover. And *Hello* and *OK!* had done numerous "at home" pictorials with her, Taye, and the twins. As for the Internet, their photos were everywhere. Taye's Facebook page had millions of followers, plus he insisted on tweeting, and occasionally posting intimate family shots he'd taken with his favorite Nikon camera—a birthday gift she regretted giving him. He was always trying to catch her unaware, then posting the stupid photos of her asleep or half dressed.

The problem was that Jeromy was right; she *was* in all the magazines, and that *was* good for business, so eventually she'd stopped complaining.

The moment Ashley invited Elise to stay at their house while they went on their trip, Elise had moved in, even though Ashley had insisted it was way too soon. "We don't leave for another week," she'd pointed out. "No need for you to be here this early."

"I know," Elise had responded, thrilled to get out of her tiny apartment. "I want the twins to get used to having me around. And *you* don't mind, do you, Taye?" she'd added, simpering at her handsome son-in-law, who—once she'd gotten over the fact that he was black—she quite adored.

Taye had nodded. Anything for a peaceful life.

Now they were sitting at dinner in their dining room, and Elise was droning on and on about how they should conduct themselves on their upcoming trip.

"You have to change outfits three times a day," Elise instructed. "Breakfast, lunch, and dinner. I read that's what these fancy people do on their yachts."

"Really?" Ashley drawled sarcastically. "Where did you read that?"

"On the Internet," Elise said, then, spitting up further gems, she added, "And don't be taking any ripped or torn knickers. They have people to do your washing, and you wouldn't want them talking about you behind your back."

"Bloody hell, they'll have a right old time with *my* drawers," Taye joked, letting forth a ribald chuckle. "Skid marks galore."

Ashley threw him a disapproving glare. "Don't encourage her," she said sharply. "And stop being vulgar."

"Lighten up, toots. I'm only jokin'," Taye said, wondering if there was any chance of him getting a leg over tonight.

"Well she's *not,*" Ashley hissed. "She believes every word of it."

"Fine," Elise said grandly. "*Don't* take me seriously, but I know of what I speak. I read all about it."

"Where exactly?" Ashley demanded.

"I Googled 'yacht etiquette,'" Elise replied, straight-faced. "Are you aware that you're supposed to tip the staff at the end of the trip?"

"Good to know," Taye said cheerfully. "I'd better go raid me piggy bank."

"It's no joke," Elise said, wagging a stern finger at the two of them. "The staff talk, and the last thing you need is getting a reputation as a cheapskate."

"Watch it, missus," Taye said. "Nobody's ever accused me of bein' cheap."

Ashley had heard enough. "I'm going to bed," she announced.

"It's not even nine, toots," Taye objected.

"I'm tired."

Too tired for a quick shag?

Maybe.

Maybe not.

"I'll join you, then," Taye said, rising from the table.

"What am *I* supposed to do?" Elise whined.

"I dunno," Ashley said. "Why don't you go Google some more useless information?"

"All I'm trying to do is help," Elise said. "Although if you don't appreciate my help—"

"You're right," Ashley said, before abruptly exiting the room.

Elise turned to Taye. "What've I done now?" she asked plaintively.

Taye felt a bit sorry for her, because when Ashley was in one of her bitchy moods, there was no stopping her.

"I think she's got one of her headaches," he said, making an excuse for his wife's bad behavior.

"I don't know why she thinks she can take it out on me," Elise grumbled. "I've done everything for that girl, made sacrifices you wouldn't believe. When her father walked out on us, Ashley was six, and I didn't give up. I kept on going for her sake." Elise's lower lip began to tremble. "My little girl never lacked for anything. Singing lessons, dancing, piano—she had it all. I used to drive her to all the auditions. And look how it paid off. If she hadn't married you, she could've been a big star."

"I bet," Taye said, wondering how to make a quick getaway before Elise continued her story of sacrifice. "Anyway, you know what, luv? Ashley's a big star to me, so that's all that matters—right?"

And with those words he was out the door.

21

I'm coming to Paris early, Xuan texted Flynn. *Please book me a hotel.*

No way, he texted back. *You'll stay with me. Send details of your arrival.*

Which is how he found himself at the airport waiting for her flight to arrive. He got there early, spent some time perusing the magazine stands, picked up a copy of *Newsweek,* and settled back to wait.

Xuan's plane was an hour late. She emerged from the gate with a purposeful stride, attracting attention wherever she went. She might be petite, but she was certainly a beauty with her almond-shaped eyes, full cherry lips, and sweep of straight black hair that fell way below her compact bottom.

Men paid attention. So did women.

Well they would, wouldn't they? Flynn thought, waving at her. *Lesbian signals are surely wafting in the air.*

Xuan headed toward him with just an oversized shoulder bag filled with everything she might need.

"Any more luggage?" Flynn asked, giving her a perfunctory kiss on the cheek.

"Nope," Xuan replied, indicating her bag. "This is it."

Flynn attempted to take it from her.

She shrugged him away with a caustic "What? You think I can't carry my own bag?"

He shook his head, amused. When it came to Xuan, nothing ever changed. She was fiercely independent. Whenever they'd been chasing a story in war zones or other dangerous places, she'd always insisted on being treated like one of the boys.

So be it.

They took a cab back to his apartment. Flynn didn't own a car; he was never in one city long enough to be bothered with the responsibility.

His apartment was a small one-bedroom. He'd already decided that Xuan could have the bed, and he'd bunk down on the couch.

When he told her, she laughed in his face. "No, Flynn. You can keep your bed; the couch suits me fine."

"Still as stubborn as ever."

"This is true," she answered with a slight smile.

Later they left the apartment and dined at a nearby bistro Flynn frequented when he was in town. Xuan drank red wine and regaled him with stories of her adventures in Vietnam. She told him about the children she'd visited and the women who had to put up with so many incredible hardships.

Flynn listened sympathetically. He understood. There was so much misery in the world, and it never saw the light of day unless someone dedicated—like Xuan or even himself—grabbed a platform to write about it.

"Maybe you should write a book," Xuan announced, devouring a plate of spaghetti, the tomato sauce dribbling down her delicate pointed chin.

"I wrote a book," Flynn reminded her, although he couldn't remember if he'd ever mentioned it before.

Apparently not, because Xuan looked surprised. "What book?" she asked.

"Bullshit stories," he replied, slightly embarrassed. "When I was younger."

"I want to read it."

"It's not your style."

"Excuse me?"

"You wouldn't like it."

"Why not?"

"I wrote it when I was very young."

"Ah . . ." Xuan said, her eyes shining bright. "And now you're so ancient."

Flynn laughed. "*You're* the one who should write a book," he said, leaning across the table and dabbing the sauce from her chin with his napkin.

She stiffened, and snatched the napkin from him.

"Okay, okay," he said, throwing up his hands. "I know you don't like to be touched unless it's sexual."

"You and I, we're never going there," Xuan stated, as if it were a well-known fact.

"You're so right," he retorted.

The bistro owner's daughter, Mai, who was waitressing, approached their table. Mai was a pretty girl who could not understand why Flynn had never invited her out. Tonight she was not pleased to see him with a woman, for he usually dined alone.

"Can I get you anything?" Mai asked, shooting Xuan a dirty look.

"More wine," Flynn said. "And maybe a look at the dessert menu."

"*Oui, monsieur*," Mai said, suddenly going all French and formal on him. "*Immédiatement*."

Flynn caught her attitude. So did Xuan.

"She likes you," Xuan said with a knowing smile as Mai walked away.

"And I like her," Flynn responded. "What's not to like?"

"Ah, yes," Xuan added. "Only *you* like her as simply another girl. *She* likes you to jump into bed with."

"No way," Flynn objected. "We're friends."

"You're so naïve when it comes to women," Xuan said, shaking back her long hair.

"Not naïve, merely careful," Flynn replied. "Haven't you heard the expression 'don't crap where you eat'?"

"You mean 'shit,'" Xuan said succinctly.

"I'm being polite."

She gave him another knowing smile. "After all we've been through together, you're being *polite*? I'm one of the boys, remember?"

"Sure," Flynn said, deftly switching subjects. "However, has it occurred to you that maybe she likes *you*?"

"Don't be ridiculous."

"Why? You're not feeling the vibe?" Flynn teased.

"No," Xuan said with a casual shrug. "I am not."

"I told you," Flynn said, continuing to tease, "feel free to take the bedroom whenever you want. It's all yours."

"It seems to me that you're very evasive when it comes to women," Xuan said.

"How's that?" Flynn answered vaguely.

"I've observed that wherever we are in the world, you might allow yourself one night with a woman, but never more than one night."

"And *you're* so different?" he retaliated.

"I'm a loner, Flynn. I always have been."

"So am I."

Mai returned and thrust menus at them.

As Flynn studied the menu, he realized it was the most personal conversation he'd ever had with Xuan, and he didn't like it. He didn't like anyone poking around in his so-called love life. It was nobody's business but his.

"Dessert?" he said stiffly.

"Coffee," Xuan replied. "Black. Nothing fancy."

"It'll keep you awake," he pointed out.

"My problem, not yours."

Standing by the table, Mai tapped her foot impatiently.

"One black coffee, Mai," Flynn said, glancing up at her. "And do you have any of that delicious tart you keep for special customers?"

Mai softened as she sensed there was nothing going on between Flynn and the Asian woman. "For you," she said softly, "*bien sûr.*"

"Thanks, Mai." And he couldn't help imagining what it would be like to sleep with the young Frenchwoman. She was certainly pretty enough, and from what he could tell, she had a nice personality.

No—it wouldn't work out. After a few weeks, he'd end it and she'd be upset and hurt. Random hookups were not worth the trouble. Besides, he planned on still frequenting the bistro when he was in town, and like he'd told Xuan, do not shit where you eat. A firm rule to believe in.

22

"Did you come?" Cliff asked as he rolled over to his side of the bed. He wasn't that concerned; on the other hand, he was not averse to a rave review.

"Oh my God, *did* I!" Lori responded, full of fake enthusiasm. She didn't believe in lying unless it was absolutely necessary, but why tell one of the biggest movie stars in the world that, once again, he hadn't hit a home run?

Cliff was okay in bed, although he was certainly no superman. He was almost fifty years old and a textbook lover. Five minutes of foreplay, followed by a quick fuck, followed by her going down on him until he came in her mouth. And woe betide her if she didn't swallow—that really pissed him off.

She knew why. He'd once relayed the story of a famous tennis player who'd allowed a random date in a restaurant to slip under the table and suck him off. But the random date was smart. She hadn't swallowed, she'd spat his sperm into a paper cup and rushed it to a friendly doctor, who'd inseminated her. And voilà! One successful paternity suit.

Cliff Baxter had to know exactly where his precious sperm was headed. And actually, who could blame him?

It was almost a week after the coyote/sprained ankle incident. Lori was fully recovered, because that's all it had been, a light sprain.

Cliff had filled her in about the amazing trip they were to take; he'd even sent her out with his personal stylist to purchase a few suitable outfits.

The thought of the Kasianenko yacht intimidated her. Everyone would either be very old, obscenely rich, or at the very least horribly famous. And there she'd be, just the girlfriend, for it was common knowledge that Cliff Baxter was a confirmed bachelor who had no intention of ever getting married. He said so in every interview he ever gave, hammering the point home.

Being just the girlfriend was starting to get old. It occurred to Lori that he could dump her anytime, exactly like he'd done with the string of girls before her.

It was a scary thought. What would she do? Where would she go?

Although Cliff paid for anything she wanted, he didn't give her actual money. He *had* given her a Visa card with a five-thousand-dollar limit, and knowing Cliff, if they split, he'd cancel it immediately. Basically that meant she'd be as broke as when she'd entered the relationship. He'd presented her with a few pieces of jewelry; nothing too expensive. Even the car she drove was only leased—registered in his company's name.

What could she do to secure her position?

Nothing much, except continue to please him.

Lately, she'd been thinking about the young man who'd rescued her on the hike. Chip, with his strong thighs and rippling muscles. What a hunk. Was it wrong to fantasize about him while Cliff was on top of her?

Funny, really: here she was getting boned by a man whom millions of women lusted after, a man she'd once thought she'd loved, and her excitement level hovered at zero. What was wrong with her?

Nothing. She simply wasn't into a man who was almost twenty-six years older than her and treated her like an accessory.

Why didn't anyone ever mention the age gap when they were busy writing about them?

Because nobody wanted to get on Cliff Baxter's bad side, that's why.

It occurred to Cliff that Lori had not been as thrilled about going on a magnificent yacht as he'd expected her to be. He'd been prepared for fireworks and raging excitement. Instead, he'd gotten a halfhearted "Sounds great."

Hmm . . . was Lori starting to take the good life for granted?

Was she getting blasé?

No. Impossible. She was living a life she could only have dreamed about. She was with him, and he knew without a doubt that most women would give their left tit to be with him. After all, he'd been voted Sexiest Man Alive in *People* two years in a row. He had an Oscar and an Emmy. A red-hot, long-standing career. Three cars. A New York apartment. A mansion in Beverly Hills. A house in Tuscany. No ties to hold him down.

In short, he had the perfect life.

Or did he?

Yes. Yes. Yes.

A resounding trio of yeses. He had enough married friends to convince him that staying single was the only way to go. He'd worked hard for his money, and how many poor schmucks had he seen lose half of what they'd earned to some greedy soon-to-be ex who demanded everything?

He could understand if there were kids involved; child support was a given. Other than that, forget it.

Was Lori reaching that all-too-familiar stage in a relationship where a woman wanted more?

Commitment.

The dreaded word.

No thank you.

Cliff made a decision. He'd take her on the trip, make sure she had a wonderful time, and then when they returned to L.A., he'd ever so gently cut her loose.

Cliff Baxter would soon be back out there. Single and ready for the next adventure.

23

They went shopping. They spent a lot of money. Or rather, Luca spent and Jeromy encouraged. They bought clothes and shoes and luggage from the designer stores, then finally they stopped by Cartier, where Luca gifted Jeromy with a black Pasha Seatimer watch for everyday use. At nighttime they both wore their gold Rolexes, but Jeromy had his eye on a more expensive model.

Luca didn't get the hint. Instead, he bought Suga a diamond-encrusted bracelet as a consolation prize for her cut-short tour.

Jeromy tried not to look pissed off, although he was. When would Luca stop spending money on the fat cow? Would that magical day ever come?

The previous night they'd had dinner with Suga and Luca Junior. Today Jeromy's facial muscles hurt from the big phony smile he'd had plastered on his face all night. Luca Junior was boring, and Suga was an embarrassment. Jeromy hated being seen out in public with her.

Of course the photographers and lurking paparazzi were all over them. Since Luca had emerged from the closet, he was more popular than ever. His superstar ex-wife and bright-eyed young son added spice to a story that everyone loved to read about. Photos of them together were gold dust.

When it came to attention, Luca lapped it up. He was

so good-looking and charming. A blond Latin god who'd risen from nothing and conquered it all. His music reached out to everyone, and he'd never forgotten his roots and the sensual salsa sounds that were so much a part of his past. He recorded his songs in both Spanish and English, and they were always worldwide hits. His lyrics inspired people.

Because Suga was still so much in the picture, Jeromy found himself the odd one out. The magazines, newspapers, and gossip sites seemed to overlook the fact that he and Luca were partners; they rarely mentioned him, and he was nearly always cut out of press photographs. It infuriated him. How come David Furnish was always pictured alongside Elton John? How come everyone knew who David Furnish was? And how about Ellen and Portia de Rossi? Never apart in the press.

Then it struck Jeromy.

Of course. They were married. They were legal.

So *that's* what he had to do—persuade Luca to marry him.

One thing he knew for sure: it would not be easy.

When Luca had come out to Suga, she had not been surprised. She'd always suspected that he preferred boys to girls. In spite of this, she'd married him anyway. Why not? He was a beauty, and he had a generous soul. Plus he was extraordinarily talented, and she'd decided it was her calling to nurture that talent and make him into a star. Which she'd done, very successfully.

Getting pregnant was a bonus. Giving birth to Luca Junior was the best day of her life. Forget about all the accolades and the gold records and the fan worship; having a healthy baby boy was the pinnacle. She'd relished sharing parenthood with Luca, while also watching his career rise.

Then one day he'd come to her and told her he was living a lie, that he was a gay man and could no longer keep it to himself. She'd understood and immediately set him free.

Only he wasn't free, was he? Slimy English Jeromy had somehow or other inveigled his way into Luca's life, and he appeared to be here to stay.

Suga did not like Jeromy. She did not trust him. And she sure as hell knew that he resented her as only an angry, jealous gay man can.

Unbeknownst to Luca, she'd had Jeromy investigated, and the results of said investigation were not great. Jeromy's design business was in trouble, in spite of the fact that he constantly boasted about how well he was doing. His personal life was also suspect. He was not at all faithful to Luca. In London he was a well-known figure at fetish and leather clubs, and he often used the Internet to trawl for fresh meat.

Did Luca know any of this? Was it up to her to tell him? Or if she did, would he resent her forever?

She knew that she had to tread carefully, and perhaps come up with a plan to get Jeromy out of Luca's life once and for all.

But how? It was something she had to think about.

24

"Thank you, dear," Hammond said as Skylar placed a mug of coffee on his desk. "I warned you there would be late nights."

"Yes, you did," she said sweetly.

"And are you absolutely certain you're okay with it?"

"Of course I am, Senator," Skylar replied, flattered that she was the only one he'd chosen to stay late. She'd been working for him for just a few days, and already she felt special. The offices were deserted except for a couple of cleaners who were busying themselves outside. Even his two assistants had left for the night.

"I'll be needing some papers copied shortly," he said, all business.

"I'll wait," Skylar offered.

"Then you may as well wait in here," Hammond said, indicating the leather couch across from his desk. "Make yourself comfortable."

"Are you sure, Senator?" Skylar asked tentatively. "I could wait outside."

"No, no, dear. Sit yourself down. I'm expecting a call, and until it comes through, I'm stuck here."

"You work so hard," Skylar ventured, her tone full of admiration as she settled on the couch and crossed her legs.

"Yes," Hammond agreed. "I suppose I do."

He noted that her thighs were a tad too heavy and her skirt was much too short. She had on a pair of wedge-heeled shoes that all the young girls seemed to favor, not at all sexy. Her legs were bare, though, which made up for the clumsy shoes. He imagined running his hands up her legs, starting at the ankle and slowly traveling all the way up until he reached her meaty thighs, then plunging his fingers into what lay beyond.

"My wife doesn't understand why I have to work so late," Hammond said, playing the sympathy card. "The truth is, she doesn't get it."

"Oh," Skylar said, thrilled that Senator Hammond Patterson was actually confiding in her, making her feel even more special.

"Relationships have their ups and downs," Hammond continued, taking a sip of his coffee. He paused for a moment and gave her a long, lingering look. "And how about you, dear? Are you in a relationship?"

"Uh . . . um . . ." Skylar faltered, thinking of her football-playing boyfriend with whom she was always breaking up. "Sort of," she managed.

Hammond's honest brown eyes twinkled. "Sort of?" he said. "What does *that* mean?"

"Well, uh . . . sometimes we're together and sometimes we're not," Skylar admitted, nervously tugging at her short skirt, wishing she'd worn something a little more circumspect. But how was she supposed to know that she'd end the day sitting in Senator Patterson's private office? It was an honor she had not expected.

"Boys," Hammond said with a meaningful chuckle. "Can't live with 'em, can't live without 'em."

"I totally agree," Skylar said, starting to feel more at ease.

"This sometime boyfriend of yours," Hammond continued, "does he push you to do things you might not feel comfortable doing?"

"Excuse me?" Skylar said, startled.

"I'm sure you understand what I'm saying."

"Uh . . . n-no, I don't," Skylar stammered.

"Sexual things," Hammond said, feeling a rising hard-on as he watched the girl squirm and blush beet red. "No need to be embarrassed," he added, adopting his best fatherly voice. "I have a teenage daughter, you know. She tells me what goes on between boys and girls. She listens to me and I give her advice."

"Oh," Skylar said, filled with relief. For a moment she'd thought the esteemed senator was about to come on to her, and how would she handle *that*?

"Boys are only after one thing," Hammond said evenly. He was tempted to yell *Pussy! Young juicy pussy!* However, he controlled himself. This one wasn't quite ready, and it wouldn't do to have her screaming rape if he touched her. "Anyway, Skylar—it is Skylar, isn't it?"

"Uh . . . yes, Senator."

"You can go now."

"But I thought—"

Don't think, you stupid little girl. Simply get out of my office before I change my mind and jam my cock into your dumb mouth.

"That's all right," he said easily. "Everything can wait until the morning."

Skylar jumped to her feet. "If you're sure . . ." she said hesitantly.

"I'm sure," Hammond replied, busying himself with some papers on his desk. "Good night, dear."

Slightly disappointed that she was being dismissed, Skylar slunk out.

Hammond immediately hurried into his private bathroom and masturbated, staring at his well-put-together reflection in the mirror while thinking of how it would feel the first time he came in Skylar's mouth, the first time he stuck it into her, the rubbing and fondling of her big breasts naked against his bare chest.

He could wait.

Why not?

He'd done so many times before.

Sierra had shopped. Reluctantly. She'd bought clothes she knew would please her husband. Although why the hell she wanted to please him was beyond her comprehension.

Oh yes. Of course. She'd given up. Given in to the threats and insults he hurled at her. She was his docile arm-piece. She was—to the general public—the perfect wife.

Hammond had caught her in a trap, and the only way out would be to end it all.

Or . . . she could run to her parents and tell them what a terrible monster her husband was, and hope and pray that he would not carry out any of his dire threats.

However, that would be taking too big a risk. Hammond was a dangerous man, and as long as she went along with what he wanted, everyone would be safe.

As each day, week, month passed, Sierra sought solace in a variety of pills. They kept her calm. They kept her going.

They were gradually sucking the life out of her.

Book Two

THE TRIP

25

Six months after the murder of his older brother, Boris, Sergei Zukov had moved to Mexico City, where over the years Boris had built many solid connections in the arms and drug world. Sergei was finished with Russia. Even though the Zukov gang supposedly had people in high places on their payroll, those people had done nothing about finding and prosecuting his brother's murderer. It seemed to be too sensitive a subject, with no one prepared to do a damn thing.

And why was that?

Because Boris Zukov was a known criminal, and even though he'd never spent more than one night in jail, it was a well-known fact that Boris was capable of monstrous crimes. Kidnapping, murder, torture, drug dealing, arms.

Neither the authorities nor the public cared that a violent criminal had been thrown from a fourteenth-floor window to his certain death.

Sergei cared. Sergei cared deeply. His brother had been everything to him. Boris had raised him when their mother had run off with a local car salesman, leaving them with their drunken, violent father, Vlad.

When their mother left, Boris was sixteen and tough as an old boot. Sergei was six, and scared.

Over the years, Boris had protected him from everything, making sure that he attended school, watching out that nothing bad happened to him. Boris had acted more like his father than Vlad had.

Vlad was a heavyset lazy oaf of a man who couldn't care less about raising his two sons, although he certainly didn't mind living off the money Boris brought home, never once asking where it came from.

Boris hated him, and he taught Sergei to feel the same.

When Sergei was ten, Vlad had arrived home one afternoon and flown into a drunken rage when he'd discovered that Sergei had finished the paltry amount of milk left in the empty fridge. He'd beaten the boy badly, cut his cheek with a razor blade, then settled back to watch TV, nursing a full bottle of vodka.

That night, Boris returned to their small apartment late. He was already creating a fierce reputation selling street drugs and making sure he was available for any other jobs that might come his way.

Collecting debts.

No problem.

Stealing cars.

A pleasure.

Even a little murder on the side if the price was right.

Yes, at twenty, Boris Zukov was a man on the come.

When he got home (having had a night of rough sex with a randy local girl), he walked in to check on his younger brother, only to find Sergei crouched in a corner, whimpering and covered in blood from the gash on his cheek, his eyes blackened, his nose broken, and his skinny body covered in welts from his father's heavy belt.

It wasn't necessary to ask who'd done it. Boris had no doubt that it was Vlad.

With a masklike face, he'd marched into the bedroom all three of them shared, taken a pillow from Vlad's bed, and returned to the living room.

His father was passed out in an armchair in front of

the TV, still clutching the bottle of vodka he'd been swigging from earlier. It was empty.

Stealthily, Boris positioned himself behind the chair, placing the pillow firmly over his father's face, ignoring the old man's muffled cries of shock.

Boris kept the pillow in place until there was no breath left in him.

Suffocation. Vlad deserved it. He was a sorry excuse for a father; they were better off without him.

When Sergei was eighteen, Boris packed him off to a college in the U.K. Sergei had liked it, what with all the pretty girls and available sex. Mastering the English language had been easy for him, and learning economics and bookkeeping was also a breeze. When he'd returned to Moscow, Boris had put him to work organizing the financial records of his various so-called legitimate businesses, most of which were merely a front for his criminal activities.

It was tricky. Two sets of books, sometimes three. Sergei had turned out to be a master at manipulating numbers.

Everything was going smoothly until Boris's untimely death. It was then that the problems had started. Sergei had attempted to take over, but there were men in the organization who did not want him seizing control. Men who were older and more experienced. Men with more clout, who thought *they* were entitled to take over. These men blocked Sergei at every turn, although they were happy to keep using his book-manipulating skills.

Sergei had burned with fury—as Boris's brother, *he* was the one who should've been in charge.

But no—he was deemed not worthy to fill his brother's boots.

It was disappointing, because Boris had been so proud of him. "My brother, the smart one," he'd often boast to whoever would listen.

Yes, Sergei was smart, all right. He'd never stolen from his brother, but with Boris gone he began siphoning money from the businesses, then moving it out of the country. After a while, he'd amassed enough to make an overnight exit.

Fuck the men who claimed to be Boris's partners. He'd taken what he considered to be his rightful inheritance and fled to Mexico, where it wasn't long before he reconnected with the people Boris had done business with in the past.

Now, at thirty-two, five years after Boris's murder, he had a new life and more money than he could ever hope to spend.

Input Denim Inc. was a clothing company he'd purchased, a line of clothes that sold all across the U.S., Europe, and the Middle East. He'd also taken over a worldwide medical supply and waste company. Both businesses were savvy fronts for his real business: the drug trade.

Over a short period of time, Sergei had managed to turn himself into a drug kingpin, with major ties to the Mexican drug cartels. He was a natural at covering his tracks and making new friends.

Apart from his crooked nose, which had never set properly, and the vicious scar on his cheek, Sergei wasn't bad-looking. He was not tall, but his build was quite muscular. He smothered his face and body in fake tan, and exhibited shining white teeth—all capped. Sergei particularly enjoyed the company of women, and they seemed to like him back. Cocaine was his drug of choice. His special kick was snorting it off the body of whatever woman or women he might be with, then packing a fair amount of coke into their vaginas before sucking it out. Good times.

His ex-wife, a Ukrainian model who'd divorced him when she'd found out he was into four-way sex, now lived in New York and headed the legitimate part of his clothing company. Their marriage had lasted barely six months.

He had no children—or at least not any that he knew of, because fucking was one of his favorite pastimes, second only to making money.

He resided in a penthouse in Mexico City. Weekends he spent at the villa he owned on the water in Acapulco, complete with helicopter pad.

Sergei made sure he was always surrounded by half a dozen faithful and dedicated henchmen. In business, a man could never be too careful.

Boris would be so proud if he could see him now. He'd seized control of his destiny, exactly as his big brother would have wanted him to do.

The one thing that continued to bother Sergei was finding out who had arranged the hit on Boris. And exactly who had carried out the plan. For it *was* a plan; he was sure of that.

Sergei wanted that person, and he wanted them badly.

Over the years, he'd never been able to find out. Not knowing ate away at him, because revenge was essential for his peace of mind.

Boris would expect him to exact revenge. Indeed, Boris would demand it.

There had been only one witness to the crime, and that was the whore Boris had been living with at the time, a young French slut who went by the name of Nona. The girl had taken off with the contents of Boris's safe the day after his demise. Sergei had been trying to find her ever since, but she'd managed to disappear.

Over the five years she'd been missing, he'd hired several detectives to locate her, and it was only in the last month that he'd received any results. She was in Arizona, living with a divorced businessman.

Sergei was currently on his way to pay her a long overdue visit.

The conniving bitch owed him the money she'd stolen from Boris's private safe. And more than that—she owed him the information about who had set up the murder of his brother.

Sergei was convinced she knew.

And he *would* get it out of her, one way or the other.

26

Sleek, sensuous, powerful, and fast, Aleksandr's new yacht was all that and more. His orders had been to create an elegant state-of-the-art yacht that could take him anywhere in the world, and that's exactly what he'd ended up with.

Luxury abounded. There were several sundecks on three levels, all with their own bars and spacious dining areas. Plus a spiral staircase leading to all levels. There was a counterflow swimming pool, a Jacuzzi, and a fully equipped gym with a Pilates retreat. On the lower deck was an authentic Finnish sauna, a steam room, a hair salon, a movie theater, and even a small medical room for any emergency that might occur. There were also many toys, from water skis and Jet Skis to snorkeling and sportfishing equipment, kayaks, WaveRunners, and scuba-diving gear. Everything was available.

The interior of the yacht was classy—all imported Italian marble, pale woods, soft beige leathers, and flattering lighting.

A giant Buddha presided over the marble entryway to the master stateroom, leading into the interior, which was more like a luxury apartment. A huge California king bed covered in exotic fur throws dominated the space, and there were rich Oriental fabrics on the walls. En suite were his-and-hers marble bathrooms, a feature Aleksandr had insisted on for Bianca's pleasure; the master also had its own private terrace, lap pool, and Jacuzzi, where Bianca could sunbathe and swim nude if she so desired.

The six other staterooms were also luxurious; however, nothing lived up to the master, which was located on the sky deck, allowing spectacular ninety-degree views.

Aleksandr had ordered the yacht three years earlier, before meeting Bianca. Then Bianca had entered his life and he'd changed the plans and also the name—the yacht was now christened the *Bianca*. He hadn't told her. It would be one of the many surprises he had in store for her.

During the course of the boat's construction at the Hakvoort shipyard in Holland, Aleksandr had visited several times to make sure everything was exactly as he'd envisioned. Later, he'd worked with a team of talented interior designers to fulfill his vision of pure opulence.

The yacht had been finished two months previously, and the captain and crew had taken it for a series of sea trial runs, finally ending up in Cabo San Lucas, where the big trip would begin.

Aleksandr had decided that rather than make the usual South of France/Sardinia/Italy run, they would embark on a different kind of voyage. They would explore the beautiful Sea of Cortez and the various small Mexican seaside towns and deserted islands along the way.

The Sea of Cortez—sometimes known as the aquarium of the sea because of its bountiful plant species, different kinds of fish, and other marine mammals—offered everything for a fantastic vacation. Aleksandr and his guests would visit uninhabited white sand beaches, experience jungle adventures, and sail far away from the ties of civilization.

Aleksandr was determined that this would be a trip to remember.

To be doubly sure everything was to his liking, he'd made one final visit to speak with Captain Harry Dickson, a ruddy-faced Englishman in his fifties. There were to be no screwups; everything had to be perfect. Captain Dickson assured him that it would be.

Flying back to Moscow, Aleksandr was fully satisfied that the captain was a man in charge, and that none of his guests, especially Bianca, would be disappointed.

Aleksandr was proud to say that he had created the perfect yacht for the perfect woman.

Bianca felt like crap as she sat on the British Airways plane taking her to Moscow. She had a horrible feeling that at any moment she was going to throw up all over the man sitting next to her. It seemed as if the plane was flying one way, and she was flying in the opposite direction. Wow! Talk about the mother of all hangovers.

Her overweight neighbor suddenly leaned over and said, "Excuse me, miss."

"Miss"! Was he fucking kidding?

"Yes," she said, backing away from his garlic breath, lowering her copy of *OK!* magazine. "What?"

"Aren't you that famous model?"

What a dumb question. Either he knows who I am or he doesn't.

"Um, yes, I am a model," she said grudgingly, glad she'd worn her blackout shades so that no one could see her eyes.

"The famous one?" the man said. "I mean if you are, then I have to tell you that my daughter loves you, but, er . . ." He hesitated for a moment before continuing. "Unfortunately, I can't seem to recall your name . . . ?"

Really? For God's sake, get a life and leave me alone.

"Bianca," she muttered, not pleased and regretting that she hadn't insisted that Aleksandr send his private plane for her.

"Oh," the man said with a note of disappointment. "I thought it was Naomi."

Please God save me from morons and tell this fucker to leave now!

"Bianca," she repeated, unclipping her seat belt, then abruptly getting up and heading for the galley, where Teddy, a languid gay cabin attendant, was discussing the size of Beyoncé's thighs with an agitated blond flight attendant who could think of nothing but her Russian boyfriend—the one with the massive appendage—who was waiting for her in a hotel room in Moscow.

"You know what?" Bianca said with an *I am very famous so kindly pay attention* scowl. "The guy in the seat next to mine is really bothering me. Do you think you can move him somewhere else?"

Teddy had attitude; this passenger was interrupting his discourse on Beyoncé's thighs, and he didn't care who *she* was or what she wanted.

Then all of a sudden he did care, because the moment she removed her ridiculously large sunglasses, he found himself staring into the feral cat eyes of Bianca.

"Oh my!" he gasped. Why hadn't anyone alerted him that the super-famous supermodel was aboard? He glared at his lovesick coworker and snapped, "What can we do, Heidi?"

Heidi managed to put on a suitably concerned expression. "We have a full flight," she said apologetically. "Would you like me to have a word with the gentleman?"

"A word's not about to shut him up," Bianca said sharply. "The man's a freaking pest."

"Oh dear!" Teddy exclaimed, waving his arms in the air. "I can't stand pests, or AP's as I call them."

Bianca frowned. "AP's?" she questioned.

"Annoying passengers," Teddy responded. "We get them all the time."

"I could ask the lady sitting across the aisle if she'd swap seats with you," Heidi suggested. "That might solve our dilemma."

"And how can you guarantee that I won't end up sitting next to another moron?" Bianca demanded.

Heidi lowered her voice to a conspiratorial whisper.

"The man in the window seat is a well-known English politician recently involved in a big scandal. I doubt if he'll be interested in making conversation."

"Once they know it's me, they're *all* interested in making conversation," Bianca said with a weary sigh. Sometimes it was tough being famous and having to deal with the general public. "But I guess anything is better than Mister Chatty," she added, putting her sunglasses back on.

"I'll go see what I can do," Heidi said, while Teddy envisioned telling his hunky Polish partner all about his encounter with the very famous Bianca. Of course he would embellish, make out that they'd swapped e-mail addresses and would definitely stay in touch.

"You're gorgeous," he managed, staring at her with envy and admiration. "More beautiful than your magazine covers."

Bianca shrugged. "Good genes," she murmured, giving him hope that maybe they *could* become friends, that it wasn't all simply a wild fantasy.

Heidi returned with the news that the woman in the aisle seat had agreed to move.

Bianca nodded; she was so used to getting her own way that it didn't surprise her. And then, because she couldn't help herself, she said, "And who exactly *is* the politician? And what was the scandal?"

Heidi and Teddy exchanged looks. Gossiping about the passengers was a definite rule breaker, but since they were now both suitably impressed that they were conducting an actual conversation with Bianca, what the hell.

"He texted pictures of his *you know what* to seven random women," Heidi whispered. "Sort of like that American politician last year—the Weiner man. Only what this one did was worse."

"Yes," said Teddy, happily joining in. "The pervert sent his texts from the men's room in Parliament, *and* he perma-marked messages on his piece of man meat."

" 'Man meat'?" Bianca said, suppressing a giggle. "That's a new one."

Teddy lowered his voice even more. "Apparently he has a huge penis."

Bianca squashed an urge to burst out laughing. What was up with these guys who thought that photographing their junk was a fine old idea? Were they the new-age flashers? Or merely horny old hound dogs with nothing better to do?

"Hmm . . ." she said thoughtfully. "Well, as long as he's not gonna show *me* the goods."

"I think we can guarantee that he's learned his lesson," Teddy said, wondering if her small but quite perfect boobs were real.

"Then let's do it," Bianca decided. "But one move from the asshole, and all bets are off."

A few minutes later, she was settled in her new seat. The politician, a thin-faced gentleman, was curled up in his window seat under a blanket, apparently asleep.

Bianca took out her iPod, tuned into Jay-Z and Kanye, leaned back, and daydreamed about Aleksandr, the yacht, and her future.

Everything was set, and if all went according to plan, one of these days in the not-too-distant future she could become Mrs. Aleksandr Kasianenko.

27

Frantically packing, throwing clothes into several open suitcases, Ashley didn't know what to take because she didn't know where they were going. She wished she did, because surely it made a difference? If it was the French Riviera or Sardinia, then only the fanciest of resort clothes would do. Chanel, Valentino, maybe even Dolce & Gabbana. However, for Greece or Sicily, she would pack differently.

"Take everything," Taye assured her. "Or take nothin'," he added with a ribald chuckle. "You'll look like a right old sexy bird in nothin'."

"'Old'?" Ashley said, turning on him, nostrils flaring. "I'm twenty-nine, for God's sake. That's hardly old."

"Just f-ing with you, toots," he said good-naturedly, sitting on the edge of the bed, watching her pack. "You'll be the best-lookin' girl on the boat. I'd bet me left ball on that."

"I wish we knew *who* was going," Ashley grumbled, throwing in a leopard-print bikini with a matching cover-up.

"I thought you was gonna give Bianca a buzz, find out."

"I tried. She's changed her cell number."

"Text her, then," Taye suggested.

"Aren't you listening, Taye?" Ashley said, irritably. "I just told you, she's changed her number."

"Oh yeah, right," Taye answered vaguely, wishing his wife would snap out of her never-ending bad mood. It was starting to piss him off.

Ashley held a skimpy white sundress up in front of her and turned to seek her husband's approval. "You like?" she questioned.

"Here's the deal, toots," Taye said, stretching. "I like anything *you* like."

"For God's sake!" Ashley snapped. "Have an opinion for once."

"Okay, okay, don't go gettin' your panties snaggled up your arse," Taye said quickly. "It's nice. Virginal."

"Who wants to look bloody virginal?" Ashley exploded. "What's *wrong* with you?"

I could tell her, Taye thought. *I could tell her that what's wrong with me is an acute case of blue balls, and no amount of whacking off seems to solve the problem.*

"How do you *wanna* look, then?" he asked.

"Sexy. Hot," Ashley said, pouting. "Like I used to before I had the twins and ruined my figure."

For a second he thought she might burst into tears, and quick as a flash he was on his feet, holding her, comforting her, feeling her boobs pressing up against his chest and liking it a lot.

Then Mammoth intruded and she hurriedly shoved him away. "Is sex all you ever think about?" she said crossly.

"Maybe," he confessed. "'Cause y' know what, toots? We haven't done it in weeks."

"Oh my God!" she said, glaring daggers. "Are you *counting* now?"

"Not counting," he said, careful not to piss her off further. "Just frustrated."

"The problem with you, Taye," she said grandly, "is that all you can think about is yourself."

Trouble loomed. There was no getting Ashley out of her usual pissy mode, and they were leaving the next day.

He didn't want to set off with Ashley all uptight; maybe if he backed down, he could bring her around. Anything for a bit of peace. "Okay, okay," he said soothingly. "I'm sorry, luv, I get it—you're wound up. Me too. We both need this break."

"I know *I* certainly do," Ashley said pointedly.

Saved by the twins, who came bounding into the room, followed by a fussy Elise, who was quite enamored with being in charge. She'd sent the nanny out on a series of errands and was in full control.

The six-year-old twins, Aimee and Wolf, were looking picture-perfect. For some reason known only to Elise, the two children were both dressed as if they were on their way to a party or a photo shoot.

"Daddy!" Aimee flung herself at Taye, wrapping her sturdy little body around his legs, clinging to him tightly. "Don't wantchoo t' go 'way!"

Wolf, a miniature version of his father, hovered in the doorway scowling and kicking at the rug.

"It's only for a week, baby girl," Taye assured Aimee. "And Daddy an' Mummy gonna buy you lotsa presents."

"Don't promise them that," Ashley hissed. "They're spoiled enough as it is."

"I wanna Ferrari," Wolf piped up.

"An' *I* wanna princess castle," Aimee said, joining in.

"Only if you're good, mind your manners, an' listen to Grandma," Taye said.

"Please do *not* call me Grandma," Elise said, throwing him a dirty look. "The children call me Moo-Moo. I've told you both dozens of times. Doesn't anyone listen?"

"Moo-Moo sounds like a cow," Ashley snickered.

"No, it doesn't," Elise objected. "It's an adorable nickname. Isn't it, children?"

"Wanna get Princess Barbie too," Aimee announced.

"You're stupid," Wolf said with a great deal of authority. "All girls are stupid idiots."

"Don't be rude to your sister," Ashley snapped.

"Yes, you heard your father—mind your manners, young man," Elise interjected.

"*Manners! Manners! Manners!*" Aimee chanted, sticking her tongue out at Wolf, who retaliated by spitting in her direction.

"Oh my *God*!" Ashley screamed. "The two of you are disgusting! Take them away, Mother. I can't stand to look at them."

"We're going for dinner at Nando's," Elise said, unfazed by the children's bad behavior. "The little ones love the chicken burgers there."

"Why're they so dressed up?" Taye asked, attempting to disentangle Aimee from his legs.

"In case they're photographed," Elise responded matter-of-factly. "You never know."

"They only get photographed when they're out with us," Ashley pointed out.

"Not so," Elise argued. "Celebrities' children are quite the vogue. Gwen Stefani's little ones are almost as famous as their mother. And Suri Cruise is simply everywhere."

"That's in America," Ashley stated.

"It's starting here too," Elise said. "And I'm sure you want Aimee and Wolf to look their adorable best."

"Whatever," Ashley muttered, more interested in getting back to her packing.

"Okay then," Taye said, finally freeing himself from his little daughter's clutches. "We'll see you all later."

Elise threw him a pointed stare.

"*What*?" Taye said, realizing she wanted something.

"Money," Elise said. "For dinner."

"Oh yeah," Taye said, digging in his pocket and coming up with a crumpled wad of bills. "How much you need?"

"Stop being a cheapskate and give her everything," Ashley said, eager to get rid of them.

"Sure, toots," Taye said, handing over a bundle of cash.

The family departed, and once more Taye found himself alone with his bad-tempered wife. He couldn't wait to get the hell out of England and into sunnier climes. Maybe a change of scenery would put Ashley in a better mood.

A man could only hope.

28

Xuan did not need to be entertained. She took off on her own every morning, not returning until late at night. When Flynn suggested another dinner, she demurred, saying that she was finishing up work on a thesis she was writing about women who become prostitutes and their reasons. He had plenty of work of his own to get to before they took off, so he didn't mind. But he couldn't help thinking that Xuan was a difficult woman to figure out. Even though he thought he knew her, he soon realized that he actually didn't know her at all. She was an enigma.

The Kasianenko plan was to meet up in Cabo San Lucas at the boat, so he was surprised to get a call from Aleksandr himself.

"I have to stop in Paris for a meeting tomorrow," Aleksandr said briskly. "So we will pick you up and we will fly to Cabo together."

It was as if they'd spoken yesterday instead of almost two years previously.

"Sounds good," Flynn responded, pleased with the change of plan. It certainly beat getting on and off a series of planes to reach their destination.

"I'll have my people call with the arrangements," Aleksandr stated.

And that was that. Aleksandr was a man of few words.

Later, Flynn told Xuan the new plan, and she nodded.

"Perhaps I can write a piece about this man with his big plane, his supermodel, and his enormous yacht," she said coolly. "Does he give back to the world, or is everything simply a prize for him?"

"No writing anything," Flynn warned. "Aleksandr's one of the good guys."

"How do you know that?" Xuan asked with a skeptical expression.

"Because I do," he retorted, experiencing doubts about whether inviting Xuan on this journey was such a smart thing to do.

"I will judge for myself," Xuan said, her beautiful face turning inscrutable.

"Don't embarrass me," he warned. "Just remember that Aleksandr is my friend."

"You think I would embarrass you?" Xuan said, amusement lighting her eyes.

"If you could," Flynn said. "Only I'm sure you wouldn't do that to me, would you?"

"We'll see," Xuan answered mysteriously.

Shit! he thought. *I've made a mistake. She's gonna try and break his balls because he's rich and powerful.*

Then he thought, *Well, at least it won't be boring. Let the games begin.*

That night he had dinner alone at his neighborhood bistro, feasting on all his favorite foods.

Mai attended to his table, and when he was finished, he invited her to sit with him while he drank his coffee.

Mai accepted his invitation, and they chatted for a while. She was beguiling and sweet in a very French way.

It occurred to him that he had the apartment to himself tonight; Xuan had informed him she would be staying with a friend and would not be back until morning. So against his better judgment, he ended up asking Mai if she would care to join him for a drink.

She accepted, and they strolled the three blocks to his place.

When they arrived, he poured her a Pernod on the rocks, and they sat around sipping their drinks and talking politics—which surprised him, because Mai was far more knowledgeable than he'd expected.

Eventually they ended up in bed. Somehow it was inevitable.

Being with Mai was not the experience he'd thought it would be. Mai was no spider-monkey girl—she was a gentle lover with a warm and welcoming body. She smelled of lavender and roses, while the Pernod on her breath added a tangy sharpness to their kisses.

He found himself making love to her with more feeling than he'd known in a long time.

She murmured that she'd been wanting to sleep with him ever since he'd first come into her family's restaurant, but she'd felt that he wasn't at all interested.

He was taken by her lilting accent, the way she touched the back of his neck, the smoothness of her hands. Mai was the first woman in a long time who was actually getting through to him.

And did he want that?

No.

Feelings only led to heartbreak.

Eventually they fell asleep, entwined in each other's arms.

When he awoke at dawn, she was gone.

For a moment he was relieved, then he was pissed. Had he not pleased her? What was the deal with walking out without so much as a good-bye?

Suddenly the realization struck him that he was actually experiencing real feelings.

It was a shocker.

Xuan arrived later in the morning, carrying a shopping bag of warm baguettes, a jar of homemade jam, and a tub of thick creamy butter.

"Breakfast," she announced, placing everything on the small kitchen counter. She paused for a moment and sniffed the air. "You had a woman here," she said matter-of-factly. "Will she be joining us for breakfast?"

"No," Flynn said evenly. "She will not. How did you know?"

"Ah . . . I smell her fragrance in the air. *And* I notice the smile on your face."

"I'm not smiling."

"Enjoy it for once."

"I am *not* smiling," he insisted.

Xuan shrugged. "Too bad she isn't here. However, that means all the more for us."

Flynn nodded; his mind was elsewhere.

"Can you make coffee while I take a shower?" Xuan asked. "I was out on the streets all night. It was worth it, because I gathered some very interesting material."

"I'm sure you did," Flynn said, finding himself thinking that he wished he'd invited Mai on the trip as opposed to Xuan. He was already looking forward to seeing the Frenchwoman again, which was a positive sign that maybe he *was* finally ready for more than a two- or three-week stand.

"It's good that you're happy," Xuan said. "This woman, she pleased you?"

"None of your fucking business," Flynn replied, finding himself trying to suppress the stupid grin that seemed to bubble up from nowhere.

"Ah yes," Xuan said with an all-knowing smile. "She pleased you."

"Are you packed and ready to go?" Flynn said, quickly changing the subject. "We're supposed to meet Aleksandr at the Plaza Athenée at three. Then we'll head straight on to the airport."

"Me? Packed?" Xuan said with a gesture of surprise. "I never unpacked. Or didn't you notice?"

"Right."

"It's nice to know that you can still summon up feelings," Xuan remarked. "Unfortunately for me, that is not possible."

He didn't need to ask why. Xuan had shared with him some of the horrors she'd experienced, and for her own peace of mind, it was best not to dredge up the past.

"I don't know about you, but I'm starving," he said, keeping it casual. "Let's eat."

"Ah yes," Xuan said. "Making love always gives one a hearty appetite."

"Will you quit?" he said, slathering butter on a baguette.

Xuan allowed herself another mysterious smile. "Of course," she said. "Only I so enjoy seeing you like this."

"Like what?" he said, attempting a frown.

"Vulnerable."

"Come *on*," he said, almost choking. "Let's not get carried away."

Yet he knew she was right. Maybe he was finally giving himself permission to move on.

And maybe that wasn't such a bad thing.

29

Even though he was a major movie star and had been for many years, Cliff Baxter did not own a plane. It wasn't necessary, because whenever he wished to go anywhere, there was always a studio plane available for his use; all he had to do was ask. So he did, and a company jet was on hand to fly him and Lori to Cabo San Lucas the following day. In the meantime, he had his valet pack his clothes, and he had Enid come to his house to go over any last-minute business.

Enid was her usual cryptic self. "I hope and pray you're not planning any surprises for me on this little jaunt you're taking off on," she said, giving him a piercing look.

"Now what kind of surprises did you have in mind, Enid?" Cliff asked, his eyes crinkling.

One thing about Cliff Baxter: he had not succumbed to the Botox and plastic surgery some of the older male stars had dipped into. He was of the George Clooney/Clint Eastwood school. You are what you are, take it or leave it. But he did look fabulous for a man approaching fifty. He had just the right amount of lines and wrinkles, and only a fleck of gray in his lustrous head of hair. Not to mention the devastating smile that had women across the world swooning.

"The marriage surprise," Enid said bluntly. "You know exactly what I mean."

Cliff roared with laughter. Perhaps his laughter wouldn't have been quite so hearty if he'd known that Lori was lurking outside the door to his study, listening to every word.

"Are you *kidding* me?" he blurted. "You better than anyone should know how I feel about marriage. Not for me. Nope. No marriage. No whiny kids. Not anytime soon or indeed ever."

"That's a relief," Enid said. "Because Lori is not for you, yet she seems to have stayed around longer than the others. I really don't understand why."

"They stay because I *want* them to stay," Cliff stated. "They leave when it suits me."

Enid could certainly believe that. "And this one?" she asked.

"Between us?" Cliff said, giving her one of his serious looks.

"No, Cliff," Enid said with a sarcastic edge. "I plan on selling everything you tell me to the tabloids."

"In that case I should be truthful with you."

"Please do."

"Okay, here's the scoop: the truth is that Lori's sell-by date is almost up."

Hovering in the hallway, Lori could not believe what she was hearing. Sell-by date. Fucking *sell-by* date. What did he think she was, a tub of yogurt on the supermarket shelf?

Bastard! Prick! How could he be so cavalier about their relationship? It hurt, it *really* hurt.

She stood there fighting back angry tears, suppressing a burning desire to march into the room and tell him exactly what she thought of him.

But forewarned was forearmed, and Lori began to formulate a plan.

Dinner was a casual affair at a megaproducer's Bel Air mansion. Cliff and the producer had worked together on several movies and were planning a franchise starring a renegade detective, a character Cliff was dying to play. He spoke about the detective all the time as if he were a real person.

Lori was sick of hearing about his upcoming movie. If there wasn't a role in it for her, why would she be remotely interested?

The two men were friends from way back. They had a wish list of leading ladies—everyone from Angelina Jolie to Scarlett Johansson.

What about me? Lori wanted to yell. *How about giving* me *a chance?*

Reality check. She knew that was not about to happen, especially now with her exit visa waiting to be stamped.

She wondered how Cliff would deal with getting rid of her. Perhaps he'd manufacture a big fight—bad enough that she'd be forced to walk.

Hmm . . . She was smart enough to realize that it takes two to make an argument work, and now that she was aware of the situation, there was no way she'd play into that scenario.

Maybe he'd be brutally honest and simply tell her that it wasn't working for him.

Did that mean a severance package? Money and an apartment?

She felt like calling a couple of his exes and checking out the deal.

Meanwhile, they were still going on the trip, so that was something. Could she salvage their relationship? It was possible.

"You're looking very girlish tonight," said the producer's wife, a Hollywood social blonde with large over-plumped lips and an unsatisfied expression. "I simply adore your dress—Kitson?"

No, Target, Lori was tempted to reply. *It cost me twenty-five bucks as opposed to the two hundred twenty it would've been at Kitson. And that's a conservative estimate.*

"The ruffles are such fun," the producer's wife continued. Then, without taking a beat, she added sotto voce, "How are things going between you and Cliff?"

Did she know something? Had Cliff confided in his producer friend?

All the wives were insanely jealous of Lori because they all secretly lusted after a piece of the famous Cliff Baxter cock. Only *she* was the one getting it and *they* weren't.

Too bad, bitches.

"Actually," Lori answered evenly, "things couldn't be better. Cliff is such a sweetheart, so generous and thoughtful." She paused, then added, "Why would you ask something like that?"

The producer's wife was flustered, but only for a moment. "Well," she said. "Cliff *does* have a reputation for moving on. Of course we all love him dearly, and we'd like nothing better than to see him settle down, but you know that our Cliff is totally anti-marriage."

Yes, I do know, bitch. Thank you for reminding me.

"That's why we're so good together," Lori said sweetly. "'Cause I'm too young to even consider marriage. I plan on having a career first, marriage much much later." *Make sure you tell that to your horny balding husband so he can relay the message to my boyfriend.*

"Oh," the producer's wife said, pursing her wormy lips. "Then you are indeed the perfect girl for Cliff."

Across the room, Cliff and the producer were discussing the advantages of shooting in New York as opposed to L.A. "Better tax breaks in New York," the producer proclaimed, adding with a ribald chuckle, "and better strip clubs."

Cliff shook his head. "Can't show my face at a strip club," he said. "It'd be all over the Internet the next day. Who needs that shit?"

"Why should you care? You're not married."

"It's not right for my image. Besides, I have a girl-friend."

The producer glanced across the room. "How's it hangin' with Lori?" he asked. "Seems like she's a keeper. She's stayed around longer than most."

Cliff nodded. His private life was all his, and only Enid was privy to certain information. However, that didn't mean he couldn't reveal a little something. "Lori gives the best head I've ever had," he confided, knowing it would drive his friend crazy. "Better than a porn star any day."

The producer's mouth quivered slightly as he digested the information. It wasn't enough that Cliff Baxter was a fucking matinee idol, and single too. Now he had a girl-friend who gave the greatest blow jobs ever. Sometimes life just wasn't fair.

Later, the producer and his wife were getting ready to show a first-run movie in their private home theater.

Cliff decided they wouldn't stay. "We're leaving early tomorrow," he explained. Then, winking at the producer, he added, "Gotta take care of a couple of things before bed."

The producer stared hungrily at Lori before moving in for a good-night hug, while the producer's wife managed to kiss Cliff full on his lips.

In the Bentley on the way home, Cliff suggested to Lori that she might like to give him head while he was driving.

"What if we're pulled over?" she asked, thinking of the consequences.

"It'll be worth it," he replied, obviously in the mood for his own particular style of lap dance.

Lori gave in and went to work, her head in his lap as he negotiated the winding roads of Bel Air, one hand on the steering wheel, the other making sure she stayed down.

Lori gave it her best shot, and he came within minutes.

Let's see if you can find a new girlfriend who'll tend to your needs the way I do, she thought. *Lotsa luck, Mister Movie Star. You're gonna find me harder to replace than you can possibly imagine.*

30

Because Suga had a concert in Mexico City, Luca decided it would be supportive and maybe even fun to attend her show before flying on to Cabo San Lucas the following day.

It was an arrangement that did not sit well with Jeromy. Watching Suga perform was akin to having a thousand sharp knives stuck in his eyes. The woman pranced across the stage like an oversized Barbie doll in ridiculous outfits that she obviously considered insanely sexy. They were insane, all right, suitable only for a five-foot-ten-inch, skinny, flat-chested model, not a short, overweight, fifty-something diva with big hair, huge bosoms, and way too much makeup.

The fans who crowded the arena obviously appreciated her over-the-topness. Jeromy certainly didn't; her voice sent shivers up his spine, and not in a pleasant way.

The most excruciating part of the evening was when she dragged Luca up onstage with her and the crowd erupted into a frenzy of whoops, screams, and orgasmic sighs at the sight of their idol.

Luca. Jeromy's blond Latin god. Onstage with the she-wolf. Not a pretty sight. Jeromy was mortified that he had to witness such a scene.

Afterward there were celebratory drinks in Suga's overcrowded dressing room. Hangers-on abounded. Young fans, old fans, managers, promoters, a couple of photographers.

Jeromy slid into a corner and stayed there. He was an observer at a freak show, certainly not a participant.

Luca didn't seem to notice or care about Jeromy's lack of interest; he was too busy making sure that Suga received the full dazzle of his attention.

Damn the woman! The more time Jeromy spent in her company, the more he loathed her. She was easy to hate.

Looking around, he soon made eye contact with one of Suga's backup dancers, a tall, thin man clad in ass-baring leather pants, his head shaved. Jeromy had noticed him onstage, and now, in close proximity, he felt that old familiar stirring. They continued making eye contact until, with a slight tilt of his eyebrow, Jeromy indicated the door.

Luca was still busy playing nice with Suga; he did not notice Jeromy slipping out, or the dancer following close behind him.

Without exchanging a word, they both headed for the men's room, where they crowded into a stall together.

Jeromy reached out and touched the man's shaven head while feverishly unzipping his own pants.

The dancer fell to his knees and accepted Jeromy's engorged cock into his mouth.

Still no words were spoken.

The sexual excitement was intense as Jeromy realized that at any moment they could be discovered.

He shuddered out an orgasm, hurriedly stuffed his member back into his pants, and rejoined the dressing-room group.

Ten minutes later, Luca finally remembered he was alive, and approached him.

"You getting bored?" Luca asked.

Getting bored! What planet did Luca live on?

"I'm perfectly fine," Jeromy said, noticing his partner in sex across the crowded room. "But since we have such an early flight tomorrow, perhaps we should think about leaving."

"Sure," Luca agreed. "I'll go say good-bye to Suga. Come with me. She adores you."

Blatant lie.

Jeromy followed Luca across the room to where Suga held court. Her elaborate eye makeup was smudged, her lip gloss caked on her obviously enhanced lips. *Vagina lips,* Jeromy thought. *Big old vagina lips.*

"Thank you for coming," Suga said to Jeromy, all fake warmth and cloying perfume.

Ah, she should only know . . .

"It was my pleasure," Jeromy lied. "And you were . . ." He searched for the right word. "Amazing."

"Of course," Suga said, adding a rather grand, "I never let my fans down." Then dismissing him, because she was well aware that he didn't mean a word he said, she turned to Luca and threw her arms around his neck, kissing him full on the lips and whispering something in Spanish in his ear.

Jeromy did not speak Spanish. His young lover spoke perfect English, so there had never been the need to learn. Right now he wished he knew what the annoying cow had said. English, Spanish—it didn't matter. It was one of those intimate whispers that put a big smile on Luca's handsome face.

Dammit. Why did the fat bitch cast such a spell over Luca? It had to be broken, that was for sure. And he was the one to do it.

31

Sierra dreaded the forthcoming trip. She loathed the thought of being stuck in a cabin on a boat, however luxurious, with Hammond in close proximity. It wasn't as if she even knew Aleksandr Kasianenko. She'd met him once—briefly—at a political event in Washington. They'd exchanged pleasantries for a moment, and that was it. Hammond had then proceeded to pursue him like a dog chasing a particularly juicy bone.

It was the night before their departure, and as usual, Hammond was once again working late. Earlier in the day, they'd attended a lunch together, and she'd acted as the perfect political wife in a St. John suit, her copper hair neatly coiffed, smile firmly in place. Oh yes, she would make an outstanding first lady, and didn't Hammond know it. That's the *only* reason he wanted her. She understood that, and it sent chills down her spine.

Hammond had a dream. And that dream was to be standing on the steps of the White House, with her on his arm.

May I present President Hammond Patterson and his lovely wife, Sierra Kathleen Snow Patterson.

The perfect wife. The perfect husband. What a couple. They would put the Kennedys to shame.

Or so Hammond thought.

Sierra was confident that day would never come. Someone would eventually expose Hammond for the phony he was. Maybe it would be her. But she didn't think so. She couldn't risk it.

No. She had to depend on someone else to take him down.

And who that someone was, she didn't yet know.

"Am I working you too hard?" Hammond inquired, pressing his fingers together as Skylar entered his office carrying a stack of papers.

"Not at all, Senator," Skylar said, quite pleased with herself, because out of all the interns, she was obviously his favorite. This was the fourth night in a row he'd asked her to work late. "I'm here to be of service."

Indeed you are, Hammond thought. *And tonight I'm going to test that theory out.*

"How's that boyfriend of yours?" he asked.

"Oh, y'know," Skylar said, gesturing vaguely with her left hand.

"Together? Not together?" Hammond pressed.

"We . . . uh . . . had a bit of a fight."

"About what?"

"I'm not sure," Skylar confessed. "Sometimes he seems so . . . inexperienced."

Hammond jumped at the opening. "Sexually?" he questioned, standing up from behind his desk.

Skylar's face reddened.

"Don't be embarrassed," Hammond continued, walking around the desk toward her. "I told you before, I discuss everything with my teenage daughter. Sex . . . well, naturally, because boys *are* inexperienced. They mature much later than girls, therefore they have no idea how to treat a woman." He took a long, meaningful pause. "And that's what you are, Skylar, a young, beautiful woman."

Skylar blushed beet red. Such a compliment! From such an important man! That very morning her brother had called her a fat-ass, and her mom had told her to clean up her room and stop acting like a twelve-year-old.

They should only know that the esteemed senator had just called her a beautiful woman. *Take that, Mom. I'm a woman. Not a freaking twelve-year-old.*

"Thank you, Senator," she murmured.

He moved closer to her, placing both his hands on her shoulders.

She didn't dare move. He reminded her of a teacher she'd had in high school. Older, nice-looking in a very buttoned-up, all-American way.

He had lovely brown eyes. Honest eyes. Eyes she could trust.

He lowered his voice and said, "Did you hear what I told you, Skylar? You are very beautiful."

Hammond had learned over the years that if you told any woman, old or young, that she was beautiful, be she rabid dog or true beauty, she would always believe you. There were no exceptions.

"Uh . . . yes . . . uh . . . thank you," Skylar muttered, flattered, yet at the same time wishing he'd remove his hands from her shoulders. It was creeping her out. She remembered hearing stories in history class about an intern at the White House way back when Bill Clinton was president—apparently he'd come on to the intern or vice versa, Skylar couldn't remember which, but whatever it was, it had gotten him impeached. Not that she thought Senator Patterson was about to do anything, but still— she wished he'd remove his hands.

He didn't.

He moved a tad closer.

He slid his hands down until they cupped both her breasts.

Skylar was mortified. This couldn't be happening. The senator was a married man. She was a teenager, and he had to be somewhere in his late thirties. This wasn't right.

She froze, unable to move.

"You have beautiful breasts," he said. "I noticed them the first time I saw you."

She opened her mouth to object, but nothing came out.

He maneuvered his hands under her sweater, and expertly lifted her bra so that it rested above her breasts. Then his fingers began tweaking her nipples.

She was so confused, fully aware that she should stop him. But suddenly new feelings began flooding her body. The way he was touching her was making her feel excited and breathless. The senator's touch was so different from the furtive fumblings of her on-again, off-again boyfriend, whom she'd never allowed beyond second base—the reason they were always fighting.

"Do you like this?" the senator questioned, circling her nipples with his fingertips. "Does it make you excited?"

She managed a strangled yes, imagining her mom's face if her mom ever found out.

The senator raised her sweater, and bent his head to suck on one of her erect nipples. He stopped for just a moment to ask, "And this?"

Her throat was dry, and she knew she should object, but the way he was making her feel was too good. She didn't want him to stop what he was doing. Never. Ever.

Hammond experienced a moment of triumph. Skylar was primed. Enough action on big-breasted girls and they were all yours. Nothing like a little nipple-play to get them creamed up and ready to go. Hammond knew this for sure.

"I cannot resist you," he crooned, seducing her with his words. "You're like a delicious candy. Your breasts are incredible."

Compliments were an important part of the initial seduction. Compliments and foreplay—a winning combination.

Sierra checked her watch. It was late, and still no sign of Hammond. She ate a solitary dinner without him and finally retired to bed.

Tomorrow they would be on their way, and who knew what would happen?

Maybe she could push him overboard in the middle of the night, and then her problems would be over.

She smiled grimly to herself.

If only . . .

32

"I dunno what you're talking about," the girl muttered, sitting stiffly in a chair in the living room of the house she shared with her boyfriend in Arizona.

"No?" Sergei Zukov questioned, a nerve in his left cheek twitching out of control. He stood in front of her, angry and disgusted that she was trying to deny who she was. They'd met only once before, when Boris had taken her to a cousin's wedding in Moscow. Five long years ago. She'd had long black hair then and dressed like a Goth. He remembered asking Boris what he was doing with such an odd creature. Boris had chuckled and muttered something about getting off on strange-looking women. After Boris's death, Sergei had discovered that the girl was a heroin addict, and unbeknownst to Boris, had been selling information about him to feed her habit. Boris had always gone for females who walked a dangerous path. It had turned out to be his downfall.

Now the girl had cropped bleached hair. She wore denim shorts, a tank top, and a long green cardigan. She had thin lips and bad skin and spoke with a fake American accent.

It was her, no doubt about it.

Sergei hated the sight of her.

"So what you are telling me is that your name is not

Nona, and that you never lived with my brother in Moscow?" he said, circling her chair. "Is that correct?"

She scowled at him, vigorously shaking her head. "My name's Margie," she spat. "I'm an American citizen, an' I know my rights, so get the fuck outta my house."

He'd arrived ten minutes earlier. She'd opened the door thinking it was a delivery. He'd had two of his men with him, and they'd grabbed her and placed her in the chair like a puppet. She hadn't screamed; instead, she'd glared willfully at him, her eyes full of hatred. She knew why he was there.

"I am Boris's brother," he'd said. "And you *are* Nona."

She'd said nothing.

"You know why I am here, don't you?" he'd continued. "I can see it in your face."

That's when she'd denied knowing what he was talking about.

"My husband will be home soon," she said, her eyes darting furtively toward the door. "He has a gun, and he's not afraid to use it."

"The man you live with is not your husband, and you are not Margie," Sergei stated coldly.

"Screw you," she said in a low angry voice. "You don't scare me, so like I said, get the fuck out."

"I will when I recover the money you stole, and get the information I require," Sergei said, quite calm apart from the giveaway muscle twitch in his left cheek.

"Whistle for it, asshole," she said, full of defiance. "The money's long gone."

Sergei was a patient man when he had to be; however, he was not about to play word games with this tough bitch all day.

It took two hours, but after a certain amount of physical persuasion, she'd finally cracked, revealing that she'd sold information to an American journalist about Boris's plans to kidnap one of Aleksandr Kasianenko's daughters, and that the journalist must have gone straight to Kasianenko with the information, because twenty-four hours later Boris was dead and Nona had taken flight, afraid for her own life.

Sergei was finally satisfied; he now had everything he needed.

The fat-cat billionaire Aleksandr Kasianenko was the man responsible for his brother's death.

It was enough knowledge to set Sergei on a vengeful path.

33

Sitting next to Aleksandr on his plane, Bianca regaled her boyfriend with tales of her commercial flight to Moscow and the many indignities she'd had to endure. "I should've stayed in Paris," she said with a rueful laugh. "'Cause here I am, twenty-four hours later, on my way *back* to the city I only just left! This is crazy time! *And* like I said, I flew commercial. What a nightmare! I don't know how people do it. It's so inconvenient."

Aleksandr seemed preoccupied, and although she was making light of it, Bianca was not thrilled that she'd traipsed all the way to Moscow to find Aleksandr quite distant. He'd been immersed in business meetings and she'd hardly seen him. Now they were stopping off in Paris to pick up friends of his she'd never met. This wasn't exactly how she'd expected her big birthday trip to start off.

"Are you all right?" she asked Aleksandr, leaning closer to him. "You seem like you've got something on your mind."

"Something on my mind," he repeated, turning and fixing her with a steady gaze.

"That's what I said."

"And how *was* your previous trip to Paris?" he inquired. "Tell me more."

"I told you everything," she said, wondering why he was suddenly so interested. "Dinner with friends, all delightfully gay, so you would've hated it. We had a ton of laughs, and I missed you madly. I always do when we're apart."

"My wife's lawyer seems to be under a different impression," Aleksandr said evenly, tapping his fingers on the side of his seat.

"Excuse me?" Bianca said, frowning. "What's your wife's lawyer got to do with anything?"

"He sent me over some very interesting printouts from various Internet sites."

"What printouts?"

Aleksandr picked up his briefcase, opened it, and laid out various photos of Bianca dancing the night away and grinding on a stripper pole, and—oh, the humiliation— crotch shots that clearly showed she was not wearing underwear.

"Oh crap!" she gasped, reviewing the photos. "I . . . I don't get it."

"Neither do I," Aleksandr said, his face grave. "You surely understand that I am going through an extremely difficult divorce, and visitation with my daughters is of paramount importance to me. Now my wife is saying she will not allow our children to be around a woman of such low character."

"Low character!" Bianca exclaimed, her humiliation turning to anger. "Low fucking *character.* How dare she! It wasn't as if I was *posing* for those shots. Somebody took them without my knowledge."

"However, you *were* in a club," Aleksandr said accusingly. "You *were* dancing on a pole like a cheap stripper. And you were not wearing underwear."

"Something you've never complained about before."

Aleksandr's face darkened. "Do not forget that you are my woman, Bianca. Your behavior reflects on *me,* and this kind of behavior is beyond disrespectful."

"Your *woman*!" Bianca burst out, stunned that Aleksandr was carrying on as if she were his personal property.

He was revealing a side of him she'd never seen before, and she didn't like it. "Who the *hell* do you think you are?" she demanded, her temper rising. "An Arab with a fucking harem? 'Cause, baby, I ain't into that game."

"Bianca," Aleksandr said, fixing her with another steady gaze. "This is serious."

"Well, *fuck* serious," she said, still full of anger. "Nobody tells *me* what I can and cannot do. I'm sorry I got photographed, but it comes with the fucking territory of being a star. You should know that."

Their first fight. They glared at each other, neither prepared to back down.

"I loathe it when you swear," Aleksandr said coldly. "It's unfeminine. It does not become you."

"Really?" Bianca retorted, furious at the way he was speaking to her.

"It makes you sound common, using the words of a streetwalker."

"And I bet you've had a few of those," Bianca snapped, unable to help herself.

"Excuse me, Mr. Kasianenko," Olga, his personal flight attendant, said, hovering because she really didn't want to interrupt. "The pilot has asked that you fasten your seat belts in preparation for our landing."

"Thank you, Olga," Aleksandr said with a curt nod.

Bianca turned away from him and grappled with her seat belt. She was seething. This was some shitty start to what was supposed to be a memorable trip.

It suddenly occurred to her that maybe she was making a big mistake.

Flying commercial was not Ashley's favorite thing to do. Going through Heathrow Airport was inconvenient, to say the least. Everyone wanted Taye's autograph, and there was no escaping the hordes of paparazzi who trailed them all the way until they passed through security.

Some of the paparazzi shouted mean things at her.

"Give us a smile, luv. You always look so bloody miserable." "Taye gettin' a leg over with any other bird?" "C'mon, Ashley, try not to look as if you're constipated!"

Rude bastards. She hated them all.

It wasn't *her* fault that Taye always managed a big shit-eating grin; she simply couldn't do it. He was mister personality. She was not.

The truth was that she wasn't miserable, merely cool. Better to look cool than to look like a fool.

Once they were through security, things calmed down, although she wasn't too happy about having to remove her shoes, her jacket, and all her jewelry as they passed through the scanner. Damn, why didn't Taye get priority treatment? He was a British football hero, a bona fide star, and stars weren't meant to suffer the indignities of ordinary people.

Sometimes she wondered if it was because he was black that he didn't get the Beckham treatment.

Hmm . . . food for thought.

Sitting in the VIP lounge, Taye chatted amiably with other passengers. Ashley settled herself at a table, sipping an early-morning coffee while leafing through a copy of *Hello* magazine, pausing to study a photo of herself at a fashion event in an extremely chic outfit. She was pleased with the image, pleased enough to tear the page out of the magazine and stash it in her Birkin purse.

Taye was dragging over someone to introduce to her, which was annoying because she wasn't in the mood for company. She soon perked up when she realized it was American movie star Billy Melina, and he was smokin' hot.

Ashley put on her animated face and began plying Billy with questions about his next movie and where he was flying to. Billy was totally charming in an all-American way, and when he left, Ashley fantasized about what it would be like to be married to an actual movie star. A handsome movie star who looked exactly like Billy Melina.

So hot and sexy, *and* he'd just finished making a movie with Cliff Baxter—another of her crushes.

Idly, she wondered what Billy was like in bed.

"What you thinkin', luv?" Taye asked.

"Oh," she said cheekily, "I was thinking about what you're gonna do to me once you get me on that boat." Her husband was right; they hadn't had sex in a while, and suddenly she was experiencing quite a tingle.

"You were?" Taye said, startled.

"Boats are sexy, aren't they?" Ashley said, tugging on his arm.

Christ! Was his wife finally feeling horny?

"Dead sexy," he managed. "Let's put it this way, toots. You an' I are gonna rock the boat from stem to stern. Be prepared."

She smiled, then glanced down and noticed the erection growing in his pants.

Taye was so damn easy, and he was all hers.

In the large black SUV on their way to the airport, Lori was on her best behavior. Cliff was thinking of dumping her, and she was having none of it. She was determined to make him see the error of his ways. A perfect blow job in the car while he was driving was merely the beginning of all the exciting things she had in store for him. Their sex life was about to heat up. On their upcoming trip, she had plans to take it to an entirely new level.

Yes, Cliff Baxter was about to see a whole other side of her. By the time she was finished with him, he'd be *begging* her to stay.

Cabo San Lucas was at its glorious, shimmering best. The sun was shining, palm trees swaying; a vacation atmosphere prevailed.

Luca and Jeromy were staying overnight with the Luttmans, acquaintances who owned a magnificent villa overlooking the bay. The Luttmans were a New York power couple whom they'd met on the social circuit several times, a couple Jeromy had been desperately trying to cultivate. So when the yacht trip had come up, Jeromy had quickly discovered the Luttmans would be in residence at their vacation home, and he'd suggested to Luca that they might stay the night. Luca had agreed, and the Luttmans had been thrilled to say yes.

Lanita Luttman, a former showgirl, now a jewelry designer and a well-known lesbian, was a true social butterfly. And her husband, Sydney, an absurdly rich investment banker and a well-known homosexual, couldn't have been happier to welcome Luca and his English partner into their home.

A uniformed driver and two eager assistants met Luca and Jeromy at the airport and whisked them to the gated villa, where Lanita waited to greet them wearing a flowing purple caftan and multiple strands of long diamond necklaces. A flamboyant woman, she had dyed-black hair and turquoise contacts and was decidedly overweight.

Servants abounded. Lanita snapped her fingers, and trays of canapés and Bellinis appeared in the hands of ridiculously handsome young waiters clad in tight shorts, with only colorful braces covering their well-defined abs and pecs.

Jeromy was in heaven. He glanced around and wished that they were spending more than one night; he could get very used to this kind of life.

Luca was already admiring Lanita's array of sparkling necklaces, while various maids and housekeepers peered from the windows and behind the bushes, desperate to get a peek at their idol, the fabulous Luca Perez.

So gorgeous, so blond, and what a voice! They were all in a state of hero worship.

Meanwhile, Jeromy was in his element. Who would have thought that his life would take such an amazing turn? The London gays in high places had written him off when he'd turned forty and didn't have a permanent boyfriend, let alone a successful business. However, since hooking up with Luca and bringing Ashley in, he'd managed to achieve it all. With Luca's backing and connections and Taye's investment, his design business had taken off, and now here he was in Cabo San Lucas with one of the richest couples in America, about to set off on an exclusive trip with a Russian oligarch and his supermodel girlfriend.

Not too shabby. Not too shabby at all.

Hammond climbed into the marital bed stinking of sex.

Sierra cowered on her side of the bed, pretending to be asleep. The bastard hadn't even bothered to wash the smell of another woman off his body.

Sierra continued to wonder how she'd allowed herself to sink to such a low point in her life.

Because of Hammond's diabolical threats, that's how. Threats she had no doubt he would manage—somehow or other—to carry out.

You have to get out of this marriage, a voice screamed in her head.

I can't, another voice replied. *I don't have the courage.*

Once she would have fought back, stood up for herself. But now she couldn't summon the strength. Playing along was the only way to go.

She closed her eyes tightly shut and prayed for oblivion.

This was her life, and there was nothing she could do about it.

34

As Flynn and Xuan entered the spacious lobby of the Plaza Athenée hotel, Aleksandr rose to his feet and enveloped Flynn in a hearty bear hug. "It is great to see you, my friend," he said warmly. "It has been far too long. I have missed your company."

Flynn extricated himself and introduced Xuan. Aleksandr gave her an appraising once-over and nodded approvingly. "You have done well," he said.

Flynn realized that he had probably failed to make it clear that he and Xuan were not a couple, merely platonic friends.

He'd have to deal with that.

Xuan proffered her hand, gave Aleksandr a firm handshake and a steady gaze. "I have heard much about you," she said briskly. "And your lady too. Where is she?"

Nothing like getting straight to the point, Flynn thought. But he had to admit he'd been thinking the same thing. Aleksandr appeared to be by himself, apart from a burly bodyguard hovering a few feet away. Where *was* the extraordinary Bianca?

"My lady is waiting for us on my plane," Aleksandr said. "She did not feel like coming into the city."

He omitted to mention that Bianca had refused to accompany him. She was in a full sulk and had locked herself in the bedroom on the plane, much to Aleksandr's chagrin. He was hoping that by the time they got back, she would have had time to think things through and realize that he was right.

"It's great to see you too," Flynn said. "It was quite a surprise hearing from you, though I can assure you it was a welcome one. Your timing was right on—I needed a break."

"Sit," Aleksandr said, indicating a comfortable banquette. "We'll take tea before we return to the plane."

"How very civilized," Xuan murmured, sitting down. Aleksandr sat himself beside her, while Flynn settled on an upholstered chair opposite them.

"Tell me, Mr. Kasianenko," Xuan said, "do you use your plane for humanitarian efforts, or is it merely for your own convenience?"

Aleksandr gave her a long, penetrating look. "So personal, so soon," he said at last, sounding vaguely amused. "Please, *do* call me Aleksandr; there is no need to be so formal."

"Aleksandr it is," Xuan said, twisting a thin gold bangle on her delicate wrist. "You haven't answered my question."

Oh shit, Flynn thought. *She's determined to score points, and she's doing it with the wrong guy.*

Aleksandr didn't seem to mind. "You tell me about *your* humanitarian efforts, and I'll tell you about mine," he said, still sounding amused.

Flynn quickly interjected. "Let's get into it later," he said, determined to avert trouble, because once Xuan got going, she *really* got going. "I heard a rumor you're in talks to buy an English football team," he continued. "Now *that's* what I'm interested in hearing. Want to tell me all about it?"

"Didja fancy him then?" Taye asked, snuggling close to his wife on their British Airways flight to L.A., where they were to make a connection to Cabo San Lucas.

"Fancy who?" questioned Ashley, all wide-eyed and

giggly because she'd been taking full advantage of the free champagne.

"You know who," Taye teased. "That American movie-star bloke."

"Dunno what you're talkin' about," Ashley said, letting forth a most unladylike hiccup.

"Billy Melina."

"Oh, *him*," Ashley said dismissively. "He's not so hot."

"Thought you fancied him."

"Not me," she said innocently.

"Is that so?"

"Yes, Taye," she said, fluffing out her blond curls. "He isn't my type."

"Glad to hear it."

"Are you?" she said coyly.

"You bet your pretty little arse," Taye said, reaching over for a quick grope of her left breast, pleased to hear that she didn't fancy the movie star. "Can't wait t' get you on the boat," he added. "We're gonna have a fine old time."

"Stop feeling me up." She giggled. "Try to be patient for once."

"Can't do it, toots. I'm too turned on."

"At least wait until the cabin lights are off," she insisted, impulsively running her hands over his shaved head, something she did only when she was feeling horny.

Holy shit! It looked like little wifey was letting her guard down and he was about to get lucky.

Mile-high club, here I come!

To Flynn's surprise, Aleksandr and Xuan appeared to hit it off. Flynn had expected fireworks, but all he got was a heated discussion between the two of them about why politicians were not doing enough to end wars, world hunger, atrocities, inhumane treatment of prisoners, and urban crime.

It turned out that Aleksandr was quite a do-gooder in his own way. He wasn't a boastful man; however, Xuan managed to pry all kinds of information out of him. She soon discovered that he supported several charitable institutions, that he'd financed a school for uneducated teenagers in Ukraine, and that on occasion he did indeed use his plane to transport food and supplies to disaster areas.

Flynn had not been aware of any of this, and it made him respect Aleksandr a hell of a lot more. The man wasn't simply a rich tycoon looking to sleep with beautiful models and throw decadent parties; he was the real deal. A billionaire with a social conscience. Surprising. Refreshing.

Xuan had her own particular way of making people talk, and by the time they'd had tea in the lobby of the Plaza Athenée and then helicoptered to the airport, she and Aleksandr were carrying on like old friends.

Bianca—not so much. She greeted them with a frosty demeanor as they boarded the plane, practically ignoring Aleksandr when he attempted to give her a kiss. She hurriedly turned away from him, announced that she had a killer of a headache, and flounced off into the bedroom, slamming the door behind her.

"Sorry about that," Aleksandr said, obviously uncomfortable. "Bianca has been working too hard lately."

"Really?" Xuan said with a sarcastic edge. "Posing for pretty photographs all day long must be extremely tiring."

Flynn threw her a warning look, which she ignored. Xuan was not one to back down; like it or not, she always said what was on her mind.

Aleksandr appeared unfazed. He ordered shots of vodka and a large silver bowl piled high with caviar. "We shall drink," he announced. "And we shall eat. Bianca will feel better later. You will see."

The studio corporate jet was luxurious by anyone's standards. Cliff joked with the two attractive flight attendants, and even visited the pilots before takeoff for a manly chat. Everyone loved Cliff Baxter. He was an American classic: handsome, smooth, and a damn fine actor. His movies made billions worldwide, and why not? He always gave his adoring public exactly what they wanted.

"This is quite an adventure for you," he informed Lori as they settled into their seats. "One I hope you'll always remember."

You patronizing shit, she thought, remaining calm on the outside, furious on the inside. She knew exactly how Cliff wanted her to behave. He required her to be the grateful girlfriend who was so very lucky to be given the opportunity to go on such a fabulous trip with her famous movie-star boyfriend. Well, screw him. She could play the crap out of that role.

"How could I *not* be excited?" she said, all bright-eyed and eager, just the way he expected her to be. "Thank you so much, Cliff, for including me."

"That's okay, sweetie," he said, nodding at her reassuringly. "You deserve it."

I do? she was dying to say. *How come? I thought you were preparing to dump me. Isn't that the next item on your agenda?*

But of course the dumping was to take place *after* the trip, *after* he'd used her as his sexual plaything and adorable arm candy, *after* a week of sex Cliff Baxter–style.

Yes, Cliff was that most dangerous of men. An attractive, famous, charming, talented, rich user of women.

We'll see, Mr. Baxter, she thought. *We'll damn well see.*

The Luttmans invited a dozen or so friends over to show off their famous star guest. Luca wasn't thrilled; he'd been looking forward to lying back and relaxing, not being put on display.

Jeromy was one happy camper. The more important people he met, the better for his design business. It seemed everyone had a second home in London, so what could be better? He flung himself into being socially adept, while Luca sat at a table surrounded by predatory, overly tanned, bored women, all married to incredibly rich men who were at least thirty years older than them, and all anxious to capture Luca's full attention.

Jeromy glanced over. Foolish women. Didn't they know Luca was gay? Didn't they get it?

Apparently the message hadn't reached them.

By the end of the evening, Jeromy had acquired three new clients, and an offer for him and Luca to join Lanita and Sydney in their luxurious bedroom later that night.

Jeromy knew Luca would decline, but there was nothing wrong with being curious. What did Lanita and Sydney have in mind?

Sex, of course. But what combination? And where did Lanita fit in?

Jeromy couldn't resist. As soon as Luca was asleep in the guest suite, he took himself to the master bedroom, where incense candles burned and Sydney lay spread-eagled on the middle of the bed with a healthy Viagra-inspired erection and an even healthier gut, which Jeromy found quite exciting in a totally repulsive way.

Lanita was also present, clad head to toe in a Day-Glo purple latex bodysuit, wielding a lethal whip with a sinister Vampira mask covering her eyes. "Welcome," she purred. "Where is Luca?"

Naturally they wanted the star. Who didn't? But tonight they'd have to make do with him.

Fortunately for them, he was *far* better at participating in games than Luca.

Nobody played a more beguiling man of the people than Senator Hammond Patterson. He had it down to a fine art. Smile at everyone, pose with their children, pick up babies, wave when appropriate, always appear amicable and approachable. He came across as idealistic and full of hope, when in point of fact he was rife with ambition and harbored a deceptive personality.

As Hammond's closest personal aide, Eddie March

had yet to discover the real man who lurked beneath the façade of decency and truth. All he saw was an upstanding man who always spoke up for what he believed in. A future candidate for the U.S. presidency. A compassionate man with high standards.

Eddie also saw the very beautiful, classy, and serene wife of the senator, Sierra Hammond. Every time he was in her presence, she took his breath away. He had a schoolboy crush, and there was nothing he could do about it except worship her from afar.

Eddie March was catnip to women. An attractive single man working next to an esteemed senator. At thirty-four he had his own boyish charm; only his was genuine.

Eddie elected to accompany Hammond and Sierra to the airport on the pretext that he had a few things to tie up before the senator's short vacation.

He sat opposite Hammond in the limousine discussing final decisions on several matters pending.

Sierra curled into her seat and gazed blankly out the window.

Eddie couldn't help sending a few furtive glances her way. She was so damn beautiful with her porcelain skin and exquisite cheekbones. How the hell had Hammond gotten so lucky?

There was a mini press conference outside the airport, not planned, but Hammond handled it with his usual style. Everyone was anxious to know when and if he was planning to run—rumors abounded.

Hammond gave them the standard well-thought-out noncommittal answers; he had no intention of revealing his strategy to announce his candidacy. When the time came, he'd decided, he would make his announcement on Jay Leno's *The Tonight Show,* just like several other important politicians before him.

After all, he was a man of the people—what could be more fitting?

35

It was Sergei's way to do things fast. Fast and thorough, with an obsessive attention to detail. Possessing a steel-trap mind, a lack of conscience, and a knack for picking the right business partners was an asset, because when he required something to be done, he expected instant gratification or there would be consequences.

So when Sergei discovered that Aleksandr Kasianenko was the man responsible for his brother's murder, he immediately had his people find out everything he needed to know about his fellow Russian. Sergei had numerous contacts, and since information was a currency he dealt in every day, it didn't take long.

Sergei was reminded that way back in the early nineties, after the fall of the Soviet Union, Boris and Aleksandr Kasianenko had been involved in some kind of business dispute over shares in an oil company that Boris had claimed he was entitled to. Sergei had no memory of how the issue was resolved, but he did recall that Boris had always held a grudge, and after brooding about it for years, he'd made plans to kidnap one of Kasianenko's daughters and hold her for ransom. "That motherfucking *pizda still* owes me money," Boris had raged. "It's been years now, and I have waited long enough. It is time to claim what's mine."

Boris's plan had never materialized because of his untimely death.

Finally, Sergei understood why. Aleksandr Kasianenko must've heard about the kidnapping plot and taken steps to prevent it from happening. Aleksandr Kasianenko had murdered Boris, taken his life as if it meant nothing. And he would pay for that.

When Sergei heard about Aleksandr's new yacht and his upcoming trip, it was like a gift laid out in all its glory for him to salivate over and relish.

Sergei could almost taste the ultimate revenge.

Could anything be more perfect?

Aleksandr Kasianenko.

One rich, lucky motherfucker.

Not so lucky anymore.

Sergei would see to that.

36

When Bianca caught sight of her name emblazoned across the side of the gleaming white super-yacht, she forgot all about her fight with her lover and melted. She turned to Aleksandr and hugged him tightly. "You didn't!" she squealed.

"Yes, my dear, I did," he said, finally breaking a smile. Their flight to Cabo had been most uncomfortable. Bianca had spent the majority of the time locked in the bedroom, which was an embarrassment, considering they had guests. At times she could be a willful woman, and it infuriated him.

"Why didn't you tell me?" she demanded, green eyes gleaming with delight.

"I decided to surprise you," Aleksandr said. "I know how you love surprises."

"Now I feel so selfish for not helping you with our guests," Bianca said, pouting. "I'm such a bad, bad girl."

"It's all right, my dear," he assured her. "Our guests slept."

"And you?"

"I fell asleep for a minute or two," he replied. "Not as comfortably as if I'd been in my own bedroom, but it was acceptable."

"Why didn't you come in and join me?" Bianca asked, experiencing waves of guilt. "I wouldn't've kicked you out."

"I was under the impression that you were in no mood to be disturbed."

"I'm so sorry," she said, truly meaning it.

"Good enough," he replied, relieved to put their argument to rest. Fighting with Bianca was not his favorite pastime.

"I'm also sorry for flashing my cooch," Bianca added with an embarrassed giggle. "You *know* it wasn't intentional. I wouldn't do that."

"I'm sure it wasn't."

"Damn cell-phone cameras," she grumbled. "They should be banned!"

"I expect my wife will eventually get over it," Aleksandr said, quite certain that Bianca's indiscretion would cost him dearly.

"You think?" she asked hopefully.

"I know," Aleksandr said, taking her arm. "Come, my dear. Let us go board the *Bianca*. The magnificent lady awaits our presence."

Away from London, their large house, the irascible twins, her interfering mother, and her design obligations—which as far as Taye could tell consisted of nothing more than picking out fancy fabrics for rich clients—Ashley was like a different person. She'd suddenly turned all giggly and girlish, groping him on the plane, even suggesting they might do it in the bathroom. His wife was actually happy *and* randy! Exactly like the girl he'd married six years ago, the girl who couldn't get enough, the fun-loving Ashley he'd knocked up in the back of his Roller one drunken night after a party.

Ah yes, he remembered that night well. Ashley in a Stella McCartney dress and no knickers, high heels and bare legs. He'd actually gone down on her in the back of the car before jamming it into her sweet wetness.

It was the night they'd conceived Aimee and Wolf. What a night!

"Oh," Ashley said, fanning herself as they got off the plane. "This place is bloody hot."

"Yeah," Taye agreed, "an' it'll get even hotter tonight when I'm givin' you exactly what you want."

"You mean what *you* want." She giggled.

They had not done it on the plane due to the fact that Ashley had complained that the bathroom was too gross. "There's three inches of pee on the floor," she'd moaned in disgust. "Why can't men ever aim straight?"

"I can," Taye had retorted with a lascivious grin.

"Oh, I know *that*," she'd replied.

And *he'd* known without a doubt that tonight he was definitely getting lucky.

Watching Xuan grill Aleksandr was quite entertaining. It wasn't until Xuan had started her inquisition that Flynn realized the charitable deeds the rich Russian was capable of. The man was full of surprises. Now that he was aware Aleksandr had a charitable side, there were many things Flynn thought he might discuss with him. For instance, would Aleksandr be prepared to sponsor the building of a school in Ethiopia for orphans who'd lost their parents in the ongoing war? It was a project that had been on Flynn's mind for a while, but raising the money was almost impossible. He was in weekly contact with people who were prepared to build and organize everything, but lack of funds was the big holdup. One school. Surely that wasn't too much for Aleksandr to manage?

Flynn decided that before the trip was over, it was his duty to ask.

Aleksandr was obviously intrigued by Xuan; they hadn't stopped talking on the flight. Finally—after they'd landed—Bianca had emerged from the bedroom, and she and Aleksandr had left the plane together, followed by Aleksandr's ever-present bodyguard, Kyril.

"I wish to take Bianca to the yacht first," Aleksandr had said. "A car will come for you and Xuan shortly."

So Flynn was left with Xuan, who couldn't wait to inform him that Aleksandr Kasianenko was a far more interesting man than he'd led her to believe.

"I didn't lead you to believe anything," Flynn objected.

"Yes, you did," Xuan insisted. "You told me he was an obscenely rich oligarch with no conscience."

"Bullshit," Flynn said, laughing. "I never said that."

"Well . . . that's the impression I got."

"Then you should listen more carefully."

"Anyway," Xuan said, smoothing back her long hair, "I find him to be an extremely knowledgeable man."

Flynn raised a skeptical eyebrow. "You do?"

"Yes, I do. Although I cannot imagine what he sees in that rude, spoiled creature he's with," Xuan said, seemingly puzzled that Aleksandr Kasianenko was bedazzled by such an exotic woman.

Flynn felt argumentative. "What makes you think Bianca's spoiled?"

"Did you *see* the way she behaved?" Xuan said. "Pouting and sulking like a teenager. I can't stand that kind of woman. They imagine their beauty excuses them from everything."

"I kinda think we caught them mid-fight," Flynn noted.

"Perhaps. But in my opinion, a man like Aleksandr deserves better."

Flynn broke a smile. "I do believe my little Xuan has a crush," he teased.

"Don't be ridiculous!" she snapped.

"These things happen," he said lightly. "Even to you."

"My goodness, Flynn. Having sex with someone you like has taken away your better sense of judgment."

"And so she turns the tables," Flynn said.

"And so he starts speaking in clichés," Xuan shot back.

"I gotta say that you and Aleksandr *would* make an interesting couple," Flynn observed.

"Oh, *please*," Xuan said, dismissing his comments with

a shake of her head. "The man is taken, in case you hadn't noticed."

So she *did* like him. Flynn was amused at the thought of Xuan and Aleksandr together. It would be the mismatch of the century. The Russian oligarch and the militant Asian girl. What a fun combination *that* could turn out to be.

Guy, the entertainment director from the yacht, personally met Cliff Baxter and his girlfriend at the airport. A gay, personable Australian, Guy was used to dealing with celebrities; it was his wish to make them feel as comfortable as possible from the get-go.

"The name's Guy," he said, offering Cliff a firm handshake. "It's a pleasure to welcome you, Mr. Baxter."

"It's a pleasure to be welcomed," Cliff responded, his famous movie-star smile thrilling every woman who hovered within ten feet of him.

"I'm Lori," Lori said, asserting herself.

"Welcome, ma'am," Guy said, reaching for her carry-on bag. "Allow me to help you with that."

"Thank you," Lori said, trying to decide if he was gay or not. He was certainly nice-looking: tall and muscular with bleached white hair worn in a spikey cut, crinkly pale blue eyes, and a deep suntan.

"Follow me," Guy said, attempting not to stare at Cliff Baxter, who was just as handsome in person as he was on the screen. "Your luggage will be taken care of. I have a car waiting. And Mr. Kasianenko wanted me to tell you that he is delighted you are here."

The Luttmans supplied a white Bentley to take Luca and Jeromy to the Kasianenko yacht. After his nighttime sexual adventures with the Luttmans, Jeromy was quite hungover. He hadn't drunk *that* much. Was there such a thing as a sexual hangover? Yes. And Jeromy was proof that it existed.

Between the two of them and their sexual perversions, the Luttmans had worn him out. Jeromy had always been partial to a walk on the wild side, but the Luttmans were something else. He almost blushed at the memory.

Luca was his usual handsome, cheerful, blond-god self. Jeromy wondered what Luca would say if he ever found out about the sexual shenanigans that had taken place the previous evening. Luca would probably be shocked; he might be gay, but in Jeromy's world, he was an innocent gay with very limited experience. *You suck my cock, I'll suck yours.* Plus a certain amount of mild penetration on special occasions.

It was no wonder that Jeromy had to venture elsewhere to get real satisfaction.

"I can't wait to relax and get away from everything," Luca said. "How about you?"

"I must say that being on the Kasianenko yacht sounds like the perfect getaway," Jeromy agreed, adjusting his dark glasses so they hid what surely must be hideous bags under his eyes. He longed to pat on some hemorrhoid cream before falling into a deep and most welcome sleep.

Alas, that would have to wait until later, because right now he had the role of attentive boyfriend to play, and nobody played it better than Jeromy Milton-Gold.

"We're here." Hammond nudged his wife awake as the plane landed. "Try to look a little less miserable, and for crissakes, put on a smile," he said, his tone a sharp command. "Do not forget, these people are all future contributors to my campaign, so attempt to sparkle."

Had Hammond just instructed her to sparkle? Was that what he expected?

Yes.

Or what?

Or he'd regale her with his threats again. Threats against her family. Threats he assured her on an almost daily basis he could definitely arrange to have carried out.

37

After exploring the luxurious yacht and falling in love with every aspect of it, especially the opulent master suite, Bianca settled on the main deck with Aleksandr by her side, and a glass of champagne in her hand, ready to greet their guests.

"This is paradise," she commented, taking in her surroundings and realizing how lucky she was to have found a man like Aleksandr. Not only was he a fantastic lover, but he was so very good to her and rich rich rich! Not that his money mattered—she had plenty of her own. However, it made a welcome change to be with a man who did not expect *her* to pick up the check.

"It certainly is," Aleksandr agreed. "And there will be more surprises to come."

"I can't wait," she said, clinging to his arm. "Tell me everything."

"Be patient, my love," he said, lifting his glass to clink it with hers.

"I'll try."

"Try hard."

"You shouldn't keep me waiting," Bianca said with a captivating smile.

"Ah, but that's exactly what I should do," Aleksandr responded. He knew how to keep Bianca interested.

Ashley and Taye were the first guests to arrive. Bianca

was pleased; she and Ashley were sometime friends, and she couldn't wait to show off the glamorous yacht. She gave Taye a quick kiss on the cheek and hoped that he'd forgotten about their one night of lust many years ago.

Apparently he had, for he never said a word, not that he would in front of his wife.

"This is amazing!" Ashley squealed, taking in her surroundings. "Your name is on the boat and everything! How fantastic is *that*?"

"My gift to my lady," Aleksandr said with an enigmatic smile. "Bianca deserves only the best."

Some gift, Ashley thought as she quickly checked Aleksandr out. She found him to be a somewhat imposing man with his close-cropped dark hair, gray at the temples, and heavy features. He was attractive in a very manly way. A bit frightening really, like the mysterious villain in a Hollywood action movie.

"This is so exciting!" Ashley said, continuing to enthuse as she and Bianca sipped champagne.

"I know," Bianca agreed, smoothing down her Azzedine Alaïa tighter-than-tight dress. "The whole yacht thing was all Aleksandr's idea, and I'm here to tell you that I'm loving every single minute!"

"Who wouldn't?" Ashley said, experiencing a sharp stab of envy.

"I know," Bianca agreed. "It's quite overwhelming."

"Can I ask who else is coming?" Ashley asked, plucking a smoked salmon canapé from a passing stewardess.

Before Bianca could reveal who the other guests were, Luca and Jeromy were escorted aboard.

Spotting her old friend Luca, Bianca flung herself at him with screams of excitement. "Look at *you*!" she yelled. "Big fuckin' star! And don't we love it!"

Luca was as delighted to see her as she was to see him. He'd known Bianca long before he was famous, and she'd always been a loyal friend to him, especially when he'd come out. He embraced her energy and spirit, and he considered her to be very special, even though they never got to spend as much time together as they would like.

"You look outrageous," he said, taking a step back to admire her. "Could your dress be any tighter?"

"You know what they say," Bianca responded with a cheeky wink. "If you got it, flaunt it!"

"I'm all over that!" Luca said, grinning.

Ashley sauntered over to Jeromy. "Bet you never expected to see *me* here," she said with a distinct note of triumph.

"Lord, no," Jeromy exclaimed, hardly able to conceal his surprise. "When did *you* get invited?"

"The same time as you," Ashley retorted, delighted to stick it to him. "Taye had the invite in his pocket all through that dinner we had. He thought if he kept it hidden he'd get a b.j. out of it."

"And did he?" Jeromy asked caustically, not thrilled with the caliber of guests. He'd expected so much more than Ashley and Taye, although he soon changed his opinion when Cliff Baxter and a vibrant young redhead appeared. Aha! A full-blown movie star. Nice one. Jeromy launched into full smarm.

Lori stood back and checked out the other guests, while a tall, skinny, anonymous Englishman played kiss-ass with Cliff.

She noticed Luca Perez and was immediately smitten. He was so gorgeous with his quiff of blond hair and golden tan. Then there was supermodel Bianca with her deep caramel skin and delicious green cat eyes. The Russian man, their host, was an overpowering presence in a very quiet, almost sinister way. And Taye Sherwin, the famous Brit footballer. What a hunk, although his wife wasn't exactly Miss Friendly. When they were introduced, Ashley Sherwin had sniffed out a hello as if it were giving her a migraine.

Bitch! Lori thought. *I'm not good enough for you, but I bet my boyfriend is.*

And bingo! Lori was right. Ashley cracked a big smile when introduced to Cliff. "I love all your movies," she simpered, tossing her long blond curls and sticking out her boobs. "I'm such a big fan."

You should see his cock, Lori thought. *Or maybe not.* She'd often taken note of Taye Sherwin's print commercials in all the best magazines, and he was certainly not lacking in the big dick department. Either that or he was stuffing socks.

Lori grinned. Fun with the rich and famous. Little Lori Walsh was doing well for herself. Maybe the Russian had a billionaire friend she could hook up with. After all, she was the soon-to-be ex of a major movie star; that had to count for something.

Flynn and Xuan were almost the last to arrive. Flynn might not have been famous, but every woman's eyes swiveled to check him out. He was dead sexy in an edgy way. Not perfect by any means, but he had the look. The two-day stubble, intense ice-blue eyes, lean body, and longish hair. Cliff Baxter was classically handsome. Taye Sherwin, boyish. Luca, gorgeous but gay. Aleksandr, an overpowering presence. And then there was Flynn. The most attractive man on the boat.

Hot, Lori thought.

Delicious, Ashley thought.

Damn! Bianca thought.

And while everyone was lusting after Flynn and wondering exactly who he was, Hammond Patterson made his entrance, trailed by the lovely Mrs. Patterson.

Flynn glanced over and suddenly felt his world spin out of control, for to his shock and surprise he was staring straight into the eyes of the love of his life.

Fifteen Years Earlier

By the time he was twenty, Flynn Hudson had been with more girls than he could remember or even count. It wasn't that he chased them; it seemed that they were always coming on to him—and he had no logical reason to turn them down. What the hell, he was young, fit, and enjoying himself while studying economics, journalism, and world affairs at UCLA in Los Angeles.

Flynn lived in a house on Westholm Avenue with several other guys. They were a rowdy bunch who liked to use Flynn as the bait to get girls. It always worked. Flynn took the prize, and they shared the leftovers. They all joked about it, except Hammond Patterson—commonly known as Ham—who often argued that he was the main attraction, considering that his dad was an important congressman, and that he too was going into politics.

Ham was the peacock of the group, forever boasting about his conquests and insisting on sharing graphic sexual details whenever he got a girl into bed.

Flynn and Ham did not get along at all. Ham was jealous of Flynn, and it showed. Flynn considered Ham to be a major asshole.

Flynn's American grandparents lived in a large house in Brentwood, and sometimes he'd spend the weekends hanging out there.

One memorable weekend while his grandparents were safely in Palm Springs, his buddies persuaded him to throw an open-house party. It wasn't Flynn's idea, but he got talked into it by Arnie, one of his best friends.

The party started out as a sedate get-together, but as word spread, it soon turned into a major rave. The beer began flowing, naked girls couldn't wait to jump into the swimming pool, and the smell of pot wafted in the air.

"Jeez, Arnie," Flynn complained after the cops had visited twice. "My grandparents are gonna go ape shit. Help me close this thing down."

And as he watched, Arnie dissolved into a useless stoned heap.

Flynn shook his head, and then he glanced up and saw her. The girl with the heart-shaped face, honey coppery hair, and large brown eyes. Pretty did not describe her; she exuded warmth and compassion. She was a showstopper, and she was busy fighting off Ham, who was trying to persuade her to take a swig from the beer bottle he was holding. Ham had her in a neck lock.

Flynn didn't hesitate; he quickly moved in. "Easy," he warned Ham. "Looks to me like she doesn't want a drink, so get your hands off her."

"Y' can fuck off," Ham slurred, hanging on to the girl with the intent to keep her. "None of your fuckin' business."

Flynn stared at the girl. "Are you with this guy?" he asked.

"No way," she said, suddenly shaking herself free and starting to run off, but not before yelling, "You know something? You're all a bunch of drunken slobs!"

And that was that. Until three weeks later, when he saw her again. She was standing outside a fast-food restaurant in Westwood with another girl, and as luck would have it, he knew the girl she was with.

The good news was that he was acquainted with her friend.

The bad news was that he was on a date, and his date was a clinger who refused to let go of him.

Flynn did not allow this to stop him. He walked over to the girl he knew, said hello, and waited for her to introduce him to her friend. Which she did.

Then he had her name. Sierra Snow. A name as beautiful as the girl herself.

Sierra barely looked at him, but it didn't matter;

he was finished, gone, helplessly, hopelessly in love or lust or whatever.

Somehow he knew that Sierra and he were destined to be together. It was fate, karma, whatever you want to call it.

But most of all, it was inevitable.

38

Women were Sergei's playthings. Like new toys, he only kept them around for so long, trifling with them until they were broken or he got bored.

His current paramours were Ina Mendoza, a former Mexican beauty queen who lived at his Acapulco villa, and Cookie, a ratty blond American D-list actress who'd once starred in a successful comedy where she'd flashed her fake boobs. Since then she'd done nothing of note.

He kept Cookie stashed in his Mexico City penthouse, where she spent her days shopping, always accompanied by a female bodyguard on the vague chance that she might be kidnapped.

"Kidnapped? You?" Sergei had sneered when she'd mentioned her fears. "Nobody would dare to fuck with Sergei Zukov. Any kidnapping to be done is done by *me*." But to placate her, he'd assigned one of his bodyguards to watch over her.

Cookie was thrilled that she had finally landed a powerful boyfriend. Finally. Her Hollywood career had not been stellar, so Sergei was her last chance of hitting the big time. She knew he had plenty of money, and she was hoping that she might get him to finance a movie—starring her. What a coup *that* would be.

Her ex-husband, a nightclub bouncer back in L.A., had written a banging script, and all she had to do was get

Sergei interested, which was no easy job. He had the attention span of a gnat.

Lately, he'd had something else on his mind, something that seemed to be taking all his attention.

Cookie hoped it wasn't the fat Mexican so-called beauty queen he kept in Acapulco. She seethed with jealousy over that one. What could Ina do that she couldn't?

She'd raised the subject of Ina once with Sergei, and he'd slapped her across the face so hard that she'd lived with the imprint of his hand for days.

Bastard! He'd pay for that.

Or maybe not. Cookie knew better than to cross boundaries. Sergei was her ticket back to the big time—if only he'd read the fucking script.

"How *is* your American *puta*?" Ina sneered, her Latin eyes filled with jealousy, hands on voluptuous hips— she'd put on twenty pounds since winning her title.

Sergei silenced her with a grim look. He did not appreciate being questioned, and certainly not by a woman. Didn't they realize that they were interchangeable? However sexy and pretty they thought they were, there was always a younger, prettier model creeping up behind.

He had an urge to slap Ina, leave the imprint of his hand on her smooth cheek, exactly as he'd done with Cookie. Women needed discipline.

He couldn't do it because Ina's brother, Cruz, was in the house, and Sergei needed Cruz, for he was an important part of Sergei's plan. In fact, Ina's brother was one of the main reasons he kept Ina around. Family connections were important.

Sergei had conducted business with Cruz before. There were many deals to be brokered when it came to drugs, and Cruz had turned out to be a reliable and useful contact for moving shipments when Sergei needed him.

How fortuitous was it that Ina had a brother who'd spent the last seven years in Somalia, amassing a fortune from pirating small ships and yachts—any vessel he and his team could hold for ransom. Anything to do with the high seas, and Cruz had it down. Therefore he was just the asset Sergei needed right now, and when Sergei needed something, things always fell into place.

He'd made Cruz an offer he couldn't resist, and now Ina's brother was living in his house, and Cruz's men were ensconced in a downtown hotel, ready to move when Cruz gave them the word.

Plans were in motion.

Soon Mr. Big Shot Aleksandr Kasianenko would find out how real men did business.

39

Once all the guests were aboard, Aleksandr instructed Captain Dickson to set sail. The captain obliged, aware he had precious cargo, and delighted to add the list of esteemed guests to his résumé. He was particularly chuffed that Taye Sherwin was on the trip. The man was a brilliant footballer—right up there with the best of them. Twice picked as the BBC's sports personality of the year, a former captain of the national English team, a brilliant player, Taye Sherwin had an illustrious career. Captain Dickson was honored to have him aboard. Of course it was not too shabby that movie star Cliff Baxter was also with them, *and* Senator Hammond Patterson and his lovely wife.

The *Bianca* had a crew of eighteen, which included everyone from an executive chef to a barman, stewardesses, engineers, a valet, a head housekeeper, deckhands, maids, and Guy, the entertainment director, whose job was to keep the guests contented and entertained at all times.

Captain Dickson was not as happy with his crew as he should have been. He'd had to say yes to the hiring of a few replacement crew members when three of his regulars dropped out at the last minute. This did not please him, as he preferred working with a crew who knew exactly how he expected them to behave.

One of the new hires was a Mexican girl, Mercedes, who Guy had seen fit to hire as a stewardess. Captain Dickson considered her too attractive for her own good. He didn't want any of the female guests getting annoyed or jealous; he'd seen that happen before. He instructed Guy to keep a close eye on her.

"No worries," Guy had assured him. "Checked out her references. Not one complaint. I'll watch her."

"You'd *better*," Captain Dickson had warned. "Her kind are inclined to give us problems."

Her kind, Guy thought, convinced that Captain Dickson was some sort of racist. Apart from one African-American engineer, the rest of the crew were all white. Besides, Mercedes wasn't *that* attractive. For a start, she was on the short side, and was it his imagination or was her left eye slightly squinty? And could he detect the beginning of a very faint mustache? However, he had to admit that she gave off a sexier vibe than most of the fresh-faced girls he usually worked with. Anyway, it was all last-minute, so he'd hired her. Big deal—he kind of liked the idea of introducing a bit of flavor to the trip. As long as she did her job, he was cool with it.

Over the last year, Guy had worked several high-profile cruises—one with a famous female talk-show host, another with a dominating captain of industry, and then there was the trip with the two NBA players.

The female talk-show titan had turned out to be a secret lesbian. The captain of industry had turned out to be a raging pervert. And the two NBA players had turned out to be hooker hounds with libidos that never quit.

Guy figured if he could handle that lot, then he was certainly well equipped to deal with one sexy little Mexican stewardess.

"Nice!" Taye exclaimed, exploring their accommodations, which consisted of a large, stylishly decorated VIP stateroom—color scheme pale blue—with a king-sized bed, plenty of closet space, a small private terrace, and an all-marble en-suite bathroom.

"Not bad," Ashley agreed, trying to conceal her excitement at actually being on the same trip as Cliff Baxter. *The* Cliff Baxter. *People* magazine's Sexiest Man Alive. *GQ*'s man of the year. *Rolling Stone*'s actor of the decade. Not to mention hundreds of other accolades.

Ashley had a major crush. And was it her imagination or had Cliff given her a long, lingering look—a look rife with sexual promise?

Ashley was full of expectations. What if Cliff Baxter came on to her? What would she do? How would she handle it?

Such delicious questions! She felt quite light-headed.

Was she capable of cheating on Taye? She never had, but this was Cliff Baxter, every woman's fantasy, so surely a quick fling was allowed?

The very thought made her tingle with the anticipation of the forbidden.

She'd relished the expression of shock on uptight Jeromy's face when he'd discovered that she and Taye were guests on the yacht. Jeromy could be such an annoying snob at times, so she and Taye being included kind of evened out the playing field.

In the meantime, she couldn't wait to have a girl's gossip with Bianca, get the scoop on everyone. She'd already decided that Cliff Baxter's girlfriend was no big deal. The girl had a nice body and flaming red hair—probably dyed—but Lori wasn't drop-dead Hollywood gorgeous. Kind of ordinary, really. Ashley had thought Cliff would have a raving beauty on his arm, someone of the Angelina Jolie caliber.

"What're you thinkin'?" Taye asked, plopping himself down on the bed and patting a spot beside him.

"I'm wondering what I should wear for dinner," Ashley mused, fluffing out her blond curls. "Do you think we're eating outside?"

"I expect so," Taye responded. "Heard someone mention dinner is on one of the decks. It's all go, ain't it, toots?"

"Cool it with the 'toots,'" Ashley said irritably. "We wouldn't want to sound like the poor relatives, would we?"

Taye shot her a dirty look. "Poor *what*?"

She'd hit a sensitive spot. Taye hated it when she intimated that they weren't good enough. She suspected it had something to do with him being black. Not that it mattered to her; she wasn't her mother's daughter when it came to racist thoughts.

"Nothing," she said, sitting on the bed beside him.

The bed was soft, welcoming. They'd been traveling all day, so she was entitled to be tired, what with the time change and all. And it was important that she look her best for cocktails at five-thirty. Yes, she wouldn't mind a nap before dinner.

Cocktails first, then dinner in the company of Cliff Baxter. If she was lucky, maybe she'd be seated next to him at the table.

Ashley couldn't wait.

"I can't believe how Taye and Ashley managed to get themselves invited," Jeromy fumed. "I should never have told them about the trip. It's quite obvious they solicited their own invitation once they heard about it."

"I thought you liked Ashley," Luca remarked. "Didn't you bring her in as your partner?"

"Only for the name value." Jeromy sniffed. "And do not forget that Taye invested money in the business too. You could say she bought her way in."

Luca stripped off his shirt and threw it on the bed, then dropped his pants.

"What are you doing?" Jeromy asked, alarmed— because after the sex marathon with the Luttmans the previous evening, he was not in the mood for more of the same. Although with Luca it would be oral and that was about it.

"I'm off to the pool," Luca said, opening a drawer and trying to discover where the valet who'd unpacked for them had put his swimming shorts.

"Oh," Jeromy said. "I was thinking perhaps a nap might be more of a plan."

Luca located his colorful Versace shorts and slipped them on. "Not for me," he said cheerfully. "I'm catching up with Bianca. Promised I'd meet her by the pool."

"Should I come with you?"

"Not necessary," Luca said, running a hand through his thick blond hair. "We'd probably bore you with our reminiscences."

Reminiscences? Luca and Bianca? Yes, he *would* be bored listening to the stories of how the two of them first met.

"Then I shall stay here and rest," Jeromy decided.

"See you later," Luca said, and he was gone, leaving Jeromy to stew over the fact that he wasn't being included.

"Impressed?" Cliff questioned, gesturing around their luxurious stateroom.

"With what?" Lori retorted, opening up her carry-on bag.

"You know what," he said, a tad irritable.

"No, I don't," she said, being purposefully obtuse.

"Oh come *on*," Cliff said, stifling a yawn. "The yacht. The other guests. This whole incredible setup."

She turned on him. "Are *you* impressed, Cliff?"

"Why would *I* be impressed?" he said, laughing and shaking his head.

"Then why would I?" she countered, taking out her makeup case.

"'Cause you're twenty-four, sweetie," he pointed out. "You've got to admit that you've never seen anything like this yacht before. You shouldn't forget that you're one very, *very* lucky girl."

"Am I?" she said, giving him a piercing look.

"For fuck's sake, what's the matter with you?" Cliff said, his handsome face suddenly scowling. "You've been acting like a petulant little bitch ever since we left L.A."

She was tempted to tell him exactly what she was pissed about. *Excuse me, Mister Big Fucking Movie Star. Correct me if I'm wrong, but aren't you just about getting ready to dump my ass? So why shouldn't I be pissed off?*

"It was a long journey," she said, deciding that backing down was probably the best way to go. "And yes, Cliff, this *is* a once-in-a-lifetime trip. Thanks so much for including me."

"That's better," Cliff said, satisfied.

And before she knew it, he was unzipping, readying himself for the inevitable blow job.

Guy personally escorted Senator Hammond and his wife to their stateroom.

Hammond glanced around and said, "This'll do."

"Is there anything at all I can get for you, Senator?" Guy asked. He was impressed with Sierra Patterson; she was quite lovely, even more so than the photos of her he'd seen in magazines and newspapers.

"A bottle of Grey Goose vodka would be very welcome," Hammond said, winking at Sierra. "Right, darling?"

Sierra summoned a weak smile. She was in shock. Total shock. Never in her wildest dreams had she ever imagined she would run into Flynn again.

Yet here he was. Flynn Hudson. The love of her life.

It was all too much.

Fifteen Years Earlier

Sierra would never forget the first time she saw Flynn. It was at a party, and he came racing over to rescue her from the man who would one day in the far-off future become her husband.

What a joke! What a travesty! Marriage to Hammond should have never happened.

But it had. Unfortunately.

She remembered getting a quick look at Flynn. Tall, with longish hair and the most incredible steely-blue eyes. She'd run off yelling that they were both drunken assholes, and then she hadn't stopped talking about him to her girlfriends. "Who is he?" she'd wanted to know.

"Give us a clue," they'd all replied. "We don't know who you're carrying on about."

She'd shrugged. She had no idea who he was or where she could track him down. A few weeks later she was sitting in Hamburger Hamlet in Westwood when she spotted him through the window.

"Quick!" she'd shouted at her friend. "It's him! Do something!"

They hurriedly made it outside and tried to appear casual.

The good news was that her friend knew him.

The bad news was that he had a girl clinging to him like a magnet.

But they exchanged names and discovered that they both attended UCLA, and Sierra knew it was the start of something special.

Flynn Hudson was her future. There was no doubt about it.

40

Lying out by the pool located on the middle deck, Bianca and Luca indulged in a major gossip fest as the sleek yacht navigated the shimmering blue waters of the Sea of Cortez.

Aleksandr had wasted no time in instructing the captain to take off. The moment everyone was aboard, he'd announced it was time to go.

"What do you think of the group we've gathered?" Bianca asked, sunning herself in a barely-there Brazilian bikini that hardly covered any of her assets, her dark skin gleaming in the sunlight.

"It's some crazy mix," Luca observed.

"Isn't it just," Bianca agreed, stretching one leg above her head. "I only know half the people."

"That's more than me. And stop flashing."

Bianca lowered her leg and grinned. "Anyway, all I can say is thank God *you're* here."

"Who's the tall guy with the two-day stubble?" Luca asked, reaching for the bronzing oil.

"Oh, you must mean Aleksandr's writer friend, Flynn. Sexy, isn't he? I just met him for the first time."

"There's something kinda cool yet so hot about him," Luca observed, rubbing oil on his legs.

"Hmm," Bianca murmured knowingly. "Could be you fancy him?"

"Maybe," Luca said with a wide grin. "Don't you?"

"I think just about everyone does," Bianca said. "Only we may as well forget it, 'cause according to Aleksandr he's totally straight. And anyway, he's with that pretty little Asian piece."

"Ah," Luca said knowingly. "Men are like spaghetti—they're all straight until they hit hot water."

"Luca!" Bianca exclaimed, giggling. "I thought you were happily joined at the ass with Jeromy?"

Luca shrugged. "I can look, can't I?" he said, handing her the oil and turning onto his front.

"Is *that* what you're doing?" Bianca said, amused.

"You can bet that Jeromy does more than look."

"*Really?*" Bianca said, obligingly smoothing the sticky oil all over Luca's bronzed back.

"Yeah, really. He thinks I don't have any idea about what he gets up to, but I know everything."

"Yes?"

"Hey, it's not as if I care," Luca said casually. "Do you see me as the jealous type?"

"I'm jealous as shit," Bianca said, rolling her eyes. "If I caught Aleksandr screwing around, I'd cut off his balls and bounce them from here to Moscow."

"You're such a girl," Luca teased.

"Guilty as charged," Bianca said, putting down the bottle of oil and wiping her hands on a towel.

"So this is what true love in all its glory is like?" Luca said, still lying on his stomach.

"I suppose you could say that."

"Ah," Luca observed. "The girl who'd do anyone has finally found *the* one."

"Yep," Bianca said, nodding vigorously. "Aleksandr is *it* for me. He's so sexy, and he treats me like a queen."

"Darling," Luca objected, "*I'm* the queen. You're just a girl in lust."

"Love," Bianca corrected briskly. "True fuckin' love."

"Okay, okay, but trust me—I know you. You'll get bored eventually."

"No, I won't."

"Yes, you will."

"Don't be such a Debbie Downer."

"If you're giving me a girl's name, make it Lucia."

"Oh my *God*!" Bianca exclaimed, once more rolling her eyes. "You're too much!"

Luca sat up, picked up his drink, and took a sip. "Hey, remember when you and I nearly—"

"Don't remind me!" Bianca squealed. "Shades of *you* couldn't get it up, and I was totally insulted."

"Yeah, but then later we became best friends."

"After I discovered you were gay."

"For your information, the *reason* I couldn't get it up was 'cause I had a hard-on for one of Suga's backup dancers," Luca confessed. "That black dude with the amazing abs."

"Had him," Bianca said matter-of-factly. "All abs and no cock."

They both burst out laughing.

As soon as she'd finished servicing Cliff, Lori decided she did not wish to sit around watching him snore. He was almost fifty; he needed his rest. She was twenty-four; she needed to explore the yacht. Why waste a moment of such a once-in-a-lifetime experience?

After changing into a polka-dot bikini and a skimpy cover-up, she put her hair up in a ponytail and left the room.

A helpful steward directed her to the swimming pool, where she came upon Bianca and Luca Perez in the middle of a full-on laughter fit.

She was reluctant to disturb them; they were obviously close. But Bianca waved her over and said, "Pull up a lounger and come join us. We're catching up on old times."

Lori immediately felt at ease. Even though Bianca and Luca were both enormously famous, she didn't feel intimidated. Besides, they were way nearer to her age than Cliff.

"You're with Cliff Baxter, huh?" Luca said. "I'm a big fan."

Oh God! She was so sick of hearing those four words. Didn't anyone have anything original to say? And surely *he* could come up with better than that?

Apparently not.

"How long have you and Cliff been together?" Bianca inquired.

Another much-asked question.

"A little over a year," Lori answered, settling on a lounger.

"Hmm . . ." Bianca mused, stretching out a perfect leg. "You think he's marriage minded?"

Lori bit her bottom lip. Wasn't that a somewhat personal question coming from someone she barely knew? Besides, she was sure Bianca must read the entertainment rags, and it was a well-documented fact that Cliff Baxter had no intention of ever getting married. He was anti-marriage. He drove the point home in every interview he gave.

Before she could come up with a suitable reply, Luca saved the day. "Stop pestering the girl with questions," he said. "I want to find out if *Aleksandr* is marriage minded. That's what *I* want to know."

"Aleksandr is still married," Bianca pointed out, turning frosty. "He's in the middle of getting a divorce."

"That's what they all say."

"Don't piss me off," Bianca snapped. "You know better than that."

"I guess that means no giant ring for Bianca," Luca teased.

"And no giant ring for me either," Lori said, quickly taking the opportunity to bond with the famous supermodel. "Cliff isn't into the whole marriage bit. And quite frankly, neither am I. I'm too young."

"Oh honey," Bianca advised, nodding sagely. "A man like Cliff Baxter, you *need* to put a ring on it."

"Yeah, a cock ring," Luca said with a raucous chuckle.

Bianca dissolved into peals of laughter. "You'd better not talk like that around Aleksandr," she warned when she'd finished laughing. "He doesn't appreciate dirty talk."

"What's dirty about a cock ring?" Luca asked innocently.

"And I thought stardom might've changed you," Bianca chided. "But no, you've still got the same old potty mouth—thank God!"

"Careful with the *old*," Luca warned. "Have you forgotten we're almost the same age?"

"I'm guessing you two have known each other a long time," Lori ventured, noting the camaraderie between them and wishing she had a friend like Luca.

"Right," Bianca said. "I was nineteen and doing a swimsuit show in Rio. Luca was one of the boys in the background. Oh my God, he was totally edible!"

"And how about you, missy," Luca said, joining in. "You were like a black Bond babe with a major kick-ass attitude."

"I couldn't *wait* to jump his luscious bones," Bianca confided. "Only he wasn't interested, even though he was supposedly straight at the time. Course, I understood immediately. Gay as a fruit fly—although he didn't come out until years later, and that was only after one marriage, one son, and a red-hot career. *Finally,* he emerged from the closet and I was vindicated."

"I love this woman," Luca said, raising his glass to toast her. "She never changes."

"And you'd better believe it," Bianca said, calling for another round of champagne.

Flynn and Xuan were shown to their stateroom together as if they were a couple. Flynn was so shocked at seeing Sierra that he didn't really notice until Xuan demanded to know why they were supposed to share a bed.

"This is ridiculous," she said, quite angry. "Did you

plan this, Flynn, just to get me into bed? If you wanted to fuck me so badly, you should've said so."

"What?" He stared at her, his mind taking him on a trip that he didn't have any desire to go on.

"We must have separate cabins," Xuan said firmly. "I demand it."

"You do, huh?" Flynn said, narrowing his eyes.

"I most certainly do," she retorted. "I will call for the steward."

"No," he said quickly. "You can't do that."

"And exactly *why* can't I do that?" Xuan demanded.

"Because I'm uh . . . kind of caught in a situation," he muttered, trying to get his head straight.

"What situation?" she wanted to know.

He didn't care to tell Xuan the sad story of him and Sierra, but if he expected her to stay with him, then he'd better tell her something. And she *had* to stay with him. There was no way he could face being on this cruise alone—he had to at least give the impression he was with someone.

Why hadn't he asked who the other guests would be?

Why had he walked blindly into hell, because seeing Sierra with Hammond was exactly that. Pure hell.

He was trapped. The yacht had sailed, and it was too late to get off.

Fifteen Years Earlier

Sierra was not easy like most of the girls Flynn encountered. After getting her number, he called her several times. She blew him off. Finally, he ran into her at a frat party, and when they got to talking, she offered to fix him up with her roommate, a raucous party girl who was more than hot to do whatever he fancied.

He fancied Sierra, and only her. There was no doubt about it. Not only was she cool and smart and achingly beautiful, she apparently had old-fashioned values, and his reputation as a player had obviously reached her.

But he persevered, and when they eventually began to date, he wasn't that surprised to discover that sex wasn't on the menu. "I'm not a casual girl," she informed him. "And I do not intend to start being one now."

Surprise, surprise.

Was she a virgin? He didn't dare ask. Instead, he developed a close relationship with his right hand and kept the faith.

Sierra Snow. He would do anything for her, and eventually she would do anything for him.

They were together six months before they had sex. And it wasn't just sex. It was a mind-blowing, loving, incredible experience of epic proportions.

Suddenly he dropped his plans of trekking around the world when he finished college. He wanted only one thing, and that was to be with Sierra forever. She told him that she felt the same way.

They swore to each other that even though they were both young, they would never allow anyone or anything to split them apart. They would drop out of college, travel the world together, and share every adventure out there.

Then one day he'd received an urgent call from his grandmother in the U.K. informing him that his grandfather had been rushed to the hospital, and that she needed him to fly to England immediately.

Sierra drove him to the airport. She hugged him tightly and pledged her undying love. He promised he would come back as soon as he could.

A week later he received a FedEx envelope marked high priority. It came from a name and address in Los Angeles he did not know. Inside the envelope were half a dozen photos of Sierra in various stages of undress with several different men.

One of them was Hammond Patterson. Sierra looked dreamy, almost happy, with the little half smile on her face that Flynn knew only too well.

She was enjoying herself.

There was a typed note enclosed.

> *STOP BELIEVING YOUR SO-CALLED
> GIRLFRIEND IS PERFECT.
> OPEN YOUR EYES AND SEE THE TRUTH.*

He felt a sickness and rage he had never experienced before. He felt betrayed and hollow inside.

Why?

Why had she professed her undying love?

Why had she spent all those months playacting something that didn't exist?

And what was she doing with Hammond Patterson?

His fury knew no bounds. He wanted to get on the next plane to L.A. and confront her.

But he couldn't; his grandfather was not expected to live much longer, and his grandmother needed him.

He was stuck in England, and there was nothing he could do about it.

41

When Cruz Mendoza wasn't out causing mayhem on the high seas, he was a lazy son of a bitch, spending his days lolling by Sergei Zukov's pool in Acapulco, wearing nothing more than a skimpy man thong while entertaining hookers he'd picked up the night before at some dubious club in town. It made a pleasant change from life in his guarded compound in Somalia, where he always had to tread carefully, because he had many enemies intent on taking over his lucrative business.

Although only in his early forties, Cruz appeared to be much older. He was stocky and balding, with weatherbeaten skin, two prominent gold front teeth, and a pronounced limp—the result of being shot in the thigh by an irate husband who'd caught him screwing his sixteen-year-old trophy wife. Cruz had gotten his revenge by persuading the sixteen-year-old to run off with him, then dumping her when he'd had enough.

Watching Cruz play was putting Sergei on edge. Cruz had insisted that everything was set, but the way Ina's brother was sitting around bothered him.

"Relax," Cruz told him. "We strike at the right moment. My contact on the yacht tells me everything, an' here in town my men wait for me to give 'em the word. We let the rich motherfuckers get comfortable on their fuckin' yacht trip, then we move in when I say so. I've done this a hundred times, an' believe me, surprise always works."

"So there's no way you'll fuck it up?" Sergei growled.

"No, Sergei," Cruz retorted with a slight sneer, a sneer that Sergei did not appreciate. "I'm as dependable as takin' a daily shit."

Sergei knew that Ina's brother was a slippery son of a bitch. He wouldn't put it past him to try and pull something.

Then again, Cruz wasn't stupid; he must realize that to fuck with Sergei Zukov would be beyond dumb.

Sergei was impatient, but Cruz was confident that everything was on course.

Only time would tell.

42

Aleksandr sat alone and thoughtful on the private deck outside the master suite, smoking a cigar. He was satisfied that the long-planned-for trip was finally under way. There had been a moment in time when he'd sensed that everything might fall apart after he and Bianca had exchanged heated words. She could be so headstrong and unpredictable—who knew *what* she might do? However, once she'd seen that he'd named the yacht after her, she'd melted exactly as he'd hoped she would, and here they were, everything on track.

Bianca was like a world-class racehorse, difficult to tame, but apart from the occasional incident—such as the inappropriate photos on the Internet—all was going well.

Unfortunately, his ongoing battle with his wife continued to heat up. What a difficult and spiteful woman Rushana had turned out to be. There had been affairs before—Aleksandr would be the first to admit that he'd never been a faithful husband. But in the past, Rushana had chosen to ignore his infidelities. It wasn't until Bianca had entered his life, and his request for a divorce, that Rushana had turned into a vindictive bitch. She was getting everything she wanted financially, but it seemed that wasn't enough for her. Oh no, the fact that he was with a world-famous supermodel infuriated her beyond belief.

Rushana was desperate to see him single and alone, pining for the family he'd once had.

Bianca's latest escapade had only fueled the fire, giving Rushana some powerful new ammunition. "I will not have my daughters in the company of such a prostitute," she'd screamed at his lawyers, along with other insults. "Until Aleksandr stops being with that tramp, there will be no divorce. And I will not allow him to see our children."

It was not a happy situation, although he was sure that once Rushana realized that he had no intention of leaving Bianca, she would be forced to give in.

Rushana's fury and jealousy had not changed his plans. He still intended to ask Bianca to be his wife, and if he had his way, by the end of the trip they would be engaged.

Drinks at five-thirty on the top deck. The sun slowly setting in the clear sky. Champagne and canapés being served on silver trays by Mercedes and Renee, the two stewardesses. Den, the barman, standing attentively behind the bar. Soft Brazilian music wafting from hidden speakers.

Bianca made her entrance in a white, backless Valentino dress, Aleksandr close behind her in a long-sleeved black sweater and black pants.

Although Aleksandr was twenty years older than Bianca, they made a good-looking couple. A fact that did not escape Guy, who was on hand, supervising his staff. As entertainment director, Guy was very hands-on, always there to anticipate the boss's every need. This was the first time he'd worked for Aleksandr Kasianenko, but of course he knew who the man was. Who didn't? Before hooking up with Bianca, Aleksandr had managed to keep a low profile, but once they were together, his cover was blown—the words *billionaire businessman* and *Russian oligarch* were forever attached to his name.

Poor sod, Guy thought, watching the famous couple. *It has to be a real downer, everyone knowing all your crap.*

Guy had recently viewed the raunchy and uncensored images of Bianca on his laptop. He considered her to be a feisty little minx, and he couldn't help wondering how Aleksandr felt about his famous girlfriend flashing her pussy for all the world to see. The man was probably major pissed. Guy knew he would be if it was *his* boyfriend flashing his dick for public consumption.

Luca and Jeromy appeared on deck at exactly five-thirty, both in white suits. Checking them out, Guy considered them to be an odd couple. Luca was hot, Jeromy not. What hidden talents did the gorgeous blond superstar see in the tall, skinny Englishman?

Oh well, everyone to his own. Although Guy had to admit that he wouldn't say no to a run around the track with Luca Perez. He was some Latin hottie!

Mercedes sprung into action, offering them champagne or a drink of their choice, speaking to Luca in Spanish.

Guy didn't know what Captain Dickson was so concerned about. The women on the yacht were all so bloody beautiful—why would a pretty young Mexican girl threaten any of them? Mercedes was perfectly suitable for her job. She was also appropriately dressed in a smart nautical uniform, so no one would mistake her for anything other than a hardworking and eager-to-please member of the crew. He liked Renee and Den too. They were fellow Australians, and they both seemed to know what they were doing.

The next couple to arrive for cocktails was Ashley and Taye. Aleksandr stepped forward to greet them. As a football fanatic, he wanted to spend time speaking with Taye, picking his brain about the team he was in talks to buy. He beckoned Taye toward him, and the two men moved over to a quiet corner of the deck.

Ashley immediately zeroed in on Luca. "I can't believe we've never met before," she enthused. "You being with Jeromy and all, and me being Jeromy's partner. It's so lovely to finally meet you. I'm a big fan."

Cliff and Lori approached just in time for Lori to over-hear Ashley's "I'm a big fan."

Here we go again, Lori thought. *Everyone's a big fan of everyone else. What a clusterfuck!*

"Luca," Cliff exclaimed. "I was making a movie in Puerto Rico last year, an' I managed to catch your concert. That was some wild performance."

Please don't say it, Lori silently begged. *Please, please, please!*

"I'm a big fan," Cliff added.

Shit! Lori thought. *You too.*

"Oh, and this is Lori," Cliff continued, introducing her as if she was some kind of an afterthought.

"Lori an' me, we're old friends," Luca said, winking at her in a knowing way like he totally got it. "Isn't that right, *cariño?*"

"You two know each other?" Cliff said, a look of puzzlement on his face.

"We go way back," Luca explained. "We were hangin' out by the pool today, catching up."

Lori experienced a small shiver of triumph. She wasn't just an appendage on Cliff Baxter's arm; she was a person in her own right.

At which point Ashley and her cascade of blond curls moved in big-time, grabbing Cliff by the arm and whisking him away.

"Thanks," Lori muttered to Luca, who patted her on the arm and said, "I get it, sweet thing. Been there. Done that. You should know that when I was first married to Suga, nobody knew who the hell I was. I was simply the pretty boy in the background, and unless I was attached to Suga's arm, nobody gave a fast shit."

"Then you totally understand," Lori said, relieved that at least someone was aware of exactly how she felt.

"You bet I do," Luca said. "Don't sweat it, *bonita.* We're all here to have fun and relax. You're one of us now. Enjoy."

"Enjoy what?" Bianca said, creeping up behind them.

"Everything!" Luca exclaimed, indicating the sunset. "This is spectacular."

"We aim to please," Bianca said with a Cheshire cat grin.

It is spectacular, she thought, looking around and taking everything in. *It's way over the top, and I love it!*

One thing about Aleksandr: he did not disappoint. He was a man of style, and she was looking forward to seven days of utter bliss.

Meanwhile, down in their stateroom, Hammond was taking his fury out on Sierra.

"WHAT THE FUCK!" he screamed at her. "You tell me what that loser bastard is doing on this trip?"

Sierra knew better than to answer him. She merely listened to him rant on about how much he hated Flynn Hudson.

"He's nothing but a low-life scumbag!" Hammond yelled. "Why is he here? How did this happen? Why didn't you get a list of guests?" He paused to take a breath. "You know something? You're useless. You probably *wanted* the son of a bitch here, the loser you used to fuck. How I could touch you after you'd had his cock inside you is beyond me." Another pause. "Let's not forget you were damaged goods and I fucking *saved* you. I've given you a life you can be proud of, and *this* is how you repay me?"

Sierra watched him closely. His face was red with fury; his eyes were bulging. He was acting like a raving lunatic and blaming her for Flynn being aboard.

She chose to remain silent. She chose to close her mind to the broken heart she'd suffered when Flynn had betrayed her. It was all too painful to remember.

Fifteen Years Earlier
Just like that Flynn stopped calling. Sierra couldn't understand why until she received a FedEx envelope marked high priority. She opened the

envelope and there they were—six graphic photos of Flynn with six different girls.

At first she couldn't believe it, but after studying the photos, she had no choice but to accept the worst. There was a typed note enclosed.

> *STOP BELIEVING YOUR SO-CALLED BOYFRIEND IS PERFECT.*
> *OPEN YOUR EYES AND SEE THE TRUTH.*

A week later she realized she was pregnant. Heartbroken and alone, she confided everything to Hammond Patterson, who had been coming around ever since Flynn left. Hammond had told her that Flynn had asked him to look out for her. At first she'd been surprised, for she'd not realized that Flynn and Hammond were at all close. But Hammond had turned out to be the rock she'd needed to lean on; he was there for her in every way. He even offered to pay for an abortion, insisting it was the right thing for her to do.

She'd declined his offer, but he'd persuaded her to go to a party with him that night. At the party they'd both had too much to drink—especially Hammond—and while he was driving her home in his newly acquired Ferrari (a present from his adoring mother), he'd started coming on to her. One hand on the steering wheel, the other groping her breasts and between her legs.

She had never considered Hammond anything other than a friend, and his sudden attack shocked and upset her. She slapped his hand away, but he was determined.

Neither of them saw the oncoming car. Neither of them realized the danger. The rest was a blur as the Ferrari hit the oncoming car and immediately overturned, throwing Sierra out.

She suffered a broken pelvis and lost the baby.

Hammond suffered a damaged ego and walked away without a scratch.

Rumors abounded, and it wasn't long before the whispers on campus were that Sierra had been pregnant with Hammond's baby. Hammond said nothing to deny it; in fact, he promoted the story.

Still in the U.K., Flynn heard the gossip and that was it for him. By the time he returned to the States, Sierra had dropped out of college and was back in New York with her parents.

Flynn and Sierra never spoke again.

43

Sierra and Hammond arrived at the cocktail gathering shortly before it ended, due to the fact that Hammond could not seem to stop himself from spewing venom about Flynn and how he hated him, and questioning why he was on this supposedly exclusive trip.

Sierra had continued to remain silent while her husband paced up and down venting his fury, although she was somewhat confused as to why Hammond was so angry. Hadn't he and Flynn been friends, even roommates, at one time? Wasn't he the one who Flynn had asked to watch out for her? Was his anger due to the fact that Flynn had treated her so shabbily? And if so, why was he taking it out on her?

It didn't make sense. She was the one who should be upset, not Hammond.

When they finally left their stateroom and joined the others, Sierra made sure she had no contact with Flynn whatsoever. She stayed by Hammond's side playing her role of good wife, although her stomach was churning and she did not dare to glance in Flynn's direction.

Not that she wanted to. He was the man who'd broken her heart into a thousand little pieces, and she could never forgive him for that.

After the car accident and the loss of her baby, she'd spent time traveling across Europe visiting relatives, finally returning to her family in New York, where she'd taken up social work, counseling young victims of rape and abuse. It was hard work, but she found it to be quite fulfilling. It was exactly what she needed.

Eventually she'd moved out of her parents' home and settled into an apartment with a girl she worked with. Soon she'd started dating sporadically—nothing serious—until one day she'd run into Hammond, now an up-and-coming lawyer with big political aspirations, at a fund-raiser.

At first he'd complained that he'd tried to contact her and she'd never returned his calls. Then he'd proceeded to court her in a way she'd found hard to resist. He'd been so damn charming, honest and committed to doing all kinds of worthwhile work, which really impressed her. No longer the drunken horny student who'd been responsible for their horrific car accident, he seemed like a changed man with a definite purpose in life, and although she didn't love him in the way she'd once loved Flynn, he'd finally worn her down, and she'd said yes to his marriage proposal. "Together we can change the world," he'd promised, and naïvely she'd believed him.

They were married in Connecticut at her family's house. It was a lavish wedding, exactly the way Hammond wanted it. Her parents had influential friends, and they all turned out; so did his family. Hammond used the occasion to cement future connections.

It took a year or so before she realized she'd made a horrible mistake. By that time it was too late. She was Hammond's wife, a major political asset. And one thing she knew for sure: he would never let her go.

"Ladies and gentlemen, dinner is served," Guy announced. He had heard that very line spoken in a series of old movies and he thought it sounded perfect. It gave him the personality and identity he imagined he deserved.

Guy hoped the guests not only noticed him, but depended on him for anything they might need, because being noticed and appreciated meant a much larger tip at the end of the voyage. He always made a bet in his own mind about who would turn out to be the most generous tipper. On this trip it would be Aleksandr, although one could never be too sure.

Luca, perhaps—famous singers were known for their generosity. However, Luca's miserable English partner was probably a penny-pincher.

The politician? No. Politicians raised money, but they were all notoriously stingy when it came to parting with their own.

Well then, there was always the movie star, Mr. Cliff Baxter himself. Except Guy knew from past experience that movie stars expected everything for free in exchange for their illustrious presence.

Which left Taye Sherwin, a fine working-class lad who'd done well for himself. And Flynn, the journalist—a man who probably didn't believe in tipping.

Guy made a note to himself to drop the word—maybe to the movie star's girlfriend—that all guests were expected to tip the crew for services rendered.

One of the things Guy most enjoyed on a cruise was getting to know everyone's secrets, and on a boat, secrets were hard to hide. If he didn't find out for himself, the maids or other crew members were always quick to fill him in.

Life on a luxury yacht with guests aboard was very much an *Upstairs, Downstairs* experience. With this group, Guy expected mucho gossip.

"Dinner is served," Guy announced for the second time, repeating his words loudly because nobody seemed to be moving; they were all having too good a time.

"Thanks, Guy," Bianca responded, waving her well-toned arms in the air. "Let's go, everyone. I'm starving!"

"What a fab table setting!" Ashley exclaimed as the guests approached an elegant oval table located on the middle deck. The table was decorated with a series of cut-glass vases holding white roses—Bianca's favorite. There was also exquisite crystal stemware, gleaming silver cutlery, black and silver dishes, and tall white candles in ornate holders. The result was a picture-perfect table.

"Please all find your place cards," Bianca announced, a tad mischievously. "I placed everyone myself, 'cause I'd like you all to get to know each other. I promise to change it up every day, so look out!"

"Trust you to mix it up," Luca said, admiring his old friend's style. "Who am *I* next to tonight?"

Bianca snapped her fingers, and Guy handed her a list.

"Looks like you've got Taye on one side and Ashley on the other," she said. "Hmm, Luca, a Sherwin sandwich. Think you can handle it?"

"You *know* I can," Luca boasted.

Jeromy scowled; he did not appreciate the thought of Luca getting too friendly with the Sherwins. "And where might I be?" he asked snippily.

Bianca consulted her list; she'd spent quite some time deciding where to seat everyone. "Let me see," she said. "You're between two beautiful women. Sierra Patterson and Lori."

"Lori?" Jeromy questioned with a slight sneer, even though he knew full well who Lori was. She was the no-body redhead attached to the movie star.

Bianca chose to ignore Jeromy because he irritated her. Surely Luca could have come up with someone more exciting than this uptight turd? She turned to Cliff Baxter. "You're sitting next to me," she said warmly. "And I expect you to tell me exactly what it's like being labeled the Sexiest Man Alive."

"Pure hell," Cliff responded with a self-deprecating grin. "Women throwing themselves at me. Guys too. It's a miracle I make it through the day."

"Ah, but I'm sure that somehow you manage," Bianca teased, licking her full lips.

"I try," Cliff said with a jaunty wink. "It's not easy."

"You're seated next to Flynn Hudson," Bianca said, turning to Sierra and taking her arm in a friendly fashion. "I thought you two might have things in common. Aleksandr says Flynn's a very smart journalist and writer, so I'm sure you'll find him interesting."

"Really," Sierra murmured, her heart skipping a beat.

"By the way," Bianca continued. "It's a pleasure to finally meet you—and your husband's charming."

Charming? Sierra thought. This woman should only know the truth.

"Yes," Bianca continued. "Aleksandr is quite a supporter. He thinks that Hammond has great potential to make big changes in America."

"Does he?" Sierra said, thinking how easy it was to fool people.

"Yes, he does, and Aleksandr is usually right."

"Good to know."

"So," Bianca said mischievously. "How would you feel about becoming the first lady?"

First lady indeed. Sierra swallowed hard. Thank God for the two Xanax she'd managed to take before leaving her cabin. The drugs had dulled her senses, leaving her in a dreamy state. Still, at the thought of sitting next to Flynn she felt her heart accelerate, and a sweep of total panic overcame her.

Stay calm! a voice screamed in her head. *Do not lose control. You can do it.*

Can I?

Can I?

Yes, you can.

Jeromy shot Lori a patronizing look. Why did he have to get seated next to the only nonentity on the boat? Would he be forced to talk to her? A word or two simply to be polite; after that she was on her own.

"How are you, dear?" he sniffed.

"I'm fine," Lori replied, thinking that it was just her luck to get stuck with Luca's uptight English boyfriend. "And you?"

"Perfect."

"Lucky you," she drawled, aware that he was as unthrilled to be sitting next to her as she was to him.

"Excuse me?" Jeromy said, not appreciating her tone.

"Well, *perfect* kind of says it all."

Jeromy's back stiffened. Was this girl screwing with him? Big mistake if she was.

"I was hoping I'd be next to you," Ashley said, leaning in to Cliff as she took her seat beside him.

"You were?" Cliff said, taking in her curvy blondness. "In that case, I'll try my best not to disappoint."

"Oh, you don't have to try," Ashley said, fluttering her fake lashes. "Just looking at you is enough for me."

Shit! Cliff thought. A boatload of interesting people, and I get the starry-eyed fan.

"I've seen all your movies," Ashley continued, twirling a strand of her long blond hair through her fingers. "My mum used to take me when I was little. She had a *huge* crush on you."

"Did she, now?"

"Well . . . even though I was only ten, I did too," Ashley admitted coyly.

"That's flattering," Cliff said smoothly.

"I still do," Ashley said, adding a quick "But don't tell my husband. He's dead jealous."

Fuck! Cliff thought. *Where's Lori when I need her?*

Glancing down the table, Aleksandr was pleased to see his guests having an engaging time. The first course—a lobster and crab salad—was being served, and the finest of wines were flowing. He stared at Bianca seated at the other end of the table. She looked so staggeringly beautiful, her dark skin gleaming in the flickering candlelight, her green eyes flashing as she spoke with Flynn.

Aleksandr was satisfied that he had captured a prize worth having. Bianca might be famous, but being with her was worth all the drama his wife was busy creating. Soon he would be free of Rushana, and then Bianca would be totally his.

Watching her, he suddenly experienced a strong surge of sexual desire. Xuan was seated on his left, Hammond Patterson on his right, and they were having a spirited conversation across him.

Aleksandr moved his chair aside and stood up. "Excuse me for a few moments," he said. "I'll be right back." He headed straight for Bianca. "I need to show you something," he said, leaning down and whispering in her ear.

"What?" she responded.

"I need to show you now."

"Now?" Bianca said, somewhat bemused.

"Now," Aleksandr stated firmly.

Bianca rose from the table. "Two minutes," she said to her guests.

Aleksandr took her hand and led her along the side of the yacht to where it was dark and deserted, the only sound the sea lapping against the stern.

"Tell me," Bianca said. "Is something the matter?"

"Not unless you consider this something," Aleksandr said, jamming her hand against the bulge in his pants.

Bianca gave a low throaty chuckle. "Oh my!" She sighed, getting excited at the thought of what was to come. "You're kidding. In the middle of dinner?"

"Are you wearing panties?"

"As if I could in this dress . . ."

Aleksandr hurriedly unzipped, grunted, and grabbed the front of her thighs, pushing her dress up high.

She leaned back against the boat railings and lifted her long slender legs, wrapping them tightly around his waist.

Without hesitation he plunged deep inside her, and after several vigorous thrusts, he was done.

"Wow!" Bianca exclaimed as they disengaged. "What's up with *you*?"

"You didn't like it?"

"Oh, you *know* I liked it."

"I will not neglect you," Aleksandr promised, his voice a deep dark whisper. "Later I will suck your pussy like it's never been sucked before. Only right now, my dear, we have guests to attend to."

"Yes, *sir*," Bianca said obediently, deciding that Aleksandr was the sexiest man she'd ever encountered, and there had been many.

Sierra took a long deep breath. Even though they were sitting next to each other, she had not turned in Flynn's direction, and he had not acknowledged her. However, with Bianca away from the table, she felt forced to say something. After all, what had happened between them was old news, many years had passed, and Flynn had obviously never cared. It had all been a game to him. Just another conquest.

Maybe he didn't even remember her.

She decided on a light approach. Let him see that the way he'd treated her had not affected her one little bit.

"Flynn?" she said. *Keep it light. Keep it casual.* "It is you, isn't it?"

44

The staff cabins on the *Bianca* were quite compact, with two bunk beds in each and a communal bathroom for every three cabins to share. There was no privacy as such, which pissed off Mercedes, because she had things to do. She was sharing with the other stewardess, Renee, a tall Australian girl who had a dark blond ponytail, long legs, and horse teeth. Renee had only been on one cruise before; she'd gotten the job because her uncle had once played rugby with Guy, and her uncle had called in a favor.

"You take the top bunk," Mercedes ordered when they'd first arrived.

Renee, a somewhat timid girl, bowed down to whatever Mercedes wanted.

This suited Mercedes fine. She liked taking the boss position, and it was good to know that Renee was no threat to what she had to accomplish. And what she had to accomplish was something she'd done many times before.

Seduce the enemy.

And who was the enemy?

Kyril, Aleksandr Kasianenko's security guard.

The burly Russian was a challenge, and Mercedes was always up for a challenge. She'd learned early on that most men were easy as shit. Offer them a blow job, a fuck, a walk on the wild side, and if they didn't think it was a trap,

they were all in. Even the married ones. *Especially* the
married ones.

It hadn't taken Mercedes long to check Kyril out. He
had his own communication room, and direct contact
with Aleksandr. It seemed Aleksandr had wished to keep
this trip low-key, so his security was not as stringent as it
probably was on land.

It amazed Mercedes that however powerful and important people were, they always operated under the illusion that vacations were safe havens.

Crap. Vacations were the best time to strike. Everyone
lying around relaxed and happy, more concerned about
their suntans than anything else. Too much food, too
much wine—it was all the perfect recipe for a short sharp
strike, which was exactly what Cruz and his team excelled at. Take the vessel over, demand a large ransom,
then as soon as it was paid, get out fast.

Yes, Cruz certainly knew what he was doing. Over the
last few years he'd become quite a legend in the piracy
business.

Mercedes had been working alongside him since she
was eight. She was now twenty-two, and a key member of
his team. The inside girl. The girl nobody ever suspected.
And that's because she was good at what she did. Very
good.

After serving cocktails and canapés, Mercedes had
told Renee to cover for her while she slipped down to
their cabin. "I have a little tummy problem," she informed
Renee, who was as gullible as a virgin locked in a hotel
room with a sailor on shore leave. "Keep 'em happy. I'll
be quick."

"What about Guy?" Renee worried. "He won't be
pleased if you're missing."

"Don't worry about Guy. He'll never notice I'm gone.
An' if he does, tell him I'm checkin' on the table."

Once she got down to their cabin, Mercedes pulled out

her iPad from under her mattress and sent Cruz an informative e-mail about activities on the yacht, plus a crudely drawn map of the layout.

Cruz was a stickler for details; he required information about the crew, the guests, every move they made, and it was up to her to supply it.

When she was done, she erased her message, and hurried back to tend to the esteemed guests.

Esteemed guests, my fine Mexican ass, she thought. *The women are all whores fucking men for their money. While the men are pathetic assholes.*

Mercedes did not have a very positive view of the human race, which was hardly surprising considering the life she'd led. Her mother had died in childbirth, leaving her to be raised by a series of her papa's conquests—women who came and went on a regular basis, most of them prostitutes. Cruz had put her to work at the age of eight, picking the pockets of tourists in Mexico City. It was more rewarding than school any day, and she'd soon become the best pickpocket in town. Realizing his young daughter's potential, Cruz had started using her for other jobs—after all, who better than a child to gain entry to his burglary jobs? His kid could slide through any open window, however small—and doggie doors were no problem either.

A day after Mercedes celebrated her twelfth birthday, Cruz was arrested and sent to prison. Mercedes found herself dumped into foster care. Not prepared to be the victim of some horny old foster dad, she'd run away and survived the streets, honing her criminal skills, until eventually she hooked up with a twenty-year-old man who'd thought she was sixteen. They'd taken up residence in an abandoned bus outside Mexico City, and two abortions later she'd dumped her boyfriend and was waiting patiently outside the prison gates the day Cruz was released. She was fifteen.

Cruz had learned plenty in prison—he considered his time in the joint an education. Number one on his list of things to do when he got out was to leave Mexico.

Taking his kid with him hadn't factored into his plans, but there she was, loyal as ever. He'd felt obliged to organize forged papers for the two of them, and they'd taken off for Somalia to meet up with a Somalian man Cruz had formed a strong connection with in prison.

And so Cruz's adventures in piracy had begun, with Mercedes right along for the ride.

45

Goddamn it, Flynn thought. *What was he supposed to do? What was he supposed to say?* The love of his life was sitting next to him and what the fuck . . .

"Hey, Sierra," he said, making out as if he'd only just noticed her. "Yeah, of course it's me. Long time no see."

Casual enough? Jesus Christ. Talk about reverting to my teenage years.

"Yes, it has been a long time," she replied, turning to him with a fixed smile. "I wasn't sure . . ."

"Do I look *that* different?" he said, keeping it cool.

"No . . . I . . . uh . . ." she stammered, lost for words.

"You what?"

"Nothing."

"You and old Ham," he said, clearing his throat. "Who'd've thought?"

"I know," she murmured, taking a hearty gulp of wine, and then holding on to her glass so tightly that she hoped it wouldn't break.

"I was kind of surprised when I heard."

Really, Flynn. Surprised? Did you just imagine I'd vanish off the face of the earth once you were done with me?

They lapsed into an uncomfortable silence.

He hasn't changed, Sierra thought. *He's still Flynn.* So handsome, with the ice-blue eyes she remembered so well. No longer a boy, he now was a man with lines on his

face that revealed traces of a life lived. His hair was longer. The stubble on his chin was new—or perhaps not.

How was she to know? He was a stranger.

A stranger whose baby had grown inside her for a few
short weeks. And he'd never known about the baby. How
sad was *that*?

"Are you and uh . . . Xuan . . . married?" she asked,
breaking the strained silence.

The moment she'd asked the question, she could've
kicked herself. Why ask something so dumb? What did
she care if he was married or not?

I do care, a voice screamed in her head. *I care because
I still love him.*

Oh, for God's sake! You do not.

Yes, I do.

Stop thinking that way.

"Not married," Flynn said, scrutinizing her beautiful
face. Was she happy? She didn't look it. Her cheeks were
flushed, her eyes seemed empty. And she was slurring her
words ever so slightly. Was she drinking too much? Way
back, one shot of anything was her limit, but now she was
gulping wine like it was going out of style.

"Why not?" she managed, continuing to ask questions
she didn't want to hear come out of her mouth.

Flynn shrugged. *Why not? Because you screwed up
my head when it came to women. You made it impossible
for me to trust in any relationship. You ruined me, Sierra.
You fucking ruined me.*

"Dunno," he answered vaguely. "It's just one of those
things."

"Well," she said, wishing she could close her eyes and
drift off into a deep sleep and not have to deal with this.
"She seems lovely."

"She is," Flynn said.

And to their relief, Bianca returned to the table, a
smile on her lips as she grabbed her wineglass and took a

long, lingering sip. "Did I miss anything?" she asked playfully.

"Nothing," Flynn said quickly. "Nothing at all."

After his brief and irritating few words with Lori, Jeromy turned his full attention toward Sierra Patterson. She was a beautiful and stylish woman, and rumors abounded that one day in the not-too-distant future, her husband, Hammond, might make a run for president of the United States. And of course, if he did, the very serene and lovely Sierra would be by his side. So she was definitely someone on top of Jeromy's "get to know" list.

He turned to her with an ingratiating smile, exhibiting his imperfect English teeth. "Tell me, Mrs. Patterson," he said, all smarm and charm, "have you ever visited our fair city?"

Dazed and confused by her conversation with Flynn, Sierra had no desire to talk to anyone. "Excuse me?" she said politely.

Jeromy repeated his question.

"Your fair what?" she asked, still thinking about Flynn.

"London, England," Jeromy said, a tad sharply. *Why wasn't she paying him more attention? Wasn't he good enough for her?*

"Oh, are you English?" she inquired, attempting to rally.

Surely his clipped and very proper accent had given her a clue? The woman seemed somewhat out of it.

"Born and bred," he informed her. And then in case she hadn't realized that he and Luca were a couple, he quickly added, "Luca and I first met in London two years ago. We've been together ever since."

"That's nice," Sierra answered vaguely. "Is Luca here?"

Good God! Was the woman drunk? Or simply dense?

"Sitting right across from us," he said, indicating Luca, who was in the middle of an animated conversation with Taye.

"Ah, yes," Sierra murmured, signaling a stewardess to refill her wineglass.

Hardly Jackie Kennedy, Jeromy thought. *Why am I even bothering? And what the hell does Luca find so interesting about Taye Sherwin?*

Since Jeromy Milton-Gold had an obvious stick up his ass, Lori decided to work her charms on Hammond Patterson. He seemed like a friendly enough dude with his neat haircut and honest brown eyes. She needed to get something going, because Ashley, the footballer's wife, was busy fawning all over Cliff.

All Lori knew about Hammond Patterson was that he was a senator, and his wife was some kind of do-gooder socialite fashion plate. But so what? Since moving in with Cliff, Lori realized she could talk to anyone and be accepted—it was one of the main perks of being a very famous movie star's number-one girlfriend. Might as well take advantage of it while she could.

"I don't know much about politics," she said brightly, attracting Hammond's attention. "But I do know that you've got the look."

"And what look would that be?" Hammond asked, his eyes sliding down to take in his dinner partner's cleavage.

"You know," Lori said with a flirty smile, "handsome. Trustworthy. The American public totally gets off on a handsome candidate. If Cliff ran, they'd vote for him tomorrow."

"I'm not sure whether I should be insulted or flattered," Hammond said, liking what he saw. And what he saw was young and pretty with nice firm tits. He had an insatiable craving for youthful flesh. It always turned him on—it was his addiction.

"Try flattered," Lori said, noting that he was easy prey. "Because let's call it like it is, Senator: you *are* a very good-looking man. But I'm sure your wife must tell you that all the time."

"Ah, my wife . . ." Hammond said, letting the words hang in the air.

"She's beautiful," Lori remarked.

"And so are you, my dear," Hammond said, suppressing an urge to reach out and touch her tender flesh, maybe even stroke her tempting red hair.

"It's all an illusion," Lori said modestly.

"Some illusion," Hammond said, ogling her breasts.

"And they're real, too," she murmured, encouraging him.

"I'm so sorry," he said, raising his eyes. "Was I staring?"

"Only a little," she said with a bold smile. "However, I never said I minded."

And while Lori and Hammond were embarking on a flirtatious journey, Xuan and Aleksandr were involved in a deep discussion about Russian politics and the fall of the Soviet Union in the early nineties.

"Without that happening, you would never have amassed the fortune you have today," Xuan pointed out.

"Maybe. Maybe not," Aleksandr countered. "It's all relative."

"Tell that to the people who lost everything."

"Have you ever been to Russia?" Aleksandr asked, intrigued by this opinionated and quite smart Asian woman. His old friend Flynn had picked well.

"Once," Xuan replied. "I was researching a story on a Russian pop singer, supposedly your version of Lady Gaga. We walked through Red Square in Moscow accompanied by a camera crew and her army of bodyguards."

"Ah, you must mean Masha," Aleksandr said. "She is quite the personality."

"Personality or not, her bodyguards shoved and threw people out of the way as if they were garbage. And no one objected. No one complained. It was as if they were resigned to the fact that being treated like shit was perfectly okay. I didn't like seeing that."

"In Russia, people know their place."

"You mean people without money and status."

Aleksandr shrugged. "Never judge a country until you have lived there."

"I prefer not to."

"Not to what?"

"Live there."

"I'm not sure I was inviting you," Aleksandr said, quite amused.

"And if you were," Xuan retorted, "I'm not sure I would accept your invitation."

Later, when most of the guests had gotten to know each other, liqueurs, coffee, and dessert were served on the upper deck.

Partners reunited under the starry sky. Bianca sat on Aleksandr's lap, rubbing the back of his neck, thinking of the love they would make later, and reveling in this amazing trip that was all in her honor.

"Cliff Baxter is *such* a nice guy," Ashley confided to Taye, still tingling with the pleasure of sitting next to the movie star.

"Yeah, so's that Luca bloke," Taye responded. "Knows a lot about sport, an' y'know somethin'—he doesn't come across as gay at all."

"But he's with Jeromy," Ashley said, glancing across the deck to see who Cliff was speaking to.

"So are you," Taye pointed out.

"I'm in *business* with Jeromy," Ashley insisted. "I'm not *sleeping* with him."

"That's a relief," Taye joked.

"Anyway, you know what?"

"What?"

"I've been thinking that it's about time I branched out on my own."

"C'mon, toots," Taye groaned. "I'm not puttin' up *more* money."

"Why not?" Ashley said, bristling. "Don't you think I'm worth it?"

Tread carefully, Taye warned himself. *If you want to get laid tonight, be mindful of what you say.*

"Course you are, sweetheart," he assured her. "You're worth every penny in my pocket."

"Then can I do it?"

"I can't give you an answer now. We gotta figure it out, talk to my business manager an' shit."

"But you're saying that you'll think about it?" she pressed.

"Sure, toots."

Ashley gave him a quick kiss on the cheek. "I have a feeling that Cliff Baxter fancies me," she said, preening.

"Why wouldn't he? You're a regular hot tamale."

"You think?" she said, going all coquettish on him.

"You heard it here first."

And yes, tonight he *would* get lucky, for Cliff Baxter had already done the groundwork for him.

Thanks, Mister Big Shot. I owe it all to you!

46

Another spectacular morning. Clear blue skies, the Sea of Cortez calm and inviting, a light breeze wafting in the air.

Breakfast was laid out on the upper deck. Mercedes and Renee were standing by, ready to be of service. Den stood behind the bar, mimosas at the ready.

Lori was the first up, leaving Cliff snoring in their room. The Sexiest Man Alive indeed. Surely they meant the Loudest Snorer Alive?

Lori giggled to herself as she imagined the headline on the cover of *People* magazine. How many of Cliff's adoring fans would believe their icon was a major snorer? Not so many.

Lori remembered the first time she'd spent the night with Cliff. She'd been in shock at the noise he'd made. The sound emitting from his mouth was like a freight train rumbling through a station in tandem with a snorting pig. And when she'd mentioned it to him, he'd casually said, "You don't like the noise, stay out of the bedroom."

So she'd purchased extra-noise-blocking earplugs, and now she hardly noticed.

At this point in time she was filled with mixed emotions about Cliff. She resented the hell out of him for what he was about to do to her when they got back. On the other hand, she still had feelings for him. It was hard not to, because when he was nice, he was very, very nice.

And there was no denying that they'd shared many wonderful times together.

Marriage would solve everything.

Fat chance. Cliff was the most vocal anti-marriage
advocate on two legs.

Random thoughts. *I hate him. I love him.*

What was a girl to do?

Renee offered her coffee. Idly she watched the Australian girl fill her cup. *That could be me,* she thought. *In fact,
it was me. Waitressing. Only not on a luxury yacht with
a bunch of famous billionaires. More like in Vegas with a
bunch of randy gamblers.*

"Morning."

Lori glanced up from her place at the breakfast table to
see the Brit footballer, Taye. And what a hunky sight *he*
was. Striped board shorts concealing a multitude of good-
ies, a sleeveless tee, glistening black skin, and arms with
muscles that defied description.

Wow! Lori thought. *Sex on a stick. What a pleasant
way to start the day.*

"Any sign of my wife?" Taye inquired, helping himself
to a plate of fruit from a long table where all kinds of
breakfast choices were laid out.

"Haven't seen her," Lori said, still admiring his impressive physique while thinking that the magazine ads
didn't do him justice. "I think I'm the first up."

"No," Taye boasted, sitting down next to her, "*I'm* the
first up. Already worked out in the gym for half an hour,
and had a dip in the pool. Forty lengths. Not bad."

"Not bad at all," Lori murmured as Mercedes poured
him a glass of juice.

"You been in the gym here?" Taye inquired, thinking
that she looked like the athletic type.

"Not yet."

"Try it. It's real high-tech. Lots of fine equipment."

"Sounds great."

"It is. Gets you all souped up for the day."

"I'll give it a shot tomorrow. Maybe I can persuade Cliff to join me."

"You won't regret it," Taye said, stretching his arms above his head, thinking that last night had been solid. Ashley had been as randy as he was, and they'd had a shitload of fun in bed, more than they'd had in a long time.

"Cliff is kind of lazy," Lori offered. "Although he does like to keep it all moving."

"Don't we all," Taye replied.

"I'll second that."

"So, Lori," Taye said, "what do *you* do? You a model or somethin'?"

"Actress, actually."

"Yeah? Have I seen you in anythin'?"

"Well, if you had, I hope you would've remembered," she answered, artfully dodging the question.

"We don't get out to the movies much," Taye admitted. "What with work, practice, appearances, commercials, an' the twins. They take up a ton of time an' energy."

"Twins!" Lori exclaimed. "That must be amazing."

"If you fancy goin' without sleep for a couple of years," he said ruefully. "Yeah, then it's freakin' amazin'."

"I'm sure it's worth it."

"Of course it is," he said with a wide grin. "Although I gotta tell you, they're two right little ravers. It's never dull around our house. Keeps me an' the missus in top shape."

"I can see that," Lori murmured, once again admiring his spectacular physique.

"Huh?"

"Well, you look . . . uh . . . fantastic."

"I bloody well try," he said, trying to ignore the fact that she seemed to be coming on to him. Ashley did not appreciate any woman flirting with him, so he was more than relieved when Luca put in an appearance.

Luca was enjoying himself. He'd been working hard all year on two new albums and a worldwide tour, and this short break was a welcome one before he continued his South American tour. He was impressed with the group Aleksandr had gathered. In fact, he was honored to be included.

Jeromy did not seem to be as impressed as he was. Jeromy was riding high on a major bitch-fest. He hadn't liked either of his dining companions the previous evening, whereas Luca had experienced a fine old time.

Lately, Jeromy was starting to get on his nerves. At the beginning of their relationship, things had been quite different. Luca had looked up to Jeromy as being someone who could teach him things, improve his mind, and protect him from the gay mafia who were jonesing to get a shot at him. With Jeromy—a respectable, cultured, older Englishman—as his partner, he'd believed he'd be out of reach. Not exactly on a pedestal, but hardly a boy to be trifled with.

So after bravely emerging from the closet, he'd fallen straight into a relationship with Jeromy. At the time, he'd thought it was the safest move to make, but lately he was experiencing doubts. Jeromy was not the man Luca had thought he was. He was way too promiscuous, and that side of him somewhat unnerved Luca, what with all the diseases out there. Jeromy was also a rabid social climber, and a caustic and sometimes cruel critic of people who he felt didn't live up to his impossible standards.

Luca, who was extremely easygoing, had finally come to realize that Jeromy Milton-Gold was a big snob—especially when it came to Suga. Luca adored his ex-wife; he would do anything for her. After all, it was Suga he had to thank for giving him the chance to have such a fantastic career. She'd discovered him, nurtured him, loved him, made sure she'd surrounded him with the best managers and producers in the business. And even after giving birth to his son, she'd let him go with never a cross word, no bitterness or ill will. Suga was a truly wonderful and selfless woman who genuinely cared about him.

But Jeromy didn't see it. Jeromy seemed to take great pleasure in putting her down. *Why is she so grossly fat? Her career is definitely over. She's the worst dresser I've ever seen. What's with that god-awful hair? Can she even sing anymore?*

Jeromy's snide comments were endless, even though he knew Luca didn't appreciate hearing the disturbing and bitchy things he had to say about Suga.

As for Luca Junior, whenever the boy was around, Jeromy more or less ignored him. This hurt Luca a lot, because he adored his son, and he would have liked his partner to feel the same way.

"Hey," Taye said, greeting the singer.

"Hey back atcha, an' good morning, everyone," Luca responded. "I guess we're the early group."

"That we are," Lori said cheerfully. "Cliff was still asleep when I got up."

"Ashley too," Taye said, joining in. "That woman can sleep the day away."

Mercedes sprang into action, offering Luca coffee, tea, or juice.

He chose juice. "Well, isn't this a beautiful day," he exclaimed to his table companions. "How lucky are we?"

"I know," Lori agreed. "If paradise existed, this would be it."

"Very poetic," Luca said, grinning. "I think I feel a song coming on."

"Really?" Lori said.

"Just kidding," Luca said, recalling Jeromy's rant about Lori when they'd returned to their cabin the previous night. *Why the hell was I the one stuck next to that redheaded tramp? She's a nobody. Why should I even bother wasting my time? It was insulting.*

Luca actually liked Lori. He found her to be refreshing and pretty with her amazing red hair and great body. So what if she wasn't important or famous? Who cared?

Jeromy did, and that pissed Luca off.

* * *

True to his promise the night before, Aleksandr had satisfied Bianca until she'd begged him to stop. Aleksandr could do more with his tongue then most men could do with a seven-inch erection.

Bianca luxuriated in bed when she finally awoke. How incredible it was to be away from it all. No phones (Aleksandr had insisted every one give up their cell phones when they'd boarded the yacht). No hovering paparazzi. No fashion fittings, photo shoots, branding meetings, or personal appearances. Just pure sheer nothing to do except nothing. She was in heaven.

Aleksandr was sitting out on their private terrace eating breakfast. Bianca slid her naked body from between the sheets and strolled out to join him.

His eyes took in every feline inch of her. "Exquisite," he observed.

"And it's all yours," she said, tossing back her blacker-than-night hair.

"To do with as I will."

"Ah, but you already have," Bianca said, licking her full lips.

"You make me want more," Aleksandr said, his voice a husky growl as he reached for her.

"Shouldn't we be joining our guests?" she ventured, taking a step back.

"They can wait. Come sit with me."

She moved closer and sat on his knee. He cupped her breasts with his large hands, caressing her nipples until she began sighing with pleasure.

"Shall I make you come?" he said. "Would you like that?"

"Only if you let me return the favor."

Aleksandr roared with laughter and stood up, tipping her off his knee.

"Later," he said. "You're right; we should be joining our guests."

"You are *such* a tit tease," she said, feigning indignation. "You're leaving me all revved up with nowhere to go."

"Take a shower and put on your bikini," Aleksandr commanded. "Today we go exploring."

"Exploring what?"

"You'll see."

On her way up to the top deck for breakfast, Ashley ran into Cliff. She had on a pink jumpsuit that showed plenty of cleavage, and her long blond hair was tied back in a jaunty ponytail.

"Oh my God, talking to you last night was such fun," she said, pouncing. "You're so down-to-earth and lovely."

"What did you expect?" Cliff asked, raising a caustic eyebrow.

"Well . . . uh . . . I thought, y'know, with you being such a big star, that you might be full of yourself."

"I try not to be," Cliff said, faintly amused. "Lori keeps me grounded."

"Lori?" Ashley questioned.

"My girlfriend."

"Oh yes," Ashley said. "I forgot that you're with someone. I mean, in the magazines you're always referred to as being single, so . . ." She trailed off. She'd chosen to ignore the fact that he was with a girl, although this one was probably only temporary like all the rest she'd read about.

"You'd better not let Lori hear you say that," Cliff chided as they approached the breakfast deck. "She's very sensitive."

"Well, I can see that it must be difficult for her."

"She can handle it."

As if on cue, Lori jumped up to greet him, planting a kiss on his mouth, while throwing the blonde with the big tits a "keep off" look. Last night at dinner she'd observed Ashley draping herself all over Cliff. Poor Taye; he must have his hands full with his flirty wife. But not to worry, because Lori was going to make sure that Ashley didn't get anywhere near Cliff, not on her watch.

Besides, Ashley had the gorgeous footballer husband. Surely he was enough to keep her busy?

By the time morning arrived, Flynn had a backache from hell. He'd elected to sleep on the couch, while Xuan had commandeered the comfortable double bed. "We'll take turns," she'd crisply informed him. "Tomorrow night you may have the bed."

He was grateful she'd agreed to go along with his plan that they present themselves as a couple. "I wouldn't ask if it didn't mean a lot to me," he'd assured her.

"It is interesting to see you so vulnerable for once," she'd observed. "This woman must have really hurt you."

"She did," he'd muttered.

So the couch it was. And since he was six-two, and the couch was somewhat shorter, it had not been a comfortable night. Plus his head was spinning thinking about Sierra.

He had imagined he was over her.

He had thought that if he ever saw her again, it would mean nothing.

Of course he was wrong.

Seeing her in person was not the same as seeing photos of her in magazines, the politician's stylish wife, so beautiful, so popular.

He remembered the shock he'd felt when he'd read about her and Hammond getting married. The love of his life had married his archnemesis, Hammond Patterson.

Really? How the hell had *that* happened?

Then he'd remembered the sickening photos someone had sent him of Sierra—in one of them she was in a compromising position with Hammond. *Jesus Christ.*

He'd burned the photos. Obliterated them.

Now here he was. Stuck on a yacht in the middle of the Sea of Cortez. And what he had to do was come up with a clever excuse to get himself off the boat.

Xuan was in the shower. She emerged with wet hair and a towel tied around her petite body, sarong style.

"You hungry?" he asked.

"I could be."

"Get dressed and we'll go for breakfast."

"You don't have to wait for me."

"That's okay," he said restlessly, prepared to hang out until she was ready.

He was *not* prepared to risk another one-on-one conversation with Sierra. And he certainly didn't want to run into Hammond. They'd barely spoken. A brief "How are you?" and that was it.

The thought of Hammond being in a position to make a run for the highest office in the land was the biggest joke of all time. How the hell had *that* happened?

"Turn your back while I dress," Xuan instructed.

He did as she asked, and started working on an excuse to get off the yacht.

Hammond hit the breakfast deck, and immediately sat himself down next to Lori.

"You look very fresh this morning, my dear," he said. "All ready for a day of sunning?"

"I get too many freckles when I sunbathe," she explained.

"Nothing wrong with a freckle or two," Hammond said with a jovial chuckle and a quick peek at her breasts, perky in a pristine white T-shirt with no bra. He could see her nipples.

Man, Lori thought. *Like the song "It's Raining Men." And they're all wildly attractive. And I'm the only single woman on the boat apart from the Asian, and she's no competition. Too serious. And short. I am about to have major fun. A little light flirting for Cliff to observe might even change his mind about dumping me.*

"I guess us ladies can go topless when we lie out to

sunbathe," Lori said, addressing the table, knowing full well that there was no way Ashley would like that.

"I don't think so," Ashley responded as expected.

"Why not?" Lori said, pushing it.

"Isn't that a decision best left to our hostess?" Ashley said, her tone quite icy.

"*I* think we should put it to a vote," Lori said boldly. "What do *you* think, Senator? Tops on or off?"

"No objections from me," Hammond chuckled. "Off sounds like a fine plan."

"I'm always topless," Luca joked.

Before the conversation could continue, Aleksandr and Bianca appeared.

"Today we are taking a magical mystery tour on an uninhabited island," Aleksandr announced. "For all those who wish to come—and I hope that will be everyone—we gather at twelve noon. Be prepared."

47

Twenty-four hours in, Mercedes already knew plenty. Observation was her strong suit. As a lowly stewardess she was invisible. Conversations took place and she heard it all. The senator was flirting with the redhead. The redhead was flirting with everyone. The Asian woman was an uptight bitch who considered herself smarter than all the other women aboard, and she was not sleeping with her boyfriend—who even Mercedes had to agree was quite a hunk—because one of the maids had informed her that he'd spent the night on the couch. Aleksandr and Bianca were fucking like rabbits, even getting it on in the middle of dinner. The footballer and his blond wife were doing it too. But not the senator and his wife, who was zonked out of her mind on an assortment of pills. Plus the senator was a screamer, berating his wife in private, while fawning over her in public. The gay boys were an odd couple. Luca Perez was a sweetheart, and the older guy was a sly fox. And finally the movie star was just that—a dumb movie star.

So . . . in twenty-four hours, Mercedes had learned plenty about the passengers, all of which she'd reported to Cruz.

She kept a different eye on the mostly Australian crew, and she foresaw no problems there. Her roommate and fellow stewardess, Renee, was all teeth with an eager-to-please personality. Den, the barman, was no problem. Guy was all mouth and no balls. Captain Dickson was a nonentity—he'd fold as soon as Cruz and his men boarded.

Kyril presented her only problem. The burly Russian bodyguard was a hard nut to crack. She'd visited his command room on several occasions, ostensibly to take him trays of food, which he always rejected.

Kyril sat in a chair in front of an array of security monitors and barely moved. He was certainly not up for any light conversation, and trying to flirt with him had gotten her exactly nowhere.

What the hell? He had a dick, didn't he? And if *she* couldn't get it hard, who could?

Kyril was an imperative part of the plan. He was the only person aboard who could cause problems.

Cruz and his team planned to strike in a few days, so there was still time. She sensed that Kyril wasn't going to be easy, and if she couldn't divert him sexually . . . well . . . drugs were her other alternative.

Fortunately, she'd come prepared. Horse tranquilizers. The only sure thing.

48

"I will not be coming on the excursion," Sierra said, standing up to her husband for once.

"You haven't left our room all morning," Hammond pointed out, admiring himself in the bathroom mirror, making sure he'd combed his hair exactly the way it suited him when he appeared on TV. "What must everyone think?" he added churlishly.

"Who cares *what* they think?" Sierra replied, determined not to give in. "I have a bad migraine and I'm not moving. You'll have to go without me."

Hammond considered the possibilities. If Sierra came with him, he'd be forced to be nice to her in front of everyone and stay by her side. If Sierra didn't come, he'd be free to spend more time with the sexy redhead and the blonde with the big tits, not to mention Miss Supermodel herself with the fuck-me lips and insane body. Then there was always the Asian piece of pie. Yes, quite a tasty cornucopia of pussy.

Sierra not coming was really not so bad. After all, there was no press around, no photo opportunities, which meant who cared if she was with him or not?

"Fine," he said, tight-lipped as he emerged from the bathroom. "Have it your way. However, I do expect you to be up and dressed when I return. Headache or not, I refuse to allow you to miss dinner."

"Very well," Sierra responded.

Five minutes later he was gone and she could breathe again. His vitriol about Flynn had spilled over her like a never-ending gush of rancid oil. She'd listened, staying silent, until finally he'd run out of insults.

She'd lain awake most of the night, having not taken her usual sleeping pills, and in the morning she'd willed herself not to reach for the Xanax.

The truth was, she had no headache. She felt remarkably clearheaded for the first time in months.

Flynn Hudson. He was here on this yacht. And if not now, when would she ever have the chance to find out why he'd treated her the way he had? So callously. So cruelly and nastily. So unlike the Flynn she'd known, the man she'd given up her virginity to, the man she'd once loved with every fiber of her being.

Suddenly everything seemed very clear. If an explanation was all she needed, then maybe she could reclaim her life and become the person she once was, not this pathetic shell of a woman who yearned for a love she could never have, a woman who lived in fear of a domineering and threatening husband.

Were Hammond's threats even real?

Who knew? He'd led her to believe that they were. But surely even *he* couldn't be such a monster.

Or could he?

It was something she might be forced to find out.

Lori was totally psyched. A visit to a mysterious deserted island—how rad was *that*?

Cliff, not so much. "If you don't mind, I think I'll sit this one out," he said. "I feel like finding a nice quiet corner and reading a script or two."

"Do you want me to stay with you?" Lori asked, although she was dying to explore the island.

"No, sweetie, you go," he said, throwing her a quizzical look. "Only you'd better watch out for the horny senator."

"Excuse me?" she said, startled.

"That randy bastard has had his eye on you ever since we got here."

"Who?" she asked, as if she didn't know.

"Aren't you listening? The senator, babe. Politicians got it goin' on. Ever since Clinton, they think they're all movie stars. Only don't forget that *I'm* the real deal. Okay?"

There were times when Cliff totally endeared himself to her, and this was one of them. He'd noticed! And he was—well—if not jealous, at least aware.

"Oh," Lori said, suppressing a smile. "I can handle him. JFK he's not."

Cliff laughed. Lori was such a good sport and so much fun to be with (not to mention the world-class blow jobs)—so much fun that he was seriously considering keeping her around for another year. Who needed the hassle of breaking in a new girlfriend when an esteemed senator seemed to get off on the one he already had? Lori was hot stuff, and she never pushed him on marriage or any of that crap.

"Go have a blast," he said, patting her on the ass. "I'm not going anywhere."

She turned around and planted a big fat kiss on his cheek. "I'll miss you," she said, genuinely meaning it.

He gave her one of his famous grins. "Try not to miss me too much."

"I'll try."

"Good girl."

"Oh, and while we're on the subject of flirting," she added, "do me a favor and steer clear of Miss Blonde Big Tits. Okay?"

"She's married!" Cliff objected.

"So's the senator."

"Get outta here," Cliff said, starting to laugh again. "The blonde's all talk and no blow. Besides, I prefer me a hot-blooded redhead."

"Hmm," Lori said, putting on a mock stern voice. "Let's make sure it stays that way."

"Yes, *ma'am!*"

"I have decided not to go," Jeromy said, pursing his thin lips.

"Why not?" Luca wanted to know.

"Because I am perfectly happy staying on the yacht and relaxing, thank you very much. I have no desire to start traipsing around some stupid island. It doesn't appeal to me."

"You're missing out," Luca said mildly.

"I think not."

Luca shrugged and gave up. Jeromy was not the outdoors type. Mr. Milton-Gold preferred indoor activities, with a martini clutched in his manicured hand and his body clad in an expensive designer outfit.

"If that's the way you want it, then I guess I'll see you later," Luca said, anxious to get going and join the others.

"You're still leaving, then?" Jeromy said, surprised and irritated that Luca didn't elect to stay with him.

"You bet your ass," Luca replied enthusiastically. "Wouldn't miss it."

Jeromy scowled. He didn't like the idea of Luca running off without him. Although the thought of sweating his way through some hideous deserted island was enough to make him stick to his original decision. This was supposed to be a leisure trip, not some screwed-up version of the TV show *Survivor*.

"Well," Jeromy said testily, making the most of an annoying situation, "try to enjoy yourself without me."

"Yeah," Luca said, looking forward to some time away from Jeromy. "I'll do that."

The *Bianca* had two luxurious tenders, each able to accommodate several crew members and eight guests.

The guests gathered, ready to disembark from the big yacht.

Guy, Renee, and Den were also on the trip, prepared to cater to the celebrity guests' every need. Guy had wanted Mercedes to come too, but when several guests had elected to stay on board, he'd had to leave someone behind to cater to them; reluctantly, he'd left Mercedes.

"You're in charge of seeing that the remaining guests have everything they need," he'd warned her. "I do not wish to hear one complaint."

"Got it covered, boss," Mercedes had said with a cheeky tilt of her chin.

"Do *not* call me boss," Guy admonished, not sure if he liked this girl or not. There was something about her he couldn't quite warm to. Maybe the captain was right, and she wasn't the perfect fit. "Mr. Guy will do nicely."

"Yes, *Mr.* Guy," she said, teetering on the edge of sarcasm.

"And don't forget to see if the captain would like you to bring him lunch," Guy said, frowning. He would not be hiring this one again. She was too fresh—and not in a physical way.

"I've got it covered, bo . . . uh, Mr. Guy."

Both tenders were loaded with supplies, including several bottles of champagne, soft drinks, snacks, and an elaborate picnic lunch.

"Where's your boyfriend?" Hammond asked as he followed Lori onto one of the tenders.

"He decided to stay on board and read," Lori said. "How about your wife? Is she coming with us?"

"Headache," Hammond answered shortly, admiring Lori's long tanned legs, no freckles in sight.

"Poor thing," Lori said, her eyes following Taye as he made his way down the ladder onto the boat, followed by Ashley, clad in some kind of flimsy leopard cover-up— which actually revealed more than it covered.

Bianca, Aleksandr, Luca, Xuan, and Flynn were already in the second tender.

As the two boats took off, Captain Dickson appeared at the side of the yacht and waved them on their way. "Have a wonderful day!" he shouted.

"We plan to!" Bianca shouted back.

And then they were off.

Cliff found a quiet corner on the top deck and settled in with a pile of scripts. A peaceful afternoon suited him just fine, since it wasn't often he had the luxury of spending time by himself. His life consisted of making movies, followed by traveling the world promoting them. There was no way he could estimate how many interviews he'd given over the last two decades, or how many photo sessions he'd posed for. Not that he was complaining, for the rewards were plentiful.

Still . . . a full afternoon where he didn't have to play Cliff Baxter, charming movie star, was sheer bliss.

Mercedes brought him an iced tea and jotted down his request for a light salad lunch.

"Will you be eating with the other guests?" she asked.

"I thought they'd all gone on the trip," Cliff replied.

"No. The senator's wife is still aboard. So is Luca Perez's companion."

"I'll stay where I am," Cliff decided, in no mood to be social.

"Yes, Mr. Baxter," Mercedes said, acting as the perfect little stewardess in her neat uniform, a practiced smile on her face.

One down, two to go. The senator's wife was still in her cabin, and Mercedes wasn't quite sure where Luca Perez's significant other was.

The truth was, she didn't much care for the gays. She considered being gay a waste of manpower, although she'd had an experience or two with girls. However, girl-on-girl action was different. Besides, Luca Perez was crazy hot, so what was he doing with some old douche who seemed to be about as much fun as a box of tampons?

With most of the guests gone, she planned on doing a quick sweep of their rooms to check out the jewelry and money stash. She'd already ascertained that the limey blonde was into diamonds, and that the footballer had several expensive watches. Nice. But the real prize would be in the main stateroom, where she'd already discovered a hidden safe.

No problem there, for among her many other talents, Mercedes knew how to crack a safe with the best of 'em.

As soon as the maids were safely out of the way, she slipped into the master suite and headed straight for the safe with her handy box of tools. Fifteen heart-stopping minutes later, she was in.

What a bonanza! A stack of cash. Papers—boring. And a small black jewel box containing the most exquisite ring she'd ever seen. A magnificent emerald surrounded by dozens of sparkling diamonds.

Mercedes almost salivated.

Oh yes, when the time came, she planned on cleaning up.

Why shouldn't she grab what she wanted? Cruz could do his thing, and she'd do hers. It was about time she seized the opportunity to make a killing and strike out by herself.

Yes, she had an agenda. No more Daddy's little helper.

Mercedes had her own plans.

49

The deserted island was a magical place. A glorious oasis in the middle of the sea. White pristine sands, crystal-clear blue water, pockets of unusual rock formations, lush greenery, and groves of palm trees heading inland.

The captain had arranged to have a tour guide meet them on the island, and the Mexican man was waiting when they arrived.

"Wow!" Bianca exclaimed, jumping off the tender and running straight onto the sand, throwing off her T-shirt to reveal a barely-there orange bikini. "This is fanfuckin'tastic! And no hidden paparazzi. I'm in heaven!"

Aleksandr smiled. There was nothing he enjoyed more than watching Bianca indulge her childlike tendencies; he found it refreshing.

"C'mon, Ashley," Bianca called out. "Join me."

Ashley, who was gingerly stepping off the tender, trying not to get her Dolce sandals wet, nodded.

"This is like a friggin' dream," Taye said to Luca. "Jesus, man, it's a bloody long way from the old Elephant."

"You had an elephant?" Luca questioned, trying to keep his eyes away from Taye's fully stocked crotch.

"No way, man," Taye said, breaking up laughing. "The bleedin' Elephant an' Castle. That's the place I was born."

Luca was even more confused, but he shrugged it off as he helped Lori from the tender.

After checking out the view, Lori wished she'd brought her camera, because this was without a doubt the most stunning place she'd ever seen. Cliff should've come. He would've loved it.

Den, Renee, and several of the crew members were busy unloading the tenders, setting up umbrellas and giant beach towels and erecting a food and drink station while Guy supervised.

Manuel, the Mexican tour guide, watched in stoic bewilderment. Tourists. They never failed to dumbfound him with their endless extravagances. It was staggering the money they must have to throw away on nonessential things. When he'd been hired for this job, he'd been informed that these were very important people. They didn't look that important to him. The women were half naked, something that didn't seem to bother the men. He would be shamed if his wife or daughters ever exposed themselves in such a blatant fashion.

Guy approached him. "The guests will be eating lunch first," he instructed Manuel. "Then we'll start the island tour. Okay, mate?"

Manuel nodded, and walked a distance away, prepared to wait. He knew from experience that he was merely there to serve.

When Flynn realized that Sierra was not on the excursion, he was torn. Should he have stayed on the yacht?

For what? So she could practically ignore him again? Treat him like a total stranger?

He had a gnawing in his stomach that was bothering the hell out of him. Maybe it wasn't the smartest move in the world, although with Hammond on the island, surely this was the perfect opportunity to clear things up with Sierra once and for all?

He needed closure. Now that he'd seen her again, he knew in his heart that he had to find out why she'd betrayed him in such a callous fashion.

Goddammit! Now he was trapped on the island when he should've stayed on the yacht. And how was he supposed to get back? Swim?

No. The yacht was too far away, at least a ten-minute trip, and that was by tender.

What to do?

Perhaps feign some kind of stomach ailment? Act like a weakling and claim to be sick? Not the most manly of actions, but it appeared to be the only excuse he could come up with.

He glanced around at the activity. The girls were frolicking on the sand as if they were just out of grade school—all except Xuan, who'd sat herself down next to Aleksandr on one of the folding chairs and was busy engaging him in conversation. Hammond was leering at the girls—typical. Taye and Luca had plunged into the ocean.

Flynn approached Guy. "I don't want to make a big deal out of this," he said quietly. "Only I got a bad case of the runs, so I'm going to have to get back to the yacht."

"Don't fancy the bushes, eh?" Guy joked. Then, realizing he might have overstepped his mark, he hurriedly backtracked. "Sorry, mate," he said with a somber shake of his head. "Not so funny, huh?"

"Any chance of a ride?" Flynn inquired.

"Sure thing. We need more stuff from the mother ship. Hop aboard tender two; one of the boys'll take you."

"Thanks," Flynn said, thinking that he'd traveled through war zones, witnessed atrocities, interviewed terrorists, and yet now, at the thought of facing Sierra, he was more nervous than he'd ever been.

Could it get any better than this? Lori didn't think so. Here she was, a girl who'd had to struggle for most of her life, on a fabulous island in the middle of nowhere with one of the world's most famous supermodels, a mega football hero, a senator (who was definitely lusting after her), a superstar Latin singer, and a Russian billionaire.

It was all totally surreal. Nobody would believe it.

She could just imagine her mom's face if she could see her now. Oh lordy, Sherrine Walsh would have a fit.

Lori often wondered why her mom had never attempted to make contact. Yes, they'd been estranged for years, but surely when Sherrine had spotted her splashed all over the magazines on the arm of Cliff Baxter she'd been tempted to make amends. They'd parted on such bad terms. Sherrine had called her every vile word she could come up with. The word that had stung the most was *worthless*.

How worthless could she be? She was living with one of the biggest movie stars in the world. She was happy. For now. She had made something of her life.

Take that, Sherrine. Who's the worthless one now?

"I can't believe that Cliff didn't come today," Ashley complained to Bianca.

Bianca raised an eyebrow. Why was Ashley bothered about Cliff Baxter when she had Taye to take care of her? After all, Bianca knew what Taye had to offer in the bedroom department, and it was all good. She shrugged and rolled over on the beach towel she'd spread out. "Movie stars dance to their own tune," she offered, allowing the silky white sand to run through her fingers. "And besides, he's no Ryan Gosling."

"He's Cliff Baxter," Ashley retorted, shocked that Bianca would even dare to compare him to Ryan Gosling. "And he's bloody gorgeous."

"Does Taye know you have the hots for him?" Bianca asked, amused.

"I so do not," Ashley said, suddenly blushing.

"Oh yes, you do," Bianca singsonged. "But that's okay—it's not as if you're about to fuck him."

Why not? Ashley wanted to say. *Just because I'm married doesn't mean I'm dead.*

"That's so rude," she managed. "He's just . . . I dunno . . . special."

"Ask Lori how special he is," Bianca said, jumping to her feet and stretching her lithe body. "They're all the same between the sheets. Given the chance, they're all up for a quick cheat, however faithful they claim to be."

"You don't mean that."

"Well . . ." Bianca mused. "I like to think that Aleksandr is different."

"So is Taye," Ashley said quickly.

Bianca shot her a disbelieving look. "*How* long have you been married?"

"Uh . . . almost seven years."

"And you're telling me that Taye has never slipped it to another woman?"

Ashley immediately flashed onto Taye's glaring indiscretion. The Page 3 bimbo with the gigantic tits. The story splashed all over the English tabloids. Did Bianca know? Had she read about it?

It was one time. One time only.

She *still* resented the crap out of him for doing it. How dare he.

How dare he!

She glanced along the beach, watching her husband in the surf with Cliff's redheaded slag.

Enough of that, thank you very much.

"Think I'll take a dip before lunch," she said, ignoring Bianca's question. "Coming?"

Hammond was making a concerted effort not to stare, but the scenery was too damn tempting. He wasn't admiring the palm trees and the pure white sand—no, his full attention was directed straight at Lori, Bianca, and Ashley. Three magnificent women. Bianca, sleek and dark-skinned with a feline grace. Ashley, the definitive blond babe with big boobs and a jiggly ass. And Lori, his particular favorite—young, athletic, with that mass of flaming red hair. He found himself wondering if the pussy matched. She was wearing a white bikini, and when she emerged from the sea it appeared to be see-through. Her pert nipples were definitely on display.

He felt himself starting to get an erection, which wasn't the brightest of ideas considering he was sitting in a folding chair next to Aleksandr, and his linen shorts were not the best at concealing a burgeoning hard-on.

"The girls look good, huh?" Aleksandr said in his gruff voice.

Hammond wondered if Aleksandr had noticed his excitement. If he was on the yacht he could've gone to his cabin and masturbated, but no such luck. He was on an island, and any kind of release would have to wait.

"Very pretty," he agreed. "Especially your lady."

"She's a good girl," Aleksandr said, nodding his head like a benevolent father. "Never believe the things you might read or see on the Internet."

Cryptic, Hammond thought. Everyone knew Bianca had slept with the world. She was a tramp who happened to be a very famous tramp.

"Aleksandr," Hammond said, clearing his throat. "I was hoping we might get a moment to talk about my future plans. I have many things to discuss that could be most advantageous for both of us."

"I am sure," Aleksandr replied. "However, Senator, there is a time and a place for everything, and that time and place is not now."

"Of course," Hammond said, furious at being dismissed. *Russian peasant! Rich prick!* "Perhaps when we get back to the U.S. we should pick a time and a place," he added smoothly. "I'll make sure to slot you into my schedule anytime you find convenient."

Aleksandr nodded. "We'll see," he said in a noncommittal way.

Hammond felt his erection deflate. Even Lori couldn't coax it up now.

50

Back in New York, Eddie March was dealing with a crisis. A crisis that could blow up in everyone's face. He'd arrived at the office bright and early, just as he did every day. And there, sitting in reception, were Mr. and Mrs. Martin Byrne, parents of young Skylar, Hammond's latest intern.

"They've been waiting half an hour," the girl at reception had informed him. "They wanted to see Senator Patterson. I told them he's abroad, and besides, they didn't have an appointment. However, since they said it was extremely urgent, I suggested they wait for you."

Wait they did. And Eddie met with them, and suddenly it was all systems on red alert, for according to Martin Byrne, Senator Patterson had sexually molested his darling daughter.

Eddie was in shock. Christ! How could this be happening? Was it true? Would Hammond be stupid enough to do such a thing?

Eddie wasn't sure how to handle such a situation. Sex scandals involving politicians were hardly unusual. He immediately thought of John Edwards, Eliot Spitzer, Gary Hart, even ex-president Bill Clinton.

The scandal had ruined Edwards's political ambitions. Hart and Spitzer were long gone. Clinton had survived being impeached, but only just. And there were numerous others who'd fallen by the wayside because of their various sexual shenanigans.

Dammit! Eddie's initial reaction was, how could Hammond do this to Sierra? She was a beloved public figure, and a rare and special beauty. Why would Hammond even consider straying? And with a teenage intern at that.

Eddie thrust his mind into overdrive. What did these people want? Was it money? Headlines? An apology?

How could he help them and keep this under wraps?

There was only one way to find out.

51

On his return trip to the yacht, Flynn rehearsed exactly what he was going to say to Sierra when they finally came face-to-face.

Hey, remember me—the love of your life? Isn't that what you assured me I was?

Or:

How could you do what you did to me? Were you even aware that you smashed my heart into a thousand splintered fragments and I never got over you?

Or:

What the fuck are you doing with an asshole like Hammond Patterson? You're too smart to be with a man like him.

Hell, he didn't know what he'd say, if anything.

He'd left the island without telling anyone except Guy. No one would miss him; they were all too busy. Including Xuan, who seemed to have taken a real liking to Aleksandr. Too bad the Russian was under Bianca's spell, for Aleksandr and Xuan would've made an interesting couple.

The tender zoomed toward the yacht while Flynn desperately tried to clear his head. Thoughts were flying.

Am I making a big mistake?

Should I be doing this?

Why dredge up the past?

Hell, why not?

* * *

After a peaceful hour of solitude, Jeromy turned up, putting paid to Cliff's precious time alone.

"Ah." Jeromy sighed, flopping down on a nearby lounger. "And I thought *I* was the only smart one. Now I can see that great minds think alike."

Cliché alert, Cliff thought. *And who exactly is this?*

"Yeah," Cliff said amiably, lowering the script he was leafing through. "Just getting some reading done while I can."

"All work and no play," Jeromy admonished, wagging a bony forefinger.

Cliff frowned. *Another cliché. What a jerk.*

"It seems that everyone else has deserted us," Jeromy said, delighted to spend alone time with the movie star. Maybe Cliff Baxter could be a future client—what a coup *that* would be.

"True," Cliff said. "But reading scripts isn't really work, especially if they're worthwhile."

"I must say," Jeromy continued, warming up, "I am an ardent admirer of your work. I'm sure I don't have to tell you that you are extremely popular in the old home country."

"Home country?" Cliff questioned, thinking that maybe he should've gone on the island trip after all.

"England," Jeromy said grandly. "Actually, I'm from London. I must assume you have graced us with your presence."

Yes, the man has just proved it: he is a walking, talking cliché.

"London's a great city," Cliff said. "I've had many a good time there. In fact, I have a cousin who lives in Sloane Square. You know it?"

"Know it!" Jeromy exclaimed. "My showroom is just around the corner."

"Showroom?"

"I hate to sound immodest," Jeromy said, sounding

immodest. "However, I am regarded as one of the premier interior designers in London."

"Is that so?"

"It is."

"And you're on this cruise because of Aleksandr or Bianca?" Cliff asked, wondering how he could escape.

"Well," Jeromy lied. "They're both *dear* friends. And as I am sure you know, my significant other is Luca Perez. He and Bianca are almost like brother and sister."

"Got it," Cliff said. This was not the way he'd planned on spending the afternoon.

Fortunately, Mercedes appeared, offering drinks and snacks.

Cliff took the opportunity to stand up and stretch. "Think I'll take a break," he said, moving toward the circular staircase. "See you later."

Jeromy frowned. Was it something he'd said? Had Cliff's nobody girlfriend complained about him because he hadn't paid her enough attention the previous evening?

Dammit! A wasted opportunity.

"Can I get you anything?" Mercedes asked.

Jeromy, in a fit of pique, ignored her. It was a big mistake.

Clarity. A feeling Sierra hadn't felt in a long time. No more drugs. Even though they were legal, they still dulled her senses, made the world a different place.

She'd once been a strong woman, opinionated and positive. Hammond had turned her into a shell of the woman she once was. Unfortunately she'd allowed it to happen, punishing herself for the past, beating herself up.

Seeing Flynn had been like standing under an icy cold shower.

Wake up, little girl. Fight the fight. Get over yourself.

It was incredible to feel so free. Just like that, the shackles were loosened and she could breathe again.

After getting dressed, she headed to one of the upper

decks. It was a glorious day, just the kind of day on which
to emerge from the frightening fog that had enveloped her
for too many years.

*Come at me with your threats, Hammond. Finally I
am able to stand up to you.*

And I will. Oh yes, I certainly will.

Being treated like a nonexistent piece of shit did not thrill
Mercedes. Jeromy whatever-his-dumb-name-was would
pay for that. She'd already scoped out his stateroom and
knew exactly what she would take when the time came.
Watches, rings, gold chains, cash. Between him and the
singer, there was plenty of loot. The senator and his wife,
not so much. But the footballer kept a stack of cash hidden in his sock drawer, which amused her. Oh sure, like
no thief worth their business would ever think of checking out a sock drawer.

Who was he hiding it from anyway? His wife, Miss
Big Tits?

Mercedes was glad the guests were off the boat; it gave
her time to snoop around. She was especially pleased that
Guy wasn't present. He was such a fussy queen and always seemed to have his eye on her. Renee and Den were
both okay—easily manipulated and a bit stupid, but if the
circumstances were different, maybe they could've all
been friends.

Australians. A different kind of species.

Flynn was sweating—unusual for him, but he was way
out of his comfort zone.

What was he going to say to Sierra?

Small talk wouldn't cut it.

Shit! This was an impossible situation.

He decided to throw himself in the shower, get himself
together, and approach Sierra in a cool and collected
fashion.

Yeah, that was the way to do it.

At the door to his stateroom, he encountered one of the stewardesses emerging.

"Everything okay?" he asked. "I thought the maid was already in here."

"Checking out your wet bar," Mercedes replied, unfazed at nearly being caught.

And your computer.

And your cash.

Ninety-three dollars.

Is that all? Really?

"This place is run like a hotel," Flynn commented.

"Full service," Mercedes replied, thinking that under different circumstances she might go for this guy. He was tall and macho, a touch edgy—exactly the way she liked 'em. "Didn't you go on the island trip?"

"I did."

"Wasn't for you?" she asked, curious as to why he was back so soon.

"Uh . . . do you know where the senator's wife might be?" Flynn said abruptly, not about to be questioned.

"I think I saw her go to the top deck," Mercedes replied, wondering what was up. "Can I get you anything?"

"No thanks," he said, entering his stateroom, slamming the door, and stripping off his clothes.

Sierra. She was all he could think about as he stood under the icy needles of the shower.

Sierra. It was definitely time they talked it out.

After her run-in with Flynn, Mercedes decided that now was the time to forge some kind of contact with Kyril. She'd already thoroughly checked out his cabin—nothing personal to discover except his spare weapon stash, which was formidable. Kyril was a man prepared. He'd even affixed a special lock on the door to his cabin—a lock Mercedes had had no problem picking. She was a talented girl. Safes, locks; she knew what she was doing.

After almost getting caught by the sexy journalist guy,

she headed for the kitchen and had the chef prepare a special meal for Kyril, informing the chef that it was for Cliff Baxter, so it had better be great. What man could resist a juicy steak with french fries on the side? The smell alone was too tempting.

Unfortunately, Kyril turned out to be just such a man. When Mercedes knocked on the door to his security room carrying a tray, he waved her away with a ferocious glare.

Mercedes was not a girl to be dismissed; she persevered with the knocking until eventually he reluctantly opened the door.

"What?" he demanded, his Russian accent thick and heavy.

"Food," Mercedes replied cheerfully. "A big fat steak cooked specially for you. You need to eat, and I noticed you never do."

"No steak," Kyril said grumpily. "I no eat meat."

"Oh!" Mercedes exclaimed. "I didn't know that. Can I get you something else?"

Kyril stared at her, perhaps noticing her for the first time. She'd unbuttoned her uniform to give him a hint of cleavage. God, he was ugly—such a big stony face with gapped yellow teeth and empty eyes.

"No," he said.

"Yes," she argued, noting he had a supply of bottled water and a stack of chocolate bars sitting on a shelf.

"No," he repeated. But she could see his empty eyes checking out her cleavage.

Yes. He would soon come around. They always did.

52

A tempting lunch was laid out on folding tables and served on the endless stretch of golden beach. Giant shrimp and succulent lobster dripping in melted butter, sumptuous salads, an array of delicious cold cuts, and deviled eggs with a healthy dollop of caviar atop. All the while the champagne and sangria flowed as the sun blazed down. But not to worry, for canvas covers were erected to shield the privileged travelers from the burning sun.

Renee and Den worked full out making sure everything ran smoothly, while Guy supervised.

Bianca lolled at Aleksandr's feet, running her hand casually up and down his leg, murmuring about how this trip couldn't get any better.

Xuan sat with Ashley, Taye, and Luca. Their conversation was lightweight, mostly about music and movies. Earlier Xuan had moved away from Aleksandr as soon as Bianca laid claim. It surprised her that a man as intelligent as Aleksandr would be with such a woman. However, Xuan was wise enough to realize that every man had his weaknesses, even Flynn, usually so strong and dedicated. Yet on this trip he'd lost it over some married woman, and that wasn't at all like the Flynn she knew. She'd noticed his absence, and assumed he'd returned to the yacht. Xuan had learned at an early age never to let your feelings rule your heart. It was something she never did.

Hammond suggested to Lori that since both their partners had elected not to come, they should stick together.

Why not? Lori thought. *What have I got to lose? He obviously has the hots for me. And Cliff knows it. Maybe I'll get Cliff so jealous that he'll change his mind about dumping me.*

The senator's conversation was full of double entendres.

Lori smiled politely, nodded attentively, and wondered what Cliff was up to and if he was missing her.

Hammond informed her in a smarmy way that she was the sexiest woman on the trip and that the other women had better watch out because she was capable of stealing all their men.

Lori kept smiling and nodding as she adjusted her bikini top in a vain attempt to achieve more coverage, because she could swear Hammond possessed X-ray vision. Flirting was one thing, but after a while Hammond was starting to creep her out with his sexist comments. Cliff was right: politicians were just as horny as the next man, probably even more so.

After lunch, Manuel was summoned by Guy, who requested that everyone wear shoes and a cover-up to start the island tour. Renee and Den handed out T-shirts and baseball caps with "The *Bianca*" emblazoned on them.

"I feel like we're taking off on a school trip," Ashley giggled, throwing on a T-shirt over her bikini. "This is *so* much fun!"

"I know," Bianca agreed, grabbing Aleksandr's hand and squeezing it tight. "It's an adventure. A big beautiful adventure. And you, my darling," she added, gazing up at Aleksandr, "planned it all perfectly."

And so they set off, the billionaire and his elite group of famous guests.

They were not exactly roughing it as they began exploring the scenic beauty of the idyllic island.

Manuel had conducted the tour before with other

groups of extremely rich tourists. He was very aware that the stark unblemished beauty of the uninhabited island was staggering. First they passed by glorious pristine white sand dunes that led on to groves of coconut and date palms. Beyond the trees, they came upon a series of natural springs and glorious cascading waterfalls.

Bianca immediately decided that she wanted to stop and swim under the most impressive waterfall—it was too incredible to resist.

"We cannot hold our group up," Aleksandr chided. "There is more to see."

"Then get rid of everyone," Bianca whispered in his ear. "'Cause I want to swim naked with you. Tell them we'll catch up. Go on," she urged when he hesitated. "Do it!"

Aleksandr couldn't say no. He snapped his fingers for Guy. "Have everyone move ahead," he instructed. "We will stay here."

Manuel did not like the idea of splitting the group, so Guy suggested to Aleksandr that perhaps they should all stay together.

"Why?" Aleksandr scoffed. "It's perfectly safe. I hardly need my bodyguard on a deserted island."

Guy nodded, but Manuel still seemed uneasy. The island was supposedly uninhabited, but over the years there had been rumors—sightings of mountain lions that came wandering down from the surrounding jungle-like hills, foraging for any food the tourists might have left behind. A dead body that had mysteriously washed up onshore.

Yes, the island had its own secrets.

"Maybe I should stay with you?" Guy suggested, eager to please his temporary boss.

"Go," Aleksandr replied impatiently. "Stop bothering me. We will catch up when we're ready."

Guy jumped. He was hot and sweaty, and the last thing he wanted was to annoy the man responsible for the large tip he expected at the end of the trip.

Lori and Luca had already taken off. To Manuel's

consternation, the rest of the group were beginning to scatter. Manuel hated it when that happened. Didn't they realize that *he* was the tour guide? They should be following him, listening to his every word as he described the wonders of the island.

But no, it was not to be. This group had their own ideas.

The lush waterfalls made the perfect backdrop for Bianca to do a slow, sensual striptease for her Russian lover. Not that she had much to take off. Merely an oversized T-shirt and a tiny Brazilian string bikini.

But Bianca knew how to milk it, and Aleksandr appreciated every single minute of her seductive play as she stripped down for him.

They were under the impression that everyone had gone off on the tour, but unbeknownst to them, Hammond had lingered behind, loitering under cover of several lush palm trees.

Watching the enticing Bianca as she put on a show for her lover, Hammond was mesmerized by her long slinky legs, small breasts with large dark nipples, tiny waist, and glistening coffee-colored skin.

He felt himself harden as the supermodel sauntered naked into the water.

And when Aleksandr stripped off and followed her in, Hammond was mortified to discover that his host was hung like a horse.

He immediately felt woefully inadequate. Wasn't it enough that the man was a billionaire? Jesus Christ! Some men had it all.

For a moment he forgot about jerking off and concentrated on the way Aleksandr seized Bianca from behind and began pounding into her, moving her toward the cascading waterfall, both of them oblivious to anything except making love. Or fucking. Because yes, that's what they were doing: fucking like a couple of wild animals.

Hammond couldn't help himself; he came in his pants like a thirteen-year-old schoolboy.

"Shit!" he muttered under his breath, attempting to clean himself up.

What if anyone had seen him? He was a United States senator, for crissakes, not some Peeping Tom getting his rocks off in the bushes.

Humiliated and furious with himself, Hammond quickly set off to find the others.

53

Sierra decided that she should call her sister. They'd always been close, just not close enough for Sierra to share what was actually going on in her marriage. She wasn't about to do so now, but since Clare had been excited when she'd mentioned the trip, she knew that her sister would enjoy hearing all about the famous guests and the luxurious yacht.

With a firm step, she headed for the satellite communication center, passing the security room where Kyril, Aleksandr's fierce bodyguard, sat, surrounded by security cameras. *What a strange man,* she thought. *Quite frightening, really.*

Captain Dickson greeted her with a jovial "Good morning, Mrs. Patterson. And how are we on this very fine day?"

She gave the captain a warm smile; it was such a relief not to be operating from a fog-filled daze. "I'd like to make a call," she said. "Is that okay?"

"Certainly," Captain Dickson replied, thinking that the senator's wife appeared to be a lot more cheerful than when she'd first boarded. Sierra Patterson was a beauty, as were all the female passengers. It was nice to see her looking as if she might enjoy herself. "Allow me to escort you," he added, gallantly holding out his arm.

"Thank you, Captain," she said, dazzling him with her smile.

* * *

After standing under the shower trying to get his thoughts together, Flynn set off to find Sierra. He was more determined than ever to clear things up. Maybe that way he could finally forget about her and move on. It was quite clear that she'd experienced no difficulty doing exactly that. She'd married Hammond Patterson, for crissakes. Surely that was enough to make him forget her?

No way.

Somewhat pissed off at himself, he took the circular staircase to the middle deck, where he spotted Jeromy lounging on a chair. Immediately he did an about-face, heading back downstairs. Not that he had anything against gays—Luca seemed like a great guy—but there was something about Jeromy he couldn't stomach. You didn't have to be a genius to notice that the man was a first-class ass kisser. It was patently obvious, and if there was one type of person Flynn abhorred, it was ass kissers.

Unfortunately, Jeromy saw him and called out, "Flynn, is that you? I thought you went on the jolly old island expedition."

Why was everyone bugging him about that? Who cared?

He threw Jeromy a halfhearted wave as he hurriedly dodged out of sight.

Finding Sierra, that's all he was interested in.

While Sierra was speaking to her sister, the captain informed her that Eddie March was on the line requesting to speak with the senator.

"I'll take it," she said, saying a quick good-bye to Clare, who'd been thrilled to hear from her. "What's going on?" she asked Eddie, aware that Hammond had informed him that he was not to be bothered unless it was urgent.

"Nothing for you to be concerned about," Eddie said, trying not to sound too agitated. "I should talk to Hammond."

"He's off the yacht on a day trip. Won't be back until later." She paused for a moment. "What is it? Perhaps I can relay a message."

Not this message, Eddie thought. *Oh no, certainly not this message.*

"It doesn't matter," he said quickly. "Have him call me as soon as he can."

"If it's urgent . . ."

"Not urgent," Eddie said, feeling mighty uncomfortable about having to lie to Sierra. "Just make sure he contacts me."

"I'll do that, but it might not be today."

"Fine," Eddie said, although it wasn't fine. How long could he stall the Byrnes before they took action? They were threatening all kind of moves, such as contacting a TV news station or *The Washington Post.* Eddie had somehow or other convinced them to do nothing until they heard the senator's side of the story.

Right now he also couldn't wait to hear what Hammond would have to say about the situation. How out of control and stupid could one man be?

Pretty damn stupid.

"Hey," Flynn said, finally coming face-to-face with Sierra as she exited the communications room.

"Flynn," she murmured softly. Suddenly it all came flooding back and she couldn't help remembering all the fantastic times they'd shared in the past, the amazing love they'd once had for each other, their incredible love-making, which had resulted in her becoming pregnant.

Oh God! A pregnancy Flynn had never found out about.

What would he say if he discovered the truth? She'd lost their baby, but it wasn't her fault. She'd been in a car with Hammond, and there was the accident . . .

Guilt overcame her.

"Yeah," Flynn said with a rueful sigh. "Once again, it really is me."

"I didn't doubt it," she replied, thinking how much he would hate her if he unearthed the truth.

"You, uh . . . look lovely," he said, noting that she seemed a lot better than the previous night.

"Thank you," she said, making a determined effort to pull herself together and not fall to pieces.

"Uh . . . I was thinking that maybe we should talk," he said, clearing his throat, nervous for the first time in God knew how many years, which was odd, because he didn't get nervous—it simply wasn't on his agenda.

"I think we should," she said, nodding her head, although she wasn't sure if she wanted to talk to him; it wasn't as if it would solve anything.

"Well," he said, "since this seems like the perfect opportunity, why don't we go up to the top deck. I don't think there's anyone around up there."

She nodded again, feeling breathless, and yet strangely excited at the same time.

Closure. It was exactly what she'd been waiting for all these years. And now that it was about to happen, she wondered if she was capable of handling the situation. Thank God Hammond wasn't present to get in her way. It was just her and Flynn, exactly how it should be. So yes, she *could* handle it.

They headed upstairs, and settled on facing comfortable chairs in the all-glass atrium. For a few minutes, they made stilted conversation until he finally said, "So, Sierra, all these years later, here we are."

"Yes, here we are," she agreed, glancing out at the endless blue sea. "What a place to meet up. It's so unbelievably breathtaking."

"Better than some of the places I've experienced," he said dryly.

"I know about the places you've been," she blurted.

"I've followed your career on your Web site, read your newsletters."

"You did, huh?" he said, surprised and more than a little pleased.

"Yes, Flynn," she murmured, thinking that getting older suited him. He was more handsome than ever, with his intense blue eyes and strong jawline.

"I'm flattered," he said.

"In spite of what happened," she said softly, "I always had this crazy urge to keep you in my life."

They exchanged a long, intimate look.

"Hey, I kept tabs on you too," he said at last, finally breaking the look. "But I was shocked when I read you'd married Hammond." He took a long, steady beat. "I guess it must've started between you and him when I left for London. And then I got the photos." He stared at her intently. "Tell me, Sierra, was that the only way you could think of breaking up with me? 'Cause it was pretty damn shitty."

"Excuse me?" she said, frowning. What on earth was he talking about? It was *he* who'd broken up with *her*.

"The photos," he said insistently. "Why'd you do it?"

"Funny, that's exactly what I was about to ask you," she said, her eyes burning bright. This was a crazy conversation, and she didn't like it.

"Ask me what?" he said, puzzled.

"Look, I understand we were both kids back then," she said, desperately trying to stay in control of her emotions. "But sending me those photos was such a cruel thing to do. I couldn't believe you would do something like that."

"What the fuck are you talking about?" he said, his temper rising. "*You* were the one who sent *me* photos."

"Oh, come on, Flynn," she sighed. "I didn't send you anything."

"*Somebody* sent them. And while we're on the subject," he said heatedly, "it might interest you to know that you broke my fucking heart."

"No, Flynn," she said, torn between tears, guilt, and anger. "You broke mine."

"Oh yeah? Photos of you making out with other guys, including Ham—"

"Are you serious? I never made out with anyone, *especially* not Hammond. He was there for me when I needed him, it was purely platonic, and let's not forget that it was *you* who asked him to watch out for me."

"Yeah? Then how do you explain the photos?" he said roughly. "What's your story?"

"How do *you*?" she said indignantly. "*You* were the one with girls draped all over you."

"*What* girls?" he said, perplexed.

"The ones in the photos."

"Now hold on," he said, realizing that they were definitely talking at cross-purposes. "Are you telling me that *you* got photos too?"

"What do you mean, 'too'?"

"I mean that someone sent *me* photos of you with other men."

"And someone sent *me* photos of you with a whole bunch of naked girls."

"Jesus Christ!" he exclaimed, smacking his forehead. "There were never any other girls after I met you. I swear it. And there were sure as hell never any photos."

"Then . . . what?" she questioned, confused and upset, wishing she were somewhere else.

"Fuck!" he said, realization dawning. "Whoever sent the photos must've been out to break us up."

"Why would anyone want to do that?"

"Jesus!" he exclaimed, shaking his head. "And here's the kicker—like a couple of morons, we both fell for it. How stupid is that?"

"I don't understand," she said, her eyes widening.

"No, but I'm beginning to," he said grimly, getting up and pacing around. "Don't you get it? We were set up."

"How is that possible?"

"Who knows? But I'm sure as hell going to figure it out. What did you do with the photos you got?"

"I destroyed them."

"Yeah, that's what I did, and you know something else? Whoever sent them *knew* that's what we'd do."

"You think?"

"I know, 'cause here's the deal: they must've been fakes."

"But you were *in* the photos, Flynn. I saw them."

"So were you, sweetheart. With several guys. Want to address *that*?"

"It's impossible."

"And in one of them you were with Ham."

As soon as he said Hammond's name, it suddenly all became clear. Ham had always been jealous of his relationship with Sierra; he'd often claimed that since he'd seen Sierra first she should've been with *him*. When that logic didn't get him anywhere, he'd taken to speaking badly about her at any opportunity, calling her all kinds of sick names. It was college guy's shit, but Flynn had made sure it never got back to her.

Then when he'd left for London, Hammond had obviously moved right in and seized his opportunity, lying to her that Flynn had asked him to watch out for her. What a low-down sneaky son of a bitch.

"You're not going to like this," Flynn said, trying to keep his anger under control. "But I think I've figured out exactly what happened."

"You have?" she said tentatively. "Please share."

"You and I were taken for one big ride. And you know who was manipulating it all?"

"Who?"

"Your future husband."

Sierra felt her heart accelerate. *Hammond* was responsible? Could this possibly be true?

She could only come up with one answer.

Yes. For Hammond had proved that he was capable of anything.

54

"It's time to move," Cruz announced over breakfast in Acapulco.

"Move where?" asked Ina, channeling her best Salma Hayek in a formfitting turquoise dress, her overly large breasts spilling out, nipples permanently erect—the result of her breast-enlargement surgery.

"Nothin' to do with you," Sergei said, slurping strong black coffee from a ceramic mug. "Me and your brother got business to conduct. You stay out of it."

Ina frowned; if it weren't for her, Sergei never would have met Cruz. She knew for a fact that they'd done many a deal together, so shouldn't she be getting a commission? Or, at the very least, shouldn't Sergei be dumping the American *puta* he kept stashed in his Mexico City apartment and start thinking of marrying *her*? It wasn't right. She felt insulted.

Now her brother and Sergei were planning something big, and they didn't care to tell her what it was, which infuriated her.

Fortunately, she'd learned the art of spying from her brother, and she knew their plan had something to do with a yacht they were about to hijack and hold for ransom. A yacht that was cruising the Sea of Cortez. A little off Cruz's regular beat, but she supposed he knew what he was doing. Her brother had *cojones* the size of Cuba.

Ina had always had a bit of a crush on Cruz, although he'd never paid her much attention. Her brother was more exciting than Sergei, who had a vicious temper and wasn't that adventurous in bed. Sergei had never gone down on her, and several of Cruz's conquests had confided in the past that her brother was a master in that department.

Truth was that if Cruz *wasn't* her brother, she would've definitely had the hots for him. Too bad they were related.

Forbidden love. Why was it forbidden when it seemed so right?

"We leave tonight," Cruz said.

"About time," Sergei said.

"Where we goin'?" Ina inquired.

Both men ignored her.

Sergei had arranged to rent a villa on a very large private estate outside of Cabo. A sprawling villa off the beaten track, with beach access and no neighbors. Cruz's team of misfits had already taken up residence, busily preparing for their strike against the *Bianca,* making sure they had everything they needed. Two powerful speedboats, supplies, rifles, guns.

Cruz had trained them well. His men were Somalians who spoke no English, but they sure as hell understood exactly what he wanted. Over the last few years, he'd made them richer than they could ever have imagined. He was their boss, and they did whatever they were instructed to do.

Sergei was unknown to them. However, if Cruz indicated he was the man, as long as there was money to be made, they were prepared to work for him too.

Sergei brought several of his personal bodyguards to the villa. Stoic men of Russian descent, they did not mix with the Somalians—they considered themselves way too superior.

The plan had not included taking Ina with them, but

since she apparently knew more than she should, Sergei had finally agreed that it would be better if she came.

Cruz had not objected. What did he care? His sister could make herself useful; she could keep Sergei busy in the bedroom and out of his way.

When taking over a boat, everyone had to know what they were doing. Gaining control was a fast and furious thing—there could be no mistakes. Cruz did not relish the thought of taking Sergei along on the ride the day they hit the *Bianca*. Sergei wasn't a professional hijacker, which meant he could well turn out to be a liability. Unfortunately, Sergei had insisted he be present. "I yearn for the joy of watchin' Aleksandr Kasianenko's fuckin' face when we take over his yacht," he'd growled. "That bastard is responsible for my brother's death, and now I will see that he pays."

The details of exactly how Aleksandr would pay were still milling around in Sergei's head.

It would be long and painful. Of that he was sure.

55

Lori was basking in her time with Luca, because even though he was a huge star and world-famous, he was so down-to-earth and so much fun. She couldn't help wondering what he was doing with the crusty uptight Englishman who had practically ignored her all through last night's dinner. What could Luca possibly see in Jeromy Milton-Gold? Jeromy was not even that attractive, with his long thin nose and small squinty eyes. And judging from the previous evening, he certainly wasn't loaded with charm.

The island was such an idyllic paradise; Lori kept on wishing that Cliff had come with her. It was an experience not to be missed. On the other hand, Luca seemed quite happy that his significant other had failed to make the effort, and she could understand why.

"Jeromy's not like us," Luca confided. "He's more into indoor activities, if you get what I mean."

"Sex?" Lori questioned, tilting her head.

"Not my kind of sex," Luca retorted, grimacing.

"You're gay," Lori said boldly. "Doesn't that mean you're up for anything?"

"Not me," Luca said quickly. "I'm a one-on-one kinda guy."

"Yet the one you've chosen is Jeromy."

"Here's the situation," Luca explained. "I fell straight out of the closet into his arms. He kind of took me over."

After a meaningful pause, he added, "Lately, I've been thinking it might be time to break away."

"Why?" she asked curiously. "Have you met someone else?"

"No, but Jeromy's lifestyle's not for me."

"And you've only just realized this?"

"Y'know, Lori," he said thoughtfully, "sometimes it takes a while to figure things out."

She nodded, feeling immensely flattered that Luca felt free to reveal his true feelings to her. They barely knew each other, and it wasn't as if she was famous or anything. Obviously he liked her, and that made her feel as if she belonged. This trip was turning out to be better than she'd expected.

"I guess being away from everything is the perfect time to think things through," she offered.

Luca ran his hand through his mop of thick blond hair. "Right," he agreed. "An' that's exactly what I'm doing."

"Then I hope for your sake that you reach the right conclusion."

"Oh, I will," he said, nodding to himself. "And you, Lori," he added, "what's up with you and Cliff Baxter?"

"Uh . . . well," she answered hesitantly. "We've been together a year."

"Where's it going? Or should I ask, where do you *want* it to go?"

"I don't know. I'm not sure," she mumbled. "It's, uh . . . complicated."

"Marriage? Children?" Luca persisted.

"Cliff's not the marrying kind," she explained.

"That doesn't mean you can't change his mind." Luca paused for a moment. "Is it something you want?"

Before she could answer, Hammond came lumbering up to them, his T-shirt drenched in sweat, his face pink from the heat, his brown hair plastered to his forehead.

Lori was relieved to be off the hook; the conversation was getting a little too personal for her liking.

"Goddammit!" Hammond complained, swatting at a flying bug. "I need to throw myself in the ocean. Isn't it time we turned back?"

Jeromy was bored. He hadn't come on this voyage to sit by himself in solitary splendor while his boyfriend ran off to an island with most of the other guests.

Jeromy did not sunbathe. His skin and the sun did not mix, so instead of becoming a sun-burnished god like Luca, he usually ended up resembling a dried-up old lobster. Not an attractive look, and one he planned to avoid.

Mercedes, the feisty stewardess, was attentive, offering him drinks and snacks whenever he felt like it. The problem was that food and drink did not alleviate boredom.

Mercedes. What kind of a name was that anyway? A Mexican girl named after a German car. How ridiculous. It was exactly the sort of moronic name movie stars bestowed on their offspring.

Thinking of movie stars, Jeromy wondered where Cliff Baxter had vanished to. Earlier they'd enjoyed a most cordial chat—surely there was more to come? Perhaps Cliff had a house in L.A. that needed redecorating. Or a New York penthouse ready for renovation. Or maybe he could use his persuasive powers to talk Cliff into purchasing a London town house.

Ah . . . Jeromy Milton-Gold, designer to the stars. It had a nice ring to it.

Mercedes appeared again. There was something about the girl that was annoying. Perhaps she wasn't subservient enough for his liking. Or perhaps she was just plain cheap.

He wondered if she screwed the passengers on the side. He wouldn't put it past her—she had that dirty girl air about her. Maybe she'd even had a go at the movie star while his cheap redheaded girlfriend was cavorting somewhere on the island with Luca.

"Where is Mr. Baxter?" Jeromy inquired, peering down his nose at her.

"Ah, you mean Señor Cliff," Mercedes said, purposely irritating him.

"No, I mean *Mr.* Baxter," Jeromy said sternly, putting her in her place. "You should *never* call guests by their first names. It's extremely rude."

Mercedes stifled a strong urge to tell him to piss off. Her time would come, and when it did, she planned to clean this one out, and maybe shove a plunger up his bony ass for good measure. Except this particular *hijo de puta* would probably enjoy it.

"Señor Cliff *asked* me to use his first name," she said innocently.

"I don't *care* what he asked you," Jeromy admonished. "It is simply not done. You are in service here. Learn, dear, it is to your advantage."

Come mierda, Mercedes thought as she smiled sweetly at Jeromy, deciding that his expensive watch might make a nice birthday present for her next conquest.

Being on the island was making Taye hornier than ever. Getting Ashley out of London and away from it all was a major move. She wasn't all Miss Design Queen and mummy to the twins, she was more like the girl he'd fallen in love with, the free spirit who got off on sexual adventures and was never averse to giving a blow job or two. Taye had to admit that getting oral sex from his wife was his favorite activity. He relished the thought of shoving Mammoth into Ashley's delicate mouth, and holding her head in place while she sucked the life out of him. Before marriage it had been a daily occurrence. After marriage it had become a special treat. And for the last few months it hadn't happened at all, until last night, when Ashley had excelled at doing what she did better than any other girl he'd been with.

Now he wanted more, and the island seemed like the perfect setup for a quick bit of sex. Ashley looked so hot in her cover-up T-shirt, her big tits sticking out, long legs on parade. Last night he'd made love to her for as long as she could take it, then he'd gone down on her and she'd moaned her appreciation. Frankly, he couldn't keep his hands off his wife.

"Hey, toots," he whispered, grabbing her hand, "follow me. Just saw somethin' you wouldn't wanna miss."

"What?" Ashley said, marveling at a pair of giant turtles crawling along in front of them; it was quite a sight.

"Back here," Taye said, steering her away from the others and toward a cluster of tall swaying palm trees.

"What?" Ashley repeated, slightly irritated.

Taye didn't give her time to think. He went for her nipples, playing with them in a way that never failed to turn her on.

"Taye!" she objected. "Not here!"

"Why not?" he said, squeezing and twirling.

"'Cause the others might see." Two seconds and then—"Oh . . . my . . . *God*!"

He had her. Quick as a flash he whipped out Mammoth, still keeping up the tit action.

"Go for it, baby," he encouraged, pushing her to her knees.

"Taye . . ." she began.

He stifled her objections with Mammoth, and within two delicious minutes he'd achieved a memorable orgasm, leaving Ashley wanting more. Which was fine with him, because he'd be happy to finish the job of satisfying her later.

As far as Taye was concerned, this was turning out to be the perfect trip.

After skimming through two scripts—both of them disappointing—Cliff realized that he did indeed miss Lori. It was his loss not to have gone on the island trip. Every day shouldn't be about work, and reading scripts was actually work. Before leaving L.A. he'd had his agent, his manager, and Enid all on his case about all the scripts he should read.

"I think you should seriously consider the spy movie," his agent had said.

"We need to make decisions," his manager had informed him.

"You'll be bored with Lori before you know it," Enid had lectured. "See if you can make a dent in those scripts you've got piling up. I've packed them all for you."

Wasn't he supposed to be on vacation with his girlfriend? Why not relax and enjoy it? To hell with work.

Cliff decided that for the next few days he was going to lie back and let himself go with the flow.

"What are we going to do?" Sierra questioned.

Flynn loved the fact that she was referring to them as "we." He shrugged. "I dunno what your situation is with Ham. You've been married a long time." He paused for a moment, then gazed at her intently. "Are you happy?"

"So!" she exclaimed, refusing to meet his eyes. "Just like that, we've gone from not talking for years to whether I'm happy. I'm confused, that's what I am."

"You're not answering my question."

"Are *you* happy, Flynn?" she said pointedly, finally looking at him. "I guess you must be. Your girlfriend seems smart enough and pretty."

"Xuan is not my girlfriend," he muttered.

"You're sharing a cabin," she was quick to remind him.

"It's a long story," he said, ridiculously pleased that she sounded vaguely jealous.

Sierra was now staring at him, unsure of what to say. Should she admit that she was miserable? Should she tell him the truth?

Oh God, she felt so vulnerable. Too much time had passed; they were both grown-ups now. Could she trust

Flynn? What if the whole fake-photos thing was merely a fantasy, a convenient story he'd made up to explain the way he'd treated her?

Was Hammond responsible? At first she'd had no doubts, but why would he do such a thing? *How* could he? She realized that she would have to confront him—it was the only way to get to the real truth.

"I'm kind of tired," she said at last. "I need to spend some time alone thinking things through."

"I understand," Flynn said, realizing that pushing her was not a good idea. "It's a lot to take in. For both of us."

"Yes, it is," she answered quietly.

And where do we go from here? he felt like asking. *Just friends, lovers no more? What's the deal, Sierra? Is there a future for us?*

Was he experiencing an urge to go back in time, rekindle the feelings they'd once had for each other?

Did he still want her?

His heart said yes.

His head said no.

Whether the photos were fake or not still didn't explain the fact that she'd been pregnant with Ham's baby when she and Ham were involved in a car accident. She'd told him that they were merely platonic friends, so how come the pregnancy? Obviously she had no idea he knew.

Jesus Christ! Why was this happening? Why was Sierra back in his life? Just when he'd gotten together with Mai in Paris and thought that maybe he was finally over Sierra, this had to happen.

Too fucking bad. He could deal with it.

He had no choice.

56

Muttering under his breath, Manuel led the rich ones back to the beach and the tenders that awaited them. He considered his current group of affluent tourists a bunch of low-life animals, although animals would never behave in such a disrespectful and lustful way.

Did the tall black man think that nobody noticed when he pulled the large-breasted blonde behind the palm trees and made her do something to him that only *putas* indulged in?

And the big Russian man having sex with the dark girl under the waterfall. Disgraceful. Couldn't they wait until they were home and it was nighttime like normal people?

Manuel was thankful for his wife and daughters. They were fine upstanding women; they would never behave in such a lewd and filthy fashion.

As the tourists got into the boats, Guy handed Manuel a healthy tip.

He took it, vowing to himself that he would go back to fishing for a living rather than continue to deal with people like this. These people contaminated him with their unbridled libidos and sexual perversions. He was a simple man, and he preferred a simple life.

Hammond jumped into the boat right behind Lori, sitting himself down beside her.

"I bet you're ready for a nice warm shower," he said, edging close. "Get all that sand out of your pretty little cooch."

"Excuse me?" Lori said, not sure she'd heard him correctly.

Hammond gave an easy chuckle. "No offense," he said smoothly. "That's what my mother used to say after a day trip to the beach. Of course, *our* beach was in the Hamptons, but that's another story."

Lori stared at him; she wasn't sure how to respond.

"You are a *very* pretty girl," Hammond continued, his eyes undressing her. "Quite the temptress."

Cliff had warned her that politicians were horny bastards, and apparently he was right. At first she'd been flattered by Hammond's attention, but now she was totally turned off; there was something off-putting about this one.

"It's too bad your wife couldn't come today," she said, putting the emphasis on the word *wife*.

"Yes," Hammond replied. "She's quite . . . delicate."

"Really?" Lori said sharply. "She doesn't look delicate."

"I know," Hammond said with a put-upon sigh. "It's a personal burden I carry." A meaningful pause, then a lowering of his voice. "Between us, Lori, Sierra has, uh . . . emotional issues. It's the sad truth I live with."

What was this? Confide in Lori Day? "Sorry to hear that," she said, brushing sand off her bare leg while not believing him at all.

Hammond leaned over, his fingers lightly touching her upper thigh.

She quickly jerked back.

"You missed a bit," he explained.

"No, I didn't," she snapped.

"I apologize," he said. "I was merely being helpful."

She was saved by Taye and Ashley, who piled into the tender. Taye was grinning as if he were eight years old and had just gotten a new bike for Christmas. Ashley seemed a bit flustered.

"Wish I'd brought a camera," Lori mused, edging away from the senator.

"Me too," said Ashley, not quite as aloof as usual.

"We could probably sell our pics to the tabloids for a fortune," Lori joked, immediately realizing it was a dumb thing to come out with.

"I don't think so," Ashley said tartly, exchanging a look with Taye as if to say *I told you she was low-rent*.

"Uh . . . I was joking, of course," Lori muttered, totally embarrassed.

"I have a hunch that our host wouldn't find it particularly funny," Ashley said as the tender took off, bouncing over the waves at a brisk pace.

"Lay off, toots," Taye whispered in Ashley's ear. "Give the kid a break."

Ashley ignored him; she was too busy thinking about what dress she would wear to dinner. Something dazzling. Something to catch Cliff Baxter's eye, because she was quite sure that he fancied her. And why not? She was certainly way sexier than his girlfriend.

Sierra was tempted to reach for the Xanax as she awaited her husband's return. She stared longingly at the bottle of vodka Hammond had so thoughtfully ordered brought to their room. Hammond preferred to see her medicated, whether it be from pills or booze. That way he felt he was in complete control.

She managed to resist both temptations. Instead, she sat by herself in their stateroom, dredging up every memory she could about the photos, and the way Hammond had attached himself to her after Flynn had left for London, claiming that Flynn had *asked* him to look out for her. What a lie that had turned out to be. According to Flynn, he had asked no such thing.

So . . . if Hammond had lied about that, what else?

The photos, of course. She'd shown them to him, and he'd carried on about how he'd always known Flynn was a cheater, and that he hadn't wanted to upset her, but now that she'd seen the proof with her own eyes . . .

Next he'd insisted on destroying the photos, taken them from her along with the typewritten note. Then he'd tried to talk her into getting an abortion.

Oh God! Of course. If the photos *were* fakes, naturally he hadn't wanted her studying them. And if he envisioned her as his future political asset, then Flynn's baby would certainly not factor into his plans.

Had he crashed his car on purpose? Had he *wanted* her to lose Flynn's baby? She shuddered at the thought.

Now that she knew what kind of man Hammond really was, she wouldn't put anything past him. He was an evil man hiding beneath the cloak of a political do-gooder.

When Hammond returned from the island trip, she was ready to face him. He barged into their stateroom spewing complaints about the heat and the bugs and how he'd had no chance to speak privately to Aleksandr. "I deserve more respect from these people," he complained. "I am a United States senator, for crissakes. I am destined for great things. If they expect any future favors, they should be aware of who they're dealing with."

The man or the monster? she wanted to say. However, she controlled herself.

"Hammond," she said evenly.

"Sierra," he said, mocking her tone as he threw off his sweat-stained T-shirt.

"I need to ask you a question."

"Do you now?" he said, pulling down his shorts and underwear, showing not a shred of modesty.

"Seeing Flynn reminded me of those photos."

"What photos?" he snapped, absentmindedly stroking his balls as he headed toward the bathroom.

"The ones you faked in college," she said bravely. "The ones you sent to me and Flynn."

"What?" Stopping at the bathroom door, he turned around and faced her.

"I was wondering how you managed such a clever job," Sierra continued. "I mean, it was before Photoshop and all the technology we have today. Did you hire a professional to help you?"

Hammond stared her down, his eyes menacing slits of anger. "Have you been talking to that son of a bitch?" he demanded.

"What son of a bitch would that be?" she answered, remaining calm.

"Do not get smart with me, woman," he said angrily. "I warned you not to speak to him."

"You warn me about a lot of things," she said, keeping her tone even. "However, we are on a yacht in the middle of an ocean, and I think I can do whatever I like."

Hammond could not believe the change in her. What the hell was going on? She seemed sober and together, not foggy and compliant. This was unlike the woman he'd grown used to. The woman who never dared to argue. The woman he'd managed to control with his constant threats of harm to her family.

"You think you can do whatever you like, do you?" he said, his voice harsh and unforgiving. "Perhaps you're forgetting who you are. You are my wife, and *as* my wife you do what *I* tell you to do, or"—he paused momentarily, his eyes narrowing even more—"you know the consequences."

"For God's sake, Hammond. How long are you going to keep this up?"

"What's come over you, Sierra? Suddenly all brave because you talked to an old boyfriend? Do you think *he* can save you? Your family? And even more important, can Flynn save himself? Think about *that* for a moment." He paused and glared at her threateningly. "One phone call, and I can make his life a nightmare. I can make sure he never works again. I can have his legs broken, his pretty face smashed in. You know I can."

"It's over, Hammond," she said, her voice steady. "The moment we get off this boat, I'm leaving you. And I will make sure everyone hears about your threats, so that if anything happens to me *or* my family, the finger will be pointed at you."

"Keep it up, dear, and we will *see* what happens," Hammond jeered.

With those words, he stalked into the bathroom and slammed the door shut.

"How was it?" Cliff asked when Lori returned to their stateroom.

"Oh my God, you were so right about the senator," she replied, flopping down on the bed. "He's a randy piece of work."

"Told you so," Cliff said. "I can spot 'em a mile off."

"But Cliff, the island was *fantastic*. I wish you could've seen it. *So* beautiful, like something out of a movie. And deserted. No houses. No people. Nothing except wildlife, greenery, and these amazing waterfalls. Oh, and giant turtles," she continued excitedly. "You would've *loved* it. I wish you'd come with us."

Cliff was pleased to see Lori so animated, like a little kid who'd just experienced her first trip to Disneyland. Sometimes he forgot how young she was. Twenty-four. A mere child. Young enough to be his daughter. Yet old enough to be his lover.

And why exactly did he think it was time to trade her in for a younger, fresher face? Because he was Cliff Baxter? Because he was a star who had to maintain a certain image? To impress his male friends and acquaintances? For his adoring public?

It was all bullshit. He liked Lori; he was comfortable with her. No need for a trade-in at this time.

"Listen, toots, have I told you lately how much I love you?" Taye said, raising his head from between his wife's thighs to take a deep breath.

"Oh, for God's sake—don't stop now!" Ashley intoned,

lying spread-eagled on the bed in their stateroom, luxuri-
ating as she experienced the expertise of her husband's
talented tongue.

"But I do love you so *much*," Taye insisted. "You're *it*
for me. No other woman. Ever."

"Okay, okay, then how about you get on with the job at
hand," Ashley implored impatiently. "I'm almost there."

"You got it," Taye answered, grinning.

This trip was doing their marriage nothing but good.

"About time you got back," Jeromy said, his tone quite
snippy.

Luca threw himself down on the bed.

"Please!" Jeromy said, curling his lip. "You're all
sweaty and nasty. Can you at least take a shower before
you mess up our bed?"

Luca placed his hands behind his head and stretched;
he had no intention of moving. "You made a mistake not
coming," he remarked, wishing he were still on the magical island.

"I think not," Jeromy replied. "Staying on board was
very advantageous for me. I had quite a long chat with
Cliff Baxter, and he might be on the verge of hiring me to
design the interior of his next house."

"Is he buying a new house?" Luca said. "Lori never
mentioned it."

"Since when are you so tight with that Lori person?"
Jeromy inquired, feeling quite envious that Luca was
busy making friends while he languished on the yacht.

"I saved her from the hands of the horny senator,"
Luca said. "And don't call her 'that Lori person.' If you
took the time to get to know her, you'd realize she's a very
sweet girl."

"Changing tracks, are we?" Jeromy said contemptu-
ously. "Dying to sneak your way into her dirty little
panties?"

"Try not to turn into a bitchy queen," Luca replied.

"Excuse me?" Jeromy huffed. "A bitchy queen indeed!"

"You know what I mean."

"How dare you!"

"How dare I what?" Luca said flatly.

"Call me names."

"Jeromy," Luca said, giving him a long, cool look. "We really need to talk."

The dreaded words—*we really need to talk*. Jeromy had heard them before, and more than once. First from his father, a stern civil servant who'd beaten him unmercifully when he'd first come out. Then from the college professor at Oxford he'd been desperately in love with. Next from the septuagenarian marquis who'd kept him as his pet for several years. And finally from the "closeted" businessman who'd financed his design firm until the man's wife had found out what was really going on between them and called a halt to all financial dealings.

Now from Luca.

No. This couldn't be happening. Luca was his future. They would grow old together. They would enjoy Luca's fame and money together. This *couldn't* happen. He would not allow it.

One way or another, Jeromy was determined to stop the inevitable.

57

For the night's festivities, Bianca had requested a Spanish theme. Guy was on it—he'd arranged for musicians and a well-known Spanish chef famous for his seafood paella to be boated in from the mainland, even though they were several hours out at sea. He'd been informed up front that no expense was to be spared on this trip. Only the best for Aleksandr Kasianenko and his lady. Guy was sure that if Bianca requested that Wolfgang Puck be flown in from California to prepare his famous smoked salmon pizza, Aleksandr would oblige.

At sunset, Bianca appeared on deck, a true dazzler in a flounced flamenco dress, white flowers in her jet hair. Aleksandr accompanied her. He wasn't a man to dress up—his usual black pants and a white shirt did it for him.

Guy was a tad envious, because once again they made a ferociously handsome couple. Between them they had everything. Looks, money, power, fame. It wasn't fair that two people had so much.

Still, he was used to it. Serving the privileged. Catering to their every need. Watching them at play. Hoping for a major tip at the end of the journey. It was the life he'd chosen, and it wasn't such a bad one.

At least he had a steady partner who professed true love. They shared a cozy apartment in Sydney, and whenever Guy was home—which was not that often—they were quite compatible and took pleasure in doing the same things.

Yes, Guy was satisfied, although he couldn't help having lust in his heart (not to mention his pants) for the gorgeous Luca Perez. What a true specimen of magnificent manhood. And talented too. Guy had Luca's latest song repeating on his iPod; it soothed him during times of stress.

By the time Hammond emerged from the shower, Sierra was no longer in their stateroom.

Dammit! Where was the devious bitch, his cheating wife, the slut who'd been talking to her ex-boyfriend?

His fury was dark and cold. Did Sierra honestly think she could escape from him just like that? A divorce—even a separation—would ruin his political future. No way would he ever allow that to happen.

One day he was going to run for president, and whether she liked it or not, she *would* support him—dead or alive.

"What happened to you?" Xuan asked when she returned to their stateroom and found Flynn there. "You could've told me you were leaving the island."

"I got the runs," he answered, still thinking about his conversation with Sierra.

"You seem to be better now," Xuan remarked, opening the closet to see if she could rustle up an outfit to wear for dinner. The women on this trip were so impeccably groomed and well dressed. Her choices were limited since she traveled so light, and quite frankly she couldn't care less. Leave it to the others to prance around in their fancy clothes; she knew that she was smarter and more caring about what was going on in the world than all of them put together.

"Yeah, I am," Flynn said, frustrated that he had to share the same space with Xuan. Much as he valued her friendship, he needed to be alone to think things through. He didn't appreciate Xuan questioning him, and he was sure that she would; it was her way. "I'll see you upstairs," he added, heading for the door.

"You know, Flynn, you should be careful what you wish for," Xuan said sagely. "Wishes do not always provide the answers we crave."

"Thanks for that," he said dryly. "It makes no sense at all."

"Think about it," she called after him. "You're too clever to get caught up in your own fantasies."

Ignoring Xuan's words, Flynn ran into Taye and his blond wife, all of them on their way to the drinks deck.

"You feelin' all right, mate?" Taye inquired, friendly as usual.

"Yeah, it was nothing," Flynn answered. "Something I ate."

"Ewh, nasty!" Ashley exclaimed, clinging to her husband's arm as they made their way up the circular staircase. "Remember, Taye, that time you got the runs on the field in front of thousands of fans?"

"Don't remind me," Taye groaned. "Talk about embarrassin'."

"Had to throw all your gear away." Ashley giggled. "Even your mum wouldn't go near it!"

"Thanks," Taye said, making a face. "You certainly know how to feed a bloke's ego."

"An' that's not all I can do," Ashley said, giggling suggestively.

Taye decided that on vacation, his wife was a whole other woman. And he liked this new Ashley a lot better than he did her former self.

Bianca surveyed her guests, all present for drinks with the exception of the senator. She observed that the senator's wife seemed more social tonight. Sierra was chatting with Cliff Baxter and Lori. Bianca was delighted to note that everyone was in a more relaxed state. Ah yes, the vacation vibe was taking over, and she couldn't be happier.

Aleksandr was at ease too, talking football with Taye, politics with the Asian woman—whom Bianca had secretly christened Miss Intensity.

Luca approached and clinked glasses with her. "You and old Alek certainly know how to throw a party," he remarked. "Everyone's having a great time."

"You too?" Bianca questioned.

"Why're you askin' me?" Luca said, pushing a lock of blond hair off his forehead.

"'Cause I know you," Bianca said, looking at him intently. "Something's on your mind. Spill."

"Okay, okay, the deal is, I'm missing my kid," he confessed. "I hate being away from him. You haven't seen him lately, Bianca. He's such a cute kid, an' I don't wanna miss anything."

"He's with Suga, right?"

"He sure is, an' she's a wonderful *mamacita*. The best. Warm and nurturing and everything she should be."

"Hmm . . . sounds as if you're missing her too," Bianca ruminated.

"Hey, I'm not missin' the sex; we gave that up pretty fast," Luca said. "But the companionship an' the fun we had together, yeah—that's what I miss."

"Well, you have Jeromy now," Bianca said sagely. "He seems like a laugh a minute."

"Ah . . . therein lies the problem," Luca admitted. "Jeromy."

"Trouble in gay city, huh?" Bianca said with a knowing nod.

"You could say there's more than trouble."

"Like what?"

"Problem is he hates Suga, an' not only that, he never pays any attention to Luca Junior. It's driving me loco."

"That's not good."

"No, it's not," Luca said, shaking his head. "If you really want the truth, I think I've finally had it with Jeromy. It's time for me to move on."

"Oh dear." Bianca sighed.

"Oh dear what?"

"We're on this very special cruise, Luca. Please don't ruin anything. Can you at least wait to dump him until we get back? Is that possible?"

"I guess I can try."

"For me," she pleaded. "No dramas."

"For you," Luca acquiesced. "Only please realize that the moment we hit dry land . . ."

"I know, I know. And you're the best!"

Luca gave a wry smile. "I try."

"Dinner is served." Once again Guy found himself saying the words he loved to hear himself speak.

Everyone gathered by the stairs and began making their way to the upper dining deck.

Sierra looked around and noted that Hammond was still absent. She wondered what he was doing. Busy planning another deluge of threats?

She shivered at the thought and determined to stay strong.

Flynn was there. She decided it was best not to talk to him. Hammond was too unpredictable—who knew what he was capable of? She didn't want Flynn getting involved in any way.

Fortunately, there were new seating arrangements. At the dinner table she found herself seated between Cliff and Luca, which suited her fine.

Hammond appeared before the first course was served. Barely glancing in her direction, he took his seat between Bianca and Ashley and immediately started talking to Bianca.

It seemed impossible, but was he going to accept the fact that she was moving on? Had he run out of threats? Was this the beginning of a new life for her?

She could only hope.

* * *

After dinner there were professional flamenco dancers for the guests' entertainment. Fierce-looking women with strong, sturdy thighs, and darkly rugged men exhibiting plenty of attitude.

Bianca sat close to Aleksandr, enjoying the festivities. Her hand lingered near his crotch—the sensual dancers were putting her in the mood.

Aleksandr absently removed her hand and turned to listen to Xuan, who, as far as Bianca could tell, was carrying on about something boring and political.

Bianca was irritated. Couples were now sitting next to each other in the entertainment area. How come Miss Intensity always managed to find a place next to Aleksandr?

Not that she was jealous. Oh no. The day she was jealous of another woman would be a day indeed.

Bianca possessed extreme confidence, and rightfully so. Her beauty was a given. Her looks had always taken her wherever she cared to go. No roadblocks. Green lights all the way. Covers of *Vogue, Harper's,* and *Vanity Fair.* Puff pieces in *People, Esquire,* even *Newsweek* and *Time.*

Bianca was the supermodel of all supermodels. A woman admired by women and lusted after by men.

Jealous. Ha! Although Aleksandr did seem to be quite taken with the petite Asian woman. Earlier he'd told Bianca that he found Xuan to be very interesting.

Interesting indeed! Bianca didn't like her; she was too serious by far. And what was with Xuan and her boyfriend? They barely appeared to notice each other. As far as Bianca could tell, there was no sexual chemistry between them, and that was strange because Flynn was smokin' hot.

She decided to pay attention to Flynn, find out what his deal was. Quietly she moved away from Aleksandr, who appeared unaware that she was on the move. He was too busy solving the problems of the world with Miss Intensity.

The flamenco music was loud, the dancers even louder and overly dramatic as they snaked their way around the dance floor stamping their feet and projecting fake passion.

Bianca made her way over to Flynn, who was sitting by himself. She squeezed up next to him determined to get to know him better. "How're you feeling?" she asked, putting on her sympathetic face.

He threw her a quizzical look. "Does the whole world know I had the runs?"

"The runs?"

"I'm quoting Ashley, a very eloquent young lady."

"With enormous tits," Bianca whispered, forming a bond between them.

"Yeah," he said wryly. "I had kind of noticed."

"You'd be gay if you hadn't," Bianca said, clicking her fingers for Mercedes or Renee, the two stewardesses who were always on duty.

Mercedes dutifully made her way over.

"Two shot glasses of limoncello," Bianca ordered, barely looking at her. "And bring the bottle."

Imperious bitch! Mercedes thought. *Puta!* She couldn't wait to see the expression on Bianca's face when Cruz's men took over the yacht. *Who'll be giving orders then?*

"I gather we're drinking," Flynn said, not averse to the thought.

"You look like you need a drink," Bianca observed.

"I do."

"Problems in paradise?" she inquired, probing gently.

"Huh?" he said, rubbing his stubbled chin.

"Well," she said casually, "you and your lady friend, you're not exactly all over each other."

For one wild moment, Flynn thought she meant Sierra. Then he realized that she was talking about Xuan. Too bad. He would have quite enjoyed relaying the saga of him and Sierra, if only to get an outside opinion. Not that he would. It was private. It was between him and the love of his life.

Yes, he was forced to admit it: Sierra was indeed still the love of his life. And it wasn't too late for them, was it?

Realization dawned like a sharp kick in the gut. He wanted her back. In spite of everything, he still loved her.

"Are you pissed that Xuan is spending so much time talking to Aleksandr?" Bianca continued, leaning toward him, keeping her voice low.

Flynn snapped back to reality. "Are you?" he countered.

"Am I what?" Bianca asked, stroking a strand of her sleek dark hair.

"Pissed that your boyfriend is all over my . . . uh . . . girlfriend?"

"Oh my God!" Bianca squealed. "I can't believe you just said that!"

"Didn't *you* say it first?"

Mercedes appeared with two shot glasses and a bottle of limoncello.

Bianca snatched one of the glasses and hurriedly downed the sweet liquid.

"Aren't you joining me?" she said, fixing Flynn with a challenging look.

"Tequila's more my style," he replied.

"A bottle of tequila," Bianca snapped at Mercedes. "And make it fast."

"So what's going on?" Flynn asked, sensing something was on her mind. "You seem disturbed. Is Xuan annoying you?"

"Are you kidding?" Bianca said, raising an imperious eyebrow. "No disrespect to you, but it would take a lot more woman to annoy *me*. Xuan is like one of those irritating flying bugs you can't get rid of. She's after Aleksandr to put up money for all kinds of dumb stuff."

"I guess you must mean the school she's trying to get built in Cambodia?" Flynn said dryly. "Or food and supplies for the thousands of refugees in Sierra Leone?"

"I'm not sure what exactly," Bianca said vaguely.

"Only please understand that this is *our* vacation, and chasing Aleksandr for money is totally inappropriate."

"You want me to tell her to lay off, is that it?"

"Yes," Bianca said firmly. "That's exactly what I want."

"I'll make an attempt," Flynn said, thinking that only a rich, spoiled, and privileged woman would act in such an insensitive way. "Although you gotta realize that Xuan is extremely single-minded. When she believes in something, it's all the way."

"Maybe you can fuck it out of her," Bianca said caustically.

"I'll take that as a suggestion," Flynn said, reaching for the bottle of tequila Mercedes brought over.

Might as well have a drink or two—maybe it would clear his head.

Two hours later, Flynn was feeling no pain. The flamenco dancers were long gone, as were most of the guests. The only ones who remained were Bianca, Aleksandr, Hammond, and Xuan. They were all drinking too much, and as the drinking progressed, so did the animosity. Hammond kept on making pointed remarks about journalists being the scum of the earth. Journalists, he announced drunkenly, staring straight at Flynn, were lying, cheating pieces of garbage who continually made up stories— especially about upstanding, honest politicians who wanted nothing more than to make the world a better place.

Xuan took umbrage at everything Hammond said, and the two of them argued, while Bianca cozied up to Aleksandr and wished he would suggest it was time for bed.

Flynn managed to keep his cool, until eventually he could hold back no longer. "Honest politicians?" he said sharply. "That's a fuckin' joke, isn't it?"

Up until this point, he and Hammond had ignored each other. But now the floodgates opened and all bets were off.

"*You* can talk about jokes," Hammond said, rising from his seat. "Everyone knows that you're nothing but a poor-ass loser, a nobody. What have *you* ever accomplished? Fuck all as far as I can tell."

"Screw you," Flynn retaliated, also jumping up. "Jesus, Ham, you cheated your way through college, an' I got a big hunch that's exactly how you're handling your so-called political career. Oh yeah, an' here's the real joke: one day you're gonna try to make a run for the presidency. My *ass*. They'll see you for what you are *way* before that."

"Y'know something," Hammond slurred. "You open your mouth an' out pours a shitload of crap."

"Hey," Flynn said, narrowing his eyes, "talking of crap, do not think I don't know what you did way back. But then I guess you couldn't get her any other way, right? You had to cheat an' lie. Fortunately, you're an expert at that, so no problem."

"I have no idea what you're talking about."

"Sure you do," Flynn taunted. "The photos, asshole. The fake fuckin' photos you sent to me and Sierra to break us up. Well, she knows all about it now, so you're screwed."

Hammond's mouth tightened into a thin line, and his face reddened. "Whatever I did was for her own protection," he said angrily. "And let me tell you this, you dumb bastard: the truth is that she *never* loved you, and Goddammit, she *never* will."

Xuan leaped to her feet, all five feet two of her. "Enough!" she shouted sternly. "Flynn, time for bed. Let's go."

"Yes, that's right," Hammond sneered. "Run away with your Chinky piece of ass. I bet she sucks you off like a true professional."

Before anyone could stop him, Flynn hauled his fist back and socked Hammond square in the face.

Hammond dropped like a dead weight.

Aleksandr was unamused. He abruptly stood up. "Come," he said to Bianca, as Kyril miraculously appeared, placing his considerable bulk between Flynn and Hammond. "It is time this evening ended."

58

Cruz's gang of Somalian pirates were a wild and dirty-looking bunch, headed by their clan leader, Amiin, the only one of them who spoke English. Amiin took his orders from Cruz, and bossed the other men accordingly. They were a motley crew of misfits who thanks to a successful pirating operation had become richer than they'd ever imagined. Half of them were former fishermen who had embraced their chosen profession with much zeal, expressing no fear when it came to boarding a vessel at sea ripe for the plucking. The fruits of their labors were plentiful, allowing them many of the luxuries in life that they never thought they'd see. As long as they had their precious khat to chew on, and a formidable supply of weapons, they were ready to face anything.

Lately, they'd been enjoying the good life while awaiting instructions from Amiin, who in turn waited for Cruz to bark his orders.

In Acapulco they'd been entertained by a few chosen hookers. Now, in the guesthouse of the rented villa, they were starting to get restless, and most of them were ready to go home to their families.

Including Amiin, there were seven of them, ranging in age from eighteen—Cashoo, Amiin's nephew—to Basra, a tall skeletal man of indeterminate age with mahogany skin, sunken eyes, unkempt dreadlocks, and very few teeth.

Basra was a man to beware of. He had no compunction about shooting to kill if anyone got in his way. He'd done so twice, even though Amiin had lectured him that it was to their advantage not to leave a trail of dead bodies.

Basra didn't care. He was a lethal weapon, and it was best to stay on his good side.

Cashoo had been working with Amiin since he was fourteen, and he'd exhibited a fearlessness that made him a useful member of the team. He was lanky, with light mocha skin, raggedy facial hair, high cheekbones, and thin lips. Cashoo's favorite pastime was sex. He had several girlfriends back home, but Cashoo was never satisfied.

The moment Ina arrived at the villa, Cashoo's libido raged out of control. Amiin saw the look of lust in his young nephew's eyes and sternly warned him to not even glance in the woman's direction, since she belonged to the big boss, and as such was untouchable.

A warning didn't stop the fearless Cashoo; he'd never seen a woman like Ina before, and he was quite smitten.

The pirates were confined to the guesthouse on the property, although they were also working on stocking their high-speed boats, loading supplies and weapons, in preparation for the strike against the *Bianca*.

As soon as Ina arrived, she took up a position by the pool in a patterned orange bikini that barely covered any of her considerable assets, and they were quite considerable, given the twenty pounds she'd gained since her reign as Miss Mexico.

Cashoo lusted from afar.

Ina threw him a flirtatious smile.

Cruz noticed what was going on and ordered Ina to get back inside the house pronto.

"Since when're you the boss of me?" Ina inquired, a steely glint in her over-mascaraed eyes. "It's not as if I'm your snivelling kid you can boss around."

There was no love lost between Ina and Cruz's daughter. Ina was jealous that Mercedes got to work with him, while she, the sister, had never been asked. Plus Mercedes was younger and prettier, and Cruz paid her plenty of money for—as far as Ina was concerned—doing nothing.

"You cause any trouble an' I'll kick your fat ass," Cruz warned her.

"What trouble?" Ina asked innocently. "You're the one who makes trouble."

She knew that the men who worked for Cruz were watching her with lust in their hearts, and she reveled in the attention.

Meanwhile, Sergei was all business. For the last few days, he'd been mulling a decision, and now that the time to strike was almost upon him, he had to make up his mind. To hold the *Bianca* for ransom was move number one. However, was that punishment enough for the son of a bitch who'd murdered his brother? The money wouldn't bring Boris back. Besides, what did money really mean to Aleksandr Kasianenko? The man was richer than God.

So Sergei had decided on a plan that would take the hijack one step further. They would certainly hold the *Bianca* for ransom, and once the money was paid and Cruz's team relinquished the boat and its passengers, the authorities would find that one key passenger was no longer aboard.

Sergei had no doubt that kidnapping Aleksandr Kasianenko was the only true way of taking his revenge.

59

The talk at the breakfast table was all about last night's fight. News soon spread, and by the light of day everyone knew about it.

Bianca was somewhat put out. She'd already told Luca that she didn't want any drama on the trip, and now this had to happen. "You've got to do something," she'd informed Aleksandr the moment they got back to their stateroom the night before. "We can't have our trip ruined by some stupid fight."

"I understand," he'd assured her. "It will be dealt with."

Now it was morning and everybody was trying to figure out what was going on. Why were Hammond and Flynn such bitter enemies? And who was the "she" Hammond had mentioned?

Bianca corralled Luca and gave him a blow-by-blow account of the fracas.

Luca wanted details. Bianca supplied what she knew.

Taye was upset that he'd missed the fight—or at least the knockout punch. Ashley wasn't; she hated any kind of violence.

Jeromy was relieved that something else was taking center stage. He and Luca had yet to have "the talk." Somehow or other he'd managed to avoid it.

The previous night, Hammond had retreated to his

room with a burgeoning black eye only to find Sierra sleeping. They hadn't spoken since their earlier confrontation, and when he awoke the next morning, she was gone.

Xuan had attempted to calm Flynn down, but it wasn't possible because he was boiling. He'd slept fitfully on the couch, and in the morning he headed straight to the gym, making a futile attempt to work off his raging aggression. He stayed there until Guy appeared and informed him that Mr. Kasianenko would like to see him.

Guy was loving every minute of the goings-on. One day, when he wrote his tell-all book, this would make a fine chapter. Yes, it could go right next to the chapter about the garment tycoon who one year had rented a luxury yacht, filled it with hookers, and barely got them off the day his wife and children arrived. The crew had had to hustle that day.

Ah, fond memories of life at sea . . .

"We missed all the excitement," Lori said to Cliff over breakfast.

He smiled at her across the table, white movie-star teeth in full bloom. "Maybe we're lucky, sweetie. Wouldn't want to get involved."

"Exactly," Ashley chimed in, pushing scrambled eggs across her plate. "I'm *glad* I wasn't there. I can't stand seeing men fight."

"Me either," said Lori, taking a bite of toast.

"Does anyone know what it was all about?" Ashley asked, curious to get the details.

Jeromy shrugged his shoulders. "Extremely childish if you ask me. And most disrespectful to our host."

"What about your hostess?" Bianca said, joining the table with Luca right behind her.

"Naturally I meant you too," Jeromy said, wondering where the hell they'd been. He did not appreciate Luca running off with Bianca. Were they talking about him behind his back? He certainly hoped not.

"I'm really glad there were no paparazzi around," Cliff said, reaching for the orange juice. "'Cause if there were, everything would've been *my* fault. I'd be splashed all over TMZ with Harvey making rude comments."

"Or if it was the bloody *English* press, *I'd* be the one to get the shitty end of it," Taye interjected, staking his claim to fame. "They get off on raggin' on me. It's a national sport."

"You're both wrong," Bianca said grandly. "I can see the headline now: 'Supermodel Causes Fight Between Russian Oligarch and American Senator.' I *always* get the blame."

"Aleksandr wasn't involved, was he?" Ashley asked innocently.

"Doesn't matter," Bianca said, tossing back her long dark hair. "All they're after is a headline to sell their story. Believe me, they like nothing better than putting my photo on the front page. Preferably in a bikini."

"She's right," Luca agreed.

"How positively juvenile!" Jeromy said with a peevish toss of his head.

Mercedes listened to them all as she hovered near the table, ready to serve. She'd already figured out what was going on. The day before, she'd eavesdropped on Flynn's conversation with the senator's wife. Well, it didn't take a genius to realize there was history there. The senator had a hard-on against the journalist 'cause he figured the journalist was out to fuck his wife. It was simple, only these *cabrones* didn't get it. They were too self-obsessed.

Late last night she'd sent her latest report to Cruz. He needed to know if she thought any of the guests would put up resistance. As far as she could tell, the journalist was the only one with balls, and she'd already checked that he had no weapons. The rest of them were easy street. Although she'd discovered that Aleksandr kept a loaded gun in his bedside drawer. And Kyril could be a slight problem—only slight, for Mercedes knew exactly how she would handle him when the time came.

After dinner the night before, she'd taken Kyril a mug of hot chocolate. She was working on a hunch that he might like it.

Right again. The big man had drunk it down, smacked his lips, and informed her that it was good. Then his beady eyes had inspected her cleavage once again, and she'd known she was on the right track.

Hot chocolate and a flash of tit. She had Kyril's number.

"Hey," Flynn said, walking out onto the private terrace of Aleksandr's stateroom. "Nice digs."

Aleksandr put down the sheaf of papers he was reading and nodded at Flynn. "I cannot blame you for last night," he said gruffly. "I also cannot condone what you did."

"No shit?" Flynn said, thinking that he didn't give a damn what Aleksandr thought. If it weren't for Sierra, he would have gotten off the yacht as soon as possible. But no, he wasn't about to walk out of her life again, not until he knew exactly where they stood.

"In Russia we toast with vodka—make the peace," Aleksandr said. "Is that possible?"

"Sure," Flynn said, Hammond's words still ringing in his ears. *She never loved you and she never will.* What a fucking piece of shit.

Aleksandr buzzed for Guy. "Bring vodka and fetch the senator," he ordered. "Now."

As usual, Guy jumped. Last night's activities had certainly broken the monotony of being on a yacht. A bit of excitement was always welcome; sometimes things went along too smoothly.

Ten minutes later, Hammond appeared, wearing dark shades and a scowl.

"Let's put this nonsense to rest," Aleksandr stated

firmly as Guy handed out shot glasses filled with vodka. "We'll toast to peace and harmony."

Flynn threw his vodka back, as did Hammond. They hardly looked at each other. Hatred lingered in the air.

Aleksandr nodded sagely. "Today is the day for water sports," he said, standing up. "Come, gentlemen, we have many toys to play with."

The day passed filled with a flurry of activities, including riding the state-of-the-art Jet Skis and WaveRunners, waterskiing, and exploring the crystal-blue waters of the Sea of Cortez.

Everyone threw themselves into having fun—everyone except Jeromy, who claimed his English skin was far too delicate to be exposed to the elements.

"C'mon, mate," Taye encouraged, climbing aboard after his third trip on a WaveRunner. "You dunno what you're missin'. It's a freakin' blast."

Jeromy rolled his eyes, indicating his lack of enthusiasm. "Oh, I think I do know what I'm missing," he said, with a supercilious smirk. "Extreme sunburn and aching muscles."

"Party pooper," Taye said with a good-natured shrug.

Luca hauled himself aboard next, bronzed and beautiful as usual. "Another race?" he said to Taye, shaking droplets of water from his mop of blond hair.

"You got it," Taye said, always up for a challenge.

Jeromy stared at the two specimens of manhood standing before him. They were both in perfect shape. Taye all gleaming black skin and defined muscles. Luca so edible in his tight swim shorts, leaving nothing to the imagination.

Jeromy was aroused. Random anonymous sex was as necessary to him as a full meal, and usually, on land, he could always find someone to satisfy him. Now he was trapped on a yacht, so where could he find the temporary satisfaction he craved?

The answer came to him in a flash. Guy. The entertainment director. He was gay, wasn't he? He was there to serve, right?

The women were lolling on a giant hooded inflatable pool mattress, bobbing around in the sea. It held four people, so Lori, Bianca, Sierra, and Ashley had taken up residence. Flynn and Cliff had gone snorkeling, while Hammond was at the pool, sitting with Aleksandr and Xuan.

Jeromy took advantage of everyone being occupied and approached Guy. "Kindly accompany me to my room," he said. "There is something I have been meaning to show you."

"Should I call the housekeeper?" Guy inquired, wondering what was up.

"No, no, it's something that you should see first," Jeromy said, smoothing down his beige linen shirt—Tom Ford, of course.

"Right," Guy said, following the uptight Englishman down the stairs to the stateroom he shared with Luca.

As soon as they were inside the room, Jeromy quickly turned, slammed the door shut, and placed himself in front of it.

"What can I help you with?" Guy asked, imagining complaints about cleanliness or not enough towels—which were really not his problem.

"Here's what you can help me with—*this*," Jeromy said, unzipping his shorts while still blocking the door.

Guy took one look and was immediately horrified. A guest exposing himself was the last thing he'd expected.

Jeromy shook free his penis, a long thin weapon of destruction. "Suck it," he commanded. "You know how to do that, don't you?"

Guy recoiled. Oral sex was not part of his job description. This untoward demand was unexpected and degrading. He was shocked.

"I'm . . . I'm sorry," he stammered, almost speechless. "I . . . I . . . can't."

"Don't be sorry," Jeromy said roughly, while continuing to block the door. "Simply do it, dear boy. It's a *cock* you're looking at. You've seen one of those before, haven't you?"

"I can't—"

"Oh yes, my dear boy, you certainly can," Jeromy said, feeling the need for an urgent release. "Because if you value your job, you'll do it, and you'll do it fast. Or perhaps you would prefer me to tell Mr. Kasianenko that *you* came on to *me*, then we'll see what he does about *that*. My instinct is that he'll fire your arse, and I'm sure you know I'm right."

Yes, Guy knew that he was. Reluctantly, he fell to his knees and did what the bony Englishman required.

Sometimes a man had no choice but to put his job first.

"Tell the truth," Bianca sighed, languidly trailing her hand in the calm blue sea. "Isn't Aleksandr the sexiest man ever?"

No, Lori was tempted to say. *Cliff possesses that title—courtesy of* People *magazine.*

"He's pretty damn sexy," Ashley chirped, blond hair piled on top of her head, bosoms fighting to stay within the confines of her minuscule bikini top. "But then so is my Taye."

"You got that right," Bianca agreed, thinking of her one night of lust with Taye and savoring the distant memory. "Taye's a hot one. I'd hang on to him if I were you."

"I already have," Ashley said with a crazed giggle. "My husband's besotted with me, in case you hadn't noticed."

"Oh yes, I've noticed," Bianca said. "He walks around with a permanent hard-on. Or is that just his normal package?"

Ashley managed a quick blush. "I am a lucky girl, aren't I?" she said, giggling again.

"You certainly are," Bianca said, turning to Lori. "How about you?" she asked. "Getting any closer to snagging Cliff?"

Oh damn. Not again. Why was everyone questioning her about Cliff's intentions? "Didn't I tell you I'm too young to get married?" Lori answered, going for the flippant approach.

"A girl is never too young to pin the guy she wants," Bianca advised. "If he asks, you gotta say yes."

"I'll remember that," Lori said, as Bianca shifted her attention to Sierra.

"How long have you and Hammond been married?" Bianca asked the senator's wife.

Sierra was lying back, enjoying the sun while trying not to think about the inevitable confrontation with Hammond, which was yet to come. She'd heard about last night's altercation between her husband and Flynn. No details—only something about Hammond insulting all journalists and Flynn striking back.

She wished she could talk to Flynn, find out exactly what had happened, but she couldn't do that. The two men were already at war—no need to add fuel to the fire.

"Uh . . . a few years," she answered vaguely.

"It must be *so* exciting being married to a senator," Ashley enthused. "And an attractive one at that."

Don't forget horny, Lori was tempted to say, but once again she stopped herself.

"Yes," Sierra said quietly. "It's a lot of work, though. Fund-raisers, endless functions, meet and greets. It can get quite tiring."

"But there are plenty of perks, I bet," Bianca said, thinking that if Sierra ever became first lady, she wouldn't mind being best friends with her. A night at the White House sounded like a fun plan. "And of course you've got all the designers offering you incredible outfits, right?" she added.

"*And* you get to meet the president, don't you?" Lori said, slightly in awe.

"Taye an' I met the prime minister of England a couple of times," Ashley said, joining in. "We've also been to a tea party at Buckingham Palace. Prince William *loves* Taye, goes to all his big games."

"What kind of tea party?" Lori asked curiously.

"It's a Brit thing," Ashley said. "All outrageous hats, an' tea and crumpets in the palace gardens."

"Wow!" Lori exclaimed. "Sounds fancy."

"Oh, it is," Ashley said boastfully. "Only special people get invited."

Sierra felt it was time to move on. She slid quietly off the Lilo and into the calm blue water. After a few moments, she swam to the side of the yacht, where a deckhand helped her aboard.

And there was Flynn, sitting on a bench with Cliff, the two of them having just finished snorkeling.

"How was it?" she found herself asking.

"Incredible," Cliff said. "A must-do. I've been around, and I've never seen an underwater scene like it. It's a wonderland."

Her eyes met Flynn's—the connection between them was white hot.

Flynn dragged his eyes away as he stood up and reached for a towel.

"Would you care to give it a try, Mrs. Patterson?" one of the deckhands asked.

"Why not?" she said quietly.

"I can dive with you," the eager deckhand offered, handing her a snorkel, mask, and fins.

"That's okay," Flynn said quickly. "I think I'll go back in."

"You're gonna love it, Sierra," Cliff encouraged.

"I'm sure I will," she murmured.

"I'd come back in, but I'm going to find Lori," Cliff said. "She'll really get a thrill."

Sierra barely heard him, because now Flynn was staring at her again, and this time he held the look.

Their eyes locked, and in those few seconds she knew that everything was about to change.

She still loved him—there was no doubt about it.

60

Eddie March was livid that Hammond had failed to call him back. He was in the middle of handling a major crisis, and the senator could not be bothered to pick up a satellite phone, or whatever the yacht he was so busy cruising on had.

The Byrne family was getting even more restless, and to top it off, Hammond's fifteen-year-old illegitimate daughter, Radical, had been thrown out of her Swiss boarding school and was on her way back to New York.

Radical was a nightmare, and Eddie was in no mood to deal with her too. The Byrnes were enough work. Keeping them from going public was getting more and more difficult. He'd even offered them money until he could sort things out. "We do not want money," Martin Byrne had informed him with a steely glare. "We want to hear the senator's side of the story."

So do I, Eddie thought.

He tried calling the yacht again, and this time he was told that the senator was unreachable.

"Where is he that he's so unreachable?" Eddie demanded.

"Exploring the ocean," the first officer replied. "I will certainly see that he gets your message."

Exploring the ocean indeed! While he, Eddie March,

was shoveling the shit. It wasn't right. If he didn't get a call back soon, he was telling the Byrnes to do what they liked.

Hammond had created a mess, and it was up to him to deal with it.

61

The underwater paradise was so peaceful and unbelievably breathtaking that Sierra forgot about everything and managed to lose herself in the array of marine life. She was too busy marveling at the vivid colors and incredible shapes of the numerous fish. Although she was fully aware that Flynn was in the ocean with her—and that made everything perfect.

When they finally surfaced, he reached for her hand, and as they touched, the electricity between them was startling. They bobbed in the water facing each other.

"You okay?" he asked, wishing she would open up to him.

"I will be," she replied softly.

"We need to talk some more."

"I know," she murmured, marveling at how good it felt being near him.

They exchanged another intense look.

The spell was broken when Cliff jumped into the sea with Lori, and the two of them swam over to join Flynn and Sierra.

"Found her," Cliff crowed. "Now I'm gonna show her the wonders that lurk below."

"Boasting about your crown jewels again?" Lori quipped, treading water beside him, her red hair piled on top of her head.

"Funny girl," Cliff replied, and they smiled warmly at each other.

Lori was delighted. Things were definitely looking up.

Sierra moved away from the group and swam toward the yacht. She couldn't avoid Hammond any longer; it was time to decide how they would handle the situation. No more threats. No more cowering. With or without Flynn, she had made up her mind that once this trip was over, she would free herself of Hammond forever.

"I told Flynn to have his girlfriend lay off asking you for money," Bianca said, snuggling close to Aleksandr as they lay out by their private lap pool. It was after lunch, and they'd left their guests to their own devices.

Aleksandr pushed her away and sat up. "You did what?" he said, raising his heavy eyebrows. Bianca was interfering with something that didn't concern her, and it annoyed him.

"I simply told him to get Xuan to stop bugging you," Bianca said. "It was getting to be too much."

"Too much for whom?" Aleksandr asked, his tone sharp.

"Well, for me, actually," Bianca answered, narrowing her green eyes. "This trip is supposed to be all about you and me, and every time I turn around, there's Little Miss Do-Gooder bugging you for money for another of her precious causes. I can't take it."

"You shouldn't have done that," Aleksandr said, his face darkening. "It is not for you to decide who I speak to, or what we speak about."

Bianca frowned. "Excuse me?" she said haughtily. *Was Aleksandr actually scolding her?*

"You heard me," Aleksandr said, getting up and walking inside.

Furiously, Bianca leaped to her feet and followed him. "What is it with you and that girl?" she demanded. "Do you want to fuck her? 'Cause if you do, just tell me an' I'll make out with Flynn. He's quite the hunk, in case you hadn't noticed."

Aleksandr stared her down, his eyes cold and disapproving. "What is wrong with you?" he said at last. "Are you so insecure that because I talk to another woman you think I want to be with her? What kind of nonsense is that? I do what pleases me, Bianca. Never forget it."

Bianca scowled. Her plan of getting Xuan to leave Aleksandr alone was failing dismally.

Luca and Taye decided to organize a Jet Ski contest. Later in the afternoon they rounded up everyone who wished to participate.

"Girls against dudes," Luca suggested with a cheeky grin. "Where's Bianca?"

"I'm here," she said, joining them. She was not prepared to spend the afternoon with Aleksandr; it was about time he realized he couldn't talk to her in such a dismissive way. He'd called her insecure, and that didn't fly. *Insecure indeed. Screw him.*

"You can head the girls' team," Luca said to Bianca. "Taye, you up for playin' captain?"

"Are you friggin' kiddin' me?" Taye said, running a hand over his shaved head. "It's my job, so get ready—'cause I'm gonna kick everyone's arse."

Soon the crew had assembled a fleet of Jet Skis and they were off.

Lori raced Ashley and, to Lori's surprise, she actually won. Then Bianca went up against Xuan—and, to Bianca's extreme annoyance, Xuan beat her.

After that it was the guys' turn. Luca and Cliff raced and Luca was the winner. Then it was Flynn and Taye, a hard battle until Flynn ruled triumphant.

Everyone threw themselves into it—except Aleksandr, who wasn't present; Jeromy, who hovered on the sidelines looking thoroughly bored; and the Pattersons, who were not around.

Guy helped the proceedings move forward, even though he was humiliated beyond belief. At least he still had his job, no thanks to Jeromy Milton-Gold.

Guy couldn't even glance in the Englishman's direction. He hated him with a deep intensity and was starting to think about how he might get his revenge. Surely there had to be a way?

The final race was between Luca and Xuan. When Xuan lost, Bianca could hardly conceal her delight.

Karma's a bitch, bitch.

Bianca smiled her satisfaction.

The moment of reckoning was near. Sierra was well aware that it had to take place soon, and she was not avoiding it. In a perverse way, she was looking forward to it. Standing up to Hammond was something she should've done a long time ago. He'd cheated and lied his way into her life, she'd lost Flynn's baby because of him, and he'd kept her a prisoner with his dire threats against her and her family. Well, no more. It was over. She was finally ready to break free.

They met up in their stateroom. She'd gone straight there after her underwater adventure, taken a shower, dressed, and waited for him to appear.

Hammond walked in wearing dark glasses, which he immediately removed to show off a serious black eye. "This is because of you," he said accusingly. "This is what your piece-of-shit boyfriend did to me for no good reason."

"He's not my boyfriend," she said evenly. "And I'm sure you gave him an excellent reason."

"You think so, do you?" Hammond sneered.

"I understand you were both drinking."

"Where did you hear that?" he said, his tone bitter. "Did your boyfriend come running to tell you?"

"No, Hammond, he didn't," she replied, determined not to break. "And I'd appreciate it if we could conduct an adult conversation for once."

"Go ahead," he said coldly. "Say what you have to say."

She took a deep breath and went for it. "I'm sure you know how unhappy I am, and that we'd be better apart, so I've made a decision. I will stay with you for the duration of this trip, present a united front to prevent embarrassing you. And then when the trip is over, so are we." She swallowed hard. "I want a divorce, Hammond. I mean it."

"Really?" he said, surprisingly calm.

"Look," she continued, her words tumbling over each other. "I understand this has political implications for you, but surely you can see that it doesn't mean the end of your career. These things happen. Divorce is not uncommon among politicians—"

"You vapid, asinine *bitch*!" Hammond exploded, his voice filled with venom. "God almighty, I knew you were stupid, but this kind of talk goes beyond stupidity. Don't you understand that it's not possible? I repeat: divorce is *not possible*." His voice rose to a vicious shout. "One day I am going to be the fucking president of the United States, and you, my dear *wife*, are going to be right there next to me. Otherwise—"

"Otherwise what?" she said bravely, holding her ground, trying not to revert to the weak-willed Sierra who'd put up with his bullying and threats for too many years.

"Otherwise," Hammond said ominously, "you'll be dead. And so will your fucking boyfriend."

Listening outside their door, Mercedes felt a shiver of excitement. Drama on the high seas. But this drama would mean nothing in comparison to what was to come. Little did they know what was in store for them.

Guy had sent her to deliver a message to Senator Patterson about someone trying to reach him via satellite phone. Guy was in a shitty mood, barking orders as if *he* were the captain. *Idiota.* He would never make captain—he didn't have the stones. Besides, he was gay, and how many gay men made captain?

Probably this wasn't a good time to interrupt the Pattersons. She knocked on the door anyway. What did she care that the *imbécil* was threatening to kill his wife? The *puta* probably deserved it, seeing that she was jumping the bones of the sexy journalist guy. Or at least it looked that way.

Hammond flung open the door. "What?" he said curtly.

Mercedes stared at his mother of a black eye, handed him the neatly typed message, and inquired if he'd like her to accompany him to the communications room.

He barely glanced at the message, said a short, sharp "No!," and slammed the door in her face.

What a cabrón, Mercedes thought, switching her allegiance to the wife, who seemed like a nice enough woman, unlike the other *putas* on the boat, who all acted as if they were better than everyone else, especially the blonde with the big tits and the hot black husband.

Yet another hot guy. If she weren't working, this could be quite a trip. However, work always came first. And at the conclusion of this particular trip she was going for it, taking everything she could get her greedy hands on.

Money and jewelry. She considered it her bonus.

62

On a boat at sea in close quarters—albeit extremely luxurious ones—friends are made, idle gossip abounds, and all thoughts of the real world drift away. Aleksandr's ploy of enticing everyone to give up their iPhones, BlackBerrys, iPads, and computers for a delicious uninterrupted week of lazy bliss was a solid one. For emergencies there was always satellite communication.

A successful vacation equals relaxation—and Aleksandr expected his guests to leave their everyday lives behind.

Personally, he was enjoying himself. Sex with Bianca was spectacular, although her nagging about Xuan was annoying. His conversations with the Asian woman were interesting and in a way quite challenging, and in spite of Bianca's objections he had no intention of giving them up. Trust Flynn to have come up with a woman who was not only very attractive but smart too. And he was most impressed that Xuan wasn't intimidated by him, not at all.

If he weren't with Bianca, Aleksandr realized, he might have entertained different thoughts about Xuan. Sexual thoughts. However, he was in a committed relationship with Bianca, so all fantasies of sex with Xuan were banished to the back of his mind. Besides, she was with Flynn, and he would never disrespect a man like Flynn, whom he considered a true friend.

He was disturbed that Senator Patterson had behaved so badly the night before. The man had deserved to get hit; the senator had enticed Flynn to do so with his ridiculous attack of words. Quite frankly, Aleksandr was pleased to see Hammond receive a black eye, for he'd already decided there was something about him that he didn't like. Hammond possessed a pleasant and ingratiating exterior, but lurking beneath was a hard core of something else.

Aleksandr had always considered himself to be an astute judge of character, and he didn't trust Hammond. He decided he would keep an eye on the man's further rise to power, then he would act accordingly when the inevitable request came to donate money and support to the senator's campaign.

Yes, Aleksandr knew for sure that the day would eventually come.

After the race, Bianca hung out with Luca and Taye by the pool. She wasn't about to run back to Aleksandr's side. He could be unpredictable and bossy. It pissed her off. How dare he get mad at her? *He* was the one paying too much attention to Little Miss Intensity.

She was particularly irritated because she'd never treated a man as well as she'd treated Aleksandr. Shouldn't he be kissing her beautiful tight ass like everyone else?

Didn't Aleksandr get it? She was *Bianca*. A superstar in her field. She was not used to being lectured and told what to do.

Damn him! And damn Flynn for bringing his Asian girlfriend aboard. The two of them were hardly the same caliber as the other guests.

Bianca sighed. It was her own fault; she should've vetted the guest list more closely. Xuan and Flynn were not a good fit for the rest of the group, although she had to admit that Flynn was wildly sexy with his action-movie-star looks—not all groomed and perfect like Cliff Baxter.

Flynn was edgier, like a roughed-up Ryan Reynolds with a touch of Alex O'Loughlin, the actor who played Steve McGarrett on *Hawaii Five-O*.

Another time, another place, and she would've definitely hit that.

And talking of hitting that . . .

Mischievously, she leaned over to Taye, who was busy sunning himself, his black skin gleaming in the sunlight. "Hey, sexy," she said in a seductive whisper. "Remember way back when you and I got it on?"

Taye shot up, startled. *Oh shit.* Where was Ashley? If she even suspected that he and Bianca had done the dirty, she would have his friggin' balls for breakfast, even though it had taken place long before he and Ashley were together.

"You don't have to worry," Bianca crooned. "Wifey's in the hair salon getting all prettied up for you."

Taye breathed again.

"We would've made incredible babies," Bianca mused, having fun playing with him. "Can you imagine how gorgeous they would've been with *our* genes?"

"Jeez!" Taye muttered, totally alarmed. "It was years ago. Best kept on the down low, right?"

"If you mean would I tell Ashley, of course not," Bianca said guilelessly. "Although we were both free agents then, so we've got nothing to feel guilty about. It wasn't like we were *cheating* on anyone."

"Who's guilty?" Taye said, manning up. "Although here's the deal—my wife has a raging jealous streak you do *not* wanna mess with. She *still* gives me crap about my first girlfriend way back when I was friggin' twelve!"

Luca surfaced from his nearby lounger, a huge grin on his tanned face. "How come you never told me?" he said, directing his words toward Bianca. "Keepin' secrets, huh?"

"Oh fuck!" Taye groaned.

"My lips are shut tight," Luca said, still grinning.

"They'd better be," Taye grumbled.

Bianca stood up and dived into the pool. Revealing other people's secrets always made her feel so much better.

What next? Flynn didn't know, and it was driving him crazy. Apart from his brief underwater interlude with Sierra—during which talking was obviously not an option—he had no idea where her head was at.

Did she feel the same way he did?

Had any of those old feelings resurfaced?

Was it even possible to go back?

He didn't know. It was up to her.

Hammond's words still reverberated in his head. *She never loved you and she never will.*

Bullshit.

Cliff was behaving like a changed man. Lori wasn't sure what had come over him, although it was definitely something. She'd never known him to be this affectionate and attentive.

Was it because of the senator's blatant flirting with her?

Was it because Cliff was on vacation and the pressures of always playing Mister Movie Star were turned off for once?

She didn't know and she didn't care, for this was a whole new Cliff Baxter. This was the man she'd fallen in love with.

After the afternoon's water sports and the under-the-sea spectacle, Cliff had taken her by the hand and suggested they repair to their room.

Fine with her. She knew what he wanted, and she was prepared to oblige.

But no, getting blown was not what he had in mind. His intent was to please *her.*

She was shocked and surprised, because making sure she was satisfied was not high on Cliff's agenda. When it came to bedroom activities, he was always the star.

"I fuckin' expect so."

"Here's the deal with my men," Cruz said, taking another long drag on his cigarette. "They're driven by the money—it turns 'em into heroes when they take home the loot."

"Fuckin' heroes?" Sergei jeered.

"You got it," Cruz replied, stamping his cigarette underfoot. "An' believe me, in the shithouse towns they come from, they *are* the fuckin' heroes, with a coupla pretty wives, a fancy car, an' as many kids as they wanna have."

"You got a wife?" Sergei asked, thinking that he didn't know much about Cruz's personal life.

"Who's dumb enough to buy the cow when y' can suck the *putas*?" Cruz chuckled. "An' Somalian *putas*?" He made a wicked smacking noise with his mouth. "Beauties, an' grateful."

Sergei liked the sound of that, although he was well aware that you took your life in your hands if you visited Somalia. It was one of the most dangerous countries in the world: lawless, with a barely functioning government. The kidnapping of foreigners was a national pastime.

"My men are scared of nothin' 'cept hunger," Cruz announced. "That's what makes 'em so fearless an' strong."

"You really fell into it, didn't you?" Sergei commented.

"You bet your ass," Cruz bragged. "Me, I live like a fuckin' king. Got in at the right time with the right connections. I'm the only foreigner they trust. An' as long as I keep makin' 'em money, they're gonna keep on trustin' me."

Sergei nodded again. He understood.

64

The evening plan was dinner on another, larger island, and this time Aleksandr expected everyone to attend. Instructions were to meet on the deck by the tenders at seven P.M.

Bianca returned to the master suite and gave Aleksandr the silent treatment as she sat in front of the bedroom mirror braiding her long dark hair while wearing nothing more than a sexy leopard-print thong. She was well aware that seeing her naked always turned him on. He had a thing for her tits, so small and perfect. She'd already decided that tonight he wasn't getting anything sexual, not until he apologized. Sex was definitely off the menu.

Aleksandr needed to realize that she wasn't just another pretty face he could boss around. She was Bianca. She was a superstar, and he'd better get that into his head.

Aleksandr had no desire to continue their argument, such as it was, although he was still determined to hold his ground as far as Xuan was concerned. Bianca could sit in front of the mirror half naked for as long as she wanted; he wasn't about to touch her until she learned that she could not tell him what to do or whom to talk to. He considered it outrageous that she thought she could, and he wasn't accepting it. Bianca had a spoiled streak, and it was his job to make her see that she could not exhibit that kind of attitude with him.

He *was* the boss, something she still had to get used to.

"What an adventure!" Ashley exclaimed, getting ready for the evening's activities.

Taye nodded his agreement. Sex with his wife on a daily basis was a hell of a lot more than he'd expected. As far as he was concerned, they could stay on the yacht for a couple more months. No problem.

"Do you like these earrings?" Ashley asked, holding a pair of diamond-studded hoops to her earlobes.

"Love 'em," Taye replied, thinking he'd love them even more when he got her naked later.

Ashley put on the earrings. She was busy thinking about Cliff Baxter. She was especially excited, as Cliff had been extremely friendly at lunch. Now she was quite sure that he fancied her. Cliff Baxter had what her mum would call "bedroom eyes," and those eyes had been all over her.

She fantasized about what she would do if he came on to her.

Well, she wouldn't turn him down, that was for sure. And as far as Taye was concerned, it would be payback time for when he'd screwed that Page 3 slag.

Careful of what you do in life, Ashley thought. *'Cause one day it can come back and bite you firmly on the ass.*

Ah yes, Ashley's fantasies were in full bloom.

A feeling of helplessness overcame Sierra as she sat in their stateroom listening to Hammond drone on about exactly how he would deal with Flynn if she ever dared to talk to him again, or repeat the word *divorce*.

"You do know that I can have him killed any way I want," Hammond crowed, sweat beading his forehead. "Skinned alive. Shot in the head. Blown up in a car. I might even give you the pleasure of choosing his fate, my dear wife. Wouldn't that be an interesting decision for you to make."

This torrent of threats had been going on for some time, and she didn't know what to do. Was Hammond completely psychotic? Had he lost his mind? Or could he actually arrange to have those threats carried out?

Was it possible?

Anything was possible.

This was exactly how he'd kept her tied to him all these years. Threats against her personally. Threats against her family. But Flynn's name had never entered into the equation, and once more, it all seemed so horribly real.

"Why are you doing this?" she managed.

"Why am *I* doing this?" Hammond replied, simmering with fury. "Why am *I* doing this?" he repeated, his bland features contorting into an angry distorted mask. "*You* are the one who is doing this to us. *You* are the one who is determined to end my political career."

"No, I'm not," she objected, swallowing hard, holding back tears because she felt so helpless against his threats. Helpless and alone. She should've known there was no way out.

"Save me the whining," Hammond said harshly. "We are going to the island for dinner with our gracious host, and it would be nice if you could try to behave like a loving wife for once. These people are my future, so try to remember that. Now get dressed. I do not care to keep anyone waiting."

Lori luxuriated under the warm shower, savoring every delicious moment of Cliff's lovemaking. What a changed man! What an unexpected delight.

Cliff had showered first and gone to one of the upper decks for a drink before their island visit. This time their trip to the island would be at night, so Lori wasn't quite sure how to dress. Should she take her bikini? Would there be midnight swimming in the ocean involved? Maybe even skinny-dipping?

She was exhilarated. How about *Mrs. Cliff Baxter*? Could that elusive title possibly be in her future?

Do not get carried away, she warned herself. *One session of cunnilingus does not a marriage make.*

Although things were definitely heading in the right direction.

Yes.

Mrs. Cliff Baxter.

Who knew *what* the future held?

"Do I *have* to go?" Jeromy groaned like a petulant child.

"Please yourself," Luca responded, keeping his tone noncommittal as he selected a sexy black frilled shirt from the closet. As each day passed, he was getting more and more fed up with Jeromy and his condescending attitude. It seemed nothing and no one pleased him. It was quite obvious that Jeromy was not the center of attention, which pissed him off. Jeromy was used to holding court, and on this trip there was no court for him to hold.

"Don't you *want* me to go?" Jeromy asked, trying to manipulate Luca into begging for his presence.

Luca was having none of it. After this trip, he'd definitely ease Jeromy out of his life.

Jeromy was giving him an expectant look.

Luca shrugged as he put on the shirt. "Like I said, do what you want."

"I want *you* to tell me what to do," Jeromy replied, going for the subservient role, which didn't suit him at all. There was a long silent beat, and then, realizing that Luca was not about to beg him, he added a reluctant, "All right, I'll come."

Luca would have preferred it if Jeromy had opted to stay on the yacht, but it was not to be. He pulled on a pair of white pants, added a narrow black crocodile belt, and headed for the door. "See you upstairs," he said, and exited quickly, wondering how he was going to manage another few days of Jeromy's company.

In retrospect, he realized that he should've invited Suga and Luca Junior on this trip with him. They would've loved it, and everyone would've loved them.

Too bad and too late. He was stuck with Jeromy.

Cliff Baxter was already on the upper deck when Luca appeared. Cliff was sipping a martini and looking very suave in a long-sleeved charcoal T-shirt and matching linen pants, his dark hair slicked back.

Idly Luca wondered if the movie star had ever taken a walk on the wild side—there were always rumors—or if women just did it for him.

"Hey," Cliff said, greeting him with a smile.

"What's goin' on?" Luca responded.

"Don't know about you," Cliff said, "but I think I just experienced one of the best days of my life."

"That's sayin' something, comin' from you," Luca remarked.

"Yeah," Cliff said. "I came to the conclusion that Lori is a keeper."

"And you didn't know that before?" Luca asked curiously.

"Outside influences," Cliff said vaguely.

"I get it," Luca said. "Shouldn't listen to the chorus. When I came out, none of my advisers wanted me to do it. 'You'll lose all your fans,' they warned me. Hey, you know what—I *gained* fans. So I did what *I* wanted, an' it all worked out."

"I admire that," Cliff said.

"You admire what?" Bianca asked, appearing suddenly. She had a way of inserting herself into other people's conversations as if it were a perfectly acceptable thing to do.

"Never mind," Luca chided. "Where's Aleksandr?"

"He'll be here," Bianca said, waving an impatient hand at Mercedes. "Who do you have to fuck around here to get a damn drink?"

Mercedes decided that when the time came, she would take Bianca's clothes. Even though the supermodel was at least eight inches taller than her, she coveted the many outfits Bianca wore. The sexy bikinis with thong bottoms; the selection of wild T-shirts and designer jeans; the long skirts and backless dresses. And the jewelry. Diamond bangles, a white Chanel watch, a large aquamarine ring surrounded by diamonds. It was all expensive and ready to be taken.

The other women's clothes were more low-key—expensive, but not flashy enough for Mercedes. When this caper was over, she planned on stepping out and enjoying herself. She was thinking of buying herself a small apartment in the Seychelles, far enough away from Daddy Cruz and his heavily guarded complex in Somalia, which she'd only visited a few times. Cruz hadn't wanted her living with him anyway. "Too dangerous," he'd informed her. But he liked having her work for him. And so far she'd always blended in as one of the crew—a crew member who'd been able to supply all the information he'd needed before conducting a successful takeover.

This hijacking was different. Who expected to get taken over by Somalian pirates while quietly cruising the Sea of Cortez? Certainly not this group.

That a·man of Aleksandr Kasianenko's wealth and importance would be traveling with just one bodyguard was loco. *And* with a group of rich famous people aboard. So crazy.

Mercedes had to admit that Cruz was one smart tiger. He'd somehow or other arranged to get his entire gang out of Somalia ready to do their thing. And Cruz's team was a ruthless bunch who always got the job done.

Screw it! she thought, licking her finger, then dipping it into Bianca's martini before delivering it to her. *I'm getting impatient. I've had enough of catering to these rich spoiled* chingados.

The only one who treated her with any kind of respect was Luca Perez. He spoke to her in Spanish, and always asked how she was doing. Unlike his *imbécil* partner with his I-am-better-than-anyone-else attitude, whom she truly loathed.

Ah, if Jeromy Milton-Gold only knew how many times she'd spat in his drinks. A small satisfaction.

Meanwhile, her relationship with Kyril—such as it was—seemed to be developing nicely. Once she'd discovered his weakness for chocolate, it was all systems go. She could get into his space anytime she wanted as long as she came bearing treats. Chocolate cake, chocolate cookies, chocolate bars, and his very favorite—a full mug of hot chocolate.

He must've been deprived as a kid in Russia. Never gotten his chocolate fix.

At least he only craved chocolate; she wouldn't have to screw him or service what she imagined might be a gigantic cock. Or maybe not—sometimes it was the big men who had tiny dicks. Anyway, thankfully she wouldn't have to find out. Chocolate had paved the way, and the time would soon come to put her plan into action.

Mercedes couldn't wait.

65

Another island, only this time it was night, and this time the island was not completely deserted. At the top of a steep hill stood a magnificent old Spanish castle overlooking the pristine beach. The grand balcony of the castle was the setting for dinner.

A long antique table made of fine wood held candles in ornate silver holders and different arrangements of exotic flowers. A trio of Brazilian musicians had been imported for the night, and the food was also Brazilian, everything from *caruro*—a delicious mix of dried shrimp, okra, and onions—to *feijoada,* a simmered meat and bean dish.

Normally Bianca would've been all over Aleksandr, since he knew she loved anything connected to Brazil, and these were a few of her favorite foods, but she was still not talking to him, while he impatiently waited for her to apologize.

The two of them were playing a dangerous game.

Bianca began flirting outrageously with Taye, who was mortified, because if Ashley got even the slightest hint that he and the supermodel had once had sex, she would go apeshit.

So that Bianca could see that she had no influence over what he did or who he spoke to, Aleksandr got together with Xuan and informed her that he had been thinking about their conversations, and he would be happy to finance the school she was involved with in Cambodia, and perhaps they should talk about building an orphanage outside Moscow. He confessed that he'd thought about it often, since he was an adopted child himself.

Xuan considered it a wonderful idea.

She was delighted that this luxury trip with all these so-called celebrities was paying off. She had already asked Taye if he would be interested in sponsoring a sports program for underprivileged kids in Haiti, and he'd said yes. And Cliff Baxter had agreed to be the star attraction at an auction to raise money for the refugees of Darfur.

Xuan was fully satisfied.

Flynn was not.

What the hell was going on with Sierra? She wouldn't look at him. She seemed to be in a daze again. She did not leave Hammond's side, which he found most disturbing. It was almost as if Hammond had cast some kind of spell over her.

Jesus Christ! What was he doing allowing himself to get hung up on Sierra again? Too much time had passed.

Hammond's words were burned into his brain. *She never loved you and she never will.*

Tomorrow he was definitely coming up with an excuse to get off the boat.

"I love your dress," Lori remarked to Ashley as they took their places at the dinner table.

I love your movie-star boyfriend, Ashley was tempted to reply. *And I have a strong suspicion he fancies me back.* Instead, she said, "Thanks. It's a Stella McCartney. I always feel fab in one of her designs; she really gets me."

"Oh," Lori said. "Does she sell her stuff in L.A.?"

Ashley shot Lori a semi-scornful look. Did Cliff's girlfriend know nothing? "Actually," she said, a tad condescendingly, "Stella has a store on Beverly Boulevard. I can take you there if you want. They all know me."

"I thought you lived in England."

"We do," Ashley said, thinking it was a wise move to stay friendly with the girlfriend just in case Cliff kept her around. "Taye enjoys L.A., so we try to fly in a couple of times a year, stay at the Beverly Hills Hotel, Taye's fave. Maybe you and Cliff can join us for dinner at the Polo Lounge next time we're there."

Why is she being so friendly? Lori thought. *This is a big change in personality.*

"Love to," Lori said brightly. "I'll tell Cliff."

As far as Mercedes was concerned, the timing couldn't've been better. Almost everyone was off the yacht, including Kyril, who Aleksandr had decided should accompany him for once. Mercedes was one happy girl, having feigned painful and debilitating stomach cramps to get out of going.

Guy had been furious; his bad moods were getting worse. "What's wrong with you?" he'd yelled. "Can't you understand that we need all the help we can get?"

"It's my time of the month," she'd replied, staring him down. "It's not my fault I suffer from bad cramps."

There was nothing Guy could do except give her the stink-eye.

Too bad, Mercedes thought. *He has the ever-obliging Renee and Den to take care of everyone.*

Apparently it was a big-deal dinner, so not many of the crew were left on the yacht, which suited Mercedes just fine. Earlier in the day she'd received a cryptic message from Cruz that they were ready. It was on.

Yippee!

Servitude would soon be over!

Cruz always operated at night. It was easier to board when most of the crew were sleeping.

Cruz gave her the time; Mercedes gave him the approximate location.

There was much to prepare.

Tomorrow, after midnight, it was definitely on!

* * *

Hammond was disappointed to note that redheaded Lori was cuddling up to her movie-star boyfriend like a limpet. He had hoped to further their flirtation, but it was not to be. All the other women on the trip seemed to be quite cozy with their significant others, which left him no options except the Asian. Xuan was not a prospect—too militant and too short. He didn't like his women short.

Sierra was by his side and silent. He'd brought her back in line fast. Did she honestly believe she could get away from him?

No chance. He had her exactly where he wanted her. Compliant and scared. Threatening her once-upon-a-time boyfriend seemed to affect her more than threats against her precious family.

The thought occurred to him that maybe he should arrange to have Flynn killed anyway. There were people for hire who took care of that kind of thing. Why not?

Hammond smiled grimly at the thought.

Damn! He hadn't called Eddie back. And he'd instructed him not to call unless it was urgent.

Too late now, thanks to Sierra. He'd call Eddie first thing in the morning.

"Can I get you a drink, Senator?"

Hammond turned to inspect Renee, the stewardess with the Australian accent. She wasn't bad-looking, although a little horsey with her large teeth and generous mouth. She was tall, though, which meant long legs. He was quite partial to long legs, especially when they were wrapped around his neck while his penis was firmly tucked inside the owner of the legs.

Why hadn't he noticed this one before?

Probably because the pushy Mexican girl had taken center stage, while this one had hovered on the sidelines.

He glanced over at Sierra. She was engaged in conversation with Ashley and Cliff.

"What's your name, dear?" he asked the stewardess, turning his back on his wife.

The girl blinked like a startled deer. "Uh . . . uh . . . Renee," she stammered, blushing slightly.

Ah, she was impressed. A United States senator was asking for her name, and she was thrilled.

Of course she was.

"Where are you from?"

"Australia."

"I gathered that from your accent. Whereabouts in Australia?"

"Brisbane, actually."

Hammond's eyes dipped to her breasts. Not too big, not too small. He would've liked them to be bigger, but maybe her nipples would compensate. Hammond had a thing about nipples; he preferred them erect and chewy—all the better to bite on.

"Renee is a very pretty name for a very pretty girl," he said, giving her the sincere smile that always worked.

"Thank you," she murmured, lowering her eyes.

He winked at her. "I'll have a glass of champagne, Renee."

More blushing. He was on her radar.

He would fuck her. She was ripe and ready. Better than the redhead. Better than the blonde with the big tits. Better than their hostess. And sure as hell better than the Asian piece of work.

Hammond knew a sure thing when he saw it.

66

Preparations were in overdrive. Cruz's men were more than ready; they were on fire and primed for action. Too much lazing around was not good for them.

Second thoughts about going along with them on their mission were plaguing Sergei. Much as he harbored a strong desire to be the first to see Aleksandr Kasianenko's expression when they boarded the *Bianca,* Cruz was right: he had no experience when it came to hijacking. What if he got shot or knifed or injured in any other way? It could all go wrong, and he might easily become a victim.

Cruz's gang of misfits were heavily armed for battle, which made Sergei seriously think about veering toward the cautious side. He didn't fully trust Cruz. If anything happened to him, Ina's brother stood to gain the full ransom, so wasn't it foolish to set himself up as a target?

He'd financed this entire operation, and it had cost him plenty, but if Cruz got greedy, he wasn't about to have it cost him his life.

Finally he came to the conclusion that the smart thing to do was back off the actual raid, and have Cruz's men bring Kasianenko to him while he stayed at the villa and waited.

When he informed Cruz of his change of heart, he thought he noticed a flash of triumph flit across the Mexican man's weather-beaten face.

Interesting. It paid to always be alert.

"I'll be sendin' two of my men with you to grab Kasianenko," he announced. "You'll arrange to have a couple of your team bring him back on one of the boats. I'll be waiting."

"That means I'm gonna be two men short," Cruz complained, spitting on the ground. "Not possible."

Sergei had not come this far to get into a pissing match with Ina's annoying brother. "Then I suggest you make it possible," he ordered coldly. "Bring Kasianenko to me, then my men'll take over, and your men can return to you."

"Chingado," Cruz muttered under his breath.

"You should be smiling," Sergei said, a note of menace in his voice. "Now you don't got me on the boat where you didn't want me gettin' in your fuckin' way. Remember?"

Cruz's mouth twisted into a hard smile. "Sure," he said. "I can work it out."

"Make certain you do that," Sergei said. "'Cause you an' me, we wouldn't wanna screw with each other, would we?"

Cruz shrugged and groped in his pocket for a cigarette. "Never," he lied.

Ina wandered down to the dock, fully aware that both Cruz and Sergei would be furious if they caught her. So what? She was bored sitting around in the villa with nothing to do. They'd warned her not to sunbathe by the pool, but they'd never mentioned anything about not going down to the dock.

She wore high-heeled silver sandals and a white mesh cover-up over her bikini. Large black sunglasses hid her eyes.

Cruz's men were busy.

Ina stood by observing. She smiled at the youngest pirate, who wasn't bad-looking in a Johnny Depp kind of way. He wore torn jeans and a sloppy T-shirt, with a colorful scarf flowing from around his neck. She noticed his beautiful high cheekbones, and wondered what it would be like to make love to someone so young. One thing was for sure: he wouldn't call her fat and whack her on the ass. He would be honored to have the pleasure of being with her.

Now he was returning her smile.

She noticed an attractive gold tooth and threw him a little wave. Then Cruz ruined everything by creeping up on her and yanking her by the arm. "Get back in the house," he growled. "An' don't lemme see you down here again."

Ina turned and walked back toward the house, but not before giving Cashoo one last lingering look.

67

"We're going to the press," Martin Byrne announced, ruddy cheeks ablaze. "This waiting around is a travesty. Skylar is nervous and upset. My wife is hysterical. We have to resolve this."

"Talking to the press will resolve nothing," Eddie said, his voice strained as he tried to figure out what to do next. "They'll jump on the story with no facts, and your daughter will be crucified, exactly like Monica Lewinsky."

"How dare you mention that Lewinsky woman and Skylar in the same breath," Martin huffed, pacing up and down. "My daughter was sexually molested. It's time the truth came out."

"I understand your dilemma," Eddie said, attempting to stay calm and in control as he tried to reason with Skylar's father. "However, I can assure you that until I speak with the senator, you should hold off doing anything."

Lurking outside Eddie's office, Radical, Hammond's illegitimate fifteen-year-old daughter, kept her ear to the door.

Shitballs! This was, like, juicy stuff. Daddy Dearest had been fiddling with some girl called Skylar.

Did stepmom Sierra know?

Was this news fresh off the block?

Could she make money from it?

Radical was all for scoring extra bucks—money made

the world go 'round, and it also meant she could stock up on grass and coke without having to blow her New York dealer, who was a Puerto Rican ass-wipe and preferred blow jobs to cash.

As it was, she'd gotten thrown out of her Swiss boarding school for making out with her French teacher, who'd gotten canned.

Now that she was back in New York, it was time to, like, live it up. And money—plenty of it—could only help.

Skylar, huh?

Radical formed a plan.

68

Yet another dinner in paradise with an array of culinary delights served in a magnificent setting. What more could anyone ask?

Taking in her surroundings, Lori had no idea how she was supposed to ease back into normal life. She was savoring every moment of this once-in-a-lifetime trip. Everything was so perfect, including Cliff. She dreaded returning to their old routine, and the daily visit from Enid when Cliff wasn't at the studio. Enid was a jealous old bag who—even though she claimed to be gay—probably had the hots for her handsome boss.

Get a life, Enid, and leave us alone.

Without Enid's interference, Lori felt that she and Cliff might have a real chance of staying together. Enid was a witch; she put the evil eye on her.

"What're you thinking?" Luca inquired, approaching her as she stood by the railing on the terrace, watching the dark waves crash on the beach below.

"I'm thinking that this is a truly wonderful experience," Lori replied. "It's . . . I don't know . . . kind of magical in a way."

"That's 'cause you're in love," Luca said, adding a wistful, "I wish I was."

"You will be," Lori assured him. "Once you're free, you'll have your pick of anyone you want."

"You think so?"

"Oh, come *on*, get with the program," Lori encouraged. "You're Luca Perez. Didn't I just read that *People en Español* magazine voted you their sexiest star of the year?"

Luca shrugged. "It makes me nervous thinking about being by myself."

"Oh my *God!*" Lori exclaimed. "If *you're* nervous, then what the hell am I? Let's not forget that you're famous, rich, *and* gorgeous. You've got nothing to be nervous about."

"And you're a sweet girl, Lori," Luca said warmly. "Your friendship means a lot to me. When we get back to the real world, we'll stay in touch, yes?"

"Nothing I'd like more."

"I can be your new gay best friend," he joked. "Every girl needs one."

"Especially me," Lori said, thinking of her lack of real friends in L.A. "I don't have many friends—gay or straight."

"How come?"

"It's just the way it is," she said with a thoughtful sigh. "I'm a movie star's girlfriend. People can't figure out how long I'll be around."

"If Cliff's smart, it'll be a lifetime deal."

"You're the best! I think I love you!"

"What are you two up to?" Cliff questioned, joining them.

"Oh, nothing much. I was just telling Luca what a babe he is," Lori said, winking at Luca. "I think I love him."

"Should I be jealous?" Cliff asked, amused.

"No!" Lori giggled. "Anyway, I thought you were busy talking to Ashley."

"*She* was talking to *me*," Cliff explained with a rueful grin. "Or rather, her tits were talking to me while *I* was trying to escape. Got a hunch she might be a bit of a fan."

"Well, *that's* the understatement of the year," Lori

exclaimed, with a quick laugh. "She's all over you every opportunity she gets. Everyone's noticed."

"Really?" Cliff said with a sly smile.

"Don't act as if you don't know," Lori scolded. "Being modest doesn't suit you."

"I feel sorry for Taye," Luca lamented. "He's such a great guy."

"Do *not* worry about Taye," Lori said. "Am I the only one to see that Bianca is practically eating him for dinner?"

"She is?" Luca said. "What about our host? He doesn't mind?"

"Our host is busy making plans with Xuan about all sorts of humanitarian causes," Lori said knowingly. "They're quite a match."

Cliff started to laugh. It pleased him to note that everyone seemed to enjoy Lori's company. "Aren't *you* the little observer," he said affectionately.

"I keep my eyes open," she responded.

"You certainly do."

"I certainly do," Lori replied, mimicking him.

They exchanged an intimate smile.

"Come, my favorite redhead," Cliff said, putting his arm around her. "Let's go take a walk on the beach."

"Will you excuse us, Luca?" Lori said, smiling happily.

"Sure," Luca said, drifting back toward the table where Jeromy was earnestly trying to talk Sierra and Hammond into purchasing a pied-à-terre in London.

"My darlings, there is nothing like a summer day in a London park," Jeromy said grandly, filled with nostalgia as he recalled his first encounter with a male sex partner behind a tree in Regent's Park. He was thirteen at the time.

"We hardly ever visit London," Sierra said, studiously trying to avoid even so much as glancing in Flynn's direction as he spoke with Xuan and Aleksandr.

It was impossible—her mind refused to be still as she imagined Flynn making love to the Asian woman. She pictured them in bed together, naked and passionate, all over each other. It was all too much, and her eyes filled with tears. She was dismayed to realize that she was jealous. Hopelessly, helplessly jealous.

"I have to use the restroom," Hammond said, abruptly rising. "Would you keep my wife company, Jeromy?"

"My pleasure, Senator," Jeromy replied, catching Luca's eye and beckoning him over.

Hammond left the table. He'd noticed Renee hovering by the ornate arched doorway and he immediately approached her. "Where is the men's room?" he asked, all business.

"Oh," she said, fidgeting nervously with an escaped strand of dark-blond hair. "Let me show you, Senator. I'm supposed to escort everyone there in case they get lost. This castle is huge."

"I'm not everyone," Hammond said mildly. "Just plain old me."

"I know," Renee said with a feeble giggle. "But you're a very important you."

Hammond smiled. He was never averse to compliments.

The interior of the castle was dark and cold. Nobody lived there—it was merely a place that could be rented out for special occasions. Long winding corridors led to a series of small rooms, and finally a semi-modernized bathroom that was completely out of sync with the rest of the castle.

"I can wait outside to guide you back," Renee offered.

Hammond studied her for a moment, moving close. "You are such a pretty girl," he informed her. "So very lovely."

"Uh . . . thank you," she mumbled, flattered that an important man like Senator Patterson had even noticed her.

"Would it be presumptuous if I were to kiss you?" he asked, deciding that he had no time to waste luring her in with seductive words.

Renee was ablaze with excitement, yet at the same time quite apprehensive.

Surely he was married? And not only that, but his wife was on the trip with him.

"Uh . . ." she stuttered, unsure of what to say.

Before she could say anything at all, Hammond's lips were upon hers, his tongue pushing its way aggressively into her mouth.

She tried to gasp, but couldn't. His hands were suddenly on her breasts. Everything felt dangerous and forbidden.

Was this really happening?

What if someone came along?

What if the senator's wife caught them?

Or Guy? He would fire her for sure.

The day Guy had hired her he'd given her a strict lecture about never getting inappropriate with a guest.

Hammond's hands had snaked their way under her uniform. He began manipulating her nipples through her bra, playing with them hard.

His lips left hers and this time she did gasp, a long, drawn-out gasp of pure desire.

Hammond knew he had her.

Young girls were so easy.

69

By the time they got back to the yacht, Bianca and Aleksandr were still not talking. Both strong personalities, neither of them was prepared to give in.

Bianca was livid that Aleksandr had spent the majority of the evening fraternizing with the enemy. Xuan. Asian bitch. Sneaky little man-stealer. Bianca hated her, and more than anything, she wanted her off the boat.

Some of their guests had gone to the upper deck for after-dinner drinks. Bianca chose to join them. Aleksandr could do what he liked—she didn't care.

Yet the truth was that she *did* care. A lot. He was her man, and he was behaving like a stubborn asshole. Typical male behavior.

On the upper deck, Taye and Ashley were all over each other in one corner. Jeromy was boring the shit out of Flynn, who couldn't stop agonizing over Sierra, while Luca was sitting with Lori and Cliff. Everyone else had gone to bed.

Bianca chose to join the Luca group. "What's up?" she asked Luca.

"What's up with you?" he replied. "Are you an' Mr. Russia in a fight?"

Bianca tossed back her long braided hair, green eyes gleaming. "What makes you think that?"

"It doesn't take a genius to see what's going on."

"Nothing," Bianca said stubbornly. "Nothing is going on."

"Bullshit," Luca responded. "It's me you're talking to."

"I think it's time for bed," Cliff said, standing up and stretching.

Lori followed his lead and said good night to everyone, and the two of them took off.

"I wish you were straight," Bianca said wistfully, gazing at Luca.

"How would that solve anything?" he asked, never sure what kind of crazy logic Bianca would come up with.

"'Cause then you an' I could fuck all our cares away," Bianca said with a flippant laugh. "Wouldn't *that* be fun?"

"Spoken like a true princess," Luca said dryly.

Bianca frowned. "Do you think I'm being petty?" she asked.

"I dunno what you're supposed to be being petty about," Luca said, getting a tad impatient, because as far as he could tell, Bianca had everything she could ever want—including a magnificent yacht named after her.

"Aleksandr and Miss China Doll or whatever the hell she is," Bianca snapped. "She's getting on my tits."

"Whoa!" Luca objected, rolling his eyes. "Let's not get racist here."

"Are you calling *me* a racist?" Bianca objected. "I'm black, remember? I've been called more names—"

"Okay, okay," Luca said, holding up his hand. "Tell me the problem."

"Only if you promise to dump Jeromy the moment we hit dry land," Bianca said. "Your boyfriend is a pompous prick, and I hate seeing him bring you down."

"How'd we get onto the subject of Jeromy?"

"Promise you'll *sayonara* him?"

"I already decided. It's a done deal. Your turn."

And so Bianca began to voice her complaints about Xuan and all the various projects she was trying to involve Aleksandr in.

Luca sat back and listened. It was good for Bianca to spill.

When the tenders returned to the yacht, Mercedes managed to stay out of Guy's way. If he saw her, she wouldn't put it past him to expect her to help unload the dishes and all the other crap from the boats. Let Renee and Den deal with it; she'd accomplished everything she needed to, and now it was time to lie on her bunk bed and contemplate the adventure ahead.

She'd had a busy night making sure everything was set for Cruz's takeover the following night. She knew exactly what she had to do, and number one was making sure Kyril was out of commission. He was the only real threat, and his usual mug of hot chocolate loaded with horse tranquilizers should definitely take care of him.

She wondered what men Cruz would bring with him. Amiin for sure—he was always by Cruz's side. And maybe Cashoo. She had a bit of a soft spot for Cashoo. He was young, although sexy as hell with his permanent boner that she enjoyed teasing him about, but that's as far as it went. Cruz had taught her at an early age—*never fuck where you do business.*

Thanks, Papa. Good advice.

Mercedes wasn't nervous; she never got scared. She was looking forward to the takeover. It was always a tense and invigorating time. She'd seen people get shot or knifed for not doing what they were told, and although bloodshed wasn't her favorite thing, if it happened it was because people didn't listen.

Dumb people didn't listen. If only they'd follow orders, everything would be okay and nobody would get hurt.

Who's dumb on this trip?

All of them.

Eventually Mercedes drifted off into a semi-sleep, and did not awake until Renee came in. The Australian girl was making too much noise, which pissed Mercedes off.

"What t' fuck," she mumbled. "I'm tryin' t' sleep here."

"Sorry," Renee said, clambering into the top bunk. "It's just that—"

"What?" Mercedes grumbled. "Spit it out!"

"Well . . . uh . . ."

"Did Guy tear you a new asshole? 'Cause if he did, you gotta learn to ignore it. I do."

"One of the passengers wants to sleep with me," Renee blurted out.

"*Whaaat?*" Mercedes sat up and burst out laughing. "You're shittin' me. Who?"

"Oh gosh!" Renee said, blushing crimson. "I don't know if I should say anything."

"You just did," Mercedes pointed out. "Who's the *cabrón* with the hard dick? Gimme a name."

"I think he really likes me," Renee moaned. "And here's the thing: he's so sweet and nice and . . . and he's very important."

"If you don't tell me who it is, I'm going back to sleep," Mercedes threatened.

"The senator," Renee whispered. "And I think I like him back."

70

"Are you Skylar?"

"Huh?" Skylar Byrne took a step back from the girl with the crazy green streaks in her short black hair and the most uncomfortable-looking piercings in her nose and eyebrows. "Who're you?"

"Name's Radical, an' I get it, 'cause I'm, like, just as pissed as you."

Skylar took another step back. Was this a case of mistaken identity? Who was this girl and what did she want?

The two of them were standing at the Fifth Avenue entrance to Central Park, Skylar dressed for jogging in yellow shorts and a pale blue T-shirt emblazoned with "I vote for puppies," Radical in ripped jeans and a gray hoodie over a red T-shirt with "Hate" splashed across the front.

"Do I know you?" Skylar asked, hopping from foot to foot.

"You don't hav'ta know me," Radical replied, squinting. "'Cause *I* know *you*."

"You do, huh," Skylar said, standing up a little straighter.

Radical reached into the back pocket of her jeans and pulled out a crumpled pack of cigarettes. She extracted one and offered it to Skylar.

Skylar shook her head.

"Suit yourself," Radical said, scrounging for a book of matches and lighting up with a defiant flourish. "I'd sooner have a joint," she remarked. "Only, like, not in public. You smoke grass?"

"Who *are* you?" Skylar repeated. "What do you want?"

"I *want* for us to make money. Big bucks," Radical stated matter-of-factly. "An' if you're down with it, I know *exactly*, like, how we can do it."

Skylar couldn't help herself. Common sense informed her that she should be walking away, but curiosity got the better of her. "What are you talking about?" she asked.

And Radical began to explain.

71

Flynn, Taye, and Cliff spent the morning working out in the gym. Flynn because he needed to purge all the angst he was feeling. Taye because he loved keeping his ripped body in fantastic shape. And Cliff because he hadn't been in such a good mood in years. Besides, he was heading toward fifty; better keep everything in working order, especially since he had a much younger girlfriend, a girlfriend he planned to hang on to.

Taye chose the music—Tinie Tempah, Jay-Z, and Wiz Khalifa. The sounds were fast and furious, blasting and full of pounding energy.

Flynn would've preferred the Stones or a laid-back Dave Matthews. Cliff was more into old-school classics such as Sinatra or Tony Bennett. However, they both went along with Taye's choice since he seemed so into it.

The three of them had a competitive time sweating it out. Three guys with nothing else to do except work on their bodies. It was a bonding experience.

Meanwhile, Bianca, Luca, Ashley, and Lori lolled by the pool, soaking up the sun and sipping on ice-cold frozen margaritas. It was one of those lazy days, and everyone felt very relaxed. Everyone except Jeromy, who was sulking in his room, because he was acutely aware of Luca's withdrawal and yet helpless to stop the inevitable. He knew it was coming. He knew the signs.

He decided to leave his room and find Guy. He had a need to release his pent-up frustration, and Guy was the only one capable of helping him out.

Too bad if he didn't want to. Guy was the entertainment director. Let him entertain.

Aleksandr was engrossed in making plans with Xuan about the orphanage he'd decided to build outside Moscow. Xuan had many innovative and intelligent ideas, and he was interested in hearing them.

It wasn't long before he found himself revealing details of his own miserable childhood, things he'd never told anyone. It was a cathartic experience to expose so much of himself, and he found it to be most comforting. He was more and more drawn to Xuan as he shared memories of a horrific childhood—a childhood he'd not even revealed to Bianca, since she'd never shown any interest in hearing about his roots.

Now that he was talking about it, he felt a burden lifting, freeing him from his past.

In return, Xuan started telling him some of *her* early stories. He soon realized that they were even more harrowing than his. Watching her as she spoke, he was starting to feel true compassion for her. She was so different from any woman he'd ever known. She was nurturing and clever, and also very sensual in a low-key kind of way. There was nothing overt about Xuan; her sexuality was a private thing.

Aleksandr started wondering about her and Flynn, and exactly how strong their relationship was.

Not that he was thinking of doing anything about it . . . or was he?

Xuan was the first woman who'd stirred his sexual interest since he'd been with Bianca.

Why was it happening now?

Maybe because Bianca was acting like such a spoiled bitch. Over nothing.

Aleksandr was angry. At Bianca. *And* at himself.

He was planning on asking Bianca to marry him. Surely he shouldn't be thinking about another woman at such a special time?

"You stay here," Hammond ordered his wife. "I'm going to call Eddie, see what's so goddamn important that it couldn't wait until I get back."

"I should come with you," Sierra suggested, not wanting to be by herself and face the temptation of popping Xanax again.

"Why?" Hammond said harshly. "So you can make eyes at your boyfriend?"

Sierra sighed and shook her head. "For the last time, Flynn is *not* my boyfriend. I have no feelings for him whatsoever. Please believe me."

"Just remember what I told you I can arrange to have done to him," Hammond taunted. "I am *not* joking."

"I know you're not," she said dully. "What happened between Flynn and me was a long time ago. You have no need to worry."

"Me? Worry?" Hammond scoffed. "Believe me, dear, it would take a better man than Flynn Hudson to make *me* worry."

Sierra hoped she'd made it clear to Hammond that she cared nothing for Flynn. If he thought she cared one little bit, who knew what he was capable of? She had to tread carefully, maybe even warn Flynn if that was possible.

"As I said, you stay here until I get back. Then we will go to lunch and present a united front," Hammond said, opening the door and stepping out. "Perhaps you can be charming for once. Wouldn't that make a pleasant change?"

Sierra watched him go with hate in her heart. He'd trapped her once again with his vile threats.

Would she ever be free?

Deep down she knew it was up to her.

Bianca could not believe that Aleksandr was taking their stupid fight all the way, even though it was ruining what should have been a perfect trip. She was determined not to be the first to give in.

After all, she was right and he was wrong.

An apology had better be forthcoming soon.

Luca was the only one who was fully aware of what was going on, although Bianca supposed the others must have noticed that their host and hostess were not talking.

She couldn't care less. It had now become a matter of principle.

Jeromy accosted Guy on the stairs shortly before lunch. "Where's your cabin?" he demanded, holding on tightly to Guy's upper arm, his nails digging into Guy's flesh.

Guy attempted to shake the Englishman's grip, to no avail. Jeromy was determined.

"I . . . I'll be serving lunch shortly," Guy stammered.

"You'll be serving nothing if I complain to Mr. Kasianenko," Jeromy cautioned. "So I suggest that you take me to your godforsaken cabin, and do it *now*. I'll only use a minute or two of your precious time."

A thousand thoughts crashed through Guy's head. Did he have to do this? Would Kasianenko really fire him if Jeromy Milton-Gold complained? Was it worth making a drama out of one forced blow job?

Then he decided—do it and forget it. Piss in the wanker's soup for the rest of the trip.

"Your choice?" Jeromy growled.

"Follow me," Guy said, compliant, for if he wanted to keep his job, what other way was there?

* * *

Making polite conversation with the captain while waiting for his satellite call to go through, Hammond inquired if there were any more island trips planned.

Captain Dickson was cagey; he didn't want to reveal to the senator that the final island trip was to take place the following night, because he wasn't sure how much Mr. Kasianenko had told everyone. It was to be a spectacular night with fireworks, famous surprise performers, and food flown in from three of Bianca's favorite L.A. restaurants. It was to be a lovefest for Bianca, and Captain Dickson had a strong suspicion that the billionaire Russian was planning on proposing to his mercurial ladylove.

Hammond gazed out at the calm blue sea and thought about the long-legged stewardess—Jenni or Renee or whatever her name was. He would definitely be partaking of that. Maybe later, when everyone had gone to bed.

Yes. She would know of somewhere they could be alone together. Why deprive himself?

He fantasized about her long legs locked behind his neck. About brushing his cock against those big horse teeth. She was young and not too experienced, exactly the way he liked them.

"Here's your call, Senator," Captain Dickson said, handing him the phone.

"Eddie," Hammond barked. "What the hell do you want?"

Lunch was tense. Bianca and Aleksandr were still at odds. After a not-so-satisfying dalliance with Guy, Jeromy was desperately trying to ingratiate himself with whomever he could. Hammond was in a foul mood, while Flynn was still trying to come up with a "get out of paradise" excuse.

Only Luca, Lori, Cliff, Taye, and Ashley seemed in the holiday spirit as they discussed their afternoon of more water sports. Fun and games was the order of the day. Diving, snorkeling, racing the WaveRunners. It was all on.

Bianca sat beside Aleksandr, picking at her lobster and crab salad, drinking a healthy amount of red wine, and stewing about Xuan.

"After lunch, all the girls are going topless," she suddenly announced, shooting Xuan a spiteful look. "Are you in?"

"No," Xuan answered quite simply. "I do not believe in mass nudity."

"Mass nudity!" Bianca shrieked. "It's hardly mass nudity when you're among friends."

"I prefer not to," Xuan said, remaining polite.

"Why not?" Bianca insisted. "You got something to hide?"

Aleksandr shot her a piercing look. "Enough," he said sternly.

Bianca took another gulp of red wine. "Oh please!" she slurred. "You know you're dying to see her tiny little Chinese titties."

Aleksandr stood up and reached for Bianca's arm to pull her to her feet. She resisted, and her wineglass toppled over, spilling red wine in a little river heading straight for Xuan's lap.

"Sorry!" Bianca mumbled, dissolving into a fit of giggles. "Accident, I swear."

"Come with me," Aleksandr said, this time getting a firm grip on her arm.

"Ooh!" Bianca mocked in a singsong fashion. "Have I been a naughty girl? I thought you *liked* naughty girls, Alek, or have your tastes changed?"

Tight-lipped, Aleksandr did not answer as he maneuvered Bianca away from the table.

An embarrassed silence ensued, broken by Ashley. "Are we really going topless?" she asked, quite excited at the thought of displaying her bought-and-paid-for assets to Cliff.

Taye threw her a grim look. "Not on my watch, toots. Those titties are strictly all mine."

72

"Once you get goin', how long before you reach the yacht?" Sergei inquired, the nerve in his left cheek twitching as he attempted to ferret out answers.

Cruz, a perennial cigarette dangling from his lower lip, shrugged. "Coupla hours," he said casually. "The fuckin' boat's not that far out. They're stayin' around an' cruisin' the islands."

"Then after you take off, I can expect my men back with Kasianenko in four hours?"

"Don't 'spect nothin'," Cruz said, ash falling from his cigarette onto the ground. "Nobody knows how it's gonna go down. We gotta secure the yacht before we go lookin' for Kasianenko. It takes time. We hav'ta plan for the un-expected."

Sergei kept a tight rein on his temper. All along, Cruz had assured him that taking over the *Bianca* was an easy hit, and now he was voicing doubts?

Sergei scowled impatiently. It was happening tonight, and for Cruz's sake it had better go fast and smooth.

For the last twenty-four hours, his own personal security had been putting together a safe room where he planned on keeping Kasianenko. The room was in the basement of the villa, a cold dank room generally used for storage. Sergei had arranged for the door to be reinforced, special locks fitted, and solid handcuffs attached to the stone wall.

It was designed to be Kasianenko's new home. Sergei couldn't wait for his sworn enemy to take up residence.

Boredom drove Ina to do things she knew she shouldn't. However, what Cruz didn't know . . .

She found a way to get out of the villa without Cruz noticing. Once out, she attracted Cashoo's attention, directing him via hand signals to meet her on the beach beyond a large formation of rocks.

Cashoo was hot to do whatever the boss's woman wanted him to do. He had no scruples or guilt; he was simply a young man with a raging libido.

Ina had no intention of going all the way with Cashoo. She merely wanted to play with him for her own amusement.

They did not speak a word of each other's language. But who needed words when unbridled lust was a suitable form of communication?

Cashoo circled her like a wary coyote.

She smiled and unbuttoned her blouse, shaking her large breasts at him.

Cashoo had never seen enhanced breasts before. So big and firm. He reached out to touch them with his bony fingers.

Ina slapped his hands away, then unzipped his jeans, directing his long thin hard-on toward her breasts.

He got the idea and plunged his penis between her huge breasts. Within seconds he ejaculated.

Ina smiled at him once more before shooing him away.

It made a pleasant change to own the power for once. It was her way of getting back at both Cruz and Sergei for treating her as if she didn't matter.

They thought they owned her.

Think again.

She knew everything about both of them.

73

After speaking to Eddie in New York, Hammond sank into a black fury. Goddammit, he was out of town for a few short days, and all of a sudden there was a girl he barely knew accusing him of sexual harassment.

Skylar Byrne, some stupid dumb intern who—as far as he could recall—had come on to *him*.

Or had she? Whatever . . .

Bitch! Fucking bitch! They were all bitches at heart.

How *dare* she accuse him? And how dare Eddie go along with it as if the girl were telling the truth?

The truth was that she was waiting for a big payout. Eddie was just too dumb to realize what was going on.

On top of that nonsense, Eddie informed him that Radical had been expelled from her strict Swiss boarding school and was now staying at his apartment until Hammond and Sierra arrived home.

Great. Radical. Such a perfect boost for his public image with her green-streaked dyed black hair and her unbearable snotty teenage attitude.

Hammond was fully aware that he would need Sierra's help in dealing with both of these problems. The public was in love with Sierra; she was their darling and could do no wrong. This was excellent, because he needed her to shut down Skylar's accusations before he shipped Radical off to another boarding school far, far away. One thing about Sierra: she kept a clear head when it came to putting out fires. She'd know exactly how to manage this crisis.

He'd told Eddie to shut the Byrnes up by promising them a meeting the moment he got back. Sierra would have to be at that meeting, supporting him while he informed the Byrnes that it was all the fantasies of a power-struck young girl with a crush, who'd used her imagination to make up silly stories. With Sierra in the room, there was no way the Byrnes would believe their daughter. It would be his word against Skylar's, and nobody played honest, moral, and upstanding better than Hammond Patterson—especially with the lovely Sierra by his side.

Unfortunately, the timing was hardly perfect, what with Sierra getting restless because of seeing Flynn Hudson, who'd apparently fed her a mouthful of lies.

Well, not actually lies. Hammond *had* doctored the photos to break them up. Flynn had not deserved a girl like Sierra, so he'd dealt with the situation. At the time, it had cost him, but the results were well worth it.

The car accident was a happy mistake, causing Sierra to lose Flynn's baby. Good riddance to that. Although the downside was that she'd taken off, and it was a few years before he'd managed to lure her back in and marry her.

Sierra Kathleen Snow. The perfect political wife. She was his ace in the hole, and there was no way he was letting her go.

It was unfortunate that Flynn had inserted himself back into their lives again, stirring Sierra up, trying to persuade her to break free.

As usual, Hammond had managed to get her under control. She always believed his threats, and so she should, because in his mind, he knew he was capable of anything. And he was *certainly* capable of getting rid of Flynn once and for all.

When they got back to New York, the demise of Flynn Hudson was number one on his agenda.

* * *

"I think I'm ready to return to the real world," Flynn remarked to Cliff as they sat on the top deck drinking Jack and Cokes before dinner. "All this luxury, it's not for me. I need to be where the action is."

"You gotta admit it's not bad, though," Cliff said, reaching for the guacamole dip. "I could get used to it. Might even buy myself a sailboat."

"I'm going to try an' leave tomorrow," Flynn said, clinking the ice in his glass.

"It's the big birthday night tomorrow," Cliff reminded him. "Why not wait?"

"Got things to deal with," Flynn said restlessly. "Besides, I'm better off on dry land."

Cliff nodded. "I get it, but I'm happy to be taking a break. No paparazzi, no interviews, no five A.M. calls to the set."

The two of them had become quite friendly over the past few days. Cliff had enjoyed listening to Flynn's stories about his world travels.

"You know," Cliff said, signaling Renee for a refill, "you should consider writing a script."

"Why's that?" Flynn asked, thinking that there was nothing he'd like less.

"'Cause you've had some damn fascinating adventures."

"Kinda," Flynn said modestly.

"You'll write a dynamite script, I'll star in it," Cliff said, getting into the idea. "It's about time I played a real character with integrity."

"What makes you think I've got integrity?" Flynn quipped.

Cliff laughed. "Y'know, I like you," he said. "You're an interesting guy. You should take a trip to L.A. Come stay with me and Lori for a couple of weeks, months, whatever suits you. Bring Xuan—that's if you can pry her away from Aleksandr."

"Uh . . . yeah," Flynn said, hesitating for a moment. "About Xuan—between us—she's not my girlfriend."

"You don't have to explain to me." Cliff paused, then added an expectant, "Although, if you're in the mood to talk, what's up with you and the senator?"

"I guess you heard about the fight?" Flynn said ruefully.

"Hey, this yacht is luxurious, but it's still close quarters. What goes on soon spreads around. Not to mention the shiner you gave him. Ever thought of doing stunt work?"

Flynn grimaced. "He deserved it."

"No love lost between you two?"

"We go back, all the way to college," Flynn ruminated. "Hammond was always a prick."

"He's done well for being a prick."

"An insidious, smart prick, I'll give him that," Flynn allowed. "Treacherous as a fucking snake."

"Suitable character traits for a politician," Cliff said dryly. "Believe me, I've met a few of those."

"You live in L.A. Why am I not surprised?"

Cliff cleared his throat and laughed. "So . . . the current battle?" he inquired, as Renee delivered his fresh drink.

"Long story," Flynn said, rubbing his chin.

"Aren't they all?"

"Wouldn't want to bore you."

"I'm an actor," Cliff said flashing his movie-star smile. "We live to listen to other people's stories."

"Okay, you asked for it," Flynn said, deciding that if he didn't tell his story to someone soon, it was going to suffocate him.

And so he began . . .

"Something unfortunate has taken place," Hammond announced, as he and Sierra moved around their stateroom getting ready to go up for dinner.

For a moment Sierra panicked. Had Hammond

somehow or other managed to throw Flynn overboard? Was Flynn dead?

Oh God! Her face paled, and she could barely speak. "What?" she muttered.

"There's this young intern," Hammond said matter-of-factly. "A new girl at the office. She's developed what you might call an obsessive crush on me."

"Why are you telling me this?" Sierra asked, relief overcoming her.

"Because," Hammond said in a sanctimonious tone, "as my dear wife, you need to be aware of these things."

"And that would be why?" Sierra asked, eyeing him warily. Something was coming, something she wasn't going to like.

"This poor deluded girl is apparently accusing me of improper conduct toward her."

Sierra almost burst out laughing. Improper conduct indeed! Had Hammond tried to fuck her and gotten caught? She couldn't be happier.

"Oh dear," she murmured. "That *is* unfortunate."

"It's nothing earth-shattering," Hammond continued. "However, we do have to deal with it."

"'We'?" Sierra questioned, taking pleasure in making him squirm a little.

"Yes, we," Hammond said sharply, not appreciating her attitude.

"And what if I don't care to help you out on this?" Sierra said coolly.

Hammond's jaw tightened as a venomous expression crossed his face. "I can tell you're not listening to me, my dear," he said, icy cold. "It seems you are forgetting the things I can arrange. It seems that perhaps you do not care about the well-being of a certain someone."

Threats.

Again.

Forever.

She was still caught in his trap.

* * *

"Exactly how long are you planning on keeping this up?" Aleksandr inquired when Bianca awoke from a too-much-red-wine-induced sleep.

Bianca slid from the bed, glared at her lover, made her way into the bathroom, and slammed the door. "Until you apologize," she yelled from behind the closed door.

Aleksandr was frustrated. Bianca and her jealous fits were ruining their trip. She was one obstinate woman behaving badly.

Was he making a mistake proposing to her?

Did she deserve the two-million-dollar rare emerald and diamond ring he had stashed in his safe?

If she didn't come around by tomorrow, he was seriously contemplating canceling the celebratory dinner he'd organized. The dinner at the end of which he'd been planning on giving her the ring.

"I am going up to join our guests," he shouted at the closed door. "We'll see you later if you're not too hungover."

"Fuck you!" a furious Bianca retaliated.

Another fine evening in paradise.

74

Cruz dressed for business. Army fatigues. Combat boots with special rubber soles. A flak jacket with plenty of useful pockets to hold his pistols and knives. He was a walking fortress, ready for anything.

Amiin was dressed in a more colorful fashion. Although his outfit was all dark brown, on his head he wore a bright orange wool cap, and around his neck were several long flowing scarves of various colors.

Cashoo opted for jeans, two T-shirts under a heavy sweatshirt to keep out the cold, and a red bandana across his forehead.

There was no dress code for pirates. They wore whatever they chose to wear; it was the weapons that mattered. Each of the two boats was fully loaded with assault rifles, semi-automatic combat pistols, rocket blasters, machetes, and an assortment of swords—a Somalian tribal thing.

Cruz didn't care how his men operated, as long as they got the job done.

Viktor and Maksim, the two bodyguards Sergei was sending to bring Kasianenko back, were both of Russian origin. They'd been with Sergei for several years and they were loyal soldiers in Sergei's army of security. Neither of them was happy about this mission. They were not seafaring men; they were security bodyguards who preferred to operate on dry land. However, Sergei paid top dollar, so they did as they were told, whether they liked it or not.

They regarded the pirates as useless scum, way beneath them.

In turn, the pirates jeered and laughed at them with their close-cropped hair, neat clothes, and Glock guns. There was no love lost. There was certainly no respect.

Sergei lectured them both before their departure. "What you gotta do is keep your eye on Kasianenko. You bring him to me, an' you'll be well rewarded. Oh yeah, an' see that those morons don't shoot him in the head by mistake. I want him alive an' kickin' like a fuckin' wild pig. Got it?"

They got it.

Meanwhile, Cruz was busy checking the weather. There was a storm brewing, only it wasn't due to hit until four or five A.M. His goal was to reach the *Bianca* by two A.M. By the time the storm moved in, they would have already boarded and taken over the yacht, and he would be on the phone making ransom demands.

Timing was everything.

Cruz was an expert at timing.

75

Dinner on the *Bianca* was a casual affair. Aleksandr had informed everyone that since tomorrow was Bianca's birthday celebration, tonight would be low-key. The theme of the night was a barbecue to take place on the upper deck. Two tables of six. Checkered tablecloths. Beer and red wine. Country music on the speakers. Couples seated together. Jeans and shorts was the dress code.

Ashley wore faded cutoffs and a pink shirt tied precariously under her breasts. Taye was in jeans and a wife-beater, muscles bulging. Lori opted for cute sequined shorts and a tank top, her red hair tied in side bunches.

"You look exactly like a little kid," Cliff told her, tweaking her chin.

"And *you* look like a grizzled old cowboy," she teased.

"That's some compliment!" he said with a self-deprecating chuckle. "Not exactly the look I was going for, but I guess it'll do. However, I take umbrage at 'grizzled.'"

"That's 'cause you haven't shaved," she pointed out, running her index finger across his chin.

"Thought I'd grow a beard. I'm that relaxed."

Lori cuddled close to him. "It's so nice to see you like this."

"Like what?"

"Like no more Mister Movie Star."

"No more Mister Movie Star, huh?" he said, amused.

"That's right. No more Mister Sexiest Man Alive."

"What? You don't think I'm sexy?" he teased.

"You know I do."

"You're cute," he said, kissing her on the forehead.

"Thanks," she purred. "I try."

"And you're pretty too. What a bonus."

"Double thanks."

"You know what, Lori?" he said, squinting at her.

"What?"

"We're damn good together."

"And you're only just discovering this?" she said breathlessly.

"Don't kick a compliment in the teeth. Just go with it, baby."

"I think I will," she said, grinning at him.

And at that moment in time she'd never felt more content. It was about to be another incredible night.

"I'm taking off in the morning," Flynn informed Xuan before they went up for dinner. "It's time for me to go."

She was silent for a moment, busy painting her toenails with a crimson polish—a very girly thing for Xuan to do.

"And that would be why?" she inquired at last.

"You know why," he said irritably. "This is fucking torture for me, watching Sierra continue to screw up her life. We finally talked, and now she won't even look at me. You've got no idea what that feels like. I have to leave."

"If you go, then what about me?" Xuan asked.

"You can do what you want. Come. Stay. Whatever. I'm sure Aleksandr enjoys having you around."

"I'm supposed to be your girlfriend, or have you forgotten?"

"Are you serious? Nobody believes we're together anymore. Not when you're hovering over Aleksandr like he's some kind of god."

"I am not," Xuan retorted, her cheeks flushing pink. "Why would you say that?"

"Listen, we're in confined quarters—nothing goes unnoticed. And for your information, Bianca is seriously pissed."

"That's ridiculous," Xuan said. "Aleksandr is merely offering his assistance and goodwill toward the less fortunate in the world. He is an intelligent man, generous and soulful."

"Yeah, yeah, sure. And you're not jonesin' to jump into bed with him, right?"

"No, Flynn," she said solemnly. "I am not."

"Then let's both leave tomorrow," he encouraged.

"No," Xuan said, taking a long, slow beat. "You do what you want. I have decided to stay."

"Fuck it," Flynn said, marching toward the door. "Like I give a shit. I'll see you upstairs."

Mercedes reviewed the situation. Eighteen crew members. Twelve guests, including Kasianenko and his diva girlfriend. The onslaught for the big party was tomorrow, so no extra bodies aboard tonight.

She relished the evening ahead, and had prepared accordingly. Drugs were not usually her thing, but to stay alert she'd gulped down several Red Bulls and snorted a few lines of coke. Coke always kept her up and at 'em. Cruz had taught her that. Who needed school when she had a papa like Cruz to educate her?

She'd also emptied two bottles of sleeping pills into the soup for the crew that the chef always had bubbling on the stove, and for good measure she'd crushed up another batch of sleeping pills and mixed them in with the baked beans being served with the barbecue. Sleepy passengers were far less likely to cause trouble, and getting everyone to bed early was of paramount importance.

She'd left Kyril until later. The timing had to be right with him. He was such a big man that she wasn't sure what level of drugs would knock him out. Better too much than too little. She'd deliver his hot chocolate later than usual. He probably wouldn't even notice. The man was a machine, a stoic, silent machine.

Guy threw her a suspicious look as they crossed paths. "*You're* lively for someone who could barely move yesterday. Had a miraculous recovery, did we?" he asked sarcastically.

"I bet you're glad you're not a girl, and don't have to go through our monthly nightmare," she said matter-of-factly. "You'd throw a shit fit, couldn't handle it."

"You got a smart mouth on you, little missy," Guy retorted, taking out his frustration regarding Jeromy Milton-Gold, for he was still steaming. "I've decided to dock you yesterday's pay since you were unable to carry out your duties."

"Ohhh," Mercedes mocked, feigning dismay. "What'll I do . . . ?"

Guy was shocked by her insolence. Captain Dickson was right, he should not have hired her.

Never again, that was for sure. She could whistle for a decent reference.

"I was thinking that after we leave the yacht, I might stay at our house in Miami with you for a week or two before returning to London," Jeromy ventured. "Just the two of us. Does that suit you?"

They were sitting at a table with Taye and Ashley, who had spent the majority of the evening whispering to each other like a couple of teenagers on a secret date. Also at the table were the senator and his wife, who apparently didn't talk at all.

Luca gazed longingly over at the next table, where his new best friend, Lori, was sitting with Cliff, Aleksandr, Flynn, and Xuan. Bianca had failed to put in an appearance. He wondered what they were all talking about, and wished he could simply get up, leave his table, and go fill the empty chair.

"What do you think?" Jeromy persisted, irritated that Luca appeared to be ignoring him.

Luca was not comfortable with confrontations, especially when it came to Jeromy, who could turn into a bitchy queen within seconds. However, since there was safety in numbers, and even though Taye and Ashley were doing their own thing, Luca felt brave enough to tell Jeromy the truth.

"No," he said evenly. "It doesn't suit me, Jeromy. Not at all."

Jeromy tapped the side of his wineglass and cleared his throat. "Excuse me?" he said peevishly, his long, thin nose quivering slightly. "I thought you would be delighted for us to spend more time together."

"Suga and Luca Junior are coming to stay with me before I take off on the next leg of my South American tour," Luca said. "I'm planning on spending as much quality time with them as I can."

"That's no problem. We'll spend quality time together," Jeromy responded, sensing his blond god slowly slipping out of his greedy grasp. "Me, you, the boy."

"His *name* is Luca Junior," Luca said pointedly. "And the four of us together—that doesn't work for me."

"Why not?"

"Because I need time alone with them." Luca paused, wondering how far he could push it. "Besides, you can't stand Suga. You've told me enough times."

"I might have criticized her once or twice," Jeromy admitted with a vague shrug. "That doesn't mean I don't *like* her. She's . . . uh . . ."

He trailed off. Who was he kidding? Certainly not Luca, who apparently had grown a new set of balls, because Jeromy knew how his young lover shied away from any kind of discord. Not tonight, though.

"Very well," he said, feeling his throat tighten. "I'll fly straight to London. I wouldn't want to get in your way."

Luca was relieved. If Jeromy flew directly to London

he could break up with him long-distance. He knew it was the cowardly thing to do, but a full blowout with Jeromy was not something he wished to contemplate.

Jeromy would not go quietly into the night, of that he was sure.

Bianca paced around the luxurious master suite like a caged tigress. How had she allowed one small disagreement to blossom into a full-fledged fight?

She was mad at herself. Then again, she was even madder at the Chinese do-gooder with the compact body and shiny black hair. Was it possible that Aleksandr actually fancied her?

No. Pure fantasy. How could Aleksandr even look at another woman when he had her? Their lovemaking alone was superlative, passionate, and mind-blowing. Nobody could beat the magic they made together.

Tomorrow was her birthday, and for the last few hours, her inner voice had been giving her a stern lecture.

Forgive him or you'll lose him.

Why should I?

Because he's a man. A proud, strong man. For once, admit you're wrong.

I'm not wrong.

Who cares? Stop ruining everything.

Okay, okay, I get it.

Impulsively, she reached for a sheet of paper and scribbled Aleksandr a short note. Then she rang for someone to take it to him.

Soon he would be all hers again.

76

By eleven P.M., Cruz had launched both boats. He'd heard from Mercedes that things were winding down on the *Bianca*; guests were retiring early and everything was on track.

Mercedes was a real asset. She'd turned out to be the son he'd always dreamed of having. She was tough as a boy in a female body. And she was his daughter. Mother dead. He'd raised her himself, trained her to take no shit from anybody, taught her plenty—all the tricks. Smart girl, a fast learner, sharp as a carving knife.

In a way he almost depended on her. As far as this job was concerned, it sure helped having someone on the inside, because this job was special. Major bucks were on the line. Not to mention Sergei Zukov hovering over him like a hawk. No fuckups allowed.

He fingered the hunting knife he kept close to his shin in a concealed pocket. On occasion, knives could be more intimidating than guns. People recoiled from knives, and so they should. The slash of steel cutting into flesh was never pretty, and Cruz had a few scars to prove it. He often recalled the whore in Guatemala who'd attempted to rob him after a wild night of sex. She'd drawn a carving knife across his stomach and almost killed him. Fortunately, he'd been found on the street where her pimp had dumped him, and a Good Samaritan cabdriver had rushed him to a nearby clinic. When he'd recovered, he'd tracked down the cabdriver and handed the surprised and grateful man five thousand dollars in cash. Next he'd returned to the whore's room, slit her throat, and shot her pimp in the balls. No regrets.

Then there was the skipper of the cargo ship who'd come at him with a steak knife and managed to slash his neck before Cruz had plunged his own knife into the man's heart. Death while protecting some rich oil company man's shit. *Estúpido*.

Yes, Cruz had experienced several encounters with knives. He was not afraid of violence.

Sergei's deciding not to be a part of the hijack pleased him. Having Sergei along would only have slowed things down, and there was no doubt he would've gotten in the way.

Meanwhile, after Googling him, Cruz had discovered that this Kasianenko *puta* was one richer-than-shit asshole, worth billions. The joke was that all they were asking as a ransom was a measly five million dollars.

It wasn't enough. By the time he'd split the money with Sergei and paid his men their share, he'd be lucky to end up with a paltry million.

He'd attempted to explain this to Sergei, who was more interested in taking Kasianenko prisoner than walking away with a king's ransom. The problem was that Sergei was so loaded down with drug money, he didn't care. All he really cared about was getting his revenge.

After thinking about it for the past few days, Cruz had begun to realize that if he played it his way, this hijack caper could turn out to be the score of a lifetime. Forget about the five mil. How about fifty? Or even one hundred?

If he was smart, it could all be his. Enough to get him out of the piracy business once and for all. He could get the fuck out of Somalia and buy himself a fancy mansion far away, in the Bahamas, Los Angeles, Argentina—anywhere in the world. He could live a life where he wasn't forced to surround himself with armed guards and watch his back at all times lest some Somalian *chingado* decide to get rid of the foreigner who was making money from their business.

Why not? This was an opportunity that would never come around again.

Cruz was conflicted. As the powerful speedboat sped across the night sea, crowded with his men and one of Sergei's guards—he'd separated the two Russians—he couldn't decide what to do. If he didn't go along with what Sergei expected, he'd be saddled with a lifetime enemy.

Yet if he handled things his way, he'd have more money than he'd ever imagined.

Sergei's way.

His way.

He didn't have much time to make the right decision.

77

"Hmm . . . y'know, I never realized making up could be this sexy," Bianca purred, twisting her long slender legs around Aleksandr's neck as the two of them lay naked and entwined on the oversized bed in the master suite.

"You took me away from our guests," Aleksandr said, shifting his body until he was able to plunge his tongue into her silky wetness.

"Umm . . ." She moaned with pleasure as he thrilled her with his skills. "Perhaps they needed an early night."

Aleksandr came up for air. "You are such a provocative woman, Bianca," he said, his voice heavy with lust. "At times you make me into a crazy man."

"Crazy with desire, I hope," she murmured, adjusting her position until she was able to take him in her mouth as he continued to pleasure her.

"Yes, my *golubushka*," he groaned. "Always desire."

After a few moments of bliss, a simultaneous orgasm occurred.

Bianca rolled over and threw her arms above her head. "That was amazing," she cooed.

"For both of us," Aleksandr said, thinking how satisfied he was that Bianca had apologized. She was truly sorry, and so was he for entertaining sexual thoughts about Xuan.

"You are without a doubt the best lover." Bianca sighed, feeling extremely content. "The best I ever had."

"You too, my sweet. And in the future, we have to make absolutely sure that petty jealousy never separates us again."

"It never will," Bianca assured him. "I promise you that."

Good-bye, Asian piece of work. He's back on my side of the court.

"I'm *so* tired," Lori said, trying to suppress a yawn as she and Cliff entered their room. "I got too much sun today. My arms are all tingly."

"You're not alone," Cliff said. "I overdid it on the Wave-Runners. Too much exercise," he added, making a face. "I'm turning into an old man."

"No, you're not," she objected.

He grinned, full of movie-star charisma. "No, I'm not," he agreed.

"So . . . no sex tonight, then?" Lori said lightly. "You don't want me to—"

"No," Cliff said quickly. "Tonight all I want to do is crawl into bed and cuddle with my girl. Is that all right with you?"

"Yes, Cliff," Lori said, glowing. "That's absolutely perfect."

Thank God these beds are king-sized, Luca thought, making sure he stuck to his side of the mattress.

Jeromy emerged from the bathroom in his pretentious silk pajamas with his initials embroidered on the pocket.

They didn't speak. There was nothing to say.

Just like that, they both knew it was over, although unbeknownst to Luca, Jeromy was not giving up without a fight.

"Who's up for a movie?" Taye asked, full of energy and ready to stay awake for another couple of hours. "There's a selection of five thousand DVDs in the screening room. Bloody hell—we can take a vote."

"Don't wanna watch a movie," Ashley said, miffed that Cliff Baxter had practically ignored her all night. "I'm off to bed."

"Me too," Sierra said, shooting a quick glance at Hammond. He didn't move. "Good night, everyone," she said, making a swift exit, wondering if she'd run into Flynn, who'd already left. Or perhaps Hammond would follow her. She prayed not.

"Dunno why everyone's such a friggin' drag tonight," Taye complained to Xuan and Hammond, the last guests left. "Aren't we supposed to be havin' fun?"

"Tomorrow is fun night," Xuan said dryly. "All the fun you could ever want." She was disappointed that Aleksandr had retired early. They had plans to make, things to discuss. Perhaps in the morning she could firm up some future meetings when they were off the yacht.

"Yeah, well I like t' have fun *every* night," Taye grumbled.

"It's almost midnight," Xuan pointed out, delicately suppressing a yawn. "It's too late for me to sit through a movie."

"Right," Hammond said, glancing at his watch and getting up. "Time to pack it in."

Taye shrugged. What was he thinking? Only a few more nights on the yacht and then it was back to Blighty and the twins and his mother-in-law. So what the hell, why was he wasting lovemaking time?

Ashley was waiting. No movie tonight.

After ten minutes of searching for Renee, Hammond discovered her on the top deck, still clearing up from the barbecue. She blushed when she saw him approaching.

Den was also there, tidying up behind the bar. Ignoring him, Hammond went straight over to Renee. "I must see you," he said in a low voice. "Where can we be together?"

Renee squirmed uncomfortably. At the beginning of the trip, her fellow Australian Den had tried to stir up a bit of a flirt. She'd shut him down, not because she didn't like him, but because she knew it would be foolish to start up something with a bloke she was working with. It was a bit embarrassing, though; she didn't want Den thinking there was anything going on between her and the senator.

"Can't talk right now," she managed in a hoarse whisper. "Can you meet me back here in an hour?"

"An hour? I can't wait that long," Hammond complained, a surly expression crossing his bland face. "Surely you understand that I've been thinking about you all day?"

Renee's stomach performed a wild somersault. She was flattered and excited all at the same time. Senator Patterson was a very important man, and he wanted to be with *her*! "You'll have to," she said, slightly desperate. "I'll be here. Promise."

"Very well." Hammond glanced over at Den. "Lost my reading glasses," he said in a loud voice. "Anyone seen them?"

"Sorry, mate," Den replied, then, remembering who he was talking to, he added, "Uh, I mean Senator Patterson."

"Not to worry," Hammond said, walking briskly away. "I'm sure they'll turn up."

Den immediately ducked out from behind the bar and made his way over to Renee. "What's up with him?" he asked, hovering beside her.

Renee shrugged. "How would I know?" she said, trying to appear super-casual but not succeeding.

"He was all up in your face," Den accused. "What's the old geezer want?"

"You heard him," Renee said, her cheeks reddening. "His bloody reading glasses. And by the way, he's not so old."

"Maybe not, but he *is* married," Den pointed out, giving her a hard look. "An' that means you shouldn't go gettin' into somethin' you can't handle."

"Oh *please*!" Renee said, quite frustrated. "You're being a dick. Nothing's going on."

"Yeah, pull the other one," Den said sarcastically. "It's got bells on."

Keeping track of everyone was not as easy as Mercedes had thought. She'd hoped that by midnight all the guests would have retired for the night. And while most of them had, there were still stragglers. Flynn Hudson, for one. Why was he taking a midnight swim? Churning up and down the length of the pool as if he were training for the Olympics. And the senator, lurking around trying to get into Renee's pants. Mercedes decided she had to do something about that, stash them somewhere secure so they wouldn't get caught in the crossfire. If there *was* crossfire, which she doubted. They were on a private yacht cruising the Sea of Cortez, not a big old tanker chugging through the Indian Ocean loaded with oil. Nobody expected pirates to descend on them. Especially heavily armed Somalians intent on gaining immediate control.

Captain Dickson had already retired, and so had most of the crew.

The yacht was anchored near one of the deserted islands; all was quiet and peaceful, although Mercedes had checked the weather report, and she had a hunch the storm was coming earlier than expected. In another life she could've been a successful weather girl on TV. She had a knack for making accurate predictions.

Adrenaline coursed through her veins as she ran upstairs to the top deck. Den was locking up the bar and leaving.

"Where've *you* been?" he said, glaring at her. "You're supposed to help Renee clear up. Jeez! You're so friggin' lazy."

"Since when did you turn into Guy?" she said irritably.

"Since *she* always lets you take advantage of her," Den answered hotly. "Renee's a beaut—an' you're a—"

"What?" Mercedes said, challenging him, her eyes flashing danger. The last thing she needed was distractions.

"Will you two shut up about me?" Renee said, hurrying over to them. "Den, I'll see you tomorrow. Mercedes, can I talk to you about something?"

"Bet I know what *that's* about," Den said, with a curl of his lip. "Some dipstick's out to get his leg over. Maybe *you* can talk some bloody sense into her, car girl."

Den had called her "car girl" ever since they'd boarded. Insulting *hijo de su madre*. He'd better get his ass down to his cabin before he got in anyone's way; she wouldn't want him getting hurt.

Renee was looking at her with a what-am-I-gonna-do guilty expression.

Mercedes waited until Den left, then, after Renee filled her in, she said, "Take him to our cabin. It's yours. Stay all night if you like."

"What about you?" Renee questioned, wringing her hands. "It wouldn't be right to throw you out of your own room."

"That's okay," Mercedes said, adding a quick, "I got my own thing going on."

"Holy crap!" Renee gulped, quite excited. "Who with?"

"It doesn't matter," Mercedes said quickly. "Just take him to our cabin."

"You're *such* a good mate," Renee enthused.

Mercedes shrugged. "Not so much," she muttered.

It was time to get back to Kyril. She'd already taken him a full plate of brownies, heavily laced with sedatives. Now came the real deal. A steaming mug of hot chocolate, or as Mercedes referred to it in her head, the horse tranquilizer special.

Soon Kyril should be sleeping like a ninety-year-old grandma.

78

Cashoo jabbered away in Somali about the boss's woman he'd ejaculated on. He pantomimed her big breasts with his hands and cackled with ribald laughter.

His cohorts in the boat licked their lips, chewed on their khat, and wondered if they'd ever get a chance to be as daring as Cashoo. He was their Casanova, with many girls back home. They were in awe of his sexual adventures. He entertained them with his stories, and they always asked for more.

Amiin was in charge of the second boat. He thought to himself how fortunate that Cashoo was not doing his boasting in front of Cruz, because obviously the young fool didn't realize that the big boss's woman was also Cruz's sister. If Cruz found out, he'd probably cut off Cashoo's dick with a rusty razor blade.

It wasn't Amiin's concern. He was here for the money, that's all.

Although he had to remember that Cashoo *was* a relative, and if anything happened to him, his sister, Kensi—a true witch—would probably place a damn curse on his head.

There were five men crowded into each boat. In Amiin's boat were Cashoo; two other pirates, Daleel and Hani; and Viktor, the Russian. Amiin wasn't sure why Cruz had chosen to break up the two Russians, but he supposed Cruz had his reasons.

The sea was calm at first, although as the boat headed farther out, the water began getting choppy. Amiin and his men were seasoned seafarers; Viktor wasn't. He started turning green as the choppiness changed into full-on bouncing waves.

Once again the Somalians laughed and jeered at him. One of them offered him a bunch of khat to chew on. When he refused, they laughed even louder. "*Kumayo,*" they muttered. "*Guska meicheke.*"

Viktor wasn't sure if he was receiving insults or sympathy. He only knew that the rougher the sea became, the more his stomach churned. This was not what he'd signed up for.

Amiin called Cruz on their two-way radio. "The Russian's getting sick," he muttered. "What should I do?"

"If he gets too sick, toss him overboard," Cruz responded.

Amiin didn't know if Cruz was joking or not. Somehow he had a hunch not.

When the rain began to fall, Cruz embraced it. He'd always looked upon rain as a good-luck omen, a cleansing.

His men grumbled and began pulling well-worn sweatshirts and old stained jackets over their heads. They huddled together like a team as Basra steered the fast speedboat through the treacherous rolling seas.

Like his partner, Viktor, Maksim was becoming seriously sick. The waves were now huge, causing the Somalians to pull out their prayer beads and start chanting.

Cruz managed to force a soggy cigarette into his mouth. He couldn't get it lit, which infuriated him. Goddammit, nothing was ever easy.

Maksim was leaning over the side of the boat groaning and throwing up.

One solid shove and he would be gone.

Cruz considered the possibilities. No more henchmen looking over him. And if he *was* changing plans, that's exactly what he had to do, dump the Russian. His crew wouldn't care; there was no love between them and Sergei's men.

Cruz did not have the stomach to do it himself, so he moved next to Basra, took over driving the boat, and pantomimed what he wanted him to do.

Basra—to whom life meant nothing—didn't hesitate. He took pleasure in violence; it had been that way since, as a child, he'd witnessed his father beat his mother to death.

After maneuvering himself next to Maksim, Basra waited for the next big wave to hit, then shouldered the Russian man overboard as if he were disposing of a sack of garbage. No emotion crossed his skeletal face. Death never bothered him.

Maksim was caught unaware, his desperate screams for help were obliterated by the noise of the storm.

Cruz glanced back to see if the second boat had noticed. The night was pitch-black; it was impossible to see your hand in front of you.

Cruz reached for the two-way radio. "Get rid of the Russian," he instructed Amiin. "Do it now."

How fortuitous that he'd thought of separating them.

In their weakened state, neither of the Russians saw it coming, although burly Viktor put up more of a struggle, and almost took one of the pirates with him.

"Done," Amiin advised Cruz.

"They needed to go," Cruz shouted over the howling wind. "Change of plans. We won't be returning to the villa."

"Yes, boss," Amiin said.

His job in life was not to ask questions, merely to obey.

79

And while the pirates were on their way to take over the *Bianca,* a story hit the front page of a New York tabloid with one of its usual stop-you-in-your-tracks headlines:

PATTERSON DOES A CLINTON.
HERE WE INTERN AGAIN!

The headline was accompanied by a photo of Skylar with another girl—both in skimpy tank tops with prominent nipples, both sticking their tongues out at the camera.

Radical had personally chosen the photo from a selection on Skylar's Facebook page. The fact that the photo was three years old didn't bother Radical; she was searching for provocative, and that's exactly what she got.

"My parents will kill me!" Skylar had said when Radical first approached her with the idea of selling her story.

"Yeah, but you'll be, like, a *rich*-as-shit dead teenager," Radical had slyly joked. "Like, so will I."

Radical had inherited the power of convincing people to do things her way from her father. He'd parlayed his gift into becoming a respected senator, while all Radical wanted to do was make lots of money.

So she'd convinced Skylar that her parents were screwing with her and were not about to do anything about Hammond's sexual indiscretions, and surely he would do the same to other girls, which made it Skylar's duty to get the word out there.

And so even though she was a few years younger than Skylar, Radical got her way. And the two of them had marched into the offices of the New York tabloid and sold their story for—as Radical put it—a shitload of money.

Now the story was out there. No stopping them anytime soon.

When Eddie started getting calls at five A.M., he flipped out.

WHAT . . . THE . . . FUCK?

How could this have happened?

And with a feeling of deep dread, he knew that if anyone was about to get the blame, it would be him.

80

The storm hit at one A.M. It was a tropical summer storm—the worst kind—violent and unpredictable.

Mercedes darted around the yacht taking note of who was still around. As the large yacht began to buck and roll, she was sure that some of the guests would get seasick and come staggering to the upper decks.

She wondered if Captain Dickson would surface. Probably not; he wasn't exactly hands-on.

Kyril had finally fallen into a drugged sleep, snoring like a freight train, his big body sliding down in his chair, hefty legs spread wide, mouth gaping open.

The timing was right on: if the storm didn't hold them up too much, Cruz and his men would be boarding the yacht in around twenty minutes.

It wasn't going to be as easy as they'd thought, what with the yacht bucking and rolling like crazy; getting aboard would be a struggle. Mercedes had no doubt that her papa could handle it—he always did.

She'd already unloaded Kyril's guns, rendering them useless. And earlier that day, she'd made it into the master suite and commandeered the revolver Kasianenko kept in a locked drawer by his bed. If anyone else on the yacht had weapons, she hadn't found them, and over the past few days, she'd conducted a pretty thorough search.

It was on, and she was ready. There was nothing else to do now except wait.

"You're not shy, are you?" Hammond inquired. He was getting impatient with this tall Australian girl, who was not giving up her pussy to him as fast as he would've liked. He had her top and bra off—nice breasts—and he figured if he played with them long enough, she'd be good to go. The annoying problem was that every time he attempted to make it downtown, she shied away from him like a nervous colt.

He had a strong urge to fuck her and get out of the miserable room she'd taken him to. If it didn't happen soon, he was contemplating *slapping* her into submission.

They were on an uncomfortable lower bunk bed, lying side by side. He was fully clothed and hard as a rock.

"I'm . . . I'm not shy," she whispered, shivering as he twisted one of her nipples a fraction too hard. "It's just that . . . uh . . . I know I should have told you before . . ."

"Told me what?"

"It's, uh . . . embarrassing."

"What?" he thundered, starting to lose it.

"I'm . . . a . . . virgin."

For some men those three words would deflate a hard-on quicker than a bucket of cold water. Hammond was not one of those men. Her words made him more excited than ever.

A virgin. Ripe for deflowering. Ah yes, he was just the man for the job.

The yacht began to rock, but Hammond didn't notice.

Now he *had* to have her.

No doubt about it.

"What's going on?" Ashley stuttered, sitting up with a start.

Taye was sleeping soundly. He'd had great sex with his

wife for the fourth day in a row, and now he was sleeping like a satisfied stallion, dreaming about winning the World Cup, then fucking Angelina Jolie. Didn't every man dream about fucking Angelina Jolie?

Ashley vigorously shook his shoulder. He groaned and opened one eye. "Wassamatter, toots?" he mumbled.

"The boat's shaking," she said in a weak voice. "I feel sick."

Taye launched himself into an upright position. He could hear the rain pounding on the porthole, and there was a flash of bright lightning followed by loud rumbles of thunder.

"It's nothin', babe," he assured her. "A bit of a storm, that's all."

"I feel sick," she repeated.

"Want me t' hold your head over the loo?" he offered.

"No, thank you," she said crossly. "I didn't say I was going to *be* sick, I just *feel* it."

"That's 'cause the boat's churnin'," he advised. "It'll soon stop."

"How do *you* know?" she said accusingly.

"'Cause it's a tropical storm. That's what they do, babe. Now spoon up against me and go back to bye-bye land."

For once Ashley did as she was told.

Sleep was impossible for Sierra. Her mind refused to be still.

Was there going to be some big political sex scandal when they got back to New York? Would she be forced to stand by her husband's side while he made a smarmy tele-vised apology?

The good wife. The obedient wife. The stupid wife who puts up with her husband's indiscretions and continues to support him.

Or perhaps Hammond would summon people adept at running damage control. He would get the girl's accusa-tions squashed before they went public. Then he'd pay off

Skylar and her parents, and that would be that. No cringe-worthy TV appearances. No fake apology. All quiet on the political front.

Which left Radical to contend with, and what were they supposed to do about her? The girl was difficult, to say the least. She hated her father as much as he hated her.

Sierra sighed. There was nothing she could do to intervene. It was what it was.

Her thoughts drifted to Flynn. The man she'd always wanted, the man she could never have—not while Hammond was still around.

It was all too much.

The storm roared outside, and the yacht was in constant motion.

She barely noticed.

Where was Hammond, anyway?

She didn't know, and she didn't care. Perhaps he'd slipped and fallen overboard. What a relief *that* would be.

Jeromy's stomach flipped and flopped. He felt light-headed and quite ill. To his fury, Luca didn't care. Luca was in a deep sleep.

Jeromy staggered toward the bathroom and collapsed onto the floor by the toilet. The boat swayed back and forth. He could hear the storm outside, and it unnerved him. Once, in the South of France, he and some acquaintances had gotten caught in a storm on a sailboat. He could still remember the nausea that had overcome him, and now it was back, that ghastly seasick sensation.

He leaned his head against the cold porcelain of the toilet and prayed for morning.

"It's okay," Cliff assured Lori when she nudged up against him. "This yacht is built to withstand anything."

"It is?" she asked tentatively. "It feels awfully rough."

"Think of it as turbulence when you're on a plane," Cliff said. "Nothing to worry about."

"You're sure?" Lori said, shivering.

Cliff held her close. "Positive."

Flynn never made it to bed. After churning fifty or so lengths in the lap pool, he'd gone to the gym and worked out with weights.

He'd made up his mind that he was leaving tomorrow. Leaving Sierra and everything she'd once meant to him. He'd finally realized there was nothing he could do about the situation. She was married to Hammond, and that's the way it was. No going back.

After a vigorous workout, he made his way up to the front of the top deck, grabbed the railing, and leaned out, gazing at the turbulent black sea, getting drenched but liking the feel of the driving rain hitting him in his face.

Lightning flashed. Thunder roared. Nature was doing its thing.

Too bad he didn't have anyone to share it with.

Xuan pulled the covers over her head. Lightning terrified her. Too many bad memories of when she was escaping from Communist China and running, running, running.

She'd gotten raped in the middle of a raging storm. Five men. Five pigs. Five penises drilling into her until she'd passed out.

Somehow she'd survived that horrific night, but the bad memories still lingered, especially when she saw lightning and heard the roar of thunder.

Where was Flynn when she needed him?

Bianca suddenly shot up in bed. "It's a storm," she announced as if she were only just making such a startling discovery.

Aleksandr was already up, sitting in a chair smoking a cigar. "I was hoping you'd sleep through it," he said.

"Don't you know?" Bianca retorted, green eyes flashing. "Storms are my thing."

"They are?" Aleksandr said. Bianca never failed to surprise him.

"Yes, ever since I was a little kid," she said, leaping out of bed. "Storms are *so* exciting! All that thunder and lightning, it's major sexy."

"What are you doing?" Aleksandr asked.

"Getting my storm on," Bianca replied, a wicked smile playing around her lips as she wrenched the terrace doors open and raced outside.

"Are you crazy?" Aleksandr bellowed as the wind blew a deluge of rain into the room. "It's dangerous out there."

"No, it's not," Bianca yelled back at him. "It's a trip."

"You're naked," he shouted. "Put some clothes on."

"Why? There's no one to see me," she said, jumping into the churning Jacuzzi. "Come, my big bad Russian. I wanna make love. Get your ass out here an' join me."

The one person Mercedes didn't want to run into was Guy.

Yet there he was, in sweatpants, a rumpled T-shirt, and a rain slicker, checking things out on the middle deck.

Before she could dodge out of sight, he spotted her.

"What are *you* doing up?" he asked, throwing her a suspicious look.

This was not good. What if he noticed Kyril slumped in a drugged-out stupor on the job? What if he figured out something was about to go down?

She managed a concerned expression. "I was worried about the guests," she said. "Wonderin' how they're coping."

"Well, well, well," Guy said, a look of surprise on his face. "Little Miss Lazy Pants actually cares."

"You never know," Mercedes said, putting on her all wide-eyed innocence expression. "Some people get quite seasick. It's not a great feeling."

"You seen anyone around?" Guy asked. "Any of the passengers?"

Mercedes shook her head.

"You're sure?" Guy said, thinking it was quite possible that he'd misjudged this girl.

"Quite sure," she said firmly.

"Then I expect we can both go back to bed," he said, stifling a yawn.

"Yes," Mercedes said, realizing that at any moment Cruz and his team would be making their play. Two boats. One on each side of the yacht. Pirates boarding. Fast and furious.

"Good night," she said, and quickly hurried out of Guy's sight.

81

The pirates were wet through and through, freezing cold, pissed off, and ready for action. They all knew what they had to do—secure the yacht—which meant herding the crew into the downstairs area so that they could be controlled, securing the guests, then keeping everyone in place until the ransom was paid and they could be on their merry way.

Amiin had supplied each of them with a crude map of the interior of the yacht. Their job was to get all of the crew into the mess hall next to the kitchen in the bowels of the boat, while Cruz took care of whoever was on the bridge—or at least in the control room, since the yacht was at anchor for the night.

The storm had held them up, but fortunately, as they got nearer to the *Bianca,* the storm had started to abate, making it easier for them to board.

Everyone had a job to do, and since the two boats were approaching from both sides of the yacht, it all had to happen at top speed. The element of surprise was crucial, which is why Cruz had decided to stage the raid in the middle of the night when most of the crew and guests would be sleeping.

As they approached the *Bianca,* Cruz ordered them to cut the engines on the speedboats, allowing a stealth landing. They secured the boats to the large yacht with strong bindings before affixing sturdy rope ladders.

Within seconds, the pirates were clambering aboard.

"Don't move," Hammond instructed, his voice thick with lust. "Stay perfectly still."

Renee did as she was told, spread-eagled on Mercedes's lower bunk bed, quite naked and a tad fearful, but mostly excited as she watched Hammond strip off his clothes. She noticed that he had a small paunch—she hadn't expected that—and his manhood was not exactly impressive. But he was a UNITED STATES SENATOR, and she was a simple girl from Brisbane. This was the most thrilling thing that had ever happened to her, and if it meant giving up her virginity, so be it.

Hammond approached the bed. He was in no rush as he savored every moment.

"Relax," he said soothingly. "It might hurt for a moment or two, but trust me, dear, when I'm finished with you, you'll be *begging* for more."

Mercedes ran to meet Cruz on the starboard side. So far, so good. Nobody had realized that invaders were busy slipping aboard. This was Cruz's easiest takeover yet.

He handed Mercedes a bag filled with heavy-duty padlocks, and told her to use them to lock the guests in their cabins until it was time to extract them.

"Somebody better secure Kyril," she worried. "Before the drugs wear off an' he goes on a rampage."

"I'll take care of it," Cruz answered.

She noticed he had his gun out. Was the big chocolate-loving Russian about to be terminated?

It wasn't her concern. She had a job to do.

At first Flynn thought he was hallucinating as he peered out to sea. What the hell? Boats were approaching. Boats in the middle of the night.

Was someone in trouble? What was going on?

The rain had almost stopped, and from his vantage point on the top deck, he could make out shadowy figures. Shadowy figures that were affixing ropes and then crawling up both sides of the *Bianca*.

Jesus Christ! Was it possible the *Bianca* was being pirated?

"I'm sick," Jeromy muttered, feeling sorry for himself. "Really sick."

Luca didn't hear him, because Luca was still asleep.

Jeromy had tried to wake him, to no avail. *Selfish blond god pop star. May his next tour tank. May his success vanish overnight. May his golden cock wither and fade away.*

Jeromy made it out of the bathroom, reached for his monogrammed silk robe, put it on, left their room, and headed for the stairs, figuring that fresh air might help him recover.

As he reached the staircase, he came face-to-face with Mercedes.

"Thank God someone's up," he grumbled. "Fetch me some seasick pills and a hot cup of tea. Perhaps some plain toast too. Do it fast. I'll be upstairs."

Mercedes was speechless, but only for a moment. "You'd better get back to your room," she said brusquely. "We have a flood going on."

"I need fresh air," Jeromy said with a petulant scowl. "Forget about your stupid flood and get me what I require. I'll be on the middle deck."

"Fine," she said, brushing past him.

"Now," Jeromy called after her. "Do it now."

She was gone.

Staff. Rude and arrogant. Jeromy decided he would complain to Guy about the girl. He'd never liked her; she'd always exhibited attitude. The Australian girl was far more polite, and prettier too.

* * *

On the next deck up, Cruz surveyed the drugged Russian security guard. He was a big man—huge, in fact. A fucking giant.

Did they really want to deal with him when he woke up?

Negative on that.

Diving under the water of the Jacuzzi, Bianca surfaced between Aleksandr's strong thighs. She resembled a sleek seal, her long black hair sticking to her back, mimicking an exotic tail.

"You, my dear, are extremely inventive," Aleksandr remarked, attempting to get his breath back after a marathon session of underwater lovemaking. When Bianca was in the mood, she could be quite insatiable. But then so could he, which made them extremely compatible in the bedroom.

"I know," Bianca purred, stroking his thighs. "I told you we'd have fun."

"The storm is over. We should go back inside."

"Not before I—"

Her words were cut short by the sound of a gunshot.

Aleksandr was immediately alert.

"What was that?" Bianca asked.

On his feet, stepping out of the Jacuzzi, Aleksandr was already trying to reach Kyril, who failed to answer.

Somewhere in the distance, he heard shouting and another gunshot.

Aleksandr's survival instinct kicked into high gear.

He immediately rushed over to his bedside drawer to retrieve his gun.

It was gone.

He turned to Bianca. "Get dressed," he said urgently, reaching for his own clothes. "Something's wrong."

82

"Shit!" Eddie March exclaimed. His phones in the office had not stopped ringing, and he could not get through to Hammond on the *Bianca*. It appeared all lines were down.

The office was pandemonium. Outside on the street, the press were assembling, waiting for something—anything—from Senator Patterson's camp regarding the sex scandal.

Radical had vanished. Taken her ill-gotten gains and no doubt skipped town. Where she would run to, Eddie had no clue. And quite frankly, he didn't care. Although he could imagine another lurid headline in the making: SENATOR PATTERSON'S TEENAGE DAUGHTER MISSING.

Martin Byrne had turned into a man possessed. He'd stormed into Eddie's office yelling and screaming about how he would sue the senator for everything he had.

"It was *your* daughter who sold her story," Eddie pointed out.

"Because that degenerate you work with had *his* daughter talk her into it," Martin shouted, ready to explode with wrath.

Eddie had no sympathy for any of them. He was seriously considering resigning when Hammond returned.

How could he stay working for a man who obviously had no respect for the position he held? Let alone respect for his beautiful wife. It simply wasn't good enough.

* * *

Meanwhile, Radical had hooked up with a boy she'd known and crushed on way back in Wyoming, before her mom had died and before she'd come searching out her father.

His name was Biff. He was seventeen and a Goth.

She'd sent him a bus ticket and booked them into a hotel room off Times Square, paying for everything with her newfound newspaper money.

Radical was happy for the first time in years.

83

Power. Yes, power was the ultimate aphrodisiac, and didn't Hammond know it as he gazed down at the naked virgin spread out in all her glory.

He hadn't had a virgin in a long while. Girls today seemed to get it on with their boyfriends earlier and earlier. It was a shame, a waste. Smart girls picked a man who knew what he was doing. Hammond Patterson—*Senator* Hammond Patterson—was just such a man.

A wolf-like smile spread across his bland face as he lowered himself onto the quivering girl. She was nervous. He liked that; it made him even harder. A delicate virgin waiting for her master to deflower her—what could be more inviting?

Hammond Patterson. Master of the universe. He recalled the Hollywood director James Cameron picking up an award for his movie *Titanic* and calling himself king of the world. Yes, that's what Hammond felt like right now as his penis thrust inside her, breaking the barrier, ignoring her sharp cries of sudden pain.

He was on a path to glory. He was about to fuck the life out of her. Give her something to think about, to remember.

Hammond Patterson was on fire.

Panic ensued. Panic as various crew members were dragged from their beds by a ferocious ragtag band of men who jabbered to each other in a foreign language and wielded lethal weapons such as assault rifles and knives.

There was hardly any resistance from the crew; they were too shocked and scared to do anything as they were hustled into the mess hall in various stages of undress.

Den attempted to grapple with one of the pirates and received a pistol-whipping across his forehead, causing a large gash. Blood dripped down his face as the housekeeper and the two Polish maids screamed in terror.

One of the maids handed him a dishcloth, and he held it to his head while searching around for Renee and Mercedes. Neither of them was there. Could it be because their room was more isolated?

Guy was marched in by a pistol-wielding pirate who shoved him to the ground. "What the *hell*?" Guy shouted as he landed on the floor next to Den.

"I think we're in trouble, mate," Den said in a low voice. "Big friggin' trouble."

Guy staggered to his feet. "Where's the captain?" he said, trying to sound authoritative.

"Dunno," Den answered, stemming the flow of blood from his forehead. "They're still bringing people in."

Guy shook his head. This wasn't happening. This couldn't possibly be happening.

Unfortunately for everyone on the *Bianca,* it was.

"Here's what I want you to do," Aleksandr said to Bianca, keeping his voice low and reassuring.

She'd pulled on black leggings and a sweatshirt. "What?" she asked, wondering why Aleksandr was suddenly so serious.

"I think there might be something going on."

"Like what?" she said, gazing at him expectantly.

"I'm not sure, Bianca," he said patiently. "I need to find out."

"Was that a gunshot we heard? Was it?"

"Perhaps," he said, purposefully sounding noncommittal. "Do not worry. Just do as I say until I find out what is taking place."

"Should we go investigate?"

"I will do that while you stay here."

"Can't we call someone?"

"The internal phone system is dead, and so are the TV monitors."

Bianca experienced a tiny shiver of apprehension. "Are we in any kind of danger?"

"I doubt it. However, in case there is a problem, I have a plan."

Settling himself in a comfortable chair in the middle deck lounge, Jeromy noted that the storm was over and the sea was almost calm again, making him feel considerably better. Once that insolent girl brought him his tea and seasick pills, he would return to bed. In the morning he would make damn sure that Luca heard all about how ill he'd been, and hopefully Luca would be filled with guilt for not waking up and ministering to him.

The room was dark—he had not bothered putting on the lights—so he did not see Cashoo until the tall, lanky boy was standing over him brandishing a lethal-looking dagger.

"Move!" Cashoo yelled, proudly using the one word of English he knew. "Move, *kumayo!*"

Jeromy almost fell off his chair. Was this some kind of joke? Some kind of bizarre plot cooked up by Suga to get him out of Luca's life?

"Move!" Cashoo yelled again, grabbing Jeromy's arm and yanking him up.

"Excuse *me*," Jeromy said, quite affronted.

Cashoo had his eye on Jeromy's robe. He imagined himself strutting around showing it off in front of his girlfriends. He had two girlfriends at home. One of them was pregnant.

He snatched the robe off Jeromy, who was too startled to struggle. Not that Jeromy would; he'd always abhorred violence unless it was of the sexual kind. Chains, whips, cock rings—all good at the right time.

Cashoo held Jeromy's arm in a vise-like grip, and, pulling him along, he marched him downstairs to the mess hall.

Jeromy's eyes swept around the room in horror. Where were the other guests? Where were Bianca and Aleksandr? For God's sake, why was he being thrown in with the crew?

This was completely unacceptable.

Flynn had been caught in many situations. Over the years, he'd traveled through war zones, interviewed masked and hooded terrorists, almost been captured by bandits twice, survived two earthquakes and a tsunami. But this—what the hell was this?

They were cruising the Sea of Cortez, for crissakes. They were in safe waters.

Apparently *not* so safe. The *Bianca* was being taken over. And what was he supposed to do about it?

He knew the drill. A couple of years ago, he'd interviewed several Somalian pirates when he'd been thinking of maybe writing a book about the modern-day piracy industry. And it *was* an industry; they shoveled in millions of ransom dollars a year.

Talking with the pirates in Eyl, the small town by the sea famous for being the center of pirate activity, accompanied by four armed bodyguards and a translator, he'd discovered that a large percentage of them were former fishermen who felt that their livelihood had been affected by illegal fishing vessels raiding their waters, so it was perfectly fine to take what wasn't theirs.

Apart from the fishermen, some of the pirates were ex-militiamen, tough as old leather, and each clan had its own technical geek to deal with satellite phones and GPS.

The pirates had enjoyed boasting about their activities, how much money they made, and how they earned respect, drove big cars, and married the most beautiful clan women.

They refused to address the violence and the weapons they amassed.

In the end, Flynn had decided against writing a book. He didn't trust any of them, and he knew that if he wasn't protected by armed bodyguards, he'd immediately be kidnapped and held for ransom. It was their way.

Usually they didn't stray far from familiar waters. So how was it possible they were running riot on the *Bianca*? This was a crazy situation.

On the top deck, Flynn knew he wouldn't be safe for long. If these intruders were indeed Somalians—and from the stray words he'd heard shouted, they were—then their next move would be securing the boat, making sure everyone was accounted for and locked away. After that it was a question of demanding the required ransom. Until then, the yacht and its occupants would remain their prisoners.

And if the ransom wasn't paid . . .

He recalled that, a couple of years ago, Somalians had hijacked a yacht with four Americans aboard. Bible-thumping Americans. The pirates had killed all four of them.

Flynn had a choice. He could try to launch one of the tenders and go for help.

Or he could stay.

Sierra was aboard. He decided to stay.

84

Usually Cliff was a heavy sleeper, so much so that he would've slept through the entire storm if Lori hadn't awakened him. He could sleep through most things—including the big L.A. earthquake in 1994—but tonight was different. After Lori nudged him awake, he couldn't get back to sleep, even though the storm had stopped and the yacht was only gently rocking.

Not wishing to disturb Lori, who was now sleeping, he got out of bed, padded into the bathroom, closed the door, put on the light, took a leak, then stood in front of the mirror above the marble sink and studied his reflection.

Cliff Baxter. Superstar.

Cliff Baxter. Soon to be fifty.

Cliff Baxter. Man alone.

His face was craggy, not as handsome as it appeared on screen. There were new lines around his eyes and jowls every day, and the gray in his hair was increasing by the week. He refused to dye it—artificial props were not for him. No Botox, fillers, or whatever miraculous shit some famous dermatologist was forever coming up with.

Cliff was comfortable with the way he looked. Most of all, he was comfortable with Lori.

Before the trip he'd considered trading her in for a new model.

Why? Because Enid didn't like her?

Because the press felt he should change it up every year? Get himself a fresh young girlfriend for even more photo opportunities? A new spectacular body to pose beside him at industry events looking pretty while saying nothing?

What the hell. If he wasn't careful, he could easily be perceived as a dirty old man, and that was *not* the image he cared to project.

Lori had been great on this trip. Warm, fun, and sexy as hell, and everyone liked her.

So, would he ever consider making her a permanent fixture?

Hmm . . . It was not such an impossible thought.

Mercedes had been under the impression that everyone was going to be rounded up and put into the mess hall—crew and guests alike. Padlocking the rich and famous into their luxurious suites was not what she'd expected.

How was she supposed to raid their rooms and take the loot she had her eye on? This was supposed to be the trip where she made her own personal score—jewelry, cash, and the big prize: the emerald and diamond ring Aleksandr Kasianenko had stashed in his safe.

In her mind she'd already mapped out her future. Enough with being Cruz's happy helper; she yearned for her own life. And counting on the score she'd make with the jewelry and cash, she could have everything she'd ever wanted. After all, she was the only one who knew about the ring. And apart from Cruz, she was the only one who could crack a safe.

What was this padlocking them into their rooms crap? This wasn't the way it was supposed to be.

She had to persuade Cruz to gather everyone in the same place, and soon.

* * *

"This is outrageous!" Jeromy objected loudly as the lanky young pirate pushed and shoved him into the crew's dining room. "I will not stand for it!"

Was he dreaming? Was this a bizarre nightmare? If he shut his eyes, would it all go away?

Cashoo was a happy young man. He slipped Jeromy's fancy robe over his clothes and pantomimed a wild and somewhat obscene dance for Daleel and Hani, the two smirking pirates standing near the door, weapons drawn.

The shocked crew watched in horror, anticipating their fate. They'd heard stories about what pirates did to their hostages, and it wasn't pretty.

"Where are the girls?" Den whispered to Guy. "Renee and Mercedes?"

Guy didn't want to think about where they might be.

As far as Cruz was concerned, he did not believe in wasting time. Everyone had a job to do, and his job was to get the ransom demand in action as fast as possible.

He was in charge, and they'd all best listen to him or else, because the faster the money was paid, the easier it would be for all concerned.

He was in possession of a yacht full of rich, famous people. It wouldn't be long before some kind of rescue mission was launched. Also, he had no doubt that when Sergei's men failed to return with Kasianenko, Sergei would go on an angry rampage.

Cruz could only imagine Sergei's fury, which he'd probably take out on Ina.

Too bad. Unfortunately, there was nothing Cruz could do about that. He had himself to look out for. Besides, he and Ina had never been close. She might be his sister, but he didn't like her that much.

The key to getting this all done quickly was Kasianenko himself. Once he had the Russian billionaire's cooperation, everything should move smoothly.

Cruz was confident that soon he'd be richer than he'd ever dreamed of.

"What the hell is this?" Bianca questioned, staring at her Russian lover.

Aleksandr had pressed a hidden button, and the mirrored wall behind his shower slid back, revealing a secret room.

"It's a safe room," Aleksandr said matter-of-factly. "For emergencies."

"Is this an emergency?" Bianca questioned, widening her eyes.

"I have no idea until I see what's going on," Aleksandr said. "And before I do that, I must make sure you are protected."

"Oh my God!" Bianca exclaimed, beginning to experience waves of panic. "You *do* think something bad is happening."

Ever so gently, Aleksandr edged her into the compact room, which was fully equipped for any kind of situation, including with a satellite phone. "I'll make a call when I know for sure what's happening," he said.

Bianca was in semi-shock. She watched in awe as Aleksandr removed a handgun from a cupboard stocked with all kinds of emergency supplies. Then he checked that the gun was loaded, and stuck it in his belt. Talk about macho! Somehow it was reassuring that he remained so calm.

"In the meantime," Aleksandr said, "do not even *think* of coming out until I return."

"Yes," she said meekly. "Hurry back and be safe."

"Oh, I will be, *angel moy*. No need to worry about me."

85

Adventure had always been Flynn's thing. Taking risks, getting himself out of dangerous situations, knowing what to do and when to do it.

Being trapped on a billionaire's yacht with a bunch of bloodthirsty pirates was not a situation he'd imagined he'd ever encounter. Only here it was, and here *he* was, bang in the middle.

Obviously, their main prize was Aleksandr, although who knew what they'd do when they discovered who else was aboard?

Flynn recalled his conversations with the pirates he'd interviewed in Eyl. At the time, they'd been holding a large oil tanker for ransom. They'd proudly informed him that all the captives aboard were being well looked after and treated like guests at a fine hotel. It was only later he'd discovered that two of the female hostages had been raped, and one of the male captives brutally murdered, even though the ransom was eventually paid.

Flynn's mind started clicking into overdrive.

Advantages: He knew every detail of the yacht. He was into martial arts. He understood the pirate mentality. So far he had not been spotted.

Disadvantages: No weapon. No idea how many pirates there were. No form of communication with the outside world. Unsettling to say the least.

He'd heard a lot of shouting and a couple of gunshots. Not good.

His main thought was *Is Hammond capable of protecting Sierra?*

No fucking way.

It was up to him to figure something out.

Roaming the yacht searching for stragglers, waving his gun in front of him ready to shoot anyone who gave him any trouble, Basra made a frightening figure with his deep sunken eyes, lack of teeth, and unkempt, rain-soaked dreadlocks.

He passed the security room where Kyril now lay on the floor, a neat bullet hole through the middle of his forehead.

Had he done that? He couldn't remember.

After a moment he doubled back, entered the room, wrenched the watch from Kyril's wrist, and put it on his own emaciated wrist. The watch was black with a red dial. Cheap and cheerful.

Next he kicked and pushed Kyril's body out of his way, and sat himself down in the command chair facing a slew of security monitors, all of them blank, for Cruz had cut the feed.

A plate of brownies stood on the shelf in front of him. Basra snatched one up and shoved it in his mouth. Sweet and tasty. He wolfed down another one, and then a third.

Sitting back, he admired his new black watch with the smart red dial. The watch of a dead man was a fine souvenir for him to cherish, especially when he showed it off at home, making his three sons jealous.

Ah . . . his sons. Lazy *wacals*. It was time to kick some sense into them as only he could.

Perhaps he'd remember, perhaps he wouldn't.

On the first day the guests had boarded the yacht, Aleksandr had generously offered everyone the opportunity to take the full tour. Flynn had accepted his offer, and now he was glad he'd done so, for knowing the layout of the yacht was imperative.

There were four levels. The lower level consisted of staff quarters, kitchens, and the engine room. On the next level were a series of luxury suites, all with their own small terraces, plus the movie theater, spa, and other facilities. On the middle deck, there was the swimming pool, the gym, and various areas for relaxing and entertaining, plus the bridge, the communication center, and the master suite with its own large terrace. And finally the upper level was all lounges, sundecks, and more entertaining areas.

Flynn realized that he had to figure out a way to reach Aleksandr, because maybe—just maybe—Kasianenko was still in his suite.

He made a dangerous but doable decision. Before anyone discovered him, he was going over the side.

After getting Bianca into the safe room, Aleksandr headed toward the door. To his consternation, it would not open more than an inch. Bending down and peering through the crack, he soon saw why. The door had been padlocked from the outside.

He wondered where Kyril was. The big man had protected him for so many years, always at his side whenever Aleksandr needed him. Indeed, Kyril had once taken a bullet for him when an irate business associate had attempted to shoot him. Kyril was loyal through and through. If he were alive, he would be here now.

Aleksandr felt a thickness in his throat. Instinct told him that Kyril was not alive. Kyril was either dead or mortally wounded.

Reaching back, he felt the reassuring presence of his gun. Motherfuckers. Whoever was on his yacht had better beware. Aleksandr Kasianenko was not going down without a fight.

* * *

Captain Dickson was hauled unceremoniously from his bed by Amiin, who punched him in the stomach and muttered a gruff "Up, mister. this boat now ours."

Anxiety overcame the English captain as he realized what was taking place. In all his years at sea, this was the moment he'd always dreaded.

"What . . . what are you thinking?" he managed, shying away from the dark-skinned man who stood before him brandishing a gun.

"Come," Amiin said. "Follow me or I shoot you in gut."

"Can I get dressed first?"

"Quick," Amiin said, waving his gun in the air. "You do it quick."

Hurriedly the captain pulled on a pair of pants and a shirt. Then, at gunpoint, he went with Amiin upstairs to the bridge, where Cruz waited restlessly.

Captain Dickson came face-to-face with the man he assumed was the leader. He immediately attempted to assert himself. "This is outrageous," he said, sounding extremely stiff-upper-lip British. "Who are you people? What do you want?"

"Whaddya *think* we want?" Cruz retorted, rubbing the deep scar on his neck. "Wanna make a guess?"

"You won't get away with this," Captain Dickson blustered, swallowing hard. "My men have already alerted the coast guard. Help is on its way."

"Your fuckin' men were all asleep on the job," Cruz sneered. "Comin' aboard was like takin' a walk in the park."

"Where are my passengers?" Captain Dickson demanded. "If you've harmed them in any way—"

"Shut your fuckin' mouth an' listen t' me," Cruz said roughly. "You're gonna fetch the Russian mothafucker, an' bring him here. Understand?" He gestured toward Amiin. "Take him with you. He gives you any trouble, shoot him in the head."

Captain Dickson swallowed hard again. Fear coursed through his body. If he survived this, he was retiring.

The *if* hung like a neon question mark before his eyes.

Meanwhile, down in the mess hall, the pirates had discovered bottles of beer, and Daleel and Hani were swigging it down, quenching their thirst, jeering at their hostages, making lewd signs at the two petrified maids and the housekeeper.

Jeromy huddled in a corner still wearing his silk pajamas, trying to make himself as inconspicuous as possible. These men were dangerous savages. God knew what they were capable of.

Guy did a quick head count. All the crew were accounted for except the captain, Mercedes, and Renee. He felt fear for the two girls. He'd heard the stories—rape was not uncommon, and Mercedes and Renee were certainly attractive enough.

Den was thinking along the same lines. In spite of his head injury, he was definitely getting his macho up. Renee was a sweet girl; she didn't deserve what might be happening to her.

"We just gonna sit here an' do nothin'?" he muttered to Guy. "These dickheads are gettin' drunker than a pig's arse. Fair go, mate, we gotta do somethin' with these drongos."

"And get ourselves shot?" Guy said, eyeing the three pirates who were supposedly in charge. "Best to sit tight and wait."

"For what?" Den said, his temper rising. "We gotta go for it."

Guy realized that Den was young—twenty-five, twenty-six. He didn't understand the danger they were in. This wasn't a TV show. This was real life. Guy knew that the smart thing to do was absolutely nothing.

If they didn't give the pirates any trouble, help would surely come. He had to keep the faith.

86

The side of the boat was wet and slippery. To Flynn's relief, the rain had stopped, the storm seemed to be over, and the sea was almost calm.

Slowly and surely he lowered himself down the side of the yacht with the help of strong ropes he'd found in a utility cupboard. He kept going until he landed on the terrace that led to the master suite.

The glass doors leading inside were locked. He could see Aleksandr. Urgently he banged on the glass with his fists until Aleksandr turned around, saw him, and hurried to open the doors.

"Jesus Christ!" Aleksandr exclaimed. "What is happening, Flynn? Do you know?"

"Pirates," Flynn answered quickly. "They've taken over the boat."

"You can't be serious?"

"Dead serious, I'm afraid."

"This is a disaster," Aleksandr said, shaking his head. "What do we do?"

"Is the door to this room locked?"

"No. Someone's secured it from the outside. I can't get out of here."

"Lock it now," Flynn said sharply. "They'll be coming for you any minute."

"Why me?" Aleksandr said, frowning.

"'Cause they'll be needing you to speak to your businesspeople. They'll want you to order them to pay the ransom immediately."

"How do you know this?"

"Trust me, I have knowledge of the way they work."

"This is some fucked-up situation," Aleksandr said, his face grim.

"It is, but we'll do our best to deal with it," Flynn said, trying to inspire confidence. "Where's Bianca?"

"I put her in the safe room," Aleksandr said, moving over to lock the door from the inside.

"Where's that?"

"Behind the shower door in my bathroom. It was a last-minute decision to incorporate it into the plans. Thank God I listened."

Flynn nodded. "How many people does it hold?" he asked.

"Five or six."

"We need to get all the women inside," Flynn said, speaking fast. "Is there a working phone in there?"

"Satellite," Aleksandr said.

"Call the coast guard. Summon help," Flynn said. "Do you have a gun?"

"Yes."

"More than one?"

"Someone took the revolver I kept by my bed."

"You think they were in here?"

"Not as far as I know."

"They might have a person on the inside. Maybe one of the crew."

"How should we handle this?" Aleksandr asked, thankful that Flynn was aboard.

"You put in a distress call to the coast guard while I try to reach the others. They've probably got no idea what's going on."

"How can you do that?"

"Same way I got in here. Who's in the suite below this?"

Aleksandr thought for a moment, his mind going stubbornly blank. "The footballer," he said at last. "Be careful."

Flynn nodded, and headed for the terrace. "I'll be back," he said confidently. "Go make that call."

"You should have put them all together in the mess hall," Mercedes complained to Cruz. "It's not safe to keep them in their rooms."

"Why not?" Cruz said, dragging on a cigarette, then spitting out fragments of tobacco. "They're secure. They don't got nowhere t' go."

"Ever think they could jump overboard and swim for help?" Mercedes said. "You never know."

"My little *idiota*," Cruz said with a benevolent chuckle, flashing his two front gold teeth while exhaling a stream of thick smoke. "Who's gonna risk swimming to a deserted island in the middle of the night? You locked 'em in. There's nothin' they can do 'cept wait."

"What if the ransom takes days?" Mercedes insisted. "You lettin' them starve to death?"

"Why you so concerned?" Cruz asked, giving her a what-are-you-hiding look.

She bit down hard on her lower lip. He knew her so well that it was difficult to hide anything from him.

"I was thinkin' I could go through their rooms, see if there's anything worth takin'," she said, keeping it casual.

"Were you now?" Cruz said with a knowing smirk. "As if you haven't already picked out what you're after."

"What if I did? I think I deserve a bonus after all the work I've put in. It's not much fun bein' stuck on this boat with a bunch of rich fuckers ordering me around."

"You spotted something good, *chiquita*?"

Cruz rarely used words of affection toward her. She kind of liked it.

"Oh, just clothes an' stuff," she answered vaguely. "These spoiled *putas* have a ton of nice things."

"Tell you what," Cruz said amiably. "Amiin took the captain to bring Kasianenko back here. Once I get the Russian to make it clear to his people they gotta pay up or he ends up on the bottom of the ocean, then we'll move 'em all downstairs. That make you happy?"

"Thanks, Papa," she said, already picturing her future.

"Don't call me that," Cruz snapped, his mood abruptly changing.

She'd forgotten for a moment that he didn't allow her to call him papa. It made him feel old in front of whatever whore he was banging.

"Sorry . . . uh . . . Cruz," she muttered. "It won't happen again."

Since he seemed to be getting nowhere with Guy, Den began canvassing other members of the crew. None of them was prepared to make a move.

"So we just sit here," Den said, staring them down. "Y'know what that makes us? Nothin' but a bunch of bloody wankers. Why stay still when we could rush 'em? C'mon, mates, there's only three of 'em against all of us."

"Yes, and get our heads blown off for the trouble," the chef—a stocky Englishman—said. "We sit here quietly and wait for the ransom to be paid. That's what we do. I got a wife and three kids to think about."

Den was frustrated. The pirates were getting drunker by the minute. If the rest of the crew cooperated, he was sure they could turn it around.

Shit! It wasn't in his nature to sit back, do nothing, and be a victim. Besides, he was still worried about Renee and Mercedes. They could be in deep trouble.

Never the heaviest of sleepers, Taye was instantly awake when he heard tapping coming from the direction of the terrace doors.

He jumped out of bed, bare-assed, which was the way

he always slept, and padded over to the doors. Flynn was standing outside.

Taye opened the glass doors. "What the hell?" he mumbled, disoriented. "You fall overboard or what?"

"Boat's been taken over by pirates," Flynn said brusquely, pushing past him. "We gotta get Ashley somewhere safe. Do you think she can manage to climb a rope?"

Taye shook his head to make sure he wasn't dreaming. Nope. He wasn't dreaming. Flynn was still standing there talking about pirates.

"Are you shittin' me?" he said, confused.

"No, I'm deadly serious. You've got to get her upstairs to Aleksandr's suite right now. There's a rope outside—help her climb it. Aleksandr has a safe room up there."

"Jeez!" Taye exclaimed. "You bloody mean it, dontcha?"

"Who's next door to you?" Flynn said urgently.

"The senator," Taye said. "Never stops yellin' at that poor wife of his."

"Okay," Flynn said, tucking that information away for later. "You take care of Ashley. I gotta try to warn everyone else. I'll see you up there."

Moving fast, he took off again, not certain how he could convince Hammond to help get Sierra to safety. But he was sure as hell going to try.

Frog-marching Captain Dickson back to the bridge, Amiin passed Kyril's room, and spotted Basra asleep on a chair in front of a slew of blank monitors.

"You," Amiin warned the captain, "no move." Then he began screaming a stream of expletives at Basra in Somali. Basically telling him to move his lazy ass and continue looking for any stragglers, which was what he was supposed to be doing.

Basra forced his eyes open, mumbled a weak excuse, stood up, picked up his gun, and set off downstairs.

His job was to inspect the crew's quarters, make sure they had them all stashed in the mess hall. Yes, and if he came across anyone, he decided in his groggy state of mind, then he might as well shoot to kill.

87

"Whaddya mean, he won't come out?" Cruz demanded, glaring at Amiin as if it was his fault. "Open the fuckin' door and *haul* him out."

"He got the door locked from inside," Amiin explained.

"Jeez! What a *cabrón*," Cruz snarled. "Gettin' him up here is for his own fuckin' good."

"Why do you want him?" Mercedes piped up.

Captain Dickson stared at her in shock. Mercedes was standing there as if she were one of them.

Then it struck him: she *was* one of them. The little bitch he'd told Guy not to hire was with the pirates! She must have been working with them all along.

Guy was such a fool. Captain Dickson couldn't wait to confront his director of entertainment—if he was lucky enough for that day to ever come, because right now he had a gun stuck in his face and a strong urge to crap his pants.

Mercedes felt the hate in Captain Dickson's eyes burning into her. "Get over it," she spat.

"I need Kasianenko here," Cruz said heatedly. "To get the ransom demand started."

Time was important. He expected the money to be paid within twenty-four hours; every moment wasted ate up precious time.

"Blow a hole in the *chingado*'s door and *drag* him up here," he ordered Amiin. "Do it now."

"Yes, boss," Amiin said.

The door to the Pattersons' terrace was not locked. Flynn opened it, slid inside, and approached the bed.

Sierra was in it. Hammond was not.

Flynn checked out the bathroom. Empty. He leaned over the bed and shook Sierra awake. She opened her eyes and gasped.

"Don't be alarmed," he said, speaking fast. "There are pirates aboard."

She sat up, coppery hair tumbling around her beautiful face. "Flynn," she murmured, her eyes widening. "Pirates. Seriously?"

"Yeah, I know, it's crazy," he said. "I can hardly believe it myself."

"You're sure?"

"Yes, I'm sure. Where's Ham?"

"I . . . I don't know. He never came to bed."

"Put on something warm and grab your tennis shoes. I'm getting you to safety."

Cashoo had been expecting to see gorgeous women on this luxurious yacht, but to his disappointment the three females sitting with the male hostages were nothing special.

As usual, he was feeling horny. He couldn't seem to get his mind off the big boss's woman with her huge breasts—breasts he could play with all day long given the opportunity.

He had a hunch that they might not be returning to the villa, since Cruz had disposed of the two Russian bodyguards. That was a shame, because he would've liked to have played around with the boss's woman some more. Still, Cruz always had a plan, and at the end of the plan there was always plenty of money to share, so Cashoo couldn't complain.

Once more Cashoo eyed the crew of the *Bianca*. A sorry-looking bunch.

He started wondering where Mercedes was. The two of them got along fine. Mercedes was a spitfire, up for anything. She was his kind of girl: pretty and dangerous.

Tired of guarding the hostages, he told Daleel that he had to take a piss and would be right back.

Daleel nodded, and Cashoo headed off to search out Mercedes.

As soon as Cashoo left, Den nudged Guy. "There's only two of 'em now," he muttered. "C'mon, mate, grow a pair. If we all move together, we can rush 'em."

"It's not going to happen," Guy said, wishing that Den would settle down and stop bugging him. "In case you haven't noticed, they've got guns—nobody wants to risk getting shot. We stay calm, they'll stay calm," Guy said, trying to convince himself.

"You think?" Den argued, jutting out his chin. "They're gettin' drunker by the minute. We don't do somethin', we're gonna be toast. Shove *that* in your stay-calm book."

Over in the corner it occurred to Jeromy that if everyone was murdered on the yacht, who would even remember that he was aboard? The headlines would be all about the famous people—Luca, Cliff Baxter, Taye, Bianca, the senator, and of course Aleksandr. There was a strong possibility that he might not be mentioned at all. Jeromy Milton-Gold, an also-ran.

For some obscure reason he experienced a strong burst of anger toward Luca. Where was his blond god? Why wasn't he doing anything?

Jeromy knew he was thinking in an unreasonable fashion because, unfortunately, there was nothing Luca *could* do. Stone-cold fact: there was nothing anyone could do.

He glanced over at Guy. Was he an enemy or a friend?

Jeromy hoped he was a friend, for he needed to be close to someone at this frightening time.

Moving like a sure-footed cat, Flynn jumped from terrace to terrace, alerting everyone and telling them to get up to Aleksandr's suite. The only two people missing were Hammond and Jeromy Milton-Gold. Flynn had no idea where either of them was, and right now they were the least of his worries.

The women turned out to be a hardy bunch, climbing the rope like veterans, crowding into the safe room with Bianca. The safe room was soundproof, and at the top of the panel was a one-way mirrored section that allowed whoever was inside to see what was going on outside.

Once everyone was assembled, Xuan confronted Flynn and insisted that she stay and face the pirates with the men.

Flynn was having none of it. "You will stay in here until we come get you. Do not come out for anything, and stay quiet. You'll all be safe if you do that."

Sierra gave him a long look. "How about you?" she asked softly. "Will *you* be safe?"

"I can look after myself," he said tersely. Then, gesturing toward the other men, he said, "We all can."

"What about Hammond?" she asked.

"We'll find him," Flynn assured her, wondering if she was asking because she cared.

On the other side of the door, Amiin yelled, "Out now or me shoot!"

Aleksandr slid the panel to the safe room shut.

Flynn looked around at Taye, Luca, and Cliff. "We gonna go for the bastard or be trapped as hostages?"

"No question. We'll friggin' take the bugger," Taye said, eyes gleaming.

Cliff nodded his agreement. "I've done it in movies enough times," he said wryly. "Let's put it to the test and see how I make out in real life."

"I'm ready," Luca said, nervous inside but determined to put on a strong front. He was worried about Jeromy, but there was nothing he could do about finding him now.

Aleksandr removed the gun from his belt. "We're all in this together," he said, full of steely determination. "Five men as one."

"Right," Flynn said. "Gimme the gun. I reckon I've had more practice than you."

Aleksandr didn't argue; he handed Flynn his gun.

Outside the door, Amiin yelled a final warning: "Open or I blast in!"

"Go for it, cocksucker," Flynn muttered. "We're ready an' waiting."

Thrusting into the girl with all the force he could muster, Hammond found himself riding high, in a state of total dominance.

At one point, the girl—what was her name, Gemma? Renna? Ah yes, Renee—had pleaded with him to stop. He knew she didn't mean it; he knew she was loving every second of his enormous member penetrating her virgin territory.

He heard muffled noises outside the room. He took no notice—he was on his way to the ultimate orgasm.

Building . . . building . . .

And YES! "Aargh!" Hammond's body shook with the exquisite release, while Renee trembled beneath him.

And at that exact moment, the door to the room opened, and a groggy Basra, not quite sure what he was seeing, staggered in, raised his gun, and shot the heaving naked figure on top of the girl.

Blood flowed.

And for Senator Hammond Patterson, death and orgasm happened at the exact same moment.

88

Pacing up and down, Sergei kept consulting his watch, muttering to himself about what he would do to Kasianenko when he had him safely shackled in the basement.

After a while, Ina emerged from the bedroom wearing little more than a short baby-doll nightie and furry high-heeled mules. "When you comin' to bed?" she whined.

"When I feel like it," he snapped back at her.

He had no intention of sleeping until Kasianenko was his prisoner, chained and trussed up like a chicken ready to be put in the oven and roasted.

"I don't feel safe sleepin' alone," Ina complained, curling a loose strand of hair around her finger. "This place is scary at night. Come to bed."

Sergei shot her a look. "Stop bitchin' like a little *pizda*," he muttered. "I'll come to bed when I'm ready."

And he wouldn't be ready until Maksim and Viktor returned with Kasianenko.

He checked his watch once more. Cruz and his men had been gone for over four hours. They should be arriving any minute now.

Sergei licked his lips in anticipation. He was more than ready.

89

"You'll never get away with this," Captain Dickson warned, desperately trying to assert an air of authority as he faced the grungy-looking Mexican man with the lethal scar running across his neck and the automatic Uzi balanced precariously on his knee. "Do you even realize who this yacht belongs to?"

"I say it was okay for you to speak?" Cruz snarled, giving Captain Dickson a long hard look.

"Here's what'll happen," Captain Dickson continued, refusing to be intimidated. "You'll be caught and punished. This is treason on the high seas."

"What century you from?" Cruz sneered, wiping the back of his hand across his mouth.

"I'm warning you, if any of my crew are harmed—"

"Shut the fuck up," Cruz said, spitting on the ground. "When Kasianenko gets here, I'm sendin' you down to *be* with your fuckin' crew. How does *that* suit you?"

Captain Dickson was silent. He'd sooner be with his crew than up on the bridge with this gun-wielding maniac.

Lie still.
    Don't move.
    What happened?
    Should I scream?

Blood trickled onto Renee's naked body as a hundred thoughts rambled through her head.

Hammond was heavy on top of her, crushing her with his full weight, his penis still inside her.

Or was it?

She didn't know.

Tears formed in her eyes and slid mournfully down her cheeks.

Something awful had happened.

She could feel Hammond's blood dripping onto her skin.

Paralyzed with fear, she found herself unable to move.

Then someone was rolling the senator off her, landing him on the floor with a thud, and she found herself staring into the eyes of the most frightening-looking man she had ever seen.

She wanted to scream. But when she opened her mouth to do so, nothing came out.

Cashoo caught Mercedes on the top stairs. She was hovering there, waiting to run down to the guest suites when Amiin got Kasianenko out. She had jewelry on her mind. And clothes. And cash, plenty of it.

Cashoo shot her a jaunty grin and gave her a quick hug. His raggedy facial hair scratched her cheek. She didn't mind; she'd always liked Cashoo, ever since they'd first worked together. He was young and handsome with his high cheekbones, piercing eyes, and smooth mocha skin, and although they didn't speak a word of each other's language, they'd always managed to communicate.

Once she'd given him a quick blow job, which had progressed to them almost having sex, until Amiin had interrupted them and screamed at his nephew to never touch her again.

Right now Cashoo was determined not to waste time. He leaned in and kissed her, his slithery tongue darting in and out of her mouth like a fast-moving snake.

Mercedes responded with equal enthusiasm. She was as horny as he was, having been on the yacht with no one to play with except herself, which wasn't easy with Renee sleeping in the bunk above her.

Cashoo touched her breasts before hurriedly pulling her shorts down, then plunging his hand between her legs.

Mercedes responded accordingly, unzipping his jeans and releasing his pulsating hard-on.

Cashoo was a big boy with plenty to offer.

Mercedes was into the distraction. She knew it would be fast and furious like the raid on the yacht. And that's exactly the way she wanted it, because she had things to get on with.

After kicking her shorts away from her ankles, she wrapped her legs tightly around Cashoo's waist, feeling him slide inside her, whereupon they proceeded to take a wild ride, both of them enjoying the ride equally.

The sound of gunfire rang out just as they were reaching the peak.

"*Mierda!*" Mercedes exclaimed, still managing to shudder to a satisfying climax.

Cashoo did the same.

Then, without exchanging a word, they grabbed their clothes and took off in different directions.

"This isn't exactly turning out to be the trip we'd planned," Bianca said, deciding that if she was going to be stuck in confined quarters with the other women, she might as well try to make light of it. "Beverage, anyone?" she offered, gesturing toward a shelf stocked with cans of Coca-Cola and 7-Up.

"Thanks," Lori said, determined not to show fear. "I'll take a Coke."

"How's everyone holding up?" Sierra asked.

"Not so good," Ashley muttered, a slight tremor in her voice. "I get claustrophobic. This is freaking me out."

"You must breathe deeply," Xuan advised. "Imagine something you take pleasure in doing. Can you meditate?"

"Never done that," Ashley said, clutching her pink velour Victoria's Secret hoodie around her.

"*I* know," Lori encouraged. "Think about your twins. Taye showed me some photos of them—they're so adorable."

"What if something happens to us?" Ashley wailed, beginning to panic. "Who'll take care of my babies then?"

"We're going to be fine," Sierra assured her. "Flynn knows what he's doing. He'll get us out of this."

"You must know him pretty well, then," Bianca said, giving her a piercing look.

"We both do," Xuan interjected. "If anyone can figure a way out of this, it'll be Flynn."

"Then I guess all we gotta do is stay calm and trust him," Bianca said brightly, the perfect hostess. "Right, girls?"

"We can only try," Xuan said.

Then they were all silent as the sound of gunfire took over.

Thinking *he* was the one in control, Amiin blasted open the door to the master suite, and was immediately set upon by several men.

Before he could even think of using his gun against them, they wrestled it away from him and pinned him to the floor. One of them sat astride him, while the others tied his ankles and wrists together with strips of sheets.

"How many of you are there?" Flynn demanded. "And don't pretend you can't understand me, 'cause I know you can."

Amiin was mortified. Cruz would blame him, although it wasn't his fault. There was only supposed to be one couple in this room and no weapons. Mercedes had given the information to Cruz. She'd made a serious mistake, and her mistake could ruin everything. *She* was the one to blame.

Amiin glared at his captors with bloodshot eyes. "No Engleesh," he muttered.

"No English, my black arse," Taye threatened. "Spit it out, moron, or you'll end up wearin' your teeth around your neck."

Basra grimaced at the naked girl.

She shrank away from him in horror and opened her mouth as if to scream.

But she didn't. Couldn't.

Basra appreciated her silence, for he was so very tired. He'd done his duty, gotten rid of a straggler who should've been in the mess hall with the others. Now he deserved to rest.

Only for a minute, he thought as he settled himself on the bed next to the naked girl and closed his eyes. *Only for a minute . . .*

Seconds later he was snoring as loudly as a snorting pig.

Cruz took stock. Where the fuck was Mercedes? He had to send her to find out why Amiin was taking so long. He'd heard the shots—surely Amiin had gotten Kasianenko by now and was bringing him up to the bridge?

It was time to alert Kasianenko's people to start getting the ransom money together. He was giving them twenty-four hours only. After that, if his demands were not met, he would put Basra to work. Basra would have no compunction about knocking off the hostages one by one. If Kasianenko could not get his people to pay the ransom, then the fuckers deserved it.

Cruz dragged on his cigarette while giving the captain the evil eye. He didn't like the man; he wanted him out of his sight. After a moment or two, he jumped to his feet and yelled, "Mercedes!"

She came running onto the bridge, looking flustered.

"What the fuck's takin' so much time?" he demanded. "Go find Amiin, an' tell him to shift his lazy ass. I want Kasianenko *here*. An' I want him here *now*!"

90

With Amiin firmly secured, Taye had persuaded the pirate to reveal that there were at least seven more men aboard. Seven armed pirates floating around, men to whom killing meant nothing.

Flynn tried to force Amiin to reveal what locations they were at. Amiin was done. He spat a bloody tooth at him and refused to divulge more.

At least they had two weapons now. Flynn kept Aleksandr's gun, and Cliff took Amiin's. It turned out that Cliff had made several movies where he'd had to use a gun, so he assured Flynn that he knew what he was doing.

Decisions had to be made, and fast. Somehow Flynn seemed to have gotten himself the title of team leader. It didn't bother him; he was used to being in dangerous situations.

"Luca and Taye, you stay here with our prisoner," he said, taking control. "Aleksandr, Cliff, and I will go on a search mission."

"It don't need two of us to stay with this prick," Taye said hotly, not one to miss out on any action. "I'm comin' with."

Flynn made a quick judgment call. Was Luca able to handle it if one of the other pirates came looking for their comrade? He didn't think so, especially if the predators were armed.

The answer? Everyone had to stick together, and they would take the captured pirate along as a human shield.

Yeah, that was it. He should've thought of it before.

"Untie his ankles," Flynn said. "New plan. We're taking him with us."

"Why's that?" Cliff asked.

"'Cause if anyone's getting shot, it'll be him," Flynn said grimly. "Okay, guys?"

Everyone nodded.

Renee attempted to move. She was naked on the blood-soaked bunk bed, squashed up against the wall. The man who'd shot Hammond was curled up next to her, snoring.

She was almost too frightened to struggle free. Instinctively she knew that to survive, it was what she had to do.

There was something horribly wrong with this scary man lying next to her. The smell emanating from him was noxious. His skin was the color of old cowhide and wrinkled with wear. His hair was matted into unkempt dreadlocks. His eyelids were black over sunken eyes and he had no eyelashes.

Repulsive, disgusting, and a killer.

Move! her inner voice screamed.

Get out!

Run!

Gingerly she made a vain attempt to squeeze past him. It wasn't possible; he had her wedged against the wall.

Renee realized that the only way out was to slide across him. Yet if she did that, what would happen if he awoke?

She shuddered to think.

Hardly daring to breathe, she carefully began moving over him, blood from her body dripping onto his filthy clothes.

For a moment he ceased snoring.

She immediately stopped moving, lying on top of him as if they were lovers, desperately trying to control her shaking body.

Basra grunted, farted, then resumed his noisy snoring.
Renee continued with her escape plan.

After making her way downstairs, Mercedes quickly
dodged out of sight the moment she saw Amiin being frog-
marched out of the master suite surrounded by several of
the male passengers.

Her heart started beating at an accelerated pace. Why
were the male passengers on the loose? How had *this* shit
happened? Things were progressing so smoothly, and now
Amiin had gotten himself *caught*? This wasn't part of the
plan.

She knew she should warn Cruz immediately, but the
pull of opening Kasianenko's safe was luring her in. Besides, Cruz was sitting upstairs with an Uzi and other guns.
He'd blow everyone's head off at the first sign of trouble.

Before that happened she could open the safe and grab
the ring and the piles of cash she knew were there. Then,
with that done, she'd go find Basra, Cashoo, and the others to take care of the passengers.

At least—whatever happened—she'd have her future
secured.

Screw it! The time had come to put herself first.

Down in the mess hall, the pirates were getting out of
control. Daleel and Hani had been away from their homes
for too long; their testosterone was raging. Plus the beer
was having an effect.

Daleel didn't bother finding a bathroom. He took out
his penis and pissed in the direction of his captives, jerking his cock back and forth so the stream of urine spurted
in all directions.

"Friggin' wanker!" Den yelled, as a spray of urine
splashed him in the face.

Daleel cackled, and reached for the assault rifle slung
over his shoulder. He then waved it threateningly in the
air.

"Still wanna do nothin'?" Den muttered to Guy, as Hani decided to take a shot at the ceiling.

The bullet missed the ceiling and ricocheted off the wall, hitting Jeromy in the shoulder.

Jeromy squealed like a stuck pig. To his horror, he'd been shot, actually shot. His face paled as he slumped forward clutching his wound, blood seeping through his fingers.

"I'm going to die," he moaned. "I'm going to die among you people. And no one will ever know I was here."

Then he passed out.

Cruz was not a man to be taken by surprise. Mercedes had always said that her papa had eyes in the back of his head. He was a crack shot too, so anyone coming at him had better watch out.

However, the last thing Cruz expected to see was Amiin, hands bound, a gag covering his mouth, being shoved onto the bridge with several men behind him.

"Drop your weapon," Flynn commanded. "Do it now or we shoot our hostage."

Amiin's eyes were popping out of his head. He knew what was coming, and there was nothing he could do to stop it from happening. Cruz would show no mercy.

Cruz was on his feet in a flash. Eyes blazing, he began shooting. Several bullets hit Amiin full on; another bullet grazed the top of Flynn's ear.

Captain Dickson cowered in a corner, too scared to do anything.

Cruz was acting like a madman, wielding the Uzi as if he were Al Pacino in *Scarface*.

"Back off, everyone!" Flynn yelled to the others. "We gotta take cover."

He didn't need to tell them twice.

"What's she doing?" Ashley whispered, peering at the one-way mirrored panel at the top of the safe room entry.

Bianca crowded next to her. "It's that stewardess, whatever her name is."

"Should we bring her in here with us?" Sierra questioned. "She needs to be protected."

"Hold on a minute," Bianca said. "It looks like she's trying to open Aleksandr's safe."

"Are you kidding?" Lori said.

"Holy shit!" Bianca said excitedly. "Seems like she knows the combination."

The women crowded near the panel, watching as Mercedes got the safe open and started piling the contents into a large garbage bag.

"That little bitch!" Bianca exclaimed. "She must be one of them. What can we do?"

"Nothing," Xuan said evenly. "Flynn and Aleksandr told us to stay in here until they get back, so that's what we should do."

Bianca shot Xuan a dirty look. She still didn't like her, and hearing the Asian woman mention Aleksandr's name infuriated her.

"Well," Bianca said sharply, "if you think I'm staying in here while some skank robs my man, then you are very much mistaken."

"You're not going out there, are you?" Ashley asked, alarmed. "'Cause if you do that, they'll find out where we're hiding. We'll be caught, and who knows what will happen then."

"She's right. We shouldn't leave here," Sierra said, the voice of reason. "This is a dangerous situation. We mustn't make it worse."

Bianca hesitated. She didn't appreciate being told what to do, yet deep down she knew they were right. It was better to be safe than to risk getting captured.

"Okay," she said reluctantly. "I'll stay in here. Although believe me, I'd sooner be out there kicking that bitch's ass."

"Right on," Lori murmured.

* * *

With one last frantic push, Renee fell off Basra onto the floor, landing next to Hammond's dead body. A terrified scream rose in her throat, but once more, no sound came out of her mouth. She was traumatized. All she could think about was running away from this room of horrors.

Without thinking about anything except escape, she staggered toward the door, her feet sliding on blood— Hammond's blood—which seemed to be everywhere.

Her hand slipped on the door handle as she wrenched it open and ran naked, streaked with blood, out into the narrow hallway.

She was looking for someone—anyone—who could possibly save her.

She was looking for sanity.

91

An Uzi was not a weapon to argue with. The man behind the automatic gun had all the power, and would use it to his advantage.

Cruz was just such a man, a man simmering with fury. One moment he was king of it all, in total control. The next, a bunch of civilians—rich motherfuckers who should have known better than to mess with Cruz Mendoza—were coming at him with threats and a trussed-up Amiin, the fool who'd allowed himself to be taken prisoner.

Cruz didn't hesitate; in his line of work he'd discovered that hesitating is what gets a man killed.

He sprayed the motherfuckers with bullets. Many of them slammed into Amiin, and maybe a couple of them hit the others before their human shield slumped to the ground and they ran like scared rabbits.

Still cowering against the wall, Captain Dickson attempted to make himself invisible, while Cruz screamed a vicious litany of swear words in his native Spanish.

The captain understood that he was trapped with a deranged man, and once more he feared for his life.

Cruz had other things on his mind. This takeover was not going as expected. At first, so smooth and easy. Now *this* complication.

Abort was the word that sprang to mind. Abort and get

the hell off this boat. The passengers had guns, and that was fucked up.

He could kill 'em all. But if he did that, who would pay the ransom?

Fucking no one, that's who.

Cruz spat on the ground, a sour taste filling his mouth.

It seemed that Amiin was dead. He'd worked with him for seven years. Amiin was the clan leader, his main link to the other pirates. Amiin was the only one who spoke English, allowing him to communicate with the Somalians. Now Amiin was gone, and it was a disaster.

Cruz made a quick decision. No use thinking about what could've been.

He had to get off this boat. And he had to do it fast.

After getting the safe open, Mercedes excitedly tipped the bundles of cash into the garbage bag. She figured there had to be at least a hundred thousand dollars in bills.

She was rich at last, and best of all, everything was hers.

The ring box stood front and center, a true prize to be enjoyed.

She recalled seeing the sparkling emerald and diamond ring for the first time, so magnificent it had taken her breath away.

Time was passing, but she couldn't resist. She opened the box and once more admired the ring. It was a thing of beauty, probably worth a fortune.

A thought crossed her mind. What if she slipped it on her finger? Then it would truly be hers.

Before she could do so, gunfire erupted, and she knew there was more big trouble.

Grabbing the ring and the garbage bag stuffed full of money, she raced from the room and set off to see what was going down.

* * *

"Get in front of me," Cruz ordered Captain Dickson, waving the Uzi in the captain's face. "We're fuckin' movin'."

Captain Dickson stared in horror at the dead pirate sprawled on the ground, the man's body riddled with bullets. The captain was well aware that he could meet the same fate, although thankfully Flynn and the others were not barbarians; they wouldn't shoot him down like a dog as Cruz had done to *his* man.

Or would they?

No. They wouldn't, he was sure of it.

He wasn't so sure about this out-of-control Mexican wild man. What if the maniac put a bullet in his back simply for the hell of it?

"Move," Cruz repeated. "An' do it now, motherfucker."

As soon as Cashoo returned to the mess hall where the hostages were gathered, Daleel lashed into him, demanding to know why taking a piss took so long and what he'd really been up to.

Cashoo considered himself just as important as the other Somalians—they might be older than him, but they were certainly not smarter.

He wasn't getting into an argument about how long it took to relieve himself. Daleel was jealous of him. Back home in Eyl, Cashoo always had the prettiest girls, while Daleel was stuck with a fat wife and two whiny kids.

Hani cackled on the sidelines. He'd helped himself to a mug of hot soup, and what with the soup and too much beer, he was feeling mighty tired.

Watching the two pirates argue, Den was burning with frustration. If only he could get the crew to take action instead of sitting around like a bunch of scared girls. If he could do that, then he knew there was a fair chance they could grab control.

Guy was busy ministering to Jeromy, who had recovered consciousness and was whimpering like a wounded puppy, clinging to Guy as if Guy were a lifeboat in a storm.

In spite of their history, Guy did what he had to do and assured Jeromy that everything would be fine.

Den had maneuvered himself next to the first officer and a couple of the deckhands, and he was urgently attempting to get them motivated to take action.

The first officer, a fellow Australian, seemed up for it. The deckhands—scared of catching a bullet—not so much.

And while the pirates were bickering among themselves and Den was in full persuasion mode, an apparition entered the room.

It was Renee. Blood streaking her naked body. Hair matted with blood. A blank look in her glassy eyes. She wandered into the room, arms outstretched, walking as if she were a ghost.

For a moment, nobody moved, until, summoning his best Tom Cruise, Den leaped into action. Throwing himself at a surprised Cashoo, he wrestled the gun out of the boy's hands, hoping that the crew would follow his lead and that he wasn't alone in his bid for freedom.

92

Six hours had passed, and Sergei was starting to get the message that something was very wrong. He couldn't reach either Maksim or Viktor, and that was infuriating enough. They both had phones. No signal. Nada. Nothing.

Had Cruz double-crossed him?

Had he dared to make the hijacking of the *Bianca* all about him?

Was he planning on keeping Kasianenko, claiming the ransom, then letting the bastard go?

If Cruz did such a thing, there was nothing to stop Sergei from ordering a hit on him, a major hit that would involve torture before death, because nobody fucked with Sergei Zukov and lived to tell the tale.

Son of a bitch!

He summoned Ina from her bed and berated her.

"It's not my fault if he's done somethin' bad," she whined. "I can't tell him what to do."

"How much does your low-life brother care about you?" Sergei demanded, his left cheek twitching out of control.

"I dunno," she said sulkily. "We have different fathers, y'know."

As if that made a difference. They'd both sprung forth from between the legs of the same whore.

"If your brother doesn't return soon," Sergei threatened, "if he's screwed me—then you can pack your shit and get out. Understand me, *pizda*?"

Ina understood.

93

After taking cover, Flynn tried to figure out their next move. He was dealing with a group of inexperienced men who knew nothing about combat. It wasn't as if they were in the midst of a battle in Afghanistan, but this was still dangerous territory and he didn't care to see anyone else get hurt.

A bullet had grazed the top of his ear—no big deal. He was more concerned about Aleksandr, who'd taken a bullet in the thigh and was bleeding profusely. They'd gotten Aleksandr into Kyril's room, where they'd discovered the security man's dead body.

Aleksandr had shaken his head and groaned his sorrow.

Two dead already. How many more? Flynn didn't want to think about it. As long as Sierra and the women were safe. That was his main concern.

"I'm afraid you're out of action," he informed Aleksandr. "Luca and Cliff, you stay here with him. If anyone comes visiting, don't hesitate—shoot 'em."

Cliff nodded. Shit! He was somewhat fearful. This wasn't playacting anymore, and the gun he was holding on to was making his hands slick with sweat. Not to mention Kyril's dead body, a signal that the pirates really meant business.

"I'd like to have a gun," Taye said, bouncing on the balls of his feet, full of nervous energy.

"And I'd like to have a cold beer," Flynn retaliated. "But we gotta make do with what we got. So you and I are gonna go see what's goin' on. You up for an adventure?"

Taye wasn't afraid. Being raised in a tough London suburb had taught him plenty about street smarts; he had a few moves of his own.

"I'll lead the way," Flynn said. "If I get my head blown off, take my gun an' mow 'em all to hell an' back. Right?"

"You got it," Taye said, hoping Flynn's words were his idea of a joke.

Blood was trickling down from the top of Flynn's ear, landing on his neck. As long as it stayed out of his eyes, he didn't care. He was on a hunt, ready to shoot anyone who got in his way.

A triumphant Den surveyed the scene. Finally, they had them! All three pirates and no injuries, other than to Jeromy, who'd gotten shot earlier.

One of the deckhands had fetched sturdy ropes after they had overpowered the three pirates, and they'd tied them up.

Now not only did they have three prisoners, they also had their guns, making Den feel more secure about everyone's future.

Guy had taken charge of an incoherent Renee, wrapping her in Jeromy's robe, feeding her sips of water, assuring her she was safe now.

Renee was unable to speak. Tears coursed down her cheeks while she clutched her arms around her body and rocked back and forth.

Guy led her over to Jeromy and sat her down next to him. "Look after her," Guy said tersely. "Who knows what the poor girl's been through."

Jeromy was about to object, then thought better of it. Guy had shown him kindness. Therefore, he had to reciprocate in spite of his injury, which was probably draining the life out of him, although Guy had fixed him up with a makeshift tourniquet that could quite possibly be saving his miserable life.

Jeromy was not a religious man; he'd been to church twice in all his forty-two years, and that was only to appease one of his ex-lovers.

Slumped on the floor in the mess hall of a luxury yacht, he suddenly found himself praying to a God he'd never conversed with before. A God he'd never believed in, only right now that God was all he had.

He reached over and touched Renee's arm. "There, there, dear," he said soothingly. "Everything will be all right."

Clutching her loot, Mercedes made it up to the bridge.

No Cruz.

A dead Amiin.

She was horrified. Amiin was Cruz's right arm. Who could have done this to him? Where was Cruz?

She skipped away from the bridge, and as she passed Kyril's room she was grabbed by a concerned Luca Perez, who held her arm and said to her in Spanish, "There are pirates aboard, girl. Get in here now. You'll be safe with us."

"I know," she said, thinking fast. "They haven't seen me. I'm . . . uh . . . looking for weapons."

"Are there guns? Where?"

"There's a place I know," she said vaguely.

"You have to stay," Luca said, reverting to English. "These people are bloodthirsty savages, they shot their own man."

"Amiin?" She said his name before she could stop herself.

Cliff stepped forward. "What did you say?"

"Amen," she muttered, crossing herself.

"You're a girl— if they catch you it won't be good," Luca warned.

"Thanks for your concern, Mr. Perez. Thing is, I know this boat pretty well, so there's no way they'll catch me."

"What's in the bag?" Aleksandr asked, leaning forward from Kyril's chair.

"Oh God! I think I hear Renee," Mercedes cried out. "I'll be back with guns. Don't worry about me. I know what I'm doing."

She ran before they could stop her.

The question was, how *had* they gotten free? Were they telling the truth? *Had* Cruz shot Amiin himself?

If so, why would he do that?

She had so many questions, and no one to answer them.

The biggest question of all was, where was Cruz?

Was he abandoning ship?

Would he do that and leave her behind?

Knowing her papa, it was quite possible.

She thought quickly. There had obviously been a confrontation. The passengers had most likely used Amiin as a shield, and Cruz had blown him away to save himself. Then he'd probably decided to make a quick getaway as things were turning sour, and right now he'd be heading for one of the speedboats to whisk him away.

Mercedes's gut feeling warned her that she'd better hurry if she wanted to catch up with him. The captain knew she was one of them, so she could hardly stay on board and bluff it out.

Screw it! She was cool. She had what she wanted. The cash. The ring.

Best to run while she still could.

"I feel like I'm in *CSI* or *Law and Order*," Taye quipped, trying to make light of a dire situation as he followed close behind Flynn, who moved stealthily with his gun drawn. "Wish *I* had a friggin' gun," Taye continued. "It'd make me feel a lot more secure."

"Here's what you do," Flynn advised. "If I start shooting, you rush 'em, tackle them at the knees, throw them off balance. Then grab whatever guns they got."

"Yeah, sure, that's if they don't shoot my balls off first," Taye said, imagining the worst.

"They won't," Flynn said with a grim smile. "We got this."

"*You* got it," Taye said, running his hand over his shaved head. "I certainly ain't."

They were doing a sweep of the top deck; it all seemed to be clear.

Taye stuck right behind Flynn, his new hero. The bloke appeared to be fearless, and Taye got off on the air of confidence Flynn exuded.

Taye wondered how Ashley was coping. If he knew his wife at all, by this time she'd be a hysterical wreck. Ashley didn't do well under pressure, although she'd managed a pretty fine job of climbing up the side of the yacht when she'd had to. He was proud of her for that.

Flynn led the way down the staircase to the middle deck. Once more, it was all clear.

"The pirates have speedboats each side of the yacht," Flynn said quickly. "One pirate guarding each boat. If we can surprise 'em, then it's two less to deal with."

"Surprise 'em? You mean kill 'em?" Taye said, trying to stay cool.

"No," Flynn answered caustically. "How about we invite them aboard for a cup of your favorite English tea?"

"Okay, okay, I get it," Taye said, duly chastised. "Where do you think the crew is?"

"My guess is they've got them all together on the lower deck. The guy upstairs was the leader. The one he shot might've been second in command. Then there's the two with the boats. That leaves four more. Two of them at least are watching the crew. The other two—that's who we gotta keep a lookout for."

Taye couldn't hold back his curiosity. "You ever shot anyone?" he asked, as once more they moved stealthily toward the stairs.

"Why don't we shut up and concentrate," Flynn muttered, feeling the sting at the top of his ear, while blood continued to drip down his neck.

"Right," Taye said quickly. "I'm way into concentrating."

"Good," Flynn said. "So let's do this thing."

94

Once Cruz decided something, that was it, no going back. Every fiber in his body warned him to make a fast getaway and haul his ass off the *Bianca*.

Amiin was dead. The other pirates meant nothing to him; they were merely the workforce. Amiin was the only one who'd mattered.

Dammit. His right-hand man had been dumb enough to get himself taken prisoner, giving Cruz no choice but to shoot, since he'd managed to get himself right in the line of fire.

Cruz headed for the speedboat on the left side of the boat, pushing and shoving Captain Dickson in front of him, using him as a shield, so that if any bullets came flying, they'd hit the captain and not him.

For one brief moment he thought about Mercedes and wondered where the hell she was. Then he remembered that Mercedes was a smart girl. She could look after herself; she didn't need him to babysit her. He'd taught her to be a survivor, exactly like him.

Captain Dickson was breathing heavily. Abject fear overcame him; he felt that at any moment he might succumb to a heart attack.

Cruz dug him in the back with the Uzi and yelled at him to move faster.

The captain struggled to do as he was told, but he still failed to move fast enough for Cruz's liking.

Cruz gave him a vicious kick, causing him to slip and fall down the stairs, whereupon Cruz muttered a litany of curses, came after him, and hauled him to his feet. "You do that again an' you're dead meat," Cruz growled.

As time passed, Ashley began to lose it, and no amount of consoling words could calm her down.

"I have to get out of here," she whimpered, thinking of her twins and how they couldn't possibly manage without her. "I can't stay in here. I feel sick. I'm about to faint."

"No, you're not," Xuan said sternly. "What you *are* going to do is sit down, shut up, and put your head between your legs."

"I can't do that," Ashley wailed. "Surely you understand? We've all got to get out of here. They'll find us anyway, so what are we waiting for?"

"We're waiting for Aleksandr and the others to come back," Bianca said, fast losing patience. "And you're not making the wait easy. So like Xuan said—shut up."

"Listen, I know we're all scared," Sierra said, sure that Flynn wouldn't let them down. "However, staying in control is the most important thing of all. Fighting among ourselves is not helping."

"She's right," Lori said. "We can't lose it."

"Oh, be quiet," Ashley snapped. "What do *you* know? You're here on a pass."

"Excuse me?" Lori said, bristling.

"Now, now, ladies," Bianca interjected. "This is no time to get into a bitchfest."

Ashley slumped down on the bench that ran along one side of the small room. "Oh my God!" she moaned. "I have a premonition. We're all going to die in here. We're getting raped, then murdered. I know it."

"Be quiet, you stupid woman," Xuan said with steely

determination. "You're talking nonsense. And you'd better stop your nonsense before I force you to."

"We gotta go investigate, find out what's goin' on," Den insisted to Guy, once the three pirates were firmly secured.

Guy, a lot braver now that he was no longer being held at gunpoint, demurred. "Let's not forget who's in charge here," he said, asserting himself. "I'm the one with seniority. I'll decide what we do next."

"Where was all that seniority when I was beggin' you to get the crew to do somethin'?" Den demanded.

Guy did not appreciate the younger man's tone. "We should stay put," he said. "It's safer for us to all be in one place."

"You're such a friggin' pussy," Den said in disgust. "Doncha understand what's goin' on here? You're not in charge of me or anyone else. This is a shit situation, an' I'm not sittin' around waitin' for it to get worse."

Ignoring Guy, he started talking to a few of the crew who finally seemed to have realized that they did indeed have balls, and even better, they now had guns.

Den proposed that several of them set off to find out exactly what was going on. The first officer and two of the crew agreed.

Den took the front position.

Jabrill, an emaciated man with slit eyes and a mean mouth, guarded the speedboat on the left-hand side of the boat. A former fisherman, he was not as bloodthirsty as his comrades. He preferred sitting on the sidelines, chewing on his khat while contemplating his Ethiopian girlfriend and the money he had coming to him.

Jabrill was anxious to get home. He hoped that the ransom would be paid fast, and that they could be on their way soon.

When Cruz appeared, Jabrill was pleased. It seemed

things had happened quicker than expected, although he hadn't heard a helicopter overhead, and usually the ransom was paid in cash and dropped off by helicopter.

Cruz was not alone. He had an unknown white man with him, a man he shoved into the speedboat ahead of him at gunpoint.

Jabrill stared at his boss and wondered where Amiin was. Cruz never made a move without Amiin by his side. Amiin was Cruz's conduit to the pirates, the only one who could translate his orders.

"Let's go!" Cruz shouted, jumping into the boat.

Jabrill continued staring, his expression blank.

"Go!" Cruz yelled. "Fuckin' take off, you moron!"

Jabrill did not understand a word he was saying.

Fully charged with the leadership gene, Den experienced no fear as he and several members of the crew began checking out the yacht. On the upper level, they came upon Aleksandr, Cliff, and Luca, and quickly exchanged information.

Once they saw Kyril's lifeless body, they all realized the seriousness and extreme danger of the situation.

Den was on fire. They had guns. They had balls. He decided that if he got through this, he was going into the security business. Maybe start his own firm. Yeah, no more barman crap; he was hot to strike out on his own.

He suggested to Cliff and Luca that they get Aleksandr down to the mess hall, pointing out that it was safer if everyone stayed together.

Luca and Cliff seemed to think it was a smart idea, and Aleksandr agreed.

"We should go find Flynn and Taye—tell them what's going on," Cliff announced, commandeering an AK rifle. "I'll do it."

"And I'll stick with you," Den said, thinking of his mum's face if she knew he was on a dangerous mission with an actual movie star.

Oh yes, his mum would have a fit! So would his married sister, who had a big crush on Cliff Baxter. She'd always considered her little brother a total loser, so screw you, big sis!

Den had never felt more alive.

The movie star and the barman set off to find Flynn and Taye, while Luca and several crew members assisted in getting Aleksandr downstairs.

Aleksandr was not happy about being a victim. He was a strong, powerful man, and not being able to walk because of his injury infuriated him.

In his mind he was going over how this could possibly have happened and who was responsible. He had enemies. Every successful businessman had enemies. And then there were his soon-to-be ex-wife's brothers. He wouldn't put it past them; they were a bunch of jealous, greedy pricks who thought he owed them a living.

He promised himself that however long it took, he would find the person who had masterminded this outrage, and they would be duly punished. Not only by the law, but by his own hand.

Aleksandr never made a promise he couldn't keep.

"He's dead!" Renee cried out, her eyes wide with fear. "A man . . . a bad bad man shot him."

"What did you say?" Jeromy asked, leaning closer to the girl. It was the first time she'd spoken, and he couldn't quite understand her; she wasn't making much sense.

"Dead," she repeated, shivering uncontrollably, her face deathly pale.

"Who is dead?" Jeromy asked, fear creeping up on him, for surely this couldn't be true?

"The senator," Renee gasped, breaking into heavy sobs. "He was on top of me . . . the man shot him . . . I could've been shot too."

Jeromy didn't like what he was hearing. He summoned Guy, who came over carrying a blanket that he wrapped around Renee.

"She's saying something about the senator being shot," Jeromy informed him. "It can't be true . . . can it?"

"God no!" Guy said. "I'm sure it isn't. She's traumatized, doesn't know what she's saying."

"There's an evil man in my cabin," Renee whispered, barely able to speak. "He's asleep on the bed. He has a gun. If he wakes up, he'll come kill us all."

Guy looked around.

Where was Den?

Moving as fast as she could, Mercedes made it to the speedboat just as Cruz was screaming at Jabrill to take off.

She shimmied down the rope ladder and jumped into the boat, clutching her garbage bag of cash, the ring stuffed into her bra for safekeeping.

"Were you leavin' without me?" she said accusingly.

"Who d'you *think* I was waitin' for?" Cruz lied. "You, of course."

"Why's *he* here?" Mercedes demanded, indicating the captain.

"'Cause he might be useful," Cruz said gruffly. "An' when he's not so useful, I'm gonna toss him overboard. Now tell this motherfucker to start the boat an' get us the fuck outta here."

Mercedes knew a few words of Somali, enough to tell Jabrill to go.

Jabrill wasn't having it. Sensing all was not right, he demanded to know where the others were. Cashoo, Hani, and especially Amiin.

Cruz screamed his frustration as Flynn and Taye appeared on deck.

Spotting Mercedes and Captain Dickson in the boat, Flynn figured they were both being kidnapped and instantly knew he had to do something.

"Get out of the boat with your hands up," he yelled at

Cruz. "It's over. The coast guard's on the way. You may as well surrender now."

"Go fuck yourself," Cruz screamed, raising his Uzi and letting forth a barrage of bullets.

Jabrill jumped to attention. Violence was not his thing unless absolutely necessary. To hell with the other pirates; they'd be okay on the other boat.

He revved the engine, and within seconds the powerful speedboat took off.

95

"Get out!" Sergei screamed, wrenching the covers off the bed.

Ina opened one eye. "What?" she mumbled.

"You heard me. Out. Now! Out of my life, you conniving cunt," Sergei shouted. "You're probably in cahoots with your thieving brother. The two of you laughing at me behind my back. I should've known better than to trust either of you."

"I've done nothing," Ina whined. "Why're you taking my brother's bad deeds out on me?"

"Bad deeds, huh?" Sergei yelled, grabbing her hair and yanking her from the bed. "So you knew all along what the *pizda* had planned. You knew it!"

"No," Ina objected. "I knew nothing. What's happened? Why are you so mad?"

"As if you don't know," Sergei snarled. "I want you out of my house. *Now.*"

"It's the middle of the night, Sergei," Ina said. "If you really mean it, I'll leave tomorrow and go back to Acapulco until you calm down."

"You'll go back nowhere," Sergei assured her. "It's over. And consider yourself lucky that I'm letting you walk away."

"But Sergei—"

"Five minutes, Ina," he threatened. "And if you're not gone by then, I promise you I'll break every bone in your body."

96

If Flynn knew anything at all, it was that he couldn't let the bastard get away with kidnapping the young stewardess and Captain Dickson. God knew what he'd do to them—the pirate had gunned down his own man, which meant he was capable of anything.

"You okay?" he said, briskly turning to Taye.

"Not a scratch," Taye retorted.

"Then we gotta go after them," Flynn said with an air of urgency. "We need to get control of their boat, take it over."

"How're we—"

Before Taye could even think of finishing his sentence, Flynn was on the move, crossing over to the far side of the yacht, motioning Taye to be quiet.

Galad, the pirate in charge of the second speedboat, was not as laid-back as Jabrill. Over the last hour, he'd heard sporadic gunshots and was on alert.

Flynn, not about to waste time, surprised the pirate with a crack shot to the man's right arm, causing Galad to drop his gun and yelp with pain.

Moving swiftly, Flynn swooped down to the boat, rendering Galad unconscious with a fast and accurate blow to the head, then quickly tipping him into the back of the boat.

Climbing down the ladder after him, Taye was shocked. It seemed Flynn had moves nobody suspected. Bloody hell! Could it be that he was a Navy SEAL in another life? Taye wouldn't be surprised.

"You coming?" Flynn shouted.

"Yeah," Taye said, still somewhat shell-shocked. "Wouldn't miss it."

Flynn tossed him the pirate's gun, and started the engine as Taye leaped in.

The chase was on.

Cashoo's mind was running riot. Hog-tied, he was angry and frustrated. How had he allowed this to happen? Hani and Daleel too. What were they all thinking?

For one second he'd lost focus, staring at a naked girl as if he'd never seen breasts before. Then a civilian had jumped him, several of the crew had rushed the others, and now the situation was reversed. Hani, Daleel, and he were prisoners.

Cruz wouldn't be happy, nor would Amiin. Any moment Cashoo expected them to come in, guns blazing, all set to free them.

He was confident this would happen, and soon. Cruz wasn't one to put up with any delays.

Crouching down next to Renee, Guy was pretty certain that she'd been raped by a pirate, perhaps more than one. Poor girl, she was certainly in a sorry state.

"Tell me what happened to you, dear," he said sympathetically, as one of the Polish maids brought her over a mug of hot tea and squatted down beside her.

"She's been carrying on about a man with a gun," Jeromy said, clutching his shoulder, making sure everyone realized he was badly injured. "Apparently this man shot Senator Patterson."

Beginning to feel more lucid, Renee felt her head clearing and knew that she'd better get her story across before the repugnant man who'd murdered Hammond came looking for *her*.

"The senator and me—we were in my cabin," she said, taking small sips of tea with shaking hands, the hot liquid spilling over the rim of the mug.

Guy frowned. "What was Senator Patterson doing in your cabin?" he asked.

Renee lowered her head, too ashamed to tell the truth.

"I . . . I don't remember," she stammered. "He . . . he might've been running from the monster with the gun."

"Oh, you must mean the monster who raped you, and shot the senator?" Jeromy said with a sarcastic edge, beginning to think that her story sounded somewhat farfetched, and wishing that Guy would pay more attention to *him*. After all, he was the one who'd been shot and almost killed. *He* should be the center of attention.

"That's right," Renee mumbled.

"You should know that the yacht's been taken over by pirates," Guy told her matter-of-factly. "The man who attacked you must be one of them. It's important that you tell us where you last saw him."

"I told you," Renee said, shivering uncontrollably. "He's sleeping in my cabin. And the senator is dead—he's lying on the floor."

Then, before they could get any more out of her, she burst into hysterical sobs.

Flynn drove the fast speedboat as if he'd been doing it all his life.

And he probably has, Taye thought. *Here is a dude who can apparently do anything he sets his mind to.*

They were not that far behind the other boat, and gaining fast.

"Tie up the asshole," Flynn ordered, using one hand to toss Taye a section of sturdy rope.

Taye presumed by "asshole" he meant the still-unconscious pirate.

He did as Flynn requested, using his best slipknot technique, although he bet that Flynn had a better method.

At least Flynn hadn't killed the man. That was a relief.

"How we gonna stop 'em?" Taye yelled over the sound of the engine.

"We'll worry about that when we get closer," Flynn responded.

"Do you have a plan?"

"People who make plans end up getting fucked," Flynn shouted. "You gotta play it by instinct."

Taye could hardly believe that this was the same laid-back guy he'd spent days on the yacht with. Who knew that Flynn Hudson was a friggin' superhero?

Dawn was breaking, and they could clearly make out the boat in front of them. The sea was calm, although the boat ahead of them was causing a swell, so their boat was bouncing over the waves, spray hitting them in the face.

Flynn began covering the gap fast.

Taye was mindful of the fact that the wild man in the boat ahead of them was carrying an Uzi.

Would the pirate use it?

Bloody right he would.

Jeez! If Taye got himself shot, Ashley would never forgive him.

"It's too quiet," Lori ventured, beginning to feel trapped in the confined space. "How long before we can get out of here?"

"Not until Aleksandr tells us we can," Bianca said, just as apprehensive as the others. She was worried about what was going on outside their safe room. She was also furious that the stewardess had robbed Aleksandr's safe. If she was not mistaken, she could've sworn she'd seen the girl open a ring box, then take the ring nestled inside, and she couldn't help wondering if it was an engagement ring.

Could it be that Aleksandr had been planning to propose?

The thought was an exciting one.

Ashley had stopped complaining. She was slumped on the bench muttering to herself.

Xuan was chanting some kind of mantra, sitting cross-legged on the floor.

Sierra was thinking that this situation was almost like a signal from God. She was not a religious person—more spiritual—however, was this a sign telling her that if they all survived, she should leave Hammond?

She would. No more excuses.

"Shitheads," Cruz snarled, as he realized the chase boat was catching up with them. "Faster!" he screamed at Jabrill. "Make this thing go faster!"

Mercedes translated to Jabrill, who wasn't happy.

Captain Dickson was hunched in the back of the boat, praying to God that he would get out of this alive and be reunited with his wife of twenty years.

What did they want with him? He was useless to them.

As if reading his mind, Cruz came up with the same thought. The captain was useless to them, so why keep him around?

Flynn had his eyes fixed on the boat ahead. He figured that if he was able to pass it, maybe he could cut them off, force their engine to stall, and rescue the hostages.

He wasn't taking into account the man with the Uzi, or the driver of the boat, who was no doubt also armed. All he could think about was persuading the pirates to relinquish their two hostages: the girl and the captain. Then, as far as he was concerned, the pirates could go on their merry way.

It wasn't going to be easy—nothing ever was.

Then he thought, what if he offered an exchange? *His* trussed-up pirate for *their* two prisoners?

Seemed like a fair enough deal if he could get the fucker with the Uzi to listen.

He was thinking all of this as he powered the boat forward, intent on catching up. Then, to his utter surprise, someone on the boat in front of him hurled what appeared to be a body overboard.

Hurriedly, he swerved the boat, immediately cutting the throttle. The boat shuddered to a halt.

"Holy friggin' balls!" Taye yelled as he was thrown violently off balance. "What the *fuck*!"

97

"I want you to bring me one of the prisoners," Aleksandr ordered Guy. He was now settled in the mess hall, his leg elevated.

"There's three of them, sir, and they don't speak English," Guy advised. "We gather from the looks of them that they might be Somalians."

"Then don't bother," Aleksandr said, shaking his head. "Are they well secured?" he added. "No chance of escape?"

"Absolutely no chance, Mr. Kasianenko." Guy cleared his throat. "The problem is that we don't know how many others there might be."

"The coast guard is on its way," Aleksandr said, surveying the room. "Everyone has to stay in one place until they get here. Is that understood?"

"Yes, sir," Guy said, then after hesitating a moment he added, "May I ask—where are the ladies?"

"Safe," Aleksandr replied. "However, I regret to tell you that my bodyguard, Kyril, is no longer with us."

"I'm sorry to hear that," Guy said, wanting more details, but afraid to ask.

"So am I," Aleksandr said gravely. "He was a very loyal and fine employee."

"To fill you in, sir, we have one stewardess still missing," Guy said. "And Renee, the other stewardess"—he lowered his voice—"I fear she's been raped. She's also saying something about Senator Patterson having been shot, but this has not been confirmed."

"Jesus Christ!" Aleksandr thundered. "This is abominable."

"I know, sir. It's a terrible situation."

"Those bastards will pay for this," Aleksandr said, his face dark with fury. "You have my word."

Cliff found himself to be quite invigorated. Not that he embraced violence; however, the fact that he and the young Australian with him were prepared to defend the yacht and search out invaders—well, it was damn energizing. After all, this wasn't a movie set. He wasn't surrounded by gofers willing to accommodate his every need. This was the *real* thing, not the *reel* thing.

For once, Cliff was in charge of his own destiny. No longer the Sexiest Man Alive, a title he would like to see buried once and for all. He was living free, doing what *he* thought was the right thing, without a bevy of advisers telling him not to do anything because the press might misconstrue his actions.

Bullshit to that.

"Middle deck's all clear," Den announced. "We should go down one."

"I'm right behind you," Cliff said, holding his gun in front of him, and feeling more of a man than he had in a long time.

"I'm so sorry this had to happen to you," Luca said, commiserating with Jeromy, who was quick to tell him that he'd almost died.

"My shoulder is extremely painful," Jeromy muttered, wincing to make sure Luca realized the full extent of his suffering.

"You're being very brave," Luca said.

"It was a ghastly experience," Jeromy sniffed. "Not to mention quite humiliating." After a meaningful pause, he added, "Can you imagine being dragged down here and thrown in with the *crew*? How degrading is *that*?"

"At least we're all safe now," Luca said, attempting to be the supportive significant other.

"Are we?" Jeromy said curtly. "That girl over there says there is a man with a gun asleep in her cabin. She claims he shot Hammond."

Luca glanced over at Renee. "Well, that doesn't make sense," he said. "She's most likely hallucinating after all she's been through."

"Where *is* Hammond?" Jeromy questioned. "Has anyone seen him?"

It occurred to Luca that nobody *had* seen Hammond.

"This story of a man asleep in her cabin," Luca ventured. "Did someone go check it out?"

Jeromy started to shrug, then flinched with pain instead. "Nobody wants to," he said shortly.

"Maybe *I* should," Luca suggested.

"No!" Jeromy admonished. "Leave it to one of the men."

"The 'men,' Jeromy?" Luca said, giving him an incredulous look. "What does that make me?"

"You know what I mean," Jeromy said, hurriedly backing off. "It's not your place. You're too—"

"Too what?" Luca interrupted, finally realizing what Jeromy really thought of him.

"Forget it," Jeromy said, switching to a long, deep moan. "My shoulder is *so* damn painful. What if I'm left with a disfiguring scar? Do you think I can sue Aleksandr?"

Luca shook his head in disgust. He knew now more than ever that if they survived this ordeal, then it was definitely time for him to move on.

Thank God it was light out, for if it had been dark there would've been no way of finding a body in the sea.

Is that what they were looking for? Flynn wondered. A dead body? Had the pirate *shot* whoever it was he'd tossed overboard?

"Can you see anything?" he yelled at Taye.

Taye's eyes scoured the sea until finally he spotted arms waving above the swell. "I'm going in!" he shouted. "There's someone out there."

"You a good swimmer?" Flynn asked, grabbing a life preserver and tossing it overboard.

"Better than most," Taye boasted, stripping off his pants and T-shirt, then making a clean dive over the side of the boat.

The current was surprisingly strong, but it didn't stop Taye. He swam powerfully toward the flailing arms and grabbed the victim in a rescue hold.

"Thank God!" Captain Dickson gasped. Taye managed to get them both back to the boat, where Flynn helped haul them aboard.

The other speedboat was now way off in the distance. Flynn decided they had to go after it anyway to save the girl.

"What girl?" Captain Dickson managed, spluttering and coughing up seawater.

"The stewardess," Flynn said. "We can't let them take her."

"Don't bother," Captain Dickson said, filled with relief that his prayers had been answered. "She's one of them."

Horse tranquilizers affect humans in various ways, depending on how much they have ingested.

Basra had taken enough to knock out any normal person for many hours. However, there was nothing normal about Basra.

The main drug in horse tranquilizers—ketamine—was a powerful mind-changer. After wolfing down several of the brownies Mercedes had laced with the stuff, Basra awoke with a lethal headache and a strong urge to puke.

His mind was a blank slate. He didn't know where he was or what he was supposed to be doing.

He sat up, swung his feet to the ground, and encountered the blood-soaked body of a naked man.

After coughing up a wad of phlegm, he spat it on the man.

Next he picked up his AK assault rifle, slung it over his shoulder, and set off to discover where he was.

Basra was in a killing daze.

98

With Captain Dickson safely aboard, and having learned that the stewardess, Mercedes, was connected to the pirates, Flynn turned the speedboat around and headed back to the *Bianca*.

Galad was still trussed up and immobile in the back of the boat, although he'd recovered consciousness and was glaring at his captors with deep loathing. They all ignored him while Captain Dickson filled them in on everything he knew—which wasn't much. Just that the Mexican man was obviously running the operation and didn't give a damn about leaving his men behind, let alone shooting them.

Flynn tried to discover more about the girl. The captain had no further information on her, other than that Guy, his entertainment director, had hired her against his wishes.

Flynn flashed back on the day he'd caught Mercedes coming out of his room. He should've been suspicious then, but why would he be? She'd had a perfectly feasible excuse about checking out the minibar, and his mind had been on Sierra.

So, Mercedes had been the pirates' inside connection. Then who exactly was the Mexican man running the show?

As an investigative journalist and a guest on the yacht,

Flynn had to find out. For his own peace of mind, he needed to know.

The big question was, who had targeted Aleksandr Kasianenko, and why.

Meanwhile, there were things to tidy up on the yacht. How many pirates were still on the loose? Maybe three or even four?

With their leader having taken flight, perhaps they'd surrendered.

Flynn sincerely hoped so; he'd had enough action for one day. Besides, he was anxious to see how Sierra was doing.

"We gotta be careful," he warned Taye and the captain as their speedboat approached the *Bianca*. "If anyone comes at you, like I told you before—shoot for the knee-caps."

The captain groaned.

Taye was totally into it.

Random thoughts crossed Cliff's mind as he and Den swept each deck, guns drawn.

How many times had he enacted a similar scene in a movie? Although in a movie, every step was choreographed, every move worked out by a professional stunt-man. There was plenty of fake blood when needed. Guns that shot blanks. Actors who made it all look too real.

Cliff had the stance down. Over the years, he'd played three detectives, two cops, a renegade gunrunner, a man out to avenge his wife's murder, and a maverick cowboy.

When Cliff was six, his mother had shot his father right between the eyes. It was a secret from his past that he'd managed to hide from the world.

Oh yes, Cliff Baxter and guns were way too familiar. Yet he refused to keep one in his home lest a visitor discover it and shoot someone by accident.

So far he and Den had encountered no lurking pirates.

"Think they've run their sorry arses outta here," Den said as they finished a sweep of the lower deck. "Must've found out we caught their mates, so they pissed off."

"You think?" Cliff said, lowering his gun.

"Bunch of cowardly wankers," Den scoffed. "We're done."

"But we didn't find Flynn or Taye," Cliff pointed out.

"They're probably in the mess hall with Aleksandr," Den said, quite full of himself. "Uh . . . I mean Mr. Kasianenko."

"Right," Cliff said.

"We should go join up," Den said, wondering if anyone had a camera so he could get a souvenir photo of himself with Cliff Baxter. What a coup that would be.

"Sounds like a plan to me," Cliff said.

Den started off in the other direction, and as he did so, Basra appeared.

The pirate made a grotesque sight, gaunt and haggard, with his matted dreadlocks and filthy clothes drenched in blood. His skin was cadaverous, his eyes manic; he looked like a feral animal caught in a steel trap.

Den had his back to him—he was already heading for the mess hall.

But Cliff was facing him.

Man-to-man.

There they were, the grisly murderous pirate and the handsome movie star.

They both raised their guns.

A shot rang out and one of them fell to the ground.

Den spun around. It was too late for him to do anything.

Too damn late.

99

The 378-foot high-endurance coast guard cutter *Sunrise* pulled up next to the *Bianca*. Several maritime-law-enforcement officers immediately boarded the vessel, guns at the ready.

Flynn greeted them. "You're too late," he informed them with a cynical shake of his head. "Guess we did your job for you."

Captain Dickson was on deck. He led the officers straight to the captured pirates—Cashoo, Hani, Daleel, and Galad—who were put in handcuffs and taken away.

Medical personnel also boarded and began getting the wounded onto stretchers before transferring them to the cutter's helicopter.

Aleksandr insisted his guests be taken care of first. Jeromy got the star treatment, with Renee next in line, then Den, and finally Aleksandr—but not before he'd made sure that Bianca and the other women were safe.

A medic attempted to tend to Flynn, but he waved her away. "I'm fine," he said curtly.

Aleksandr personally gave Sierra the news about Hammond. Her reaction was not what he'd expected. She'd remained dry-eyed and surprisingly calm.

Then came the morbid part. The photographing and removal of the dead bodies from the yacht. First Senator

Patterson, then the bodyguard Kyril, and finally the two dead pirates.

Cliff Baxter was hailed as a hero, for he was the one who'd shot and killed the man who'd brutally raped Renee, then murdered Senator Patterson.

In her mind, Renee had convinced herself that this was exactly how it had all gone down. She was a victim, and she told her story with much conviction. It was all about how she'd been in her cabin when the pirate had entered and attacked and raped her. Then Senator Patterson had burst in to try to save her, only to get himself shot.

Nobody questioned why the senator was naked. Aleksandr had spoken on the phone to certain people in power, and the investigation was cursory.

Case closed.

Nobody cared about a dead Somalian pirate.

Den, the barman, was somewhat bummed. Just his luck that the friggin' movie star had been the one to shoot the wanker. It should've been *him*. He was the person who deserved hero status.

The guests were all anxious to get off the *Bianca* as soon as possible. The crew also couldn't wait.

Captain Dickson headed back full speed ahead to Cabo, where chaos waited.

The world press were in ecstasy. What a story! One of the greatest ever. A gaggle of stars. Power. Money. Fame. Sex. Murder. Luxury.

Headlines roared across the world. The Internet blew up.

Senator Patterson's sex scandal was forgotten. Along with Cliff Baxter, the senator was now a hero. A dead hero, but a hero all the same.

Aleksandr made arrangements for an army of bodyguards to meet the *Bianca* when it docked. A fleet of private jets awaited to take his esteemed guests wherever they wished to go.

Aleksandr's personal doctor had flown in to tend to him. Fortunately, the injury to his thigh was not as serious as he'd feared, and he jetted off to Moscow with Bianca by his side.

Ashley and Taye flew back to England, where the British press descended on them in full force. So many photographers; so many flashbulbs blinding them as they stepped out of the airport.

Their two mums were waiting to greet them, accompanied by the twins, Aimee and Wolf, in matching girl/boy outfits.

Ashley let out a yelp of pure joy as she bent down to cuddle both her children. "Mummy's home," she crooned. "And I promise you that Mummy will never leave you again."

"You got that right," said a grinning Taye.

To Jeromy's chagrin, Luca left him languishing in a hospital in Cabo while he flew back to Miami. "If I stay, the press'll drive us crazy," Luca explained. "It's better that you recover quietly without all the fuss of me being around."

Jeromy was not a happy camper.

Cliff, feted as a hero, avoided the press altogether. He and Lori returned to L.A. and holed up in his mansion while the furor died down. "I'm no hero," he kept on protesting to his inner circle.

But everyone—including Lori—knew that he was.

Xuan refused the offer of a private jet and took a commercial flight to Syria, where she had an assignment to write an in-depth piece for *The Huffington Post*.

Which left Sierra and Flynn.

And where exactly *did* it leave them?

Not in a perfect place, for although outwardly calm, Sierra was horrified at what had taken place. She might have hated her husband, but she'd certainly never wished anything like this on him.

Flynn made an attempt to comfort her.

She rejected him. Turned away from anything he had to say.

They parted ways without resolving anything.

Sierra traveled to New York.

Flynn took off to Paris.

Both understood that for now—sadly—it was not to be.

Epilogue

THREE MONTHS LATER

Scandals come and go. There is always something outrageous going on in the headlines, whether it be political, sexual, or financial. Sometimes all three combined.

The *Bianca* debacle was up there with the best of them, much as the main players involved tried to leave it in their wake.

Aleksandr Kasianenko would always be known as the Russian oligarch whose yacht was taken over by pirates.

Bianca—the famous supermodel whose name was synonymous with the scandal—would always be known as the girl after whom the infamous yacht was named.

The press never tired of writing about the pirating of the *Bianca*. Especially as the main pirate and the mystery girl who was apparently working on the inside were never captured. Their speedboat vanished, and since a second storm came in later that same day, the most popular theory was that they had been caught in the storm mid-ocean, and that possibly their boat had gone down and they'd both drowned.

Mercedes couldn't help smiling when she read the stories on the Internet. Talk about a clean getaway!

After Cruz had tossed the captain overboard—a move she considered genius—he'd disposed of Jabrill the same way, although the ill-fated Jabrill had no one to rescue him.

As soon as that business was taken care of, Cruz had landed the boat on one of the less tourist-filled islands and sold it to a local fisherman with the stipulation that he hide the speedboat until the name was changed and the boat repainted. Then he'd taken off on his own with hardly so much as a good-bye. "I'll be in touch, *cariño*," he'd said to his one and only daughter.

Really? Where and when?

Mercedes hadn't minded. Why would she? She had the money and the ring. Cruz had been too concerned with plotting his getaway to even bother asking her what was in the garbage bag.

After making it to Madrid, where she knew people with connections, she'd gotten in touch with a man who was able to get her a new identity and passport, then she'd flown to Argentina, because it was far enough away, and she'd read about how beautiful it was in a magazine.

Now she was happily ensconced in Buenos Aires, living with a young polo player she'd met while sitting at the bar in one of the big hotels. The boy was twenty-two and his parents were major rich! Naturally, they didn't approve of her.

Did she care? No. *He* loved her. And so he should. She knew sex tricks he'd never even thought of.

Yes. Mercedes was perfectly content. On her new passport, her name was Porsche. She was a girl with a hot boyfriend, some money, and—tucked away in a safe-deposit box—the emerald and diamond ring. Her lucky prize. Her retirement fund.

Mercedes was ready for the next chapter.

Captain Dickson decided that the time had come for him to retire. He did not like the notoriety that now surrounded him; nor did his wife. Much as he'd enjoyed his many years at sea, the events that had taken place on the *Bianca* were too much for him to stomach.

He settled comfortably in his house in the Cotswolds, and never took to the sea again.

Cashoo, Daleel, Hani, and Galad were arrested and thrown into jail, where they were repeatedly questioned through an interpreter.

None of them spoke a word. They upheld the code of silence.

In his heart, Cashoo was convinced that Cruz would come and rescue them.

Three months later he was still hoping.

Cast out in the middle of the night from the remote villa, with only the clothes on her back, Ina was burning to get her revenge on Sergei. He'd crossed the wrong girl. She wasn't her brother's keeper. It wasn't her fault that Cruz had screwed him.

Freezing cold and soaked by the storm, she'd made it to a narrow road and huddled under a tree until early in the morning, when a gardener's truck had stopped and picked her up.

She'd lost everything. Her home. Her clothes. Her life.

But Ina was not Cruz's half sister for nothing. The vengeful streak Cruz possessed ran in the family.

If she was to end up with nothing, then so was Sergei.

He was a drug lord. She knew plenty of his secrets, and she was prepared to reveal them.

With the one credit card she had concealed on her person, she purchased a ticket to Mexico City and went straight to the police.

There she went into hiding at the expense of the government, waiting to testify at Sergei's trial.

Unfortunately, this never happened, because even though she was in protective custody, an assassin managed to get past her two bodyguards, and shot her to death while she slept.

At least she never knew what hit her.

Guy returned to his hometown of Sydney and his faithful partner. He'd decided to take a month or two off before going back to work.

Guy was frankly confused. How had Renee been able to change her story and get away with it? She'd quite clearly told him *and* Jeromy Milton-Gold that Senator Patterson was on top of her when the pirate had entered her room. Then she'd switched, and said it was the *pirate* on top of her, raping her, when Senator Patterson had burst in to save her.

That's when the senator had gotten shot. In the back, no less.

Neither story made sense. And what certainly made no sense at all was Senator Patterson being naked.

Guy realized it was not for him to ask questions. He'd got a right dressing-down from Captain Dickson for having hired Mercedes in the first place. The inside girl. The insolent little twat. Who'd have thought?

Reflecting on all the drama, Guy realized that Mercedes had been a squirrely piece of work, always skiving off, never around when he needed her.

He'd done nothing about getting his revenge on Jeromy Milton-Gold. Wasn't it revenge enough that the pervert had gotten himself shot?

Karma was a right old bitch.

Den seized every opportunity he could. Returning to his native Australia, he appeared on countless TV shows, giving interviews and becoming quite a mini celebrity in the process.

Den reveled in the spotlight. So did his family. Unfortunately, it didn't last. So what next?

He took a chance and sent a letter and résumé to Aleksandr Kasianenko, reminding him of his part in the *Bianca* fiasco and requesting a job in security.

To his amazement, several weeks later he received a response with a job offer. He was currently packing up and preparing to move to Moscow.

Like Guy and Den, Renee returned to Australia, but unlike Den, she refused to do any interviews. She was still shell-shocked after all that had happened.

Before leaving the yacht, Aleksandr Kasianenko had taken her aside and handed her a check for one hundred thousand dollars. "It's best you keep your story to yourself," he'd cautioned her. "The press have a way of making things up, and you wouldn't want that, would you, dear?"

No. She wouldn't want that.

Silence was golden. Especially when it came to protecting a U.S. senator's reputation.

Cruz considered going back to his guarded compound in Eyl.

Then he reconsidered.

Sergei would know exactly where to find him. And how about the friends and relatives of the missing pirates?

Seven pirates had left. None had returned.

There would be mothers, fathers, wives, and other relatives hot to tear him into a thousand little pieces.

Cruz ran to Brazil, planning to lay low for a while. His life was in danger, so like his daughter, he forged himself a new identity and began scheming about what he would do next.

Whatever it was, he would make money. Cruz always landed right side up.

Like a snake waiting to pounce, Sergei sat back and bided his time. He could be patient when he had to. He'd waited long enough to track down his brother's killer. Now he would wait for the pond scum, Cruz, to surface, and only then would justice be done.

Just as he'd dealt with Ina, so Cruz would be next.

And sometime in the future, Aleksandr Kasianenko.

It wasn't over . . . not at all.

Dateline: London

Jeromy Milton-Gold eventually returned to London after spending a week in a hospital in Cabo. A week alone. A week during which Luca seemed to think a phone call or two would suffice.

Jeromy could not believe that Luca would dare to treat him in such a cavalier fashion after all he'd been through. Damn the trumped-up pop singer with delusions of superstardom. Luca was nothing but a lucky boy plucked from the chorus line to feed Suga's enormous ego.

Jeromy was angry. And bitter. And filled with envy that only the stars who'd been on the cruise were getting the headlines.

He was the one who'd been shot. Yet it seemed that nobody cared.

Except Lanita and Sydney Luttman, who'd come to the hospital to visit him. They'd wanted to hear *everything*.

Jeromy had obliged as best he could, digging up whatever salacious details came to mind.

The Luttmans arranged to meet up with him in London, where they'd decided to buy a town house.

"You'll be in charge of everything," Lanita had informed him, waving a diamond-encrusted wrist in the air. "Sydney pisses money. Spend whatever it takes."

Jeromy knew he was capable of doing exactly that.

Two weeks later, Sydney Luttman was felled on the tennis court by a massive heart attack. He died instantly.

A few weeks later, Lanita arrived in London, and Jeromy soon found himself spending more and more time with her. She found him to be the perfect walker, and sometime sex partner when she was up for an orgy or two. Lanita was going ahead with her town house, and was ready to spend an outrageous amount of money.

One day she'd sat herself down in Jeromy's showroom, given him a long penetrating look, then made him a proposition he couldn't refuse.

Well, he could've. But who would?

Lanita was super rich.

Lanita was a sex freak.

Lanita was generous.

Lanita wanted a husband by her side, and Jeromy was the man she had in mind.

"You do understand that I'm gay?" Jeromy said.

"Honey, gay, schmay—we can work it out."

And so—with a meticulously put-together financial agreement—Jeromy became Mr. Lanita Luttman. A role he was most suited to.

Dateline: Miami

"We should have another baby," Luca announced.

The *Bianca* debacle was long past. Jeromy was history. And recently he'd persuaded Suga to sell her Miami mansion and move into his. Luca Junior was thrilled to see his parents back together.

"I'm too old, *cariño*," Suga responded, stroking his cheek. "Besides, you and I—our lovemaking days are over."

"That's not what I was thinking," Luca said. "I was thinking adoption."

"You were?" Suga said, noting how much more relaxed and happy Luca was since he'd finally gotten rid of Jeromy. Recently he'd been seeing a young man nearer his own age. Their partnership was a much better fit. And the best news of all was that Suga and he actually got along.

"Imagine what a blast it would be to have a baby in the house again," Luca said, full of enthusiasm. "A little girl. A little Suga."

"If it's what you want, then let's do it."

"Should we ask Luca Junior what *he* thinks?"

"Perhaps, or we could surprise him."

"Then tomorrow I'll speak with my lawyer and set everything in motion."

They smiled at each other, comfortable in a relationship that suited both of them.

Luca was happy to welcome Suga back into his life.

Suga brought the sunshine, and after Jeromy, that's exactly what he needed.

Dateline: London

"Wolf's a right talented bugger," Taye said, walking in from the garden with his six-year-old son balanced precariously on his shoulders. "One of these days this little bastard's gonna outdo me on the football field."

Father and son were both in their football gear, both grinning at Ashley with identical grins, which gave her a shiver of pleasure.

Kids. Wasn't that what life was all about? Raising them. Teaching them. Nurturing them.

Ever since their trip on the *Bianca*, Ashley had changed her outlook on life. She'd resigned from Jeromy's design firm, then shortly after that, she'd fired her children's nanny.

"All I want is to spend time with our family," she'd informed a delighted Taye.

"If it's what makes you happy, toots, then I'm all in," he'd said.

Ashley was happy. Happier than she'd ever been.

Aimee came running in wearing a pink tutu, grandma

Elise—or, as she preferred to be known, Moo-Moo—behind her.

"I'm not staying," Elise said, winking saucily at Taye. "I'm having dinner with a very fine gentleman I met on an Internet dating site."

"Get you," Taye said, raising a skeptical eyebrow. "You'd better be sure to keep your knickers on!"

"Oh, you are *awful*," Elise responded with a coy giggle. "And in front of the children too!"

"Bye, Mum," Ashley said, kissing her on the cheek. "See you tomorrow."

"Yeah, that's if she's still alive," Taye joked. "You never know about geezers you pick up on the Internet. Could be a serial killer."

"Is Moo-Moo gonna die?" Wolf piped up.

"Of course not," Ashley said, frowning at Taye.

"Don't want Moo-Moo to die," Aimee whined.

"See what you've done," Ashley said, shaking her head.

"They know I'm only teasing," Taye said, laughing as he released Wolf from his shoulders.

"Go watch TV, kids," Ashley said crisply. "Special treat."

Aimee and Wolf raced off.

"What about me?" Taye asked, moving close and nuzzling his wife's neck. "Don't *I* get a special treat?"

Ashley smiled. A warm smile. A loving smile.

"As a matter of fact, you do," she said softly.

"What?" Taye asked, seizing the moment. "Do we get to go upstairs for a nooner? C'mon, toots. That'd be a *very* special treat."

"Even better," Ashley whispered, still smiling. "Guess what?"

"What?"

She took a long deep breath. "We're pregnant," she announced.

Taye's whoop of joy could be heard for miles.

Dateline: Los Angeles

The Golden Globes. A true Hollywood night.

Cliff Baxter. A true Hollywood movie star. A true-life hero too. Handsome, charming, a fine actor, and extremely popular.

Cliff Baxter. An unmarried man.

The press loved him. The hostesses of all the popular entertainment shows creamed their thongs over him. He was *their* Cliff. His long list of girlfriends were merely along for the ride. And hopefully not too long a ride.

Until Lori.

Lori with the spectacular mane of red hair, racehorse legs, and athletic body.

Lori, the girl who'd lasted longer than most.

But wasn't her time about up?

Enid seemed to think so. As did Cliff's PR people, his agent, his manager, and the wives of all his many friends.

It was time for Lori to go.

Or was it?

Cliff always enchanted at award ceremonies with his self-deprecating grin, his air of sophistication mixed with just that tiny sliver of bad boy.

Oh yes, Cliff Baxter was a man of the people with a sexy edge.

Tonight he was at the pinnacle of his fame, with Lori—clad in a sleek silver dress and sky-high Louboutins—by his side. It was his first public appearance since the tragedy on the *Bianca*. Expectations of what he would say and do were high. Whom would he speak to? What lucky journalist would get an exclusive?

Nobody knew.

Everyone cared.

He chose Jennifer Ward out of all of them. She was

smart and feisty, and he'd always enjoyed being interviewed by her.

"So, Mr. Baxter," Jennifer said, head tilted, mildly flirting. "Want to tell us all about your summer vacation?"

Cliff smiled. Movie-star smile. Movie-star teeth.

Standing next to him, Lori felt a warm glow.

"No, Jennifer," Cliff said amiably. "I think enough has been written about that already, don't you?"

"Our viewers are dying to know more," Jennifer said, gently pushing the mic toward him. "You're quite the big hero—and yet so modest."

"I know you're anxious, so I do have something for your viewers," Cliff said, pulling Lori into the shot. "In fact, we both do."

Jennifer's eyebrows shot up. "Both?" she questioned, because usually Cliff did not include his girlfriends in his interviews.

"Yes," Cliff said. "Listen, I know I've said I would never do this, but"—he leaned into Lori and gave her a full-on kiss—"this beautiful redhead and I, we're getting married. So ladies, you can cross me off your lists. I am now well and truly taken."

Dateline: Paris

Bianca would always be a superstar. She did not need a billionaire Russian oligarch to give her credibility.

After the pirating of the *Bianca,* things between her and Aleksandr had not gone well. First of all, Bianca had no patience with illness. Not that Aleksandr was ill, but he *was* on crutches, and that did not sit well with her. She had a certain image to maintain, and that image did not include a bloody cripple by her side.

Harsh, yes.

But Bianca was nothing if not honest.

Back in Moscow, they fought constantly, long screaming matches about how much time he was spending with
his children, and why his divorce was taking so long. They
did not make love. Aleksandr was never in the mood.

The thing that really irked Bianca was that he'd never
mentioned a ring, and she could've sworn she'd seen that
girl on the yacht steal a ring from his safe.

One cold Moscow morning, she'd woken up and
thought, *What am I doing here?*

Later that day she was on a plane to Paris. And that's
where she'd been ever since.

Aleksandr never chased after her.

She didn't care.

Within weeks, she'd hooked up with an Internet nerd
who'd made billions selling a series of complicated apps
and Web sites.

A month later they were married in Tahiti.

Internet Nerd did not ask her to sign a prenup.

Dateline: Moscow

Two weeks after Bianca left Moscow, Aleksandr called
Xuan. They made polite conversation on the phone, until
Aleksandr suggested that he send his plane for her to visit
him in Moscow. "We have much to discuss," he said,
sounding very formal.

Xuan was cagey. "We do?" she asked carefully.

"Yes, we do. The orphanage, among other matters.
Where are you?"

"Vietnam."

"Of course. I'll send the plane."

"No. I'll make my own way there."

"As you please."

Xuan took her time. She arrived in Moscow ten days
later and checked into a hotel. Only then did she text
Aleksandr to inform him she was there.

"I'll send a car for you," he said.

"I'll walk," she said.

"Don't be so stubborn. The car will pick you up in twenty minutes."

Xuan stopped arguing and thought about all the good she could do in the world if she were with a man like Aleksandr.

But he was with Bianca.

Or maybe not. She'd heard rumors that Bianca had left him and was currently with someone else.

She prepared herself. If Aleksandr wanted more than a business relationship, could it possibly work?

He was a very attractive and intriguing man.

There was no harm in finding out.

Dateline: New York

Sierra returned to New York and the loving arms of her family. She was no longer perceived as the good political wife. She was now the Widow. A tragic but beautiful figure, feted by all as the brave woman who'd always stood by her husband's side.

The sex scandal was long gone, wiped off the front pages in an instant.

Senator Hammond Patterson had lost his life defending the virtue of a young, innocent girl. He was an American hero.

Eddie March rallied to Sierra's side. He tracked down Radical, sent her Goth boyfriend back to Wyoming, and made sure she was front and center at her father's funeral, standing right next to Hammond's grieving widow.

Sierra went through it all in a daze. It was all too much for her to take in. Had she wished Hammond dead? Was his untimely demise her fault?

She didn't know. She was confused. She was suffused with sadness. And when Flynn tried to contact her, she told him that she needed time to get her head straight and that she would call him when she felt up to it.

In the meantime, she threw herself into her work. The rape crisis center. The battered women's homes. And anything else to keep her fully occupied.

Eddie was always there for her. Kind and understanding. The man that Hammond never was.

Sierra had no idea what her future held. She was living it day by day.

Dateline: Paris

Flynn returned to Afghanistan, a place where, strangely enough, he felt safe. He was working on a story about a rebel leader and staying in a hotel with other journalists from across the world. The camaraderie was just what he needed. None of them gave a shit about the *Bianca* and what had taken place, although one female journalist did ask him what Bianca looked like in real life.

He stayed there for several weeks before returning to his Paris apartment.

Sierra had blanked him—it was painfully obvious she did not want a connection.

He was fine with it. It was her choice, and if that's what she wanted, so be it.

Enough obsessing over one woman. Finally, he was beginning to realize that the past could never be recaptured. Too much had happened. Too many roadblocks.

Aleksandr contacted him and offered him whatever amount of money it would take to track down the mastermind behind the taking of the *Bianca*.

"I don't want your money, Alek," Flynn told him. "But I will look into it, see what I can find out."

He still had his connections in Eyl, and since the pirates were probably from there, a little investigation might go a long way.

"Xuan is here," Aleksandr informed him. "Is that all right with you?"

"Perfectly all right," Flynn assured him. "I always thought you two would be a great match."

Since getting back to Paris, he'd gotten together with Mai a couple of times.

Their relationship, such as it was, stayed on a casual level. She was exactly what he needed.

For now.

Somewhere out there was the right girl for him, and one of these days he would definitely find her.

Read on for an excerpt from

Confessions of a Wild Child

A Prequel to the Lucky Santangelo Novels

by

Jackie Collins

Coming soon in hardcover from St. Martin's Press

1

How does a girl get through school stuck with the name Lucky Saint?

How does a girl answer questions about her family when her mom was murdered and her dad was a once infamous criminal known as Gino the Ram?

Beats me. But if I have to, then I absolutely can do it. I'm a Santangelo after all. A freaking survivor of a major screwed-up childhood. A girl with a shining future.

Now here I am—a week before my fifteenth birthday—about to be packed off to L'Evier, which I'm informed is a very expensive private boarding school in Switzerland, so I'd better like it or else.

I am totally pissed. My brother, Dario, is totally pissed. The truth is we're all we've got, and separating us is simply not fair. Dario is younger than me by eighteen months, and I've always felt that I should look after him.

He's sensitive.

I'm not.

He's artistic.

I'm a tomboy.

Dario likes to paint and read.

I like to kick a football and shoot baskets.

Somehow our roles got reversed.

We live in a huge mausoleum—sorry, I mean house—in Bel Air, California. A house filled with maids and housekeepers and tutors and drivers and security guards. Kind of like a fancy prison compound, only our backyard features a man-made lake, a tennis court, and an Olympic-size swimming pool. Yeah, my dad has a ton of money.

Yippee! Luxury. You think?

No way. I'm kind of a loner with very few friends, 'cause my life is not like theirs. My life is controlled by Daddy Dearest. Gino the Ram. Mister *"Everything I say is right, and you'd better listen or else."*

It sucks. I am a prisoner of money and power. A prisoner of a father who is so paranoid that something bad will happen to me or Dario that he keeps us more or less locked up.

So I guess being sent off to boarding school isn't such a bad thing. Maybe a modicum of freedom is lurking in my future.

However, I will miss Dario *so* much, and believe me, I know he feels the same way.

We're very different. I resemble Gino with my tangle of jet black hair, olive skin, and intense dark eyes, whereas Dario inherited my mom's calm blondness.

Yes. I do remember my mom. Beautiful Maria. Sunny and warm and kind. Sweet-smelling with the smile of an angel, and the softest skin in the world. She was the love of my father's life, even though he's had legions of girlfriends since her tragic death. I hate him for that, it's so wrong.

I miss my mom so much, I think about her every day. The problem is that my memories are akin to a frightening dark nightmare because *I* am the one who discovered her naked body floating lifelessly on a lilo in the family swimming pool—the pool tinged pink with her blood.

I was five years old, and it's an image that never leaves me.

I remember screaming hysterically, and people running outside to see what was going on. Then Nanny Camden picked me up and hustled me inside the house. After that everything is a blur.

I do remember the funeral. Such a somber affair. Everyone crying. Dario clinging to Nanny Camden, while I clutched on to Gino's hand and put on a brave face.

"Don't *ever* forget you're a Santangelo," Gino informed me with a steely glare. "Never let 'em see you crumble. Got it?"

Yes, I got it. So I managed to stay stoic and dry-eyed, even though I was only five and quite devastated.

Ah yes, fond memories of a screwed-up childhood.

Now the limo sits outside the Bel Air house, idling in our fancy driveway, ready to spirit me away to the airport.

Dario has on a sulky face—which does not take away from his hotness. My brother might only be thirteen, but he's almost six feet tall, and once he gets some freedom, girls will be all over him.

It pisses Gino off that Dario doesn't look like him. He always wanted a son—a mirror image of himself—instead he got me.

Ha ha! I'm the son he never had.

Too bad, Daddy. Make the most of it.

Gino is sending me away to school because he's under the impression I'm a wild one. Just because I occasionally manage to escape from the house and hang out in Westwood—driving one of the house cars without a license—does not label me as wild. It's not as if I do anything crazy, I simply wander around the area checking out what it would be like to be a normal teenager. And yeah, I have to admit that sometimes I do get to talk to a boy or two.

Unfortunately, one memorable night I was pulled over by the cops, and that was a disaster. When Gino found out, he went loco. "I'm sendin' you off to a school that'll drill some sense into you," he yelled, having conferred with my Aunt Jen. "What you need is an assful of discipline. I'm not puttin' up with your crappy behavior anymore. You're drivin' me insane."

That's my dad, so unbelievably eloquent.

Marco is standing next to the limo, speaking with the driver. Marco is kind of Gino's shadow and a total babe. He's way over six feet tall, lean and muscular, with thick black curly hair and lips to die for. He's old. Probably late twenties. It doesn't matter because I have a major crush. He's handsomer than any movie star and major cool. Problem is that he talks down to me, treats me as if I'm a little kid, which I suppose in his eyes I am.

I'm on a mission to make him notice me in a different way. I want him to see me as sexy and cool; in fact everything I'm actually not.

Our guardian emerges from the house. Dario and I have christened her Miss Bossy. She's been around for three years, and has given us about as much affection as a plank of wood. She's so annoying that I can't even be bothered to hate her.

"Get in the car, Lucky," Miss Bossy says, fussing with her hair. "Dario," she orders tartly, "say good-bye to your sister, and make it quick."

Miss Bossy has been assigned to accompany me to Europe in spite of my protestations that I am quite capable of making the trip on my own. However, Gino insisted. "You go, she goes," he'd barked at me. "When she delivers you safely to the school, she leaves. That's it, no discussion."

Gino. King of the no discussion.

Miss Bossy opens the car door and climbs inside.

Dario pantomimes "Jerko!" behind her back and starts kicking pebbles from the driveway toward the limo. They ping off the front of the car.

"Quit it," Marco says sharply.

Dario continues scowling. Like I said, he's not happy I'm leaving.

I run over, hug my brother, and whisper in his ear, "Stay cool, don't let 'em get you down. I'll be back before you know it."

Dario tries to keep it together, but I can see the frustration and sadness in his blue eyes; he's actually holding back tears. I feel terrible.

"C'mon, Lucky," Marco says, sounding impatient like he really can't be bothered with this. "You don't wanna miss your plane."

Ah yes, Mister Handsome, that's exactly what I want to do.

I give Dario one final hug and blurt out, "Love ya," which of course embarrasses the crap out of him.

Dario mumbles something back, and suddenly I find myself sitting in the limo and we are off.

Gino is nowhere to be seen. He's away on a business trip.

What else is new?

2

The plane ride to Europe is endlessly long and boring. Fortunately, to Miss Bossy's annoyance, I am not seated next to her. I am seated beside a voluptuous bimbo in her forties who seems to be freaked out by flying. The woman has overly bleached blond hair and is wearing an astonishing amount of caked-on eye makeup. Her skirt is so short that it barely covers her leopard thong. I get several unwelcome flashes before she downs two mimosas, covers herself with a blanket, and falls into a drug-induced sleep. Earlier I noted she slurped down a couple of sleeping pills with her booze. Nice.

To my delight I score a window seat, which means I don't have to bother with her. Instead I gaze out the window thinking about Marco. Even though he escorted me to the airport, does he even realize I exist? He never speaks to me except to bark orders. He barely looks at me. Does he have a girlfriend? What does he do when he's not busy trailing Gino? What exactly is his deal?

Marco's attitude toward me sucks.

I sneak a *Cosmopolitan* magazine off sleeping bimbo's lap, and read about how to give a man the orgasm of his life.

Hmm . . . sex . . . not a subject I know a ton about. To my chagrin I've never even been kissed—and that's because I've never spent time in the company of boys—

thanks to Gino and his protective ways. Like I said—since my mom's murder, me and Dario have been kept virtual prisoners.

Oh yes, you can double bet that I plan on making up for my life of seclusion. Indeed I do. An adventure lies ahead, and I'm totally ready to run with it.

Halfway across the ocean, sleeping bimbo awakes and immediately turns into Chatty Cathy. She starts giving me an extremely tedious rundown of her extremely boring life.

I attempt to appear interested, but it doesn't work and, halfway through her discourse on why all men are dirty dogs, I drift off into a welcome snooze.

She doesn't speak to me again.

Upon landing, Miss Bossy discovers there is another girl from Los Angeles aboard, also on her way to L'Evier. She is a tall girl, taller than me, and I'm five seven. She has long red hair worn in a ponytail, and a pale complexion. I hate her outfit, all neat and buttoned-up, while I have on jeans and a Rolling Stones t-shirt—much to Miss Bossy's annoyance. She'd tried to get me to change before we left L.A., but I was having none of it. It wasn't as if she could *force* me. No way.

The girl and I stare at each other while waiting for our luggage and the arrival of the L'Evier car that's supposed to meet us.

"I'm Lucky," I finally say.

She frowns. "I'm not," she says with a bitter twist. "My parents are forcing me to do this."

"Uh . . . I mean my *name* is Lucky," I explain.

She gives me a disgusted look. "That's your *name*?" she says, as if she's never heard anything quite so ridiculous.

She should only know who I'm named after—the notorious gangster, Lucky Luciano, whom I guess Gino must've hung with way back in his criminal days.

"Yup," I say. "That's my name. What's yours?"

She hesitates for a moment before revealing that her name is Elizabeth Kate Farrell, only most people call her Liz.

Not a bad name, although no way as cool as Lucky.

The truth is that I *love* my name, it's a one-off, nobody else has it. Besides, if my mom agreed to name me Lucky, then it's all good. It's the Saint I'm having a problem with.

"Why are your parents forcing you?" I ask, curious as ever.

"You want the truth or the story I'm supposed to tell?" she says, tugging on her red ponytail.

"Uh, let's go with the truth," I mumble, delighted that someone else might have something to hide.

Liz gives me a long penetrating look, obviously trying to decide if she can trust me or not.

I stare right back at her, challenging her with my eyes, willing her to go for it.

"Got pregnant. Had an abortion. Now here I am. Banished."

Liz says this all in a very matter-of-fact way. I am totally stunned. Pregnant. An abortion. How old is she anyway?

"Wow," I manage. "That's heavy."

"You think?" she says with a sarcastic grimace.

And then Miss Bossy brings over an elderly emaciated man with pointed features, watery eyes, and a thin moustache. Apparently he is a teacher from L'Evier sent to drive us to the school, located a good hour and a half away from the airport.

The man speaks English with a thick foreign accent. "Come you with me, young ladies," he says, mouth twitching, which causes his whiskery moustache to do a funny little dance. "I am Mr. Lindstrom."

We follow him, trailed by a fat porter wheeling our luggage while breathing heavily as if near to a major collapse.

By this time I am tired, confused, and filled with questions I wish to ask Liz. If she was pregnant, that meant she'd had sex. And if she'd had sex, that meant she knew all about it.

As a virgin with absolutely no experience, I need to know *everything*.

It's essential.
Details, please.
Everything!

Today things were different. Today Cliff was heading in a whole other direction.

He started kissing her the moment they entered their room. The kissing was dreamy, and soon led to him removing her bikini top and caressing her breasts, paying special attention to her nipples as his mouth moved downward.

Lori shivered with the unexpected pleasure of it all, reveling in his touch. After a while she reached down to fondle his crotch. He quickly pushed her hand away. "Not yet," he said, his voice a husky drawl. "Lie down on the bed, baby. I want to look at you."

She did as he asked, feeling totally turned on.

Cliff stood over her, gazing at her taut body clad in nothing but the bottom half of her bikini. "I never get to see you like this," he said. "You have a really beautiful body."

Compliments too! This was unbelievable.

Then he bent down and began slowly peeling her bikini bottom off until she was completely naked. Next he rose and stood back, once more admiring her, his eyes taking in every inch.

Lori shivered with the intensity of it all. She'd never felt more exposed and yet filled with excitement.

She gazed up at him as his hands settled on her thighs, gently pushing her legs apart. And after that he did something that he'd only ever done to her once before, and that was the first time they'd made love. He actually began performing oral sex on her.

Lori threw her hand across her eyes and writhed across the bed.

"Keep still," he commanded. "You know you like it, baby. You know you do."

Who wouldn't? Cliff Baxter, star of a million women's fantasies, was going down on her, his tongue darting in and out of her most private places.

A mind-blowing orgasm was swift. And the moment

she reached the pinnacle, he dropped his shorts and moved on top of her, lazily fucking her until she came again.

It was the best time they'd ever had in bed.

Somehow, Lori had a strong suspicion that dumping her was no longer on Cliff's mind.

63

Sergei grunted like a soon-to-be-satisfied pig as he screwed his ex–beauty queen girlfriend doggie style. Ina was getting fat. It didn't bother him; he got off on squeezing the rolls of flesh gathered around her waist, then digging into her giant ass with his penis, which was not as large as he would've liked. Although who needed a big cock when a man had endless drug money and a certain amount of power?

Ina was adept at providing other girls for sex when he was in the mood, which was a bonus. His skinny American cunt girlfriend, Cookie, felt that she was too special to be shared, and Sergei had always been partial to a threesome.

Lately, he'd been thinking of cutting Cookie loose. All she ever did was whine, complain about inconsequential shit, and spend his money shopping for ridiculously expensive shoes and bags.

The upside was that she was an American girl who'd once been in a successful movie; therefore, showing up with her boosted his ego when he was invited to grand functions in Mexico City. She was the arm candy to get him noticed.

Over the years, Sergei had done "favors" for a lot of important people, including well-placed politicians and high-ranking members of the police force. In return he was invited everywhere. It was a side of his life he enjoyed. It swelled his chest with importance, and a dressed-up

Cookie was the perfect girl by his side. Ina wouldn't cut it—too obvious and trampy.

After finishing the task at hand, he pulled out and favored Ina with a couple of hefty slaps on her generous butt.

"You're a sow," he growled, not unaffectionately.

"'Scuse me?" she said, reaching for her robe.

"Big titties. Big ass," he guffawed. "I like it all."

"So does everyone else around here," she boasted, flouncing across the room, not sure she was down with his so-called compliments.

Sergei's eyes went dead. "I've warned you, and so's your brother. Stop paradin' around the pool shakin' your stuff at the workers."

"What's wrong with them looking?" Ina argued. "They can look, but they can't touch."

Sergei grabbed a fistful of her hair, causing her to cry out in pain. "*I* look. *I* touch," he spat. "You stay in the goddamn house when I tell you. Got it?"

"What's that leafy shit your guys chew on all the time?" Sergei wondered.

Cruz shrugged, a cigarette hanging precariously from his bottom lip. "Khat. It's a stimulant—keeps 'em alert an' happy."

"You want 'em happy?" Sergei snorted his disgust. "What t' fuck?"

"I want 'em ready t' do anything I tell 'em to do," Cruz replied, taking a long drag on his cigarette, his small eyes ever watchful.

Sergei nodded.

"They're dangerous men—stupid an' reckless as shit," Cruz continued, blowing out a stream of smoke. "That's t' way they get the job done."

"I should hope so," Sergei grumbled, the nerve in his left cheek starting to twitch. "This deal is costing."

"You'll get it back an' plenty more when we go for the ransom," Cruz assured him.